BOTTLE BLONDE

Mercy Watts Mysteries Book 11

A.W. HARTOIN

Bottle Blonde

Mercy Watts Mysteries Book 11

ALSO BY A.W. HARTOIN

Historical

The Paris Package (Stella Bled Book One)

Strangers in Venice (Stella Bled Book Two)

One Child in Berlin (Stella Bled Book Three)

Young Adult fantasy

Flare-up (An Away From Whipplethorn Short)

A Fairy's Guide To Disaster (Away From Whipplethorn Book One)

Fierce Creatures (Away From Whipplethorn Book Two)

A Monster's Paradise (Away From Whipplethorn Book Three)

A Wicked Chill (Away From Whipplethorn Book Four)

To the Eternal (Away From Whipplethorn Book Five)

Away From Whipplethorn Box Set (Books 1-3, plus bonus short)

Mercy Watts Mysteries

Novels

A Good Man Gone (Mercy Watts Mysteries Book One)

Diver Down (Mercy Watts Mysteries Book Two)

Double Black Diamond (Mercy Watts Mysteries Book Three)

Drop Dead Red (Mercy Watts Mysteries Book Four)

In the Worst Way (Mercy Watts Mysteries Book Five)

The Wife of Riley (Mercy Watts Mysteries Book Six)

My Bad Grandad (Mercy Watts Mysteries Book Seven)

Brain Trust (Mercy Watts Mysteries Book Eight)

Down and Dirty (Mercy Watts Mysteries Book Nine)

Small Time Crime (Mercy Watts Mysteries Book Ten)

Bottle Blonde (Mercy Mysteries Book Eleven)

Mercy Watts Mysteries Book Set (Books 1-3, plus bonus short)

<u>Short stories</u>

Coke with a Twist

Touch and Go

Nowhere Fast

Dry Spell

A Sin and a Shame

Paranormal

It Started with a Whisper (Sons of Witches

The law of unintended consequences says that you make a choice and something unexpected happens. Makes sense, unless you're me. In Mercy Watts' world, some dude I don't know makes a whack-ass choice, and I end up in a basement hunting turtles for six hours. That's right. Turtles. 'Cause it's me and I live in St. Louis. Grandparents keep turtles in their basements. I swear to God, it's a thing.

Turtles happened because exactly one week ago, I was mid-way through the annual Bled baking day, which is actually three days long, but let's not quibble. Decades ago, my godmothers, Myrtle and Millicent Bled, started baking for friends and family at Christmas time and it's gotten a bit out of hand. We now bake for staff at the Children's Hospital and all the families stuck there over the holidays. I'm sorry to say that's a lot of kids and we can't hire anyone to help. It has to be friends and family so on the first weekend in December I was trying to figure out how to roll gingerbread effectively with one arm in a cast. Like so many things, it didn't work out for me.

My gingerbread was wafer thin on one side and super fat on the other. It seemed like I was pushing down with equal force, but, clearly, I wasn't. I sighed and looked up at Stella Bled Lawrence's portrait. She watched my failure with pale blue eyes over the stacks of Christmas tins that reached up to her nose. The breakfast room was what my mother called the staging area because we did all the packing and labeling in there. The enormous kitchen was where all the action happened, but not that year, not for me. I got exiled with a lump of dough, wax paper, and a rolling pin, because I was in the way and pretty much useless. I thought I'd prove them wrong, but thirty minutes later the opposite was true.

I'd first broken my arm while doing a favor for family friend Big Steve and rebroken it three weeks ago during another favor for Myrtle. I'd looked into the death of The Girls' childhood friend Sister Maggie with some pretty unexpected results, including breaking my nose, uncovering the origin of the serial killer network with ties to the Kansas graveyard, and, last but not least, the answer to the question of what Stella had sent back from Europe on the eve of WWII. People had died because of that secret, my great grandparents, just for starters, and it was in Great Grandma Agatha's purse, hidden away in the St. Sebastian police station attic, that we found it. Stella had shipped back the liquor cabinet that had been tucked away in my parents' butler's pantry and right under our noses the whole time.

Three weeks had gone by and we still hadn't gotten in that cabinet and not for lack of trying. Getting into my parent's house when it was empty was more of a challenge than you'd think. My mother knew everything I was doing, but my father, the great and difficult detective, didn't.

After serious problems with the FBI and the media, Dad was trying to rebuild his business and the way he'd chosen to do it was a problem for us. My grandad came out of retirement as did Avery Sampson and Leo Frame to help him. The geezers had a system and it included our kitchen table, just about twenty-four hours a day. My mom had to sneak out of bed at three in the morning to search the cabinet because that was the only time nobody was looking and even then Dad turned up, asking what she was doing.

Mom didn't find anything, no secret compartments, nothing, but it was the dead of night and her eyesight wasn't great after her stroke so she may have missed something. Bled baking day was our last shot for the next week at getting in that cabinet and searching it completely. My dad was off tracking a rapist in Hannibal, and Avery and Leo were in Memphis chasing down leads in a missing persons case. My grandad was the only conceivable problem. He was home recovering from a broken ankle. He'd slipped off a curb and broken it in three places, revealing that he had osteoporosis, but he wasn't buying the diagnosis. In Grandad's opinion, osteoporosis was a woman's issue akin to menopause, not that he uttered the word menopause. He'd rather break the other ankle than refer directly to anything that had something to do with a woman's nether regions.

Because he didn't believe his doctor or me, Grandma J had to take away his car keys, relegating him to the couch with orders to eat and sleep while she helped us bake. He wasn't happy and threatened to walk over to my parents' house so he could get at work files. I wouldn't put it past him. Did I mention that Grandad was a workaholic? The man could not not work. If he wasn't hobbling out to an Uber, he was probably taking apart the plumbing looking for hairballs or oiling hinges that didn't squeak or attempting to break into his office to go through old files, looking to unearth clues in unsolved murders from his father's and grandfather's time as policemen. He coveted those ancient cases and collected more whenever he had the chance like some kind of ghoul. Occasionally, he tried to rope me into finding out what happened to Maude in 1921, but I always managed to slip the net, which is why I was trying to make gingerbread. Grandma J said I should hang out with Grandad since we were both broken. Nope. Not falling for that. I'd rather roll gingerbread badly for seventy-two hours than be picking the lock on Grandad's office and looking into Maude's mysterious end. If I'd known turtles were coming, I'd have chosen differently.

Instead of balling up my dough for another attempt, I texted Chuck, "Are you in yet?"

"Almost," he wrote back.

"What's taking so long?"

"Carlson had a breakdown. Delayed. Be in in a minute."

That damn Carlson. He was always having a breakdown and it wasn't about work either. Carlson was the squad-designated wreck. On his third divorce and in a custody battle that made Brexit look like a tiff, that idiot got some woman he met at the DMV pregnant and then to cope, he started gambling. The squad put him on a desk and then leave, but he kept coming to work, trying to explain that he was really okay and could do the job while snotting all over the place.

Yesterday, my parents' house was empty, too, but Chuck and his partner, Sidney, had to lure Carlson out of the station with the promise of chili dogs and ended up sitting at a bar for four hours, listening to how all these women shouldn't hate him, because Chuck was afraid he might hurt himself, and we missed our first chance to get in the liquor cabinet. If he ruined our second chance, I'd start hoping one of those women would take him out and protect the rest of womankind from the plague that was Daniel Carlson.

"In?" I texted.

"No." Chuck was irritated with me, but I couldn't help it. We were so close. Whatever had The Klinefeld Group coming after us since WWII was in that cabinet and I was on the edge of insanity with the waiting.

I slammed my rolling pin onto the dough and bent over, putting my casted hand's fingers on the wood and trying to inch it forward evenly. I should've just said yes to the doc when she said I could take the cast off a couple of days ago. The rebreak wasn't bad and had healed well. She assumed I couldn't wait to get it off and she wasn't wrong, but something held me back. I didn't want that cast off. There was this weird attachment, a need for the cast that I couldn't explain, and I said no. The doc shrugged and said to come back in a week. I wasn't at all sure I'd want it off in a week, but I said I would. I told Chuck and everyone else that I had to keep it on. Nobody doubted me except Fats Licata, my sometimes bodyguard and newly-minted best friend. Fats raised an eyebrow, but quickly got distracted by morning sickness.

She was in the second trimester now, but her nausea wasn't letting up. If anything, she was getting worse. I could hear her in the kitchen, where she'd gotten the honor of rolling the cinnamon rolls with her two good hands, making noises like a drowning yak. The Girls were trying to get her to take a break, but Fats Licata didn't take breaks.

What she lacked in delicacy, she more than made up for with size and determination.

"I can do it," she said. "I just have to breathe."

"You don't have to do it," said my mom. "You're pregnant. Relax. Put your feet up."

"I can't do that," said Fats.

She was right. She couldn't. I'd never seen Fats relax. That wasn't a thing for her. We went to a movie last week and she did squats while we were in line and bicep curls during the movie, when she wasn't in the bathroom throwing up, which was at least half the time.

"Please, Fats," said Clarence, the little nun who'd gone to St. Sebastian with us and had turned out to be a good friend to a woman who didn't have female friends before us. We were an odd trio, I'm not gonna lie.

"Make way!" yelled Aunt Miriam and I only had a second to step aside before Fats came barreling through the breakfast room with wild eyes and both hands clamped over her mouth.

I heard her run to the nearest bathroom and prayed she made it. Sometimes she didn't. It was that bad.

My mom walked in and leaned on the table. "Can't you talk to her?"

"About what?"

"This isn't normal."

"Correct," I said.

"What did the obstetrician say?" Mom asked.

"That it should be getting better."

"It's not."

"Nope."

Mom glared at me and wiped her frosting-covered hands on her apron. "You have to talk to her."

"And say what?" I asked.

"Isn't there medication?"

"She won't take it. She's afraid the baby will be affected and grow a nipple on her forehead or something."

"That's not going to happen," said Mom.

"When I said that, she said, 'That's what they said about Thalidomide.'"

"What does Fats know about Thalidomide?"

"Everything. She's been researching."

"Oh, Lord."

"Exactly."

The sound of retching echoed through the Bled Mansion for a second time and Clarence came in wringing her hands. "Is she okay?"

"I'm going with no," I said.

"Can't you do something?"

"I got her to drink ginger tea."

Clarence bit her lip and then said, "I don't think it's working."

"It works," I said. "But not enough."

"You should go in there," said Mom.

"Why me? I haven't had a baby."

"You're a nurse."

"I was a nurse. Now I'm a licensed PI, whose father doesn't trust her to do more than background checks."

Mom came over and hugged me fiercely. In a strange way I think she was mourning the loss of my nursing career, but I don't think she was ever that into it. She just didn't want me to follow in my father's footsteps, that much she knew, but I had to earn a living. With all the events of the last few months, I was persona non grata in the nursing world, not because I sucked, but because I was a disaster waiting to happen and everyone in St. Louis knew it. Nobody wanted to hire me, at least not until I could be normal for a while and not get a clinic rammed with a tractor or something else equally ridiculous. So in a moment of weakness I agreed, after a tremendous amount of badgering from my dad, to take the PI license test. Now I was employed by my dad and, in his words, working my way up. It didn't matter how many cases I'd cracked for him in my so-called spare time or how many murders I'd solved, I got to start at the bottom as a glorified file clerk. I was bored out of my mind, making less money than I did as a student nurse, and just about ready to pay the Columbia clinic to take me back.

Clarence came over and hugged me, too. "You'll be a nurse again."

"I don't know," I snuffled, getting all weepy.

"You will," said Mom. "Or I'll make your father give you something good."

That did it. I was an adult and my mom had to help me get a decent job. I started crying for real and that's when Aunt Miriam came in and smacked my legs with her cane. "I never heard so much caterwauling about good news."

"Good news? What's the good news? Fats can't stop barfing. We have less than forty-eight hours to fill these tins and we're not even close. I can't get a real job and..."

She gave me the stink eye. "And what?"

I was going to say we can't get inside the liquor cabinet, but Aunt Miriam was in the dark and she had to stay that way or else. "Nothing. I just feel rotten and useless."

"You are useless."

"Aunt Miriam!" exclaimed Mom.

"I mean with baking, but I have a job for you." Aunt Miriam glared at me and whatever the job was I wouldn't like it.

"Oh, yeah?" I asked. "Is it clean out the gutters or unclog a toilet?"

"Don't be ridiculous. You can't even roll dough."

"Then what?"

Aunt Miriam pulled a large bottle out of her apron pocket. "You can make yourself useful by getting some more vanilla."

"We're out?" I asked. "That's a lot of vanilla."

"We have some," said Mom.

"Aaron says it has to be his cognac vanilla."

With that, my weirdo partner, Aaron, trotted into the breakfast room wearing a pink hairnet and a frilly apron that once belonged to The Girls' mother. He was pulling on my hoodie, which is to say Chuck's hoodie, and it hung halfway to his knees.

Mom stepped in front of him. "Oh, no. Back you go."

Aaron stopped, looked to the left, and said, "Vanilla," before attempting to bypass my mother.

"We'll get it. You are not leaving us with that crazy Baumkuchen."

Aaron look confused, but that was nothing new. The only thing I was confused about was why we were making Baumkuchen. It's a

German cake that's baked in layers and takes four hours. Like we didn't have enough things with delicate timing.

Mom turned him around and Aunt Miriam stripped off the hoodie before handing it to me.

"Go and hurry."

"My dough will get dry." The gingerbread was kicking my butt. It could not be allowed.

"That ship has sailed, Mercy," said Mom.

"Fine," I said, but before I could zip up, Fats staggered into the room. She was pale, sweaty, and her usually perfect hair had come loose from its slicked back ponytail, sticking out around her face like wilting petals on a flower. If it hadn't been for her tremendous size and the hot pink leopard spandex she was wearing I might not have recognized her.

"I'll go," she wheezed.

"Not happening," said Mom.

"You can go to bed," said Aunt Miriam, primly tucking a few ginger hairs back into her veil.

"We have work...to do." Fats tried to lean casually against the door-frame, but instead sort of toppled into it and the wood made a worrisome snapping noise.

I went over to check her temperature and heart rate. Not great but not sick, in the regular sense anyway. "You have nothing to do but drink tea and rest," I said.

"No, I've got to get ahead of it," said Fats.

"Ahead of what?"

"The sick. I need some exercise."

"The last thing you need is exercise."

She straightened up and, for a second, looked normal, minus the sweaty. "I'll go and you roll the crap out of that gingerbread."

It's you and me, gingerbread. Let's do this thing.

"Hey!" My cousins, the Troublesome Trio, stuck their red heads in the door to the kitchen.

"Are we taking a break?" asked Sorcha aka Weepy, although she didn't weep much anymore since becoming engaged.

"No," said Mom. "Don't get any ideas."

"I'm not getting any ideas. I love this."

Jilly looked like she thought she was crazy, but my cousins were thrilled to be included in something Bled for the first time and weren't complaining…much.

"What about lunch?" asked Bridget. "Rodney says he has some crab that he wants to use up before it goes bad. Crab cakes?"

Crap on a cracker.

Before I could squash that, Fats made a horking noise and ran for the bathroom again.

"What did I say?" asked Bridget.

"Crab," we said in chorus.

"I thought it was coffee that made her sick."

Aunt Miriam shooed my cousins back into the kitchen saying, "It was. Now it's crab."

"Does that mean I can have a latte?" asked Sorcha.

I didn't catch the answer since Aaron tried to dart past me and I had to grab him by the apron. "You have to do the Baumkuchen."

A timer, one of about twenty-eight we had going, went off and I turned him around. "I'll get it."

"Sto-Vo-Kor," he said.

"I know."

"Six months."

"Of course," I said, not really knowing what he was referring to, but I figured the meaning would become apparent. Or not. Whatever.

Mom pushed him back into the kitchen toward the enormous La Cornue stove with its multiple ovens all fired up. "And take Pick with you. He hasn't been out for hours."

"Anything else?" I asked sarcastically.

"Hurry. We've got the next batch of sugar cookies to do."

I saluted my mother, wrapped my crusty gingerbread dough in the wax paper, and headed for the library. Pickpocket, Chuck's giant poodle, was curled up on a cushion next to the fireplace. He desperately needed a haircut, so it really just looked like someone dropped a pile of black curls in the dog bed. I couldn't make out so much as a foot.

"Time for walk," I said, picking up his leash.

Nothing.

"Walk."

Pick didn't move. I didn't even get a wag and he loved walks. To be fair it was flipping freezing out and he was a poodle with poodle-type sensibilities.

"Come on," I said. "I gotta put on your booties."

Taking Pick out for a walk was a whole thing. Booties and a red-checked jacket. He was adorable, but it was a pain.

The poodle opened one dark eye and then firmly closed it before putting a paw over his face.

"Fine, but don't come crying to me if you have to pee five minutes after I get back," I said.

Nothing.

I tossed his leash on the settee and went to the receiving room to try and suit up in my puffer coat, hat, and scarf. It was freezing, but I wasn't convinced the five-minute walk over to Aaron's bakery was worth the effort to get my jacket over my cast, so I forgot the coat and stuck with the hat and two scarves.

I went out the back of the Bled Mansion, leaving the incredible smells of fifteen different kinds of pastries behind and dashed through the rose garden to the stables that would soon be my home. Chuck and I had decided to move into the apartment above the stables, but, true to form, The Girls had insisted on renovating it for us. The sound of sawing and hammering echoed down the street as I passed though the stables and went into the alley, slipping on the ice but catching myself in the nick of time.

My phone buzzed and it was Chuck. Finally.

"I'm in," he said.

"Nobody's there?" I asked.

"Who would be here?"

"No idea, but I never count my dad out."

I heard a door close and a zipper unzip. "Yeah, you never know with Tommy. I was half-expecting him to be at the table with your Grandad."

"You and me both," I said.

"I'm going to make a coffee. I'm freaking freezing."

I rolled my eyes. "Will you just search the cabinet?"

"Maybe I should make sure nobody's here."

"Nobody's there."

"You just asked me if somebody was here," said Chuck.

"I was paranoid."

"Well, now I'm paranoid." He paused. "Wait."

My stomach twisted. "What?"

"I heard something."

"It's probably the Siamese." I turned the corner toward Sto-Vo-Kor. "You can take them."

"I...don't think it's the Siamese unless they gained a hundred pounds," said Chuck.

"Get out."

"Let me see who—"

A voice behind me called out, "Mercy!"

I turned and a man rushed at me. I put my hands out to fend him off, but I slipped when I stepped back, falling on my back. I knocked my head on the concrete and the wind rushed out of my lungs with an oomph. He was on me, shoving a wet rag over my face. I was screaming and clawing at him, but he was bigger than me and had the advantage. My vision narrowed and he started dragging me by my hoodie, keeping the rag over my face. Then he had me in a chokehold and I was lifted, thrown into something. The rag came off my face for a second. A trunk. He shoved me down and pressed the rag back over my face. I must've blacked out for a second because the next thing I knew, he'd flipped me over and was grabbing at my arms.

"Son of a bitch," he said as he twisted my casted arm behind my back and tried to force my hands together, muttering obscenities and attempting to tie me up. I screamed with everything I had, he let go, and I looked over my shoulder to see with blurred vision a man in a parka with the hood up looming over me.

"Fuck it!" He slammed the trunk.

I don't know what happened or how long it was happening. I remember sort of rerealizing where I was, so I must've passed out. The car was moving. Fast. Highway speed.

This was one of those times when being Tommy Watts' daughter comes in handy. Dad was always worried about me getting kidnapped when I was little. He dealt with some pretty bad guys during his police career and some of them got out of prison. Dad lived in fear that I'd be taken in retribution, so he trained both Mom and me in self-defense. It didn't work out in the alley, but his training included how to get out of a car. I still had my glass-breaking tool in my purse at the mansion, not that it would've helped me in a trunk. Luckily, trunks were big in Dad's training and I did not appreciate it at all. What eight-year-old wants to spend Saturday afternoon being tossed in various detectives' trunks to see if she can escape under different variables? I got timed and graded. Dad didn't reward. Living was my reward, he said. But Mom was all about the reward. I got so much ice cream for those trunks, so I learned it. I can learn anything if Ben and Jerry's is on the line.

So without any thought at all, I started searching the trunk and used Dad's annoying breathing techniques to calm myself. The trunk was empty. No tools or rubbish of any kind, but it was dirty and smelled of trash and tools. Not new, not a rental, but maybe it would have a trunk release anyway. They'd been required forever.

I looked for the glow-in-the-dark lever but didn't see one. Then I felt around where the release would normally be, but, when I found the spot, the lever had been clipped off.

Stay calm. Dad taught you what to do.

I felt to the edge of the trunk liner and tried to pull it down so I could maybe get ahold of the wire. I couldn't do it. The cast rendered my hand useless and I couldn't do it with only one. I wasn't strong enough.

Taillight it is.

"Alright then. It's a good thing I've got boots on," I said to myself.

I angled myself with my feet toward the right tail lamp and started kicking. The plastic cracked. Encouraged, I kicked with both feet at the same time. Something snapped and I had daylight. I turned myself and began prying at the plastic covering. I yanked out the light apparatus and peered out to the road whizzing away under the car. It was a highway and a busy one at that. There was a truck directly behind us and another vehicle in the left lane that we were passing. I stuck my hand out of the taillight and instantly horns started honking. I waved frantically and wished I knew sign language or something. All I could've done was given a thumbs-up or an okay sign and that was hardly helpful.

The car started swerving, jerking in and out of lanes. Then slowing and speeding up wildly. The other drivers must've been trying to stop him. I loved them for it but prayed they didn't cause a crash. I didn't know what the survival rate was for crashing in a trunk and I didn't want to find out.

It seemed like forever before I heard sirens and the guy behind the wheel was panicking. I was rolling around in that trunk like a number ball on bingo night. Then there was an abrupt swerve, an acceleration, and we were going up. An exit ramp. More sirens from every direction and then he touched the brakes before flooring it. There was a bump followed by a weird thwacking and slappy sound. Strip spikes. They'd punctured his tires, but that changed nothing. He kept speeding to who knows where, toward who knows what, as the tires peeled away.

Who is this idiot?

A sudden thump and then the sound of metal grinding filled the trunk. I covered my ears as best I could. We were on the rims and I could smell the burning metal.

Oh, come on, dude. It's over.

Apparently, the guy in the driver's seat didn't agree because we yanked to the right and were going over rough ground. I was bumping up and down so fast. Now I know how popcorn feels.

What was the point? Driving through a field was not an effective escape route. I knew it was a field because I'd accidentally driven into a cornfield in high school when we were out at a party and everyone was yelling directions in a panic because we were going to miss curfew. I took a turn too fast and drove into the bumpy furrows. It stopped me, but it didn't stop this guy. We were going slower and slower, but we were still going. It seemed like miles and miles of bumps.

And then he stopped. I was actually surprised when he did. It'd gotten to the point where I'd started to think it would last forever. I know, I know, that's crazy. Hey, I was locked in a trunk. Don't judge me.

The sirens surrounded us and people were yelling. Then gunfire. Three shots and then nothing. I could hear people yelling but couldn't make out what they were saying. I hoped to God a cop wasn't hit, but I didn't really think that was a possibility. It was probably fifteen armed-to-the-teeth cops against one moron. I liked our odds.

I laid there patiently for a while until it seemed the reason for the chase had been forgotten. Namely, me.

Is somebody going to open this damn trunk?

I started yelling and yelling, working myself into a fury. I could've been bleeding out. Choking to death on my own vomit.

Over my caterwauling, I heard a click and the trunk popped, flooding my prison with blinding light. I blinked up at a large figure looming over me. Was it possible the cops had not won the day and this was the moron getting ready to axe me to death? I didn't think my heart rate could go higher, but it did. It really did.

"Calm down," he said. "We've got you."

I shielded my eyes. "Calm down? Are you serious? I'm kidnapped here."

"You're alive, aren't you?"

"So I have to be calm unless I'm dead? Is that what we're saying?"

He chuckled and reached for me. "You're alright. Come on."

I slapped his hands away. "Get off me, ya dickhead." I climbed out of the trunk on my own and I'd like to say I was elegant about it. But no, I wasn't. I flipped over the end of the car and lay splayed out on dried corn stalks. There was some small satisfaction of being right on that count. Very small. There were at least five cameras on me. I'd gotten so I could feel the lenses. Bastards.

"Do you want help?" the cop asked.

"EMTs on their way," said a woman and then she was at my side, kneeling on the crunchy stalks and quickly assessing my condition.

She clicked her walkie and said, "Mid-twenties white female. Head injury. Possible broken nose."

I felt my face and it was bloody. Dammit. She said some other stuff, but I was thinking about my poor nose. How many times can you break a nose before it gives up and decides to look like meatloaf? I know the head injury should've been my first concern. But I *had* a head injury, thinking straight wasn't my thing just then and I'm vain. There I said it.

"Check it out." The other cop held up a rag and sniffed it, making a face. "Jesus, what the hell is this?"

"Bag it, Derek," she said.

"Yes, ma'am."

Then there were other cops talking about the suspect who was dead. A guy squatted by my head. "Mercy Watts. First major crime in three years and it's you."

He said it like it was my fault and I wanted to say, "Drop dead," but I was getting more and more dizzy. It came out like a croak.

"Ah, shit," he yelled. "Where's that ambulance? We can't have Tommy Watts' daughter dying on us."

Die?

I croaked again.

"She's not going to die," said the female cop. "She's tough. She's been here before."

To be fair, it was my first straight-up kidnapping. Even thinking that isn't a good sign. When you say "first" it means you expect it to happen again and I pretty much did.

"Alright. Alright. Let's not get worked up," he said. "You survived to wreck shit another day."

I hate you.

"Jesus, Dustin," she said. "She's the victim."

He stood up and walked away. She put her hand on my forehead and said, "The ambulance is arriving. You're fine. You're going to be fine."

I managed to croak out, "I hate him."

"Yeah, I know. He's not usually like that. I'm Sam, by the way. Samantha Samuelson."

I held up my good hand. "Mercy Watts. I think I'm going to throw up."

Sam turned my head for me and I threw up just as the EMTs

turned up in an amazing display of professional and unprofessional behavior. They assessed me, got me on a gurney and IVed, all the while discussing how I'd managed to get myself in this fix. I was kinda out of it, but I'm pretty sure one looked inside my hoodie and whistled.

They rolled me over to the back of the ambulance and I got a glimpse of a clump of cops standing around a body lying in the field, toes up. It was the oddest sensation. He was trying to kill me, I assumed, and he ended up dead. How did this happen? Dustin thought it was my fault. Was it? My head injury must've been bad because it seemed reasonable. I made that dude kidnap me.

"Alright," said one of the EMTs. "You're going up and in. It's okay."

They slid me in, strapped the gurney down, and away we went with siren wailing, bumping slowly over some soon-to-be irate farmer's field. Three weeks. It'd been three weeks since something crazy happened to me. Not a record, but still.

The EMTs chattered back and forth and, in a stunning move, got out their cellphones.

"Dude, Justin isn't going to believe this. She is Marilyn Monroe."

"It's totally whack."

"We are so gonna trend."

"Number one, baby."

They wouldn't.

They would. Two EMTs in the back of an ambulance took selfies with me, a head injury with nausea and blurred vision, and started posting to Instagram.

This cannot get any worse.

One EMT held up his phone to the other one and said, "Hey, that weird stuff on her face really shows up. I didn't even use a filter."

Crap on a cracker.

—————

CHAPTER TWO

—————

I like working in ERs. I don't like *being* in ERs. Bad memories like to visit because what else do you have to do when you're in a cold room alternately alone and scared or with a bunch of medical pros and even more scared.

At the moment I was alone and could not, absolutely could not stop thinking about my mom and her stroke, my cousin Tiny and his stabbing, my broken bones, Dad crying in the bathroom after Mom's stroke, and a multitude of patients that I watched die since graduating nursing school. I tried my therapist's breathing techniques for anxiety and Dad's for a crisis situation. Neither did a thing to stop the images.

So far, I'd had a CT, X-rays, and bloodwork. I had six heated blankets because I couldn't get warm because of the shock, which wasn't helped by a tech who tried to convince people that I needed a catheter, which he'd be happy to install. For a second, I thought it was going to happen and I would have to make a break for it somehow, but Dr. Harris stepped up and yelled at him. The tech slunk out the door with a sad backward glance, saying, "I was only trying to help."

Had everyone gone insane? Maybe I had and none of this crap was happening. I'd almost convinced myself that this was a nightmare when Dr. Harris came in with my chart and a hangdog expression.

"I'm sorry about that, Mercy," she said. "May I call you Mercy?"

I didn't say anything and she got concerned. "Miss Watts?"

"So that really happened?" I asked.

She sighed and said, "It did. I'm afraid Jordan lost his mind when he saw you. We don't get a lot of celebrities here at St. Joseph's."

"I'm not a celebrity."

She tilted her head to the side and a lock of dark brown hair with grey roots fell across her cheek as her brow furrowed. "Can you tell me your name, your full name?"

"I don't have memory loss. I'm just not a celebrity."

"You sing with Double Black Diamond," she said.

"Not on purpose. Trust me, that was not the goal."

The furrows got deeper because who ends up singing and posing for album covers for a world-famous band by accident? "Please tell me your name."

It was my turn to sigh, but I gave her all my vital statistics.

"When can I leave?" I asked.

"We've decided to keep you overnight as a precaution," she said.

I didn't like it, but it was the right decision. I had a pretty good concussion, a cranking headache, and I still had blurry vision.

"It may be longer," she said.

"Why?" I asked slowly as my stomach tightened and my shivering got worse.

Dr. Harris called out the door for another blanket and forcefully told someone they couldn't come in yet.

"Is that my family?" I asked.

"No, but they are here in the waiting room." She smiled. "Your father's signing autographs."

"For crying out loud."

"He's a charmer."

"So they say."

A nurse came in and put another blanket over me that didn't help one bit and then suggested peppermint tea for my stomach. I agreed so she would leave and the doc would tell me the bad news.

"So?" I asked.

"So your attacker used a substance on your face."

"I remember. What was it?"

"We don't know, but it's being analyzed. We are concerned by the mask-like pattern of welts it left on your face. I've never seen anything like it and your bloodwork is off. I'm concerned it's gotten into your system."

"When will it go away?" I asked.

"I don't know."

"Long term effects?"

"Your guess is as good as mine," she said.

I pulled my hands out from under the blankets and accepted the tea that the nurse kindly offered. "Do you have any good news?"

"Well, you survived a vicious attack. That's good and your nose isn't broken."

"Swell."

"I'm sorry I don't have anything more concrete, but we'll get you up to a room and your family can see you. You've got quite a collection."

"What do you mean?" I asked.

She showed me a picture of the waiting room and there they were, my family, everyone from Dad to the Troublesome Trio to Fats and Tiny.

"We've had a hard time holding them back, but the detectives insisted," she said.

"Detectives?" My head was hurting so bad I had a hard time thinking of why there were detectives.

"They're pressing hard to come in for an interview and I'm going to have to let them in."

"Can I have something for my head?"

"I already ordered it. It'll be up from the pharmacy any second."

"Thanks."

"Are you ready for them?" she asked.

"As long as it's not Dustin," I said.

"Who?"

"Never mind." I sipped my tea. "Let 'em in and let's get this over with."

"They want to help," said the doctor.

"That remains to be seen."

She was puzzled, having most likely lived a life free of law enforcement. When you grow up with my dad and have as many run-ins as I have, a wait and see approach is best. You never know who's going to walk through that door. But that time I had a sneaking suspicion that it would be Dustin the blamer. It was that kind of day and I wasn't wrong.

The doctor walked out and two detectives in wrinkled suits walked in. One was all gentle concern. The other wasn't. Dustin, of course.

"Miss Watts, I'm Detective Joe Campbell and this is my partner, Detective Dustin Rich," said the concerned one.

"We've met," I said, blowing forcefully onto my tea.

Campbell glanced at Rich and said, "Oh, right. At the scene."

"Yeah, at the scene of my *abduction*."

Concerned, Campbell shifted his feet and to give himself something to do, he got out a notebook. "I have to say we were shocked that it was really you."

"Can't stay out of trouble, can you, Miss Watts?" said Rich.

"It's not a conscious choice," I said.

"Really?"

"We all make choices," said Rich.

"Not me. Not today."

Both detectives tilted their heads to the right. It was a cop thing, also a Dad thing. If you were in trouble, you did something, however small, to put yourself there. Complete innocence was not an option. I wasn't surprised. I'd seen it happen before, particularly to rape victims I treated in the ER, but I'd never seen anyone quite so blatant as Dustin Rich.

"What's it been?" he asked. "Three weeks since St. Sebastian?"

"Does that matter?" I asked. "I was attacked by a stranger in broad daylight."

That got the desired result, even Rich seemed a bit cowed. I was a real person, a real victim, not a headline. They shuffled around and got a couple of chairs while keeping their faces averted.

Fine. Look away. You're still a douche.

"Alright, Miss Watts," said Campbell with exaggerated kindness. "Are you okay to talk to us now?"

"My head feels like it's being split open with an axe, but sure, why not?"

On cue, the nurse came in with a syringe and I got a much-needed painkiller right in the IV. Thank God for small favors.

The detectives waited and it hit almost instantly taking the edge off.

Campbell leaned forward and asked, "Do you recognize the name Anton Thooft?"

"Is that him?" I asked, leaning back on the pillows and taking a breath. Anton Thooft. Anton Thooft tried to kill me. People tried to kill me before, but I usually had a clue who they were.

"Do you know the name?"

"No."

"Is it familiar at all?" asked Rich with a surprisingly even tone. Somebody decided to do his job.

"No."

"Think about it for a minute," said Campbell.

As requested, I thought and sipped my tea, but it wasn't necessary. "I'm not going to forget a name like Anton Thooft. Is he the guy?"

"You have a head injury. Doctor says you may have memory issues," said Rich, more harshly than he should have, and Campbell shot him a look.

"I don't know him. I'd tell you if I did," I said.

"You've been known to hold information back from authorities," said Rich.

Douchebags love that word, authority. I rolled my eyes and the pain just about knocked me out. "And the *authorities* have been known to screw over my family. In this case, I never heard of Anton Thooft. Now is he the guy?"

"Miss Watts, we've heard about the problems with the FBI and—"

"Can you just tell me? Is this a State secret or what? The guy is dead, isn't he? You shot him."

"Yes," said Rich. "The man in the car is dead."

There was something in the way he said it, like there's the guy in the car and maybe some other guy. I took another sip of tea and let the painkiller percolate in my bloodstream for a second before I said, "Was there another guy?"

"You tell us?" Campbell poised his pen over his pad and waited expectantly.

My head had stopped thumping and what I wanted most in that moment was them out and my mom in. "Fine, but you're not going to be happy."

"What's happy got to do with it?" asked Rich.

I smiled at him for the first time and it was genuine, believe it or not. "Exactly. Thank you."

Rich was taken aback by my smile and whatever had iced his soul against me melted a little. "Tell us what happened."

I did and I was right. They weren't happy. I didn't know crap. I didn't even get a good look at the guy. Here's what I had. Male. Bigger than me. Deep voice. No accent. In other words, nothing.

"So is Thooft the guy you shot?" I asked.

"He is," said Campbell. "We were trying not to taint your memory."

It was a weird approach, but whatever. "Alright. Are we done?"

"I'm going to show you a picture."

"If it's of the body, no thanks I'm good," I said.

They chuckled, even Rich.

"It's a work photo." Campbell got out his phone and brought up a picture, holding it out to me. "Ring any bells?"

I tried. I really did. It was a picture of a balding, blond fifty-something white guy with good bone structure that had gotten kinda jowly. I could've seen him before, but he wouldn't have made a huge impression.

"No. Sorry. He had a hood up. So that's him?"

"It appears to be," said Rich with a touch of sarcasm.

"What does that mean?" I asked with more than a touch of irritation.

"It means that it's hard to believe this guy attacked and kidnapped you."

If you are implying that I wasn't attacked, I will flipping scream until your eardrums burst.

"I *was* attacked and kidnapped," I said.

"Yes," said Campbell hastily. "We may have gotten off on the wrong foot."

"Ya think?"

"I don't know...exactly how that happened, but we are here for you to get answers preferably before the press descends."

"Or my father," I said.

"Him, too."

I laughed and relaxed completely. Painkillers are good. "He's the least of your worries."

"Is that a threat?" asked Rich sharply.

Paranoid much?

"It's a fact. I know a lot of people and they're all weird."

The detectives leaned back and relaxed for the first time. They should relax. It was a solved crime, a gimme. Campbell held up his phone again. "You're sure? Not hanging around your apartment, the grocery store?"

"To be honest, I haven't been out much since St. Seb."

"Where have you been?"

I told him and it was a depressingly short list. I wasn't living it up and both detectives looked faintly astonished that my life included such excitement as going to my parents' house, the Bled Mansion, and my therapist. The grocery store hadn't even happened. Chuck did all the regular stuff so I could rest and I didn't have a real job anymore. My biggest thrill was a baking marathon that I couldn't really do.

"Kinda a bummer, eh?" I asked.

"I thought...you'd be doing something," said Rich.

"If you think I'm what's on those DBD album covers, you're dead wrong."

He blushed and it was the tiniest bit adorable. With the red hair, he reminded me of my dad without the charm. "It's not that."

We looked at each other for a second and I had the weirdest feeling Rich knew a lot about me and he wasn't thrilled about it. "So... are you going to let me in on the big secret of Thooft?"

"Huh?" Rich asked.

Campbell glanced back and forth between us and then said, "He was a teacher. High school civics, AP government. Fifty-four years old, unmarried, no children. Originally from Whiskey Ridge. Now living in Germany."

"Seriously?"

"Yes. Unless he has some kind of doppelgänger, Anton Thooft, a boring, middle-aged teacher, flew from Germany to St. Louis for no other reason than to kill you."

"I...I don't see why that would happen," I said.

"We don't either," said Rich. "Have you ever been to Stuttgart, Germany?"

"Probably."

"You don't know?"

I asked for more tea and the nurse brought it in with a wary eye on the cops that they felt and it made them uncomfortable. It made me happy. At least I wasn't the only one.

"So Stuttgart," said Campbell.

I picked up the teabag string and bobbed the bag up and down in my cup. "How much do you know about me?" I asked.

Campbell rattled off a few facts, not very specific and nothing about The Girls.

"I'm Millicent and Myrtle Bled's goddaughter," I said.

"Is that significant?" asked Rich harshly.

"Only if you want to know about Stuttgart."

"We do," said Campbell with his soothing voice, but I saw the edge in his eyes and it wasn't for me. Neat.

I decided to throw the guy a bone. His partner was an asshat, but it wasn't his fault. "They've taken me all over the world searching for Holocaust survivors," I said and then explained about the Bled Collection, specifically about the Stella pieces.

"You're saying they're really looking?" asked Rich.

"I don't know why you would ever doubt that," I said. "Or do you believe the press implicitly?"

"I don't," he said. "It's just doubtful that a family like the Bleds would—"

I sat up straight. "Let me stop you right there. The Bleds give away millions a year to charity and I wasn't kidding when I said I was in the middle of a three-day baking marathon for the Children's Hospital. We do it every year and all Bleds in St. Louis pitch in. Veronique Bled was making a gingerbread house when I left to go get kidnapped."

"Isn't she the CFO?" asked Rich.

"Yes, she is and furthermore, the hunt for survivors started in 1946 and it has never ever stopped. If you doubt me, you can come to the mansion to see the photos of me as a toddler having snacks in cemeteries and libraries and archives. We've got a certain Dr. Wallingford searching through the Kindertransport list right now trying to see if there are any fresh connections that got missed. Any questions?"

"So you might have a connection to Stuttgart?" Campbell asked.

"Like I said, probably, but it's nothing recent. I've been all over Germany a dozen times."

"And there's that group," said Rich quietly.

"What group?" Campbell asked.

"You know about The Klinefeld Group?" I asked.

Campbell wrote the name down. "Who's that?"

I didn't have to say anything. Rich told him that they were a not-for-profit group out of Germany that had tried to get ahold of the Bled Collection by several means, including smearing Stella Bled.

"I remember that," said Campbell. "It was all BS, right?"

"Yes," I said, very aware of how Rich was looking at me. He wanted more, but I wasn't about to give it. This was about Anton Thooft.

"Are you involved in the search for survivors?" Campbell asked.

"I help. Nothing major." I didn't mention that it was pretty apparent that I was expected to carry on the hunt once The Girls were unable to. That responsibility was one of the reasons I had to know about The Klinefeld Group, my father, and what they were after. It was all linked to who I was to the Bleds and why I, of all people, would carry on the search.

"You've never come across the name Thooft in reference to the art?"

"Not that I remember. Was Thooft Jewish?"

"Evangelical Christian."

I shrugged. "And from Whiskey Ridge. I don't see a connection, but you never know."

"You didn't seem surprised when we asked about whether you'd seen Thooft around your apartment," said Rich.

"I wasn't."

"Have you ever had a stalker or dealt with harassment before?"

I started laughing and the bloody hospital memories that had been lurking around the edge of my brain during the entire conversation vanished. "Every day, give or take."

The detectives' mouths dropped open and were quickly snapped shut. I guess they didn't know me much at all. "You had a stalker?" Campbell asked.

"That's plural. Stalkers."

"How many?"

"I don't keep track," I said. "My uncle monitors my threats on the phone and social media."

"So Thooft might've been stalking you online?"

"Sure. I just don't recognize the face or name, but you should know that my stalkers are generally harmless."

"Stalkers aren't harmless," said Rich in disbelief.

"Not everybody's, just mine," I said with a small smile. "They usually go away when they realize I'm boring and ordinary. If they don't, the STLPD invites them to beat it."

"And they leave?" asked Campbell.

"Pretty much. My boyfriend has had to have a few testy conversations to get the point across," I said. "And sometimes they come in handy. Stalkers, that is."

Rich and Campbell laughed until they realized that I wasn't.

"Wait...are you telling me you like your stalkers?" Campbell asked.

"Not all of them. Did you hear about the City Museum situation?" I asked.

"It was more than a situation," said Rich with a look like it was wholly my fault.

"Indeed," I said. "My mother was held hostage, but the point is that one of my stalkers stepped in and tried to help. Jimmy Elbert. Sweet guy. A little nutty, but I'm not going to hold that against him."

The detectives clearly didn't know what to say to that. At least, Campbell didn't know what to say. Training certainly said there wasn't an upside to stalkers, but my life defied normal in more ways than one. Jimmy Elbert was a good example. He now emailed me once a week, happily telling me about his new job and general how ya doing stuff, and I was happy to reply. We'd become friends of a sort.

Detective Rich didn't know what to say either, but his feelings flashed over his face in an odd, confusing way. He didn't like me. He didn't trust me. And he didn't believe me. But I don't think it had anything to do with Anton Thooft. I meant something to him. I hate to say it, but, like a stalker, he had an idea of me and it was now at odds with the person before him and he wasn't happy about it.

Dr. Harris came in and said they had to get me up to a room because my family was about to rush security. Rich and Campbell reluctantly agreed to beat it after they asked me a few more questions, in the usual attempt to see if I'd change my story. It was a story in their eyes and they couldn't quite believe it.

CHAPTER THREE

And then there were turtles. A week later, I was on a turtle hunt in the basement of the Bled Mansion. Why, you ask. Because The Girls stick by the old ways of pest control. In other words, turtle in the basement. In St. Louis, if you're over the age of say…seventy and you've got bugs in your basement, you put a turtle down there to take care of it. You don't spray poison or get useless roach motels. Turtles are the way to go. It's a pragmatic solution to an ongoing problem. The Girls, being well over the age of seventy, had six turtles in residence. Since they thought it cruel to put a turtle in a basement in perpetuity—not wrong there—they'd devised a system of turtle swapping and since I was recovering from the attack with them, I got to do it, because I wasn't doing much else. Thanks, Anton Thooft.

The mansion had two ginormous conservatories on either side of the house filled with palm trees and all sorts of tropical plants. Two turtles went in each conservatory and two went in the basement. Every month they were swapped out so the turtles took turns in the basement. I'm not sure how I ended up turtle swapping. I woke up that morning, Millicent handed me the turtle schedule, and then I was in the basement. Families are like that. We all have our parts and, for some reason, we play them. If I'd given it much thought, I would've seen me and turtles as more proof that I was family. You don't have family friends swap your turtles, now do you?

So now I was in the basement on what seemed like a never-ending search for one particular turtle, Thaddeus. I know it sounds simple. Turtles aren't fast, but the Bled basement wasn't typical. It was huge. Bigger than the house actually. The Girls' father, Nicolai, built the basement bigger with hidden doors to the secret section that extended beyond the foundation of the house. It was prohibition time and he wanted a place to continue to make beer and store his vast wine collection, so the basement was about fifty percent bigger than it should've been. That's a lot of turtle territory.

Usually, it wasn't a problem or so Millicent said. The Girls, ever concerned about turtle welfare, had rocks and heat lamps set up for comfort. It was a sophisticated system connected to a computer so the lamps came on with the sunrise and went out at sunset. Turtles have to know what time of year and day it is, don't ya know? About fifty percent of the time they found the basement duo on their hot rocks having a good roast, but not this time. Valentino was there, but Thaddeus wasn't. I expected to find him under the wine racks. That was supposed to be their prime hunting ground, but no luck and I'd been searching for hours. He had to be there. It's not like he could get out.

I sat down at the tasting table in the third wine cave and stretched.

"Wherever you are, Anton Thooft, I hate you," I said to the racks of dusty wine bottles.

My back hurt and my quads were burning, but I couldn't come up without that turtle. It was just my luck that Thaddeus decided to go rogue on a day when I was there and everyone else was busy. Bastard.

I was trying to think of who I could hire to hunt that damn turtle when my phone buzzed.

Yes! Tell me I have to go somewhere. Tell me I have to go somewhere.

"Ah, crap."

It was Detective Rich, my least favorite detective. But it wasn't all bad news. Maybe he needed me to come in. Immediately. That very minute.

"Hello," I said, trying not to sound hopeful.

"Miss Watts, this is Detective Rich." He sounded kinda funny. If I didn't know better, I'd have said nervous.

Since he didn't say anything else, I said, "I know. Um...what's up?"

"I...I have information I'd like to pass on to you."

"Okay. Lay it on me."

Rich didn't say anything, but I could hear him breathing. If he wasn't a cop, I'd have said it was creepy.

"Are you waiting for something?" I asked.

"No, but I'd like to talk to you in person."

Yes! Yes! Yes! See ya, Thaddeus, you reptilian pain in my butt.

"I can meet you and Detective Campbell in say an hour," I said.

"Actually, it's just me." He sounded oddly chagrined.

Swell.

"Fine. I'll be there as soon as I can."

Rich took a rather jagged breath and said, "Actually, I'll come to you. Are you available?"

"I guess. When?"

Not too soon. Not too soon.

"Now," he said.

Dammit.

"When is now?" I was thinking about my face. I still looked like I had a rancid case of Poison Ivy on the lower half. I could cover it up and I had to cover it up. I felt and looked disgusting. Worse than the hospital to be honest and he didn't like me. I couldn't be gross to boot.

"Now, now," he said.

"Now?"

He hung up and the doorbell rang. I couldn't hear it, but the lights flashed in the basement to alert The Girls in case there was no one up top.

"Holy crap," I said, looking down at myself covered in dust, spiderwebs, and more than a little turtle poop. All that and a raging case of hideous face. Dammit, Thaddeus. I was going to take a shower after finding him and now it was too late.

Joy pounded down the stairs and peeked over the bannister. "There's a cop at the door. What did you do?"

"How do you know he's a cop?"

"He looks aggravated," she said.

"It might not be about me," I said.

She rolled her eyes. "Mercy, please."

"Don't answer it."

The lights flashed again and Rocco Licata, The Girls' chauffeur and Fats' brother, yelled down the stairs. "I've got it."

"No!" I yelled, but it was too late.

"Time to face the music," said Joy.

"There's no music." I stood up. "At least I get to come upstairs for a while."

"You still have to find that turtle."

"How much would it take to get you—"

"You don't have that much money. Besides, it's in my contract. I do not hunt turtles at any price," said Joy with a wrinkled nose.

"You put that in your contract?"

"I did."

"May I ask why?"

She shivered. "Reptiles. I just can't."

I glanced at Valentino snoozing on his rock and wondered what the big deal was, but I guess everybody has a thing. "Should I talk in the library?"

She looked back and said, "Nope. Here he comes."

I dropped back onto the bench. "What the…"

"Should I bring some coffee or tea?" Joy asked.

"Down here?"

"You have to find that turtle."

I groaned and said, "Why not? Coffee, please."

She started to go up and then stopped to ask, "Is it that one from the hospital?"

"The very same," I said.

She scowled and went up squeezing past Detective Rich as he came down the stairs looking more nervous than he sounded. Joy's scowl probably didn't help. "Did she say turtle?"

"She did."

"I don't mean to state the obvious, but…" He pointed at Valentino.

"That's Valentino. I'm looking for Thaddeus."

"That turtle is named Valentino?"

"He's the best looking one," I said.

"I...uh...okay," he said. "So I wanted to update you on your case."

I sat up straight and tried to look dignified, which I certainly was not. "Okay. Go for it."

"It's closed."

I waited. Nothing else was forthcoming. "That's it? You came all the way here to say that?"

"It's not that far and traffic wasn't bad," said Rich.

"You could've called."

He looked like he wanted to say something but couldn't quite bring himself to do it. "Yeah."

"But you came all the way here?"

"Can I sit down?" he asked.

"Sure."

Rich sat down on the bench across from me at the tasting table and was silent.

"You're gonna have to tell me, 'cause I've got a turtle to find," I said with more patience than I felt. He could've gotten me out of the basement. Instead, he was wasting my time. Only The Girls got to do that.

"I wanted to update you on what we found out," he said.

"And that is...bad news?"

"Not exactly."

I'm so tired.

"Okay. What's the bad news?" I started worrying that he'd run my DNA and found out I had a wacky genetic disease.

Rich took a breath. "First, I need to apologize."

I'm awake.

"Do tell."

"I behaved in an inappropriate manner at the crime scene and at the hospital," he said.

"Did you get a reprimand or something?" I asked. "I didn't make a complaint."

Two spots of pink bloomed on his cheeks. "I know and I appreciate that."

"I have to ask why you were hostile. I don't think we'd ever met before."

"We haven't. It's complicated."

"Enlighten me," I said.

"My uncle was Orson Imich."

Orson Imich? It was the tiniest bit familiar, but it wasn't ringing a big bell. "I'm sorry. Did I do something to him?"

"No, but I thought you did."

Joy came down the stairs laden with a silver coffee service that she didn't usually break out unless she or The Girls were angry. Rich was lucky she didn't dump it in his lap. I heard a few stories about that happening, although I'd never seen it.

Then she did what she never did, she poured, like a servant on *Downton Abbey*, including sugar and cream. Joy was a servant, technically, but she certainly wasn't servile or formal. She wanted to impress upon him my status and I had to suppress a smile. My status. A cop's daughter and widely acknowledged nitwit, thanks to my face. Break out the silver.

"Thanks, Joy," I said.

"You're welcome." She shot Rich a withering look and left without another word.

"I don't think she likes me."

"She thinks you're here to hassle me again," I said.

"I'm not." He looked at his cup. "Should I drink it? I feel like I shouldn't drink it."

I laughed. "Go ahead. It'll be great coffee."

He took a tentative sip, like there might be hemlock in it and then smiled. "Wow. That's good coffee."

"She has a knack. Now tell me about your uncle. His name is familiar, but I can't really place him."

It didn't take more than fifteen seconds to understand what Rich's deal was. Orson Imich was a member of the Art Museum's board involved with The Klinefeld Group's attempt to get ahold of the Bled Collection, but he also died right before the lawsuit was filed by the board. Nobody knew why the board members got on board with The

Klinefeld Group, but several died around that time and the others were now mum on the subject.

But they hadn't been mum before. The board members that sided with The Klinefeld Group had been pretty loud about what they thought the Bleds were up to, hoarding art, hiding it from rightful heirs, and straight up accusing Stella Bled of stealing it. When Imich died, the papers said it was brought on by extreme stress over the Bled Collection situation, like he wasn't part of the reason it was happening.

"Your uncle would've sided with The Klinefeld Group had he lived," I said.

"I don't know if that's true. He was under tremendous pressure to vote with the others. He did think the museum was best to care for a collection that wasn't purchased and he was open about his opinions," Rich said diplomatically.

No kidding.

"Because he didn't think we were still searching for the real owners?"

"The Bleds wouldn't talk to the board members about the collection."

Shocking.

I narrowed my eyes at him. "What about me?"

"You avoided his lawyer's calls."

"I instinctively avoid lawyers," I said "and your uncle and the board were trashing us. They could've asked about what was happening, but they decided to attack and sue first. They only asked questions later."

Rich squirmed and said, "I'm aware of that."

"So you decided your uncle's death was our fault?" I asked. "My fault. Is that it?"

Rich took a breath and said, "The situation, the stress was at fault, and you were a part of that situation."

I took a big drink of Joy's delicious brew and looked him over. "But you don't think so now."

"No, not anymore. I started asking around and got in touch with my uncle's secretary. I'd seen her at the funeral and she also blamed his death on the stress. This time I asked about the Bleds in particular and what was going on right before he died. She reminded me that she was on maternity leave and Uncle Orson had a temp when it happened. I found the temp and she said that he'd talked about the Bleds in positive terms. He changed his mind and told her none of the accusations were true. Something about the Smithsonian and research. I guess he must've told the other board members and that's why the lawsuit was ultimately dropped."

That wasn't why, but I let it lie.

He threw back his coffee like a tequila shooter and asked, "Mind if I get some more?"

"Go ahead."

He was stalling, but I could afford to wait while he slowly poured in cream and added lumps of sugar while eyeing the writhing figures on the coffee pot with trepidation.

"So about the case," he said.

"Hold on there, Jethro," I said. "We're not leaving that sleeping dog lie."

He chuckled down into his cup. "SpongeBob fan, are you?"

"Not really. The Girls think *The Beverly Hillbillies* is hilarious and they practically raised me."

"Really? Why?"

"Don't try to change the subject. You were apologizing for being an asshat after I was assaulted and kidnapped. Let's stick with that. I know there's more to it."

"Uncle Orson and I were very close. He was...like a father to me. I believed what he said about the Bled Collection completely. I didn't know he'd changed his opinion and we're Jewish. Did you know that?"

"No. Is it important?" I asked.

"Definitely. The art and whatever else the Bleds are holding onto, Uncle Orson said it belonged to our people. He thought that stuff about Stella Bled was true and he was convinced that the Bleds would sell if it suited them because they're not Jewish, so they had no reason to be attached."

"And?"

He frowned. "Now I'm wondering why he was so convinced."

There it is.

I got up and snatched Valentino as he made a break for a wine rack. I put him on the table and he closed up his shell real quick.

"I'm sorry I talked to you the way I did," he said.

"It's alright," I said.

"No, it's not."

We drank our coffee and I debated whether I should put a bug in the detective's ear. He was already suspicious. Orson Imich's heart attack seemed a little too convenient, considering the timing and if he wasn't wholly on board with The Klinefeld Group...

"So my case is closed," I said instead.

"Yeah, it is," he said as he poured another cup.

"You sound disappointed."

"I am, but it all fits."

"Campbell called a couple days ago and said Thooft had been stalking me," I said.

"He was," Rich said, his frown deepening, "and it wasn't a spur of the moment thing either. He bought the car he used with false identification immediately after he got here, so he had a plan."

I waited for the troubled detective to say something else, but he didn't.

"Do you...have a feeling?" I asked.

"I might," he said. "You don't? I've heard about those Watts' instincts."

"Nope. Nary a one. What have you got?"

Valentino started trucking toward the edge of the table and Rich turned him around. "Nothing, it's just this Thooft character. Normal guy. No hint he'd do this. None."

"But he had pictures of me, my address, etcetera..."

"We found more on his laptop and browsing history," said Rich, but he didn't look happy about it.

I drained my cup and asked, "What else do you need?"

"Something's not right about it."

"Anything specific?"

"It's just wrong, but Thooft is dead and the case is closed." He gave me a hard look. "*I* can't do anything else."

"You think I should look into it."

"I would if I were you. The whole thing is off. Have that uncle of yours take a look at Thooft's laptop. I heard he has a way with computers."

I tipped my chin down and batted my eyelashes. "You act like he can get access to anything."

Rich laughed and saved Valentino from nosediving off the table again. "I didn't think I could ever like you."

"Surprise," I said, and he laughed again. "What does the family say?"

"Not much. If Thooft hadn't had you in his trunk at the time he was shot, they wouldn't have believed it at all. Even so, it was iffy. They wanted to see reports on fingerprints, fluids, the whole shebang."

"And you have all that?"

"The phrase *dead to rights* was invented for this situation. Your blood was all over him." He checked the time on his phone. "In fact, I'm due to meet with them in an hour."

"How are they doing?" I asked.

"Interesting that you care."

"I'm not sure if I care, but I'm curious about them. Who are they?"

"Regular as can be. We gave them a hard look because they're so damn perfect."

The Thoofts were a normal family. A hog farmer and his stay-at-home wife married almost sixty years with four kids, three boys and a girl. Anton was the oldest. No criminal history period. Nothing. No warning signs or indications that Anton was working up to kidnapping anybody, much less me.

"How are they acting?" I asked.

"Disoriented, like they can't catch their balance."

I grabbed Valentino and turned him around again. "Did he ever talk about me?"

"No. I think they were only vaguely aware of your existence. They're not news junkies."

"Did they know he was back from Germany?"

"No. He flew into Lambert and stayed at a Motel 6. From his cellphone pings we can tell he never went out to see them and spent most of his time during the week before lurking around the Central West End."

"Looking for me, you mean."

"I assume so, but you said you never saw him," said Rich.

"I didn't. My skills are highly overrated."

"Tell me more about what you were doing that week? Did you remember anything else?"

"Not really. I was still recovering from St. Sebastian. I did some background checks for my dad, some wedding planning with Fats, went to the doctor with my mom."

"Were you ever alone?"

"Sure."

He drummed his fingers on the tabletop. "So leaving the Bled Mansion that morning wasn't the first time you were alone? I had the impression that it was."

"Well, I walked to my parents' and to the mansion alone." I slapped my forehead. "Wait a minute. I had Pick with me."

"Pick?"

"Pickpocket. My boyfriend's dog."

"Pitbull?"

I pictured that big fuzzy goofball and laughed. "Giant poodle."

"Are you kidding?"

"I am not."

The drumming got harder. "And you didn't have him that morning?"

I shook my head. "My mom told me to take him, but I didn't want to mess with his coat and booties."

"I'm not even going to ask about the booties. So that was the first time you were completely alone? No dog, no witnesses?"

"I guess so. I never thought about it. I was on the phone with Chuck," I said.

"He told me. That's why the alert went out so quick. He heard you screaming. I don't know if he's going to get over that," said Rich with a softness to his voice that was new to me, but I suspected most victims got to hear it early on.

"Why do you think I'm living here and hunting for turtles? My dad and uncle did the security system."

"I don't blame them, considering what could've happened."

"Do you know what he was planning to do? I mean, other than kill me, I assume."

He shook his head with some frustration. "We don't."

I touched my bumpy chin. "How did he know how to make that concoction he put over my face?"

"Nothing has turned up on that."

"Nothing?"

He shook his head. "How are you feeling?"

"I look bad, but I feel good. My bloodwork's normal again, but the doctors have no clue about that stuff. What did you find out?"

"It was a form of insecticide, but the chemical makeup is unusual. Our lab thinks it may be a new compound recently discovered."

"How would an AP Gov teacher get ahold of that?" I asked.

"We asked the same question. The Stuttgart Polizei searched his apartment and they didn't find anything. It looks like he just got a wild hair and flew over to come after you. He was looking at several Incel sites detailing kidnapping and rape scenarios. Insecticides are mentioned."

My chest tightened up and my vision got a little funky. It'd been happening less and less over the last week, but there it was again. Anton Thooft was one of those psychos that hated women and wanted to destroy us for not liking them.

Rich touched my hand gently. "Are you alright?"

"I didn't know Thooft was an Incel. Your description didn't sound like the kind of guy that builds bombs to blow up hot cheerleaders."

"He visited Incel chatrooms, but he wasn't active in terms of contributing."

I put down my cup with a clank. Thankfully I didn't chip the china. "Where was he taking me?"

"We don't know. There was no indication from anything on his phone or in the car." He frowned at me and looked like he wanted to say something else but was worried I couldn't take it.

"What?" I asked.

"This guy was stable and six weeks ago he starts going to radical websites and decides to stuff you in a trunk. It doesn't track."

"But your investigation is done?"

"Thooft is dead. He did it without a doubt."

"So there's nothing left to investigate," I said.

"There's no need to get an exact motive when there's not going to be a trial. I was reminded this morning that Campbell and I have other fish to fry." Rich stood up.

"And I have a turtle to find, but I'll walk you out," I said, gathering up Valentino, who closed up tight.

Rich picked up the tray and smiled. "Do they usually use this set 'cause it's really something."

We went up the rickety stairs and I said, "Not usually."

"I'd have thought a cop would get the cheap stuff," he said.

I opened the basement door, letting warm light and the scent of fresh flowers and cinnamon wash over us. "It's not about you being a cop. It's about you giving me a problem at the hospital."

Rich brought the silver service into the back foyer next to the breakfast room, frowning again. "I was awful, so why'd she bring out the good stuff?"

"It's not the good stuff. They hate that set."

"I don't understand. It must cost a fortune."

"You weren't intimidated by that?" I pointed at David on the coffee pot taking down Goliath. Even though it was all heavy silver, you could see the blood in the incredible detail. Don't get me started on the dragon slaying on the sugar urn.

"It is a little...overwhelming."

"The family, including Joy, like to get their points across in unusual ways."

Rich looked over the scary silver. "So I'm Goliath and you're David?"

I put Valentino down and took the tray. "You could be the dragon."

"I'll pass."

I laughed. "You'll keep me updated about the case?"

"I will, but I doubt anything will happen."

"When it comes to me, you never know."

Millicent came rushing into the foyer, wreathed in smiles. "I didn't know you had a guest. You could've had the library for coffee and—oh." She looked at the silver set and gave Detective Rich the once over.

"Joy thought that perhaps something was wrong," I said quickly. "The detective and I had a bit of a tussle at the hospital but it's all good now."

Millicent relaxed. "Joy is very protective of our Mercy as are we all. I'm sure you understand."

"I'm beginning to," said Rich. "Thank you for seeing me, Mercy."

"No problem."

"I'm sorry," said Millicent. "I didn't catch your name."

He hesitated and then said, "Detective Rich. Dustin Rich." He waited to see if she'd recognize the name, but she merely thanked him for handling my case.

"Millicent," I said, knowing full well I couldn't let the connection go unmentioned. She'd find out later who he was and I'd be in trouble. "Detective Rich is Orson Imich's nephew."

"Oh." She threw up her hands. "That poor man. To die so suddenly like that. Such a shame. He was a great talent."

"Talent?" I asked.

"Yes, of course. Mr. Imich was an art historian. He was one of the experts they called on when a piece of Nazi-looted art turned up. He was passionate about the Holocaust. His parents survived Buchenwald."

Rich looked at her with pure astonishment. Millicent was guileless and sincere. The Girls didn't hold grudges, which is more than I could say for me.

"He..." Rich stuttered. "I'm sorry he questioned your motives over the art."

Millicent took his hand and patted it. "There's no need to apologize. Your uncle already did so before his death."

"You met with him?" I asked.

"We did. Myrtle and I decided it was churlish not to explain the situation directly and we had met Dr. Imich several times before so we thought he would be the most open to a meeting."

"What did you talk about?" Rich asked.

"Everything to do with our cousin, Stella, and the pieces in her collection. We showed him our research, including our discussions with Dr. Wallingford. He's researching the Kindertransport lists for us. We gave Dr. Imich a list of people to contact, but he died before he talked to most of them."

"His temp secretary said he'd changed his mind."

"I believe he did," said Millicent.

"Do you know why he was against you in the first place?" Rich asked.

"Someone persuaded him that we were hiding something and that we intended to sell pieces from the collection. He staked his reputation on those false accusations."

"Who told him that?" Rich asked.

"We asked him, but he declined to say," said Millicent. "Such a shame that he didn't have time to go public with his change of heart. He should've been honored by the museum for his lifetime of work."

Rich got a little misty at that and appeared to be at a loss for words.

"Do you have an interest in art?" Millicent asked kindly.

"I do," he said. "I spent more time at museums than anywhere else growing up."

"Would you like to see the objects in question?"

Rich's mouth dropped, but he recovered quickly. "You'd let me?"

Millicent patted his hand. "They've never been hidden. They're right here, so we see them every day and don't forget what happened and why."

"I'd love to see them."

Millicent took the tray from me. "Mercy dear, will you do the honors? Imogene is looking rather peaked. I must look after her."

"Of course." I led Rich into the grand foyer and started pointing out various pieces. Some were from the Stella Collection and others were regular Bled pieces.

"Who's Imogene?" he asked when we stopped in the library and I handed him a small photo album belonging to the Hermann family.

"One of the turtles," I said.

"How would you know if she was peaked?"

"Beats me, but I'm sure she is if Millicent says so."

Rich looked down at the album. It wasn't fancy with only a simple cardboard cover stamped with a diamond pattern. "What's this?"

"A family album." I took it back and flipped it over so he could see the label carefully pasted on the back.

"I didn't know they had things like that."

"It's not a headliner. The museum didn't care about things like albums and children's toys. Stella brought out a lot of stuff nobody talks about. Other agents, too. It wasn't just her. We also have objects that British pilots brought out with them after the resistance saved them."

"Money?"

"Absolutely. It's labeled the same way in the family vault," I said.

"She was different than I thought," he said.

"Most people are."

Rich's phone rang and it startled him. "Ah, shit. I have to go meet the Thoofts. Campbell's pissed. Rain check?"

"Sure. The Girls won't mind," I said.

He took the album from me and tentatively opened it. A wedding invitation pasted on the first page. The beginning of a life together. The album was only half full.

"You don't think it's too late?" Rich asked gazing down at the wedding photo on the next page.

"We'll never think it's too late," I said.

"No?"

"This album belongs to someone. We just haven't found them yet."

"I wouldn't know where to start and that's coming from a detective."

"The library. Always start in the library."

He laughed and then got serious. "Do you want me to tell them anything?"

"Who?" I asked puzzled. My mind was on the Hermanns who went into the Theresienstadt ghetto and never came out.

"Thooft's family. I only ask because victims sometimes do."

Victim.

I took a breath and put the Hermanns away on their shelf. "Like say that I forgive them or something?"

"You don't have to say anything."

"It's not their fault."

"Do you want me to say that?"

I sighed. "Sure. Why not?"

"You don't owe them anything. It's fair to say they owe you," he said.

I led him out into the hall and then to the front door. "I don't want to point fingers like that. You can't stop what you don't know."

"Have you gotten any help with this?" he asked.

"I have a therapist."

"Helping?"

"I don't even know," I said. "I feel okay."

"If you don't mind me saying, you look a lot like the Thoofts. Unbalanced."

"It's just that he came out of nowhere," I said.

"Except he didn't. It happened for a reason."

Exactly.

Rich took his coat off the ornate rack and I opened the door. I wasn't going to do it. I wasn't going to say it, but something about the way he came to the Bled Mansion to admit he was wrong, to apologize when he didn't have to. He could've never laid eyes on me again. I'd never have known why he was nasty. He was just one more guy who thought he knew me and felt entitled to judge. But he showed up. He changed it.

"Rich?"

He stood in the open doorway and flipped up his collar. "Yes?"

"I don't want to ruin this new rapport we have."

He stopped and got that eagle-eyed look I knew so well from my dad, Grandad, and Chuck. "What?"

"Did you have an autopsy done on your uncle?"

You know how in novels they talk about the color draining from someone's face? Well, that really happens. Rich looked at me and I watched the color drain out of his face. There was a line. I swear to God, a line where his rosy hue turned abruptly to printer paper white.

"He had a heart attack," he said barely above a whisper.

"I know."

"What are you saying?"

"Your uncle was going to side with The Klinefeld Group, but he may have changed his mind after meeting my godmothers. Millicent certainly thought he did."

"Did you hear something?"

I hesitated and he saw it. His face went from pale to red and sweaty just like that.

"Yes, I did. Nothing concrete on your uncle though."

"Who told you?" he asked.

"I wouldn't like to say, but it doesn't matter. A few board members died unexpectedly, didn't they?"

"Accidents and a suicide."

I bit my lip.

"Uncle Orson was old, really old and..."

"I'm not saying they killed him," I said.

"Who's they? The Klinefeld Group? They're a charity."

"If you use the word charity loosely."

Rich shook his head. "I know you've got an instinct for these things, but this is way out."

I crossed my arms and leaned on the door frame. "It really isn't and I think you were already suspicious."

"You think a charity murdered my uncle?"

"I think that if he was murdered, they did it. No question."

He squinted at me, his flushed face full of doubt. "What makes you say that?"

"Because they've done it before."

Det. Rich listened with increasing agitation as I told him about Lester, The Girls' chauffeur, and my great grandparents being murdered. I hated to send him off to the Thoofts so unsettled, but it couldn't be helped. I had to tell him.

Once he was gone, I helped Myrtle and Millicent down the basement stairs and led them through the warren of wine racks, whiskey casks, and beer barrels to the last door inside the prohibition extension. I closed the door and pointed at Thaddeus who, defying all expectations and reptilian norms, was in the corner behind the door next to a pile of dust and dirt. Visible inside the pile were eggs.

"Oh, my goodness," said Myrtle.

"It's a miracle," exclaimed Millicent.

It wasn't. I'd found the real Thaddeus dead about a week after Lester's murder and there was no way I was going to march upstairs and say, "Hey, ya know that turtle you love and have had for fifty years, he's dead." Nope. Not doing that. Plus, Thaddeus was a common box turtle. *Common.* So I took myself out to country roads near St. Seb and drove around until I spotted a turtle crossing the road. I popped that sucker in the passenger seat and took him home. It never occurred to me that he might be a girl. The original Thaddeus could've been a girl for all I knew.

So I went back to the mansion and put Thaddeus II in the basement. Thaddeus I went to my parents' backyard for a proper burial in a shoebox. Was it the wrong thing to do? Maybe. Do I stand by it? Absolutely.

"Yeah, well, miracles happen," I said.

"Dr. Halifax said he was a boy."

"Er...Dr. Halifax?"

"You know, Dr. Halifax. The curator of the Zoo's reptile house."

Crap on a cracker.

"We should call her," said Myrtle. "This has to be rare. She thought Thaddeus was about seventy."

"Maybe it was Valentino," I said.

"Valentino is a boy. That's why we named him Valentino," said Millicent.

"I'll call Dr. Halifax."

"Do you know Dr. Halifax?" Myrtle asked.

I'm about to.

"Sure. He's great."

"She."

"Right. Of course," I said quickly.

Millicent didn't notice the mistake, but Myrtle sure did. Her mouth turned into a frown, but as soon as her sister looked at her with shining eyes the frown was upside-down.

"Well, this certainly is a *surprise*," Myrtle said, giving me a mild version of Aunt Miriam's stink eye.

"We've never had eggs before," said Millicent. "All these years and no eggs."

"Because they were all boys." Myrtle kept looking at me and I had a feeling my next coffee was going to be in the angry silver.

"Maybe we should go up," I said. "It's cold down here."

"We can't just leave them," said Millicent. "They're babies and Thaddeus is trying to keep them warm. We have to do something."

If Thaddeus II was trying to do anything, it was taking a nap. She just happened to be next to the eggs, but Millicent was certain of her maternal instincts.

"Come on, dear," said Myrtle. "You shouldn't be down here. You know what the doctor said. You're still recovering. Mercy will call Dr. Halifax and tell her about this *interesting* development."

We got Millicent upstairs, not without a whole lot of protests, but we kept at her. Finding out how Sister Maggie had died so many years ago had been a huge blow to Millicent. Myrtle thought only the discovery of the liquor cabinet and me moving into the stable with Chuck kept her going, but she seemed so old. It's stupid to say that. Myrtle and Millicent were old. They were old when I was born, for crying out loud, but I was having a hard time thinking of them that way.

I helped Millicent over the threshold and Joy spotted us, rushing over all in a tizzy. "What happened? Oh, Lord, why were you down there? Did you fall?"

"Eggs," cried Millicent. "Thaddeus laid eggs."

Joy stared at her and I could see what was going through her mind. Dementia. The worst has happened.

"He laid eggs," I said. "I found them."

Joy shivered. "There are eggs in the basement?" She said it like she was talking about rabid baby rats.

"Mercy will handle it," said Myrtle. "But we should get Millicent up to bed so she can rest."

"I don't need to rest. I feel wonderful." Millicent was beaming, absolutely beaming. "It's a miracle."

Joy looked at me and I said, "I'm going to handle it."

"How?"

"I don't know. They're turtles. How hard can it be?"

Myrtle and Joy walked Millicent up the stairs and I spun in a circle. What was I going to do? Bribe Dr. Halifax to say she made a mistake? How much would it take to bribe a reptile keeper?

When in doubt call your mom. I called my mother and she was not happy about it. I didn't even get to ask her about the turtle situation.

"Where have you been?" Mom demanded.

"Um…here where you told me to be."

"You haven't answered for ten whole minutes. I thought something happened. I was just going to call Joy. What were you doing?" Mom said in an incredible rush of slurred words and irritation.

"Did something happen?"

"Yes. I'm delivering those turkeys to the mission with your father."

"That's…not exciting," I said.

"The fact that the house is empty is," Mom said. "Get over there pronto and don't scare the Siamese. Chuck gave them a real start when he was in there. There's your father. I have to go." Mom hung up.

Get over to the house and don't scare the Siamese. Like I could scare the Siamese. Chuck didn't scare them. It was the other way around. Swish and Swat were up in Dad's office knocking files on the floor when Chuck was talking to me. He'd discovered them just as Anton Thooft came at me. I don't know if my screaming triggered it, but they came at Chuck like starving tigers, jumping onto his back as he ran down the stairs to find me. He had to shed his jacket to get them off and Mom was sure they were traumatized. As they're her favorite children, she was very concerned. They'd been to the vet three times for stress and exhaustion.

I took a peek up the stairs and the coast was clear, so I whistled for Pickpocket. The poodle scampered down the hall, sliding on the area rugs and yipping for no good reason.

"Shush. We're going out." I grabbed his leash and my coat, trying to get a clean getaway.

I got the door open with one hand and had Pick's collar in the other.

"Where do you think you're going?" Rocco Licata came out from under the stairs, wearing golfing clothes and spinning a driver in one hand.

"Out," I said.

"I don't think so." Rocco came over and neatly took Pick and his leash off me. "You're going nowhere."

"Says who and what were you doing under the stairs?" I asked.

"Waiting. I heard that ruckus about that turtle. I knew you'd try to book it." He clipped Pick's leash on and grabbed his jacket. "It ain't happening."

"Why do you care?"

"Since Chuck let my little cousin Wally walk on a prost bust with a warning. He asked me to make sure you don't leave the house."

I rolled my eyes. "Chuck wouldn't do that."

"Wanna bet? Besides, Wally's only thirteen. What's the harm?"

"You're telling me Chuck found your thirteen-year-old cousin with a prostitute and he didn't do anything about it?"

"Hell, no. Wally was just on the premises."

"Doing what?"

"Stacking firewood."

"At a..."

"Brothel," said Rocco. "You act like you haven't ever heard of such a thing. You've been to Amsterdam. I've seen the pictures."

"They don't have fireplaces." Actually, I couldn't swear to that. I'd been through the De Wallen area because if you're a tourist you've got to do it, but I was looking as little as possible. It made me sad.

"It's a nice place," said Rocco. "The girls like a crackling fire."

"Does Calpurnia know?" I asked.

Calpurnia Fibonacci was the local mob boss. Both Rocco and Fats worked for her on and off. I worked for her, too, but I was doing my best to forget about that.

"It's not her trade," said Rocco.

I shook my head to clear the cobwebs. "Why was Chuck there? He's homicide."

"One of the girls stabbed a guy."

"So a super nice place."

Rocco scoffed. "It didn't happen at the house. He cut her off in traffic."

"I don't know how to talk to you," I said, "if you think that's normal."

"Well, I know how to talk to you. Go into the library and call that turtle nerd 'cause I'm taking Pick and you're going nowhere." He opened the door with a flourish. "You got that?"

"Maybe I'll go without Pick."

Rocco might not have the size or skill set of his sister, but he was no fool, which led me to wonder what the Licatas could accomplish if they went straight. "You won't leave without Pick. He's your security blanket."

"I don't like you."

"Sure, you do." Rocco grinned at me. "I'm good to The Girls. I would fuck anyone up if they messed with them and you know it."

I did know it and it made me a little misty.

Rocco's eyes narrowed again. "I don't know what's going on with that detective, but I don't like it."

"What do you mean?"

"Somebody killed his uncle, you knew, but it was news to him."

I pushed Rocco out the door. "Just walk Pick, will ya?"

"I'm going," he said, stepping outside.

I went to close the door and he said, "But I want to know what you did to that turtle."

Son of a bitch.

CHAPTER FOUR

My mother was not happy. She delayed Dad, using all her feminine wiles for three hours and I still didn't get into that liquor cabinet. Rocco came back and started practicing his swing in the rose garden, but he'd set his own special alarm and it went off when I tried to get out and Joy caught me. I didn't have the code. Everyone was conspiring to keep a handle on me after the Thooft incident, even though the guy was dead as a door nail, knob, or knocker. Even Uncle Morty was on the case, handling security while recuperating at his girlfriend Nikki's house from his surgery.

Nikki'd returned from Greece when she heard he was on death's door and Uncle Morty said nearly dying was worth it. She was charmed and gave him a second chance, saying that if he ever lied to her again, she'd come to his funeral in a red dress. Nikki didn't say she'd be the cause of his funeral, but it was implied.

Other than The Girls security, Uncle Morty was under strict orders to take it easy. He wasn't writing or doing any work for Dad or me. I thought he'd miss his hacking, but he didn't seem to. He was eating heart healthy and doing his therapy. It was a brand new Uncle Morty. I saw him wearing jeans once. It was disconcerting.

I tried all day to get out of the house unseen and failed miserably. I had to try a different tact. Early the next morning, I called in my secret weapon, my hacker, Spidermonkey. Surely, he'd be on my side and, even more convenient, he'd taken over Dad's business at Uncle Morty's recommendation or rather Nikki's. She said he had to hand it over for a while and he did, to the competition no less. I wasn't sure what to make of that, but I hadn't been yelled at for three weeks and I quite liked it.

I looked out my window at the frigid avenue and told Spidermonkey, "You've got to get me out of here."

"I don't have the new codes," he said.

"You can get them."

"I happen to think your father is right."

"About what? Thooft is super dead. What are we protecting me from?"

"You have a head injury," he said. "Rest. Eat too much. Enjoy the holidays."

"I need to walk. Mom wants me to walk," I said.

Walk was now our euphemism for getting in the liquor cabinet. We'd agreed not to ever refer to it, my great grandparents, or what I'd found in Agatha's purse, just in case The Klinefeld Group was listening. Spidermonkey had a pretty tight lock on our cyber security, but you never know. We only spoke of it in person, which was pretty hard since I couldn't get out without an escort.

"Chuck can walk you some other time," he said.

"He's in court. I have an hour window for a walk before The Girls get going."

"Fats?"

"With Tiny at his therapy," I said with triumph.

Spidermonkey took a breath. "You'll just have to wait. There will be other opportunities to walk."

"I'm tired of waiting. Waiting sucks. I'm going stir crazy."

"Embrace leisure."

"Swell."

I hung up in a huff. After the turkey delivery, Mom had dragged Dad to her therapy, instead of Aunt Tenne, saying she felt a little shaky and nervous. Dad called me wanting to know what was going on and I said it was a stroke thing. He bought it. I don't know why. It was super vague. But Mom still couldn't drive, so it was a good way to get Dad out bright and early before the geezers showed up at the house for work at nine. I had to get there. I had Pick. Rocco had set the alarm, but he was up in the gym lifting. He wouldn't see until it was too late.

Joy. That was the answer. She was in the kitchen baking turtle treats. I'm not making that up. Dr. Halifax gave me the recipe after I explained the Thaddeus situation. She agreed to say that she'd made an error when she said the turtle was a boy in exchange for a huge amount of DBD junk, signed albums, concert tees, posters, the whole shebang. I didn't know what I'd have to do to get that stuff from Mickey Stix, but it wouldn't be pleasant.

But it was worth it to see Millicent so happy. She was like her old self. Under Dr. Halifax's direction, we moved the eggs to the left conservatory and made a nest at the foot of a palm tree. Millicent spent a good amount of time checking the ambient temperature and discussing the eggs with Thaddeus II. The turtle had zero interest in her offspring, but Millicent more than made up for her lack of enthusiasm. I was a little worried she'd taken to sleeping on a lounge in the conservatory so I checked to make sure she wasn't there before I tied Pickpocket to the front doorknob and went into the kitchen to reheat some hot chocolate that Aaron had brought by in his favorite Mauviel copper pot. He seemed to think the key to my healing was gallons of hot chocolate and he kept bringing it. I couldn't drink that much. Nobody could and chocolate burps aren't as pleasant as you'd think they'd be.

"I thought you already had some hot chocolate this morning," said Joy as she poked a gnarly-looking cookie with a wooden skewer.

"I did," I said, "but Aaron keeps bringing it. I don't want to throw it out, so I thought I'd take it to the guys working on the stable apartment."

"That's not a bad idea."

The pot started to bubble and I took it off the flame. "I'll be right back."

"Oh, no, you don't." Joy slid the turtle treats onto a cooling rack. "I'll take it. You're supposed to rest."

I sighed dramatically. "Fine. But can you take it now while it's hot?"

"Sure. Can you watch those things in the oven?"

"I can," I said and Joy slipped on her jacket and took the chocolate from me. The minute she went through the breakfast room door, I sprinted through the house to the front. I yanked Pick's leash off the knob and watched the security panel.

Beep. Beep. Beep. Beep. Beep. Ding.

And the alarm was off. I scooted out the door with Pick and closed it a second before Joy put the code back in to lock it.

Am I good or what?

Pick and I ran down the walk, whipped open the gate, and stepped onto the frosted sidewalk in triumph. Like most of my triumphs, it didn't last.

"You are so easy." Rocco was leaning on one of the brick pillars, bundled up like he was the little brother on *A Christmas Story*, and knitting a lime green scarf.

"What the..."

"I knew you'd try it when I heard you talking to your dad."

"Since when do you knit?"

"Since I got anxiety. You got a problem with that?" Rocco asked with his needles clicking.

"No. I just..."

He eyed me.

"No."

"Good. I'm ready. Where are we going?"

Why God why? Don't you want me to find out what's in that cabinet?

"For a walk."

Rocco snorted and he looked adorable doing it, especially with his scarf.

"It's true," I said.

"No, it's not. You and Princess Porks-a-lot are up to something. You've been trying to get in your parents' house since you got back from St. Sebastian."

"Hey, Miss Watts!" yelled a man from across the street. "Lookin' good!"

I was so astonished I froze. People do not yell on Hawthorne

Avenue. I'd gotten more than a few disapproving looks for speaking in a normal tone. There was a lot of whispering on the avenue. It was that kind of street.

"Hey Wally!" Rocco waved at a guy standing on the front porch of the Calumet-Clausen mansion across the street. Wally, a guy with an enormous belly and bushy beard, held a coffee mug the size of a small thermos and smoked a cigarette while he directed some workman who were putting up Christmas lights. And they weren't just any lights. They were red pepper and cactus Christmas lights and there were about five million of them.

"How ya doin'?" Wally yelled.

"Great! Got time for a beer later?" Rocco yelled.

"Sure thing!"

I returned a wave and walked toward my parents' house a little stunned. "Who the heck was that?"

"Wally Klemp. They just moved in," said Rocco.

"That's Walter Klemp, the IPO guy? It can't be."

He laughed. "You fell for it. Everybody does."

"Fell for what?"

"The marketing. That guy's Wally Klemp, owner and founder of Klemp Elite Hunting, but he was marketed as some slick Wall Street type for the IPO. Banks and investors trust suits and haircuts."

"The avenue must be freaking out," I said.

"Yeah, the snobs are pissed," said Rocco, "but he's a great guy. Nice wife. Six kids. Distills his own whisky *and* he knits."

"That guy knits?"

"Did you hear me? He's got six kids."

"He's not the style the avenue's looking for."

"Nope. One generation away from the trailer park and proud of it."

"There's going to be meetings."

"Already happened," said Rocco. "Don't try to change the subject. I know you and Fats are up to something."

"We're not up to anything."

"Why was Chuck in the house the day you were kidnapped?" Rocco walked beside me, knitting rapidly without dropping a stitch. He wasn't even looking at his hands. Freak.

"I don't know."

"Yeah, right," he said, clicking away. "What are we looking for? Their will? Did your parents write you out of the will?"

"Give me a break."

"Commitment papers?"

"For who?"

"You."

"Me? Nobody wants to commit me," I said. "Why would you even say that?"

"You do some pretty wacky shit. Look at what we're doing right now. Any normal person would stay in bed in that mansion being patted and fed imported pâté."

"I hate pâté."

"See. You are clearly insane. Fats says you're throwing her a baby warming, too. Even my mom wouldn't dare do that. Fats won't be happy unless there's tofu and squats. Everyone will have to wear spandex and measure their thighs. You'd have to expect to be murdered in your sleep after doing that to women."

"A what?" I asked.

"A baby warming."

"It's a baby shower," I said.

"Not where I grew up."

"You're from St. Louis."

Rocco grinned at me, still clicking away. "Not your St. Louis."

"Clearly." I turned to go toward the alley beside my parents' house and then abruptly did an about-face. I still couldn't go down there. Mom lying on the ground. Blood in the flower bed. I could see it like it was happening.

"What are we doing?" Rocco asked and then froze. "Did you hear that?" He dropped his knitting and pulled his Ruger.

I did hear it. A weird little thwump and then a high-pitched squawk. "What the crap?"

Rocco crept forward and scanned the alley, listening intently. I thought I heard some faint cussing and he turned back to me with a grin. "Sounds like somebody's having a bad morning."

"Sandy must've dropped something on her foot. She's a sculptor. It happens," I said. "I hope she's okay."

"Who's Sandy?"

I jabbed my thumb toward the house next door. "Neighbor."

"Ah." He holstered his weapon and picked up his knitting. "So you don't like the alley?"

"My mom was attacked there."

He nodded and we went around to the front door. Happily, Dad and Morty hadn't changed the codes and we walked in to find piles of cardboard boxes stacked in precarious towers.

"Whoa," said Rocco. "Your parents are hoarders. No wonder you're a wreck."

"I am not a wreck and they're not hoarders." I squeezed in between two stacks. "This is Christmas stuff. My dad just brought it down from the attic."

"So they're Christmas hoarders." Rocco pointed to a ratty fake Christmas tree poking out of a half-crushed box.

"My mom just keeps stuff. It's still good."

"It smells like roach spray and feet in here."

He wasn't wrong, but I wasn't going to admit that. My mother loved garage sales and almost all our Christmas stuff came from her years of bargain hunting. She got some expensive pieces for pennies and it was a source of great pride when she did. We didn't have much money when Dad was a cop and if my mom could save a nickel, she did with gusto.

"We need to get real storage containers," I said as I headed for the kitchen.

"And a dumpster."

"You make me glad I'm an only child."

Rocco was right behind me and said, "If only I got a vote. Only child is the way to go."

We went into the kitchen, which was free of my mother's bargain addiction and my mind started pinging around for ways to boot Rocco. "You love Fats."

"You don't know," he said.

I turned around and he sat down at the kitchen table, resuming his knitting.

"You don't love her?" I asked with disbelief.

"I love her but imagine being *me* growing up with *her*. I got beat up because guys wanted to beat her up and couldn't."

"That really happened?"

"Yeah. Why ya think I got anxiety?" He looked at me standing there awkwardly and said, "What are we doing here?"

"I wanted to do some paperwork for my dad," I said.

"In the kitchen?"

I pointed at the laptops and files piled up on the table. "The old guys like to work in here."

Rocco clicked away and watched me unblinking.

"You could go in the living room. My dad bought an enormous TV to compensate for my mother's eyesight issues. She hates it."

Still no blinking. "I'm good."

"The paperwork is of a private nature and pressing."

"Well, get to it then," he said.

Get out. Get out. Get out.

"I like to work alone," I said.

"No, you don't."

"Yes, I do. It's just that nobody lets me."

He grinned at me in the way that made the ladies of Hawthorne Avenue quiver. Rocco was a looker in a bad boy kinda way. "And the trend continues."

Damn and double damn.

"Can't you just beat it?"

"Are you kidding? I'm not missing out on—" The alarm system started beeping. "Who knows the code?"

"Family, the whole stable of detectives," I said as some gruff male voices came into the kitchen. I checked the time. It was eight-thirty. Come on, guys.

Then the yelling started. "Son of a bitch!"

"Shit!"

"What the frack is wrong with these things?"

The cussing continued coming our way and Rocco jumped to his feet, pulled his weapon, and got in front of me a second before two old guys dressed for winter in Alaska burst in pursued by the Siamese. Swish and Swat attacked their ankles with fangs and claws. Avery Sampson and Leo Frame spun in circles, whacking them with their balaclava hats.

"You know us!" yelled Leo.

"Where are those cat treats?" yelled Avery.

They didn't see us as they knocked into the stove, counters and table until Rocco yelled, "Enough!"

Everybody froze.

Rocco snapped his fingers. "Get off, you cats."

The Siamese detached from the guys' pant legs and made odd little whiney mews. Then even more astonishingly, they slinked across the kitchen to slither around Rocco's legs, purring and acting like some kind of feline sluts.

"What the?" I asked.

"That's better," said Rocco. "Hey, guys. You're early. *Mercy* wasn't expecting you."

The geezers stripped off their parkas, much to my dismay, and tossed them on a chair.

"What are you doing here?" Leo asked as he smoothed down his few remaining hairs.

"I was going to do some paperwork," I said.

"Since when?" Avery asked.

"This morning."

"You're on bedrest."

"No, I'm not."

Leo flipped on Mom's espresso maker. "Well, that's what Tommy said. No matter. It's convenient you're here." He pointed at Rocco. "Put that weapon away, son, unless you want a problem."

Rocco stuck his Ruger back in his shoulder holster and reached down to pick up Swish. The Siamese purred like I'd never heard before and head butted his hand. We stared and Rocco said, "Cats like me."

"The Siamese don't like anyone, except my mother," I said. "Last week they pooped in my Dad's office chair and he lives here."

Rocco shrugged and sat back down. Swat jumped onto his lap and started rolling around, purring. It was like they were on the largest dose of catnip ever and it made me nervous for when they noticed me. I kept my distance from Rocco and got out the milk steamer. "Why is it convenient that I'm here?"

The guys exchanged glances and I answered a series of frantic texts from Joy, wanting to know where I was. I answered, but she wasn't satisfied so I told Rocco to call her. He got up and wandered out to explain the situation, taking the Siamese with him. Avery went over and closed the door behind him and I got a whole lot more nervous.

"What's going on?" I asked.

"It's not a big deal," said Leo.

"That's right," agreed Avery. "Not a big deal at all."

So it's a big deal. Got it.

"Spill it, please," I said.

"Now you can say no," said Leo.

"You should say no," said Avery.

"Absolutely."

"No problem at all."

"No one thinks you should say yes."

"Yes, isn't the answer."

"Simple." Leo finished making a latte and handed it to me. "You want a dash of cinnamon?"

"No, thanks."

"So it's settled," said Avery. "Good. Done and dusted."

Leo started on a second latte. "Stick a fork in it."

"No use beating around the bush."

"Calling a spade a spade."

What are we doing?

I sat down and eyed the detectives. "Guys, what—"

"No use having a chip on your shoulder," said Avery.

"Barking up the wrong tree," said Leo.

"Close but no cigar."

Leo gave Avery the second latte. "Cut to the chase is what I always say."

"What chase are we cutting?" I asked.

"Dead in the water," said Avery.

"Can't pull the wool over your eyes, Mercy," said Leo as he pushed the button for regular old black coffee.

I plunked down my cup. "What wool?"

"Straight from the horse's mouth."

"Thinking outside the box."

"Shipshape in Bristol style."

"Gotta get while the gettin's good."

"Writin's on the wall."

Are we just saying stuff now?

Leo picked up his coffee cup and said, "Take it with a grain—"

"Hey!" I yelled. "What on Earth are you two talking about?"

The guys stopped, looked down, and drank their coffee.

"I'm waiting," I said.

It took a couple of minutes, but Avery practically whispered, "Tommy wanted us to pass on a message to you since he's doing the therapy with Carolina and then they've got a mea culpa meeting with the Feds."

I sipped my latte and waited but the message wasn't forthcoming. "Well?"

"Tommy didn't think you'd want a phone call or a text," said Leo.

"Okay."

"And we were coming in," said Avery.

"We came early, in case the press got wind."

Oh, no.

"Please just tell me. I'm freaking out a little here."

"You can say no. Tommy says to say no," said Leo.

"We all understand," said Avery.

"Are you gonna tell me or what?" I asked.

The guys exchanged a glance and did a little back and forth between them on who was going to handle me, I guess.

"So..." said Leo, "you've been through a lot and we don't want to upset you."

"Neither of us has kids," said Avery.

Kids? Do they think I'm pregnant? Am I pregnant? I don't think so.

"What's it got to do with kids?" I asked.

"And we're not women," said Leo.

"It was traumatic, we understand," said Avery.

"We don't understand."

"We were trained though."

"I wasn't," said Leo. "They didn't train us for shit."

"Who did the victim stuff?" asked Avery.

"Ace. He was good with victims. Always knew what to say."

"I hear ya. Tommy was our guy for the victims."

I waved at them. "Still waiting."

Leo wiped his brow with a napkin and took a breath. "I'm not good with this stuff. Never was."

"What stuff?"

"You're like a daughter to us," said Avery.

"A granddaughter," said Leo.

"For God's sake," I said.

"We just don't want you to feel upset."

The kitchen door flew open and Rocco walked in with the Siamese draped over his shoulders. "So you're having a sit-down with the Thooft family?"

"Jesus!" yelled Leo.

"You can't ask her like that," said Avery. "Oh, God damn. Oh, hell."

"That's it?" I asked. "I thought I had cancer or something."

"You're not upset?"

"It's better than pregnant," I said.

"Pregnant?" Leo asked.

"Never mind. What is up with you two?"

It turned out that Leo and Avery had had various bad reactions to such requests. Yelling was expected, but it got worse. The husband of a rape victim got so upset that he shot Leo in the leg with a BB gun. Avery got smacked and spit on before my dad took over the duty. Even Dad had a bad reaction or two. One family disagreed about meeting the perp's family and came to blows over it. Arrests were made.

"Well, I'm okay," I said, "and I'm not a spitter."

"I didn't know you were suing the Thoofts," said Rocco.

"Who said that?"

"Channel Five."

I rolled my eyes. "I'm not suing them. What would I sue them for?"

"Some lawyer said you had a case," said Rocco.

"This is bad enough without bringing lawyers into it."

"You're really not upset?" Avery asked.

I'm not going to lie. The moment Rocco said Thooft, my chest got a little tight. I pictured him coming at me, but it was a relief at the same time. So confusing. "I'm okay."

"Okay isn't good enough, Mercy," said Leo.

Avery came over and put a warm hand on my shoulder. "I'll tell her no."

"Her? The mother?" I asked.

"No. It's his sister who wants to meet."

"Why exactly? I'm not suing."

The guys were quiet and even Rocco looked away. I didn't know he did that. He and Fats were a right-in-the-eyes type duo.

"She's having a hard time accepting it," said Avery.

"Accepting what? He died doing it," I said.

"We know," said Leo with profound sadness. His beloved nephew, Scott Frame, had attacked my mother and orchestrated Avery's wife's murder. Grandad thought it would kill him. The pain of having mentored such a person, having trained them and loved them would be too much, but somehow Leo was sitting in our kitchen. Forgiveness had happened. He and Avery worked together every day. Their grief seemed to bind them together instead of tearing them apart. That wasn't supposed to happen, but it could happen.

"I'll meet her," I said.

"You don't owe her anything," said Leo.

"So I've heard."

Rocco gave Swish a good scratch and said, "It'll be good."

"I don't know about that," said Avery. "These victim/offender reconciliations can be rough and it's only just happened."

"The sister didn't do it," pointed out Rocco.

"It's not as big a difference as you think," said Leo. "You can trust me on that."

"What's her name?" I asked. Names were good. A name made her a person.

"Kimberly," said Leo. "I think you should say no for now, but leave it open for a later time."

"She wants to meet now or soon though?"

Leo sat down and rolled his cup between his gnarled hands. "Yes, she does."

"She was pretty insistent about it," said Avery with distaste. "I don't think it's a good idea. I didn't even want to mention it, but Tommy was afraid she'd turn up on the doorstep."

"What's the hurry?" Rocco asked.

"I don't know, but she's been calling everybody and their brother to get to you." Leo wiped his brow. "I don't know how she's going to treat you."

"You'd be surprised at how people manage to blame the victim," said Avery.

"No, I wouldn't," I said firmly.

The men went quiet.

"Set it up for tonight."

"You want Campbell and Rich there?" Rocco asked.

"No. Tell her to come to Kronos," I said. "If she throws a hissy, I want my people around me."

"Done and dusted," said Leo.

"No use beating around the bush."

"Calling a spade a spade."

"Barking up the wrong tree," said Leo.

"Close but no cigar."

Rocco pointed at me. "Call 911. I think they're having strokes."

I burst into laughter and soon they joined me. Sometimes you've got to laugh while you still can.

CHAPTER FIVE

That night I sat down in a booth with Pickpocket wearing a faux therapy dog vest and a face with so much makeup I was afraid it was going to crack if I smiled, not that smiling was on the agenda.

Kronos was packed with the dinner rush, extra packed actually with my crew. Avery and Leo insisted on coming, so did Chuck, Fats, and Rocco. My parents weren't there. Mom got upset at the very idea and I told Dad to stay with her. He listened and I nearly passed out from the shock.

I made everyone sit away from us and waited by myself for Kimberly Thooft Stackhouse to show up. I sat there and realized I didn't know what she looked like. I hadn't thought to ask. All I had was the image of her brother in my head, so I pictured her as blonde, overweight, and professorial. I was wrong on all counts.

But I did spot Kimberly the second she walked in. Her shoulders were up around her ears and she clutched a purse in front of her like a shield as her eyes darted around. She was blonde, but it was a dye job. I could always tell. As for the other two guesses, Kimberly was thin with a heart-shaped face, a dimpled chin, and a pouty lower lip bitten to shreds. Given her nondescript black coat, Mickey Mouse sweatshirt, khakis, and white Keds, I'd have picked overworked homeroom mom instead of professor.

The crowd parted and she saw me looking at her. Her internal struggle showed on her face. Kimberly was about to turn tail and run, so I smiled and the makeup didn't crack, thanks to Fats' skills. She had to work hard to cover up the rash that had stopped erupting to become scaly and red. Awesome.

Kimberly slowly walked over, carefully putting one foot in front of the other, like she had to think about each step to make it happen. I don't know if she was aware of all the eyes on her, but there were plenty of them. The closer she got the less worried I got. Kimberly Thooft Stackhouse wasn't going to berate me. I'd be lucky to get anything out of her and I very much wanted to know why her brother happened to me.

When she arrived at the table, Pick wiggled with excitement and wagged his stubby tail, thumping it against the plump seat back. It was hard to imagine that goofball was what stood between me and kidnapping.

Kimberly stopped about two feet from the table, biting her poor lip, and Pick could hardly stand it. There were pets to be had. Get with the petting.

"He wants you to pet him," I said. "If you don't, he's so excited, he might pee."

A tiny smile appeared on the corners of her mouth and she whispered something.

"Sorry," I said. "It's too loud. I didn't catch that."

"Can I? Pet him?" Kimberly asked.

"Please do. I don't want him banned for life."

Kimberly Thooft Stackhouse gave Pick a good scratch and some tugs on his ears. She knew dogs and Pick was certainly a fan. I decided that meant something and asked her to sit down.

She took off her coat, hung it on the hook by our booth, and slid in to face me, unafraid for the most part.

I started to say something, but Aaron came through the crowd and trotted up to our booth. No hairnet, thank goodness, but he was wearing Millicent's apron circa 1962. There were ruffles. He didn't say anything, naturally, and Kimberly stared up at him in confusion.

"Have you ever been here before?" I asked.

"No, but I've seen the reviews. There was one in the Sentinel."

"The St. Seb Sentinel?"

"Yeah. He loved it."

Tank Tancedi did love Kronos and Aaron, in particular. Aaron had seen his wife, Mallory, and how upset she was about her dogs and the fires. Typical of Aaron, the little weirdo designed a romantic dinner for the two of them and it soothed the pain. Tank had called me in the hospital. Mallory was doing a lot better.

"Well, this is Aaron. He's the chef," I said.

"Um...really?"

Aaron started bouncing up and down on the balls of his feet. If you knew him, you knew he was itching to feed somebody. If not, well, in need of a psych hold might come to your mind.

"You hungry?" he asked.

I wasn't. I hadn't been since it happened, but not eating wasn't an option. "Absolutely."

Aaron glowed. "I've got a new Warhammer menu."

"My son loves Warhammer," said Kimberly. "He's totally obsessed."

He looked at her, sort of, and asked, "Fish?"

"I love fish."

Aaron turned tail and ran for the kitchen.

"Hey!" I yelled. "What about me? I hate fish."

Nothing. Not a glance back. I was so screwed.

"What's on the Warhammer menu?" Kimberly asked.

"Beats me. I didn't know there was one until five seconds ago. Knowing Aaron, nobody else did either," I said.

"What will he bring?"

"Don't worry. It will be amazing. I just hope it's not crab."

Kimberly's shoulders left her ears and she took a breath. "Thanks for meeting me."

"It's fine," I said. "Not a problem."

"Everyone said you wouldn't."

"I defy expectations."

"You do. I've seen plenty pictures of you. DBD and...the other stuff, but I didn't really expect you to look so much like Marilyn."

"You started looking into me," I said. "After?"

"Yes, but I knew who you were before." She fiddled with her napkin. "I feel silly saying this, but I took a picture of you to my stylist when I wanted to update my color. My mother always used Marilyn as her example, but her color's too light for me."

"I'm flattered," I said and it was true. It was a nice compliment. "She did a good job."

Kimberly wrinkled her nose. "Now that I see you in person, I'm not so sure. It's got a lot of depth, your hair."

"She can try again."

"She can, but now I think that I should go back to my natural color. My mom says she can't go back. It's grey now." Kimberly began fiddling with her napkin. "It would be weird to see her as a brunette. Actually, it'd be weird to see me as one. I've been blonde forever."

"My mother tried red once. It didn't work out as well as your blonde," I said, patiently. This could go on for a while.

The fiddling got worse until Kimberly finally said, "I thought about what to say to you and I wrote it down, but now I can't remember a word of it."

"That's okay."

A tear slipped down her cheek. "I'm so sorry. My parents, my brothers, everyone, the whole family. We can't. We don't. We never..."

Pick craned his neck across the table and gave her hand a lick. She reached over to pet him and broke down. I gave her a packet of tissues I brought in case of emergency. I thought it was going to be my emergency. It was nice to be wrong.

"I know," I said. "Detective Rich told me you were having a hard time."

She snuffled into a wad of tissues and asked, "Do you believe me?"

"I have no reason not to."

"That's not the same."

"I'm working on it," I said.

Kimberly got herself together and then she said the thing I dreaded.

"My brother wasn't the type to do that. He just wouldn't."

"But he did." Out of the corner of my eye, I saw Chuck shift in his seat. My guy was about to come over. He couldn't possibly hear what she said, but he knew me. I must've shown my distaste.

"I know. I do know," she said forcefully, trying to convince herself. "It's just not like him. Those detectives, they showed us all the evidence. I know it's true. There was even surveillance footage. I saw him with my own eyes."

"Was there?" I didn't know that. Nobody mentioned it. "What did it show?"

"You didn't see it?" Kimberly asked.

"No. The case was pretty much open and shut."

The footage Kimberly described was pretty damning. Even if my body had never been found, Thooft could've been convicted on that alone. Although they didn't have the actual attack on film, there was no one else in the vicinity and Thooft was on camera heading toward me and then peeling out so fast he took out a parking meter.

"Can I ask you something?" Kimberly asked.

"Sure."

"Did he say anything to you? The detectives said no, but surely he must have said something."

I took a breath and put my arm around Pick. His heart beat strong under my hand and it was okay. I was okay. "He called my name and cursed a little when I was fighting him, but that's it."

Kimberly balled up the tissues in her hand and her eyes pleaded with me. "I don't...he just attacked you?"

"Yes. It happened so fast I could never have identified him. I had no idea who he was until they told me."

Her lower lip trembled and I feared she'd burst into wails when Aaron trotted up with two mugs. He plunked them down and ran back to the kitchen.

"Did we order hot chocolate?" Kimberly asked. "I don't even remember."

"He knows when I need it and I guess you need it, too."

"Need hot chocolate?"

"Taste it."

Kimberly tasted Aaron's latest creation and her face changed. It filled with wonder. She was a very pretty woman. I hadn't noticed before. "That's amazing."

"He has a way with hot chocolate," I said, "and all food really."

We sipped in silence until Aaron came out with an enormous platter that made the surrounding tables groan with envy. I didn't know a thing about Warhammer, but it was meat heavy. Kimberly got three kinds of fish, including some kind of weird croquette thing with tuna. I got kabobs and lamb gyros.

The neighboring tables demanded the mysterious Warhammer menu and people stopped looking at us, but Kimberly didn't stop looking at me. Usually, it's because of my face. People can't quite believe it. They look for surgical scars or hints of how I did it with makeup, but Kimberly wasn't doing that.

"There's something else, isn't there?" I asked, finishing my last rib.

"No, no. Nothing," she said hastily.

"You might as well say it. We're here and I'm so bloated I'm not going anywhere soon."

She speared her last bite of battered cod and said, "Well, I've changed my mind. You're not what I expected. I mean, you're *really* not."

"I get that all the time. What did you expect?"

"I've read about all the things that happened to you. That crazy murderer that attacked your mom and you. That kid in New Orleans."

I raised an eyebrow. "Yeah?"

"I thought you'd be, I don't know, tougher," she said. "Hard or something."

I didn't know what to say to that. At least she didn't say she expected a breathless dingbat.

"Sorry. I hope that's not rude. I don't mean it to be. You are tough. You've had to be."

"I never think of myself as tough," I said. "I'm surprised you did. People usually think I'm a moron that gets lucky."

"You mean *20/20*. They're obviously sexist about you. Like a woman can't look good and do anything else at the same time. It's ludicrous."

I'm starting to really like you.

"I appreciate that," I said. "Now go ahead and say what you wanted to say. I can take it."

Kimberly took her napkin off her lap and twisted it into a knot. "This terrible thing happened to you and I think, my family thinks, that you must want to know why."

"Yes," I said slowly.

"And the police don't care about that."

"The motive?"

"Yes," she said.

"It doesn't matter now. Open and shut like I said."

She untwisted the napkin and laid it back on her lap. Her pretty face had become resolute and I had a sneaking suspicion of what was coming next. "Open and shut for them, not for us. Or you."

"You want me to investigate the man that was going to kill me," I said.

She shook her head so violently it must've hurt her neck. "I can't believe that. It isn't who he was."

"And yet here we are." I drank some more hot chocolate. Aaron was right. I definitely needed it.

"Anton never did a violent thing in his whole life," she said.

"Well, he started with a bang."

"But why? I'm telling you that my brother was gentle and kind. He never so much as kicked our dog and she was a biter."

"Kimberly, look, I know this must be absolutely wrenching, but some things are unknowable. They just are."

"But this isn't. The police didn't even bother to really interview anyone in Germany. Anton had friends they never spoke to. We talked to them. He didn't talk about you. His friend Sherri was in his apartment with the Polizei. There wasn't anything on you. No pictures, plans, or maps. His school laptop had nothing on you whatsoever."

Fight the feeling. Fight the feeling.

"That makes sense. You wouldn't want your obsession on your work computer. It was probably monitored."

"Most of Anton's friends were women. He was a teacher for God's sake. None of his friends said anything about him being even remotely violent."

"He kept it on the down low," I said.

"You are so good at what you do and you have a PI license now. We'll pay you. We can afford it."

I took a breath and fought the swirling tight tornado in my chest. Kimberly was so sincere. She knew her brother. But other murderers had brothers, friends, and family that were none the wiser. Leo had no idea what his nephew Scott was up to. None at all.

"I'm still not the person to do this job," I said. "I can refer you to other firms, excellent firms."

Kimberly's mouth twisted and she looked down at the table.

Oh, I get it.

"I'm not the first person you asked to take the case."

The crowd parted and Chuck was on the edge of his seat, still ready to spring into action. I gave a slight shake of my head and his eyes narrowed, but he didn't move.

"No, you're not," said Kimberly hesitantly. "But nobody else will touch this case with a ten-foot pole."

"Really? I'm surprised. There's publicity in doing it. I'd have thought you'd have people lining up."

"We thought so, too, but it's about you. A couple said they know your father and don't want to cause your family any additional pain. Others said it wasn't interesting. Case closed and who cares why. My brother was a psychopath and that's the end."

"From where I'm sitting," I said, "I can see it."

She leaned over the table and Pick licked her hand, getting himself an absentminded scratch. "He wasn't though. Everything was normal until six weeks ago."

"Something happened."

"Nothing happened."

"I'll give you a list of firms. You can't have tried them all."

"We talked to fifteen. Fifteen. The only ones interested were sketchy and my dad said no. They seemed like they would take our money and do nothing. They weren't going to come out to us for interviews or even think about going to Germany. Dad asked what they would do and they said various versions of stuff and things. Nothing concrete. It'd be a waste of time."

"It probably *is* a waste of time," I said.

"Not to us. We can't go the rest of our lives not knowing what happened to Anton," she pleaded.

The swirl in my chest grew and I thought about The Girls and Aunt Miriam. Not knowing what happened to Sister Maggie haunted them. She was the victim, but would it be any different for the perpetrator's family? Having seen what that crime did to Robert Snider's family, manifestly not.

"Kimb—"

"You're the only one that would care as much as us about why he did it. To everyone else, it's simple. But it's not."

"It looks fairly simple." I heard myself say the word *looks* and it stung a bit. Didn't I hate that surface crap? "He was in Incel chatrooms, reading about kidnap, rape and murder fantasies. Don't get me started on the Deep Fake porn starring me."

"He wouldn't do any of that stuff."

This was so hard. It hurt to be looking at her pained and innocent face. Why was I sitting there? Why didn't I listen to the geezers? I never listen. That's why. Idiot.

"He did," I said firmly. "The evidence was on his computer."

"*My* brother would not do that. I know he attacked you. I know that's true. Detective Rich proved it to me, as hard as it is to believe, but those other things, they just can't be true."

"Maybe you didn't know him as well as you thought you did. Incels have a lot of hate brewing inside them."

"I was his sister. Anton didn't hate women. I never heard him say a nasty thing about a woman in his life. His friends were women. Incels don't have female friends."

Interesting. No, Mercy. Don't get interested. It's not enough. Not even close.

"People hide things, especially men who are into that violent stuff," I said.

Kimberly glanced around as if someone might be eavesdropping. "Yes, they do. But for Anton, it's not possible."

"Alright, I'll bite. Why not? Why couldn't Anton Thooft have been a violent woman-hating involuntary celibate?"

"Because my brother was gay."

Aaron whisked away our platter and plates, replacing them with an entire pot of hot chocolate on a warming rack with a tea light underneath. He struggled to get his lighter to ignite and it gave me a minute to process what Kimberly had said. Well, I say process, try to comprehend was more like it. Why in the world did Campbell and Rich leave that out? To keep me in the dark? Why? What would be the point? To make their lives easier? It would, for certain, but Rich didn't seem like he was in the market for easy.

Aaron lit the tea light and stood there bobbing up and down, waiting.

"I love the Warhammer menu," I said automatically.

The bobbing continued.

"You should add it to the regular menu."

Still going.

Oh!

"Kimberly, how did you like the Warhammer menu?" I asked pointedly.

"Um...what? Yes, oh, yes." She turned her head slowly, like she was barely able to recall how to do it. "It was amazing. I feel like I've never had fish before today."

"You think I should add it?" he asked.

"Yes, absolutely."

Aaron poured us some more hot chocolate, popped what appeared to be a sugar wafer in our cups, and then spooned some stiff whipped cream on top of the wafer. He topped it with tiny housemade marshmallows and something he'd recently invented, honey sprinkles. "There," he announced and waited until I dutifully picked up my cup.

He didn't move and I raised an eyebrow at Kimberly. She started and then picked up hers. "Thank you. It's beautiful, almost too good to drink."

Aaron went up on the balls of his feet.

"But we will drink it," I said quickly.

He nodded and dashed off.

We sat there, mugs in hand, in silence until Kimberly said, "You heard me, right?"

"Yeah, that's um...new information," I said before tasting Aaron's latest creation. I swear to God my brain went on the fritz for a second. It was that good. The honey sprinkles were infused with some kind of liquor, but not really sweet. The whole thing together was dark and kinda meaty, if hot chocolate can be meaty.

"I know." She took a sip. "Oh, oh my. What..."

"This might be the best yet," I said when my brain could focus again.

"No kidding. I feel better. Do you feel better?"

"I do," I said.

"But it's not better."

"No."

She looked at the chocolate pot. "It's like he made a pot of hot fattening Prozac."

I smiled and it felt good. Everything felt good. "You're not wrong."

"Please don't tell anyone."

"About the Prozac?"

"My brother," she said. "Nobody knows."

"When you say 'nobody'?"

When Kimberly said nobody, she meant nobody. Her brother was gay and it wasn't a new thing either. Anton had always known, like he knew his name, she said. Although her brother was fourteen years older, they had always been extremely close. He came out to her when he was thirty, but Kimberly had already figured it out. Anton had dated women, but it was always more like a friend situation and never went anywhere. Her other brothers were intense about relationships, constantly bringing girls home and falling in love at the drop of a hat. You couldn't shut them up about who they were going out with. Rachael was so pretty. Theresa was the best at soccer. Lauren scholarshipped. It was tedious to listen to at every family dinner and it made Anton's silence more noticeable, at least to Kimberly.

"He was so secretive about his private life, but I just knew," she said.

"But he never told your parents or your other brothers?" I asked.

"He never told anyone, except his partners, of course."

"Why? It's not the sixties."

"My parents, well, we're a very religious family. We were raised that homosexuality was against God's law. Anton didn't want to put the family in a position where they had to choose, but, later, I think it became a habit. He didn't talk about himself hardly at all. I knew he was gay and had partners from time to time, but I got the impression that he kept everyone at arm's length."

"He was secretive," I said.

"I know what you're thinking, but I'm telling you he was just extremely private, not crazy."

Secretive people have secrets.

"Would your parents have booted him out of the family?" I asked.

"No way. I told him that, but he couldn't open up. He was built that way, keeping everything in. Honestly, it was sort of a relief. My other brothers tell you everything that's on their minds. It's exhausting."

I drank that amazing hot chocolate, letting its warmth run through me as I patted Pick and let him lick a little whipped cream off my finger. It'd been so easy before I sat down with Kimberly Thooft Stackhouse. Detective Rich wasn't satisfied with what happened, but I could ignore his poke to do something about it. Anton was dead. No amount of information would change what he did. But would *why* change the way I felt about it? How did I feel about Anton? And perhaps more importantly, when did he become Anton, instead of Anton Thooft.

"You've changed your mind, haven't you?" Kimberly gave me a sad smile. She wanted to know. She had to know, but it would give her more pain and she knew that, too.

So did I.

Chuck slid into Kimberly's seat about three seconds after she vacated it. He was exceedingly attractive in his going-to-court suit and tie, even his scowl didn't ruin the fancy effect. "I don't know what you're going to do but don't do it."

"What makes you think I'm going to do something?"

"I've seen that look before and I'm not having it."

"Like you're in charge," I said with an exaggerated eye roll.

"I should be. Look at you. You've got a rash, a broken arm, and I don't know why your nose looks normal. That's not normal."

"It's fine and my cast is off." I waggled my newly-freed fingers at him.

"Mercy, why did you meet her? No good can come of it. You're a victim. You get to feel any way you want to feel."

I picked up my mug and batted my eyes at him over the lip. "What if I feel curious?"

"Son of a bitch," he growled and his blue eyes grew more brilliant in response to the flush taking over his face. "That's how she hooked you, huh? There's nothing to be curious about. He did it. Done. Over."

"Detective Rich came to see me," I said.

"That asshat? Why?"

"He thinks something's off."

Chuck slammed a hand down on the table making the chocolate pot and everyone nearby jump. "I will hurt him. First, he treats you like some kind of lying piece of crap when you're the victim and then he lays this on you. I'm calling his CO. I know you said to leave it, but I'm not leaving it."

"It's fine."

"How can it be fine?" he asked. "You were kidnapped and I wasn't there."

I wrinkled my nose. "It's not about you."

He backtracked quickly, but it was still there. Chuck failed me somehow. My dad failed me. Uncle Morty. Spidermonkey. Leo. Avery. All the men failed me. I never appreciated Fats so much. She didn't blame herself for something she didn't do. She didn't own me in some weird way like I was a child who must be looked after.

"You can't watch me every minute," I said, "and, if you try, we're going to have a problem."

"The case is closed."

"I want to know why he came after me."

"But do you need to know?"

"Yes."

"Need to know is very different than want to know."

I scowled back at him. "I know the difference. For instance, I wanted to know what The Klinefeld Group was after, now it's become a need."

"That's different."

"How? 'Cause they didn't throw me in a trunk? They murdered Lester and my great grandparents."

Chuck held up his hands in defeat. "Can you give me one good reason that can get me on board?"

"More than your fellow cop thinking it's not right?" I asked.

"Yeah, more than that douche saying it for who knows what reason."

"Just between us?"

He frowned and my heart melted a little, but the fact that he was a big pain in my butt held my resolve firm.

"I'm waiting," I said and I put out my hand to shake.

"We have to shake on it?"

"Yes."

He shook my hand. "Fine. What's your reason?" Chuck's voice had the distinct sound of "this is going to be nonsense."

"Anton Thooft was gay."

"Ah, crap!"

Half of Kronos turned and looked at us and Pick yipped in alarm. Leo and Avery were ready to leap into action, although I doubt leaping anywhere would work out well for either of them.

I took Chuck's hand again. "I know, right?"

"Campbell and Rich didn't mention that to me," he said.

"Kimberly didn't tell them."

"Witnesses, I swear to God, the bane of my existence."

Pick scrambled off my seat and went over to Chuck's to give him a comforting if slobbery lick on the cheek.

"I'm okay, ya big dingus."

More licks and Chuck made the poodle lay down after wiping off the spittle.

I told him everything Kimberly said and he listened without interrupting. That was a first. "So you see why I have to do this."

"I do," he said reluctantly. "So what's your theory? He had a psychotic break?"

"Maybe. I'll start with who Kimberly says her brother was and go from there."

"A lot of killers appear normal until they're caught," said Chuck.

"But they aren't misogynists with white supremacist tendencies and rape fantasies that show up out of the blue six weeks before a kidnap murder attempt, especially when they're gay."

"You got me there." He ran his hands through his thinning hair and then eyed me closely, his face, despite its hard edges, was worried and sweet. "I don't have any vacation time coming. I could take a leave of absence."

"Nobody's asking for that," I said. "You can't investigate off the clock anyway. I'll do it. She's paying me." I slipped out of my seat, snapped my finger, sending Pick over to my bench, and slid in next to Chuck. "I have my first paying PI gig."

He wrapped his arms around me and kissed my forehead. "Tommy was paying you already."

"To do background BS. I can do more than that."

Leo and Avery came over and pushed Pick into the corner.

"Alright," said Leo. "We can't take anymore. What did she want? Absolution?"

"No," I said, rather proudly. "She hired me. Officially. My first one."

"She has a band?" Avery asked.

"No."

"Modeling agency?" Leo asked.

"What?"

Avery threw up his hands. "Oh! Private nurse."

"Private Detective," I said.

The geezers drew back. "No, no. That's not. No."

"I'm not asking you."

Leo took a look in my mug, sniffed it, and asked, "What did the little guy put in this?"

"Chocolate," I said.

The geezers tilted their heads to the side like Pick when I asked him to roll over and he decided not to know what on Earth I was hinting at.

Chuck waved at Rodney who was at his former table with a couple of plates. "It's true, guys. She's investigating her own kidnapper."

"You can't investigate your own murder," said Leo.

"I wasn't murdered," I said.

"For all intents," said Avery.

"No, not really."

"Close enough," said Leo.

"Close enough to what?" I asked.

"Dead." Avery patted my hand. "We took a vote. You're not doing it."

"There's no vote." I looked at Chuck. "Hello? Not helping."

He kissed me again. "I don't want you to do it. I voted in absentia. It was unanimous."

"Bummer."

Chuck shrugged at the geezers, who were completely aghast. "Say some stuff from your vast experience and convince her. I got nothin'."

I put on my stubborn face and then it was my turn to be aghast. Rodney came over and put a huge plate of boiled eggs, poached chicken, and cottage cheese in front of Chuck. "There you go. Aaron says if you ever do this again, you're banned."

"Duly noted," said Chuck, picking up a fork and spearing a whole egg.

"Ew," I said. "What is that?"

"An egg."

"Are you sick? Do you have an ulcer?"

"On that note," Avery got out of the booth quick, "we'll leave you to it."

"You're supposed to help me," said Chuck.

I leaned away from him. "You said you'd help me get through this however I wanted to get through it. Did you mean however *you* wanted to get through it?"

Leo got out of the booth so fast he was a bald blur. "See ya, Chuck. God bless."

"God bless? What the heck is that?" Chuck asked. "Help me."

"Oh, no," said Avery. "I saw that look on my wife's face. Mercy means business. I don't intend to be collateral damage in this war."

I poured some more hot chocolate, the fancy way, from a distance and with a flourish. "There's no war. I'm going to root around and see what I can find."

"I feel like that's probably been said before," said Leo.

"Because it has," said Chuck.

"And we've had this talk before, too," I said. "This is who I am. I root around."

"But, Mercy, whenever you root around you kick up a shit storm," said Avery.

"May I remind you all that I'm the victim," I said. "If I want answers, I'm entitled to kick up any kind of storm I want."

The geezers' whole demeanor changed. The tension went right out of them and Leo reached over and cupped my cheek. "Sweetheart, I can't argue with that."

"Thanks, Leo."

The guys left me with Chuck and his plateful of weird, unappetizing food. I tried to slide away from the white pile. It smelled...bland. But Chuck grabbed me and pulled me tight to his side.

"What can I do to make this not happen?" he asked.

"Pay for dinner."

He brightened right up. How could someone so smart be so dumb? "Really?"

"No, you big dufus."

"Dammit, Mercy." The cords in his neck got so taut I feared they might snap and take out an eye. "I can't stand it. These things keep happening to you. I just..."

I put a hand on his thigh and squeezed. "What do I have to do to make you comfortable with this job?"

He gave me the side eye. So suspicious. "Really?"

"Yes. I'm doing it, so what do you need?"

"I want Pick with you."

"Seriously?"

"Yep."

I crossed my arms. "Is this just because you don't want to walk him?"

"It's a side benefit, but no."

"Anything else?"

"You don't go alone," he said. "Ever."

"I'll take Fats."

"She's pregnant."

I snorted. "So? She kicks more butt than any man I know."

"Any man?"

I shouldn't answer that.

Chuck gave me the stink eye.

"I love you," I said.

"You think Fats can beat me up," he said.

Hell, yeah.

"Maybe, if she wasn't barfing."

He wasn't satisfied but decided not to pursue it further. "So you'll take her with you?"

"Absolutely."

"And if she's barfing?"

Aaron appeared at the table, staring at Chuck's abominable plate. He made it, but I think he hated himself for it. I didn't blame him.

"I'll take Aaron," I said.

"Come on." Chuck looked up. It wasn't very far. "No offense, Aaron."

"You can't offend him," I said. "He probably didn't hear you."

"He's right there."

"Aaron?" I tugged on his apron.

"You hungry?" the little weirdo said.

"See."

"I can't believe it," said Chuck. "Aaron, focus."

"I've got some dogs." Aaron clasped his hands together. "New recipe. Andouille and cabbage."

Odd combo.

"Yeah, eat that." I started to slide the bland pile to Aaron, but Chuck stopped me.

"I can't eat that," he said.

"Why not?"

He looked away. "I'm on a diet."

"Since when?" I asked.

"Right before Thooft. You really didn't notice?"

"I noticed the tremendous gas."

"That you noticed?"

"How could I not?" I asked. "Didn't *you* notice I've been sleeping on the sofa?"

"I thought you had a nightmare," he said.

"I did and it smelled terrible."

He and Aaron got into a tug of war over the plate, which surprisingly Chuck lost. Aaron ran off with the plate and Chuck savagely ate his one remaining egg in one bite.

"Why are you on this diet?" I asked.

"I'm going to be thirty," he said with anger.

Better than the alternative.

"In two years," I said.

"Exactly and my metabolism will start going down," he said in all seriousness.

"And the solution is boiled eggs?"

"Muscle mass. I've got to build muscle while I can. I've always wanted to add bulk. Time is running out."

"So you're eating massive amounts of boiled eggs and stinking me out of the bedroom."

"My system will adjust," he said.

Or I'll smother you, whichever comes first.

"This isn't a healthy diet," I said.

"You don't know."

"Actually, I do. I'm a nurse."

My guy leaned back and crossed his arms. He was not bulky and he wasn't going to be. "No, Miss Watts. You are a PI."

Touché. Dammit.

CHAPTER SIX

I heard the voice, but I figured it was a nightmare. I'd gotten used to nightmares and I was okay with it. Except this nightmare kicked my bed and shook me violently.

"What are you doing?" asked the voice.

It seemed pretty obvious. I was sleeping. I was in bed and everything.

"Mercy!"

I rolled over and sat up. "Dad!"

"Finally," he said from the foot of my bed. "Did you take a pill or something?"

"No. What time is it?"

"Morning."

I glanced at the drawn curtains in my bedroom. Not a hint of light. Not a sliver. "Define morning."

"It's a quarter to seven. Get up." Dad leaned against my bedpost dressed in a three-piece grey flannel suit, an overcoat with a winter liner to give him bulk and held a fedora in his hands.

"Where are you going? 1952?"

"I've got a parole hearing."

"Who's it for? Bugsy Siegel?" I asked.

"Greta."

"Really?"

Greta was an inmate at Hunt Hospital for the Criminally Insane. My father had put her there, a move I suspected he regretted. We both visited her and I'd gotten more fond of a woman that killed her children in the throes of postpartum psychosis than I thought possible.

"Is she getting out?" I asked as I yawned and winced at the scabs cracking on my chin.

"Not a chance," he said. "Are you getting up or what?"

"Or what." I pulled the covers up to my nose. "Am I supposed to be going to the hearing?"

"No. There's no point."

"Then why are you going?"

"She requested that I be there so I'm going to be there," said Dad. "Get up."

"Am I missing something?" I asked.

"Work."

"I don't have a job, thanks to my life."

"A little bird told me you do."

Crap on a cracker.

"Was this a wrinkly bird that likes to sit at our kitchen table?"

"Could be." Dad whipped the covers off me and pointed at the closet. "Now get up and get going. You're on the clock. Clients expect results. We don't pad our bills and we don't sleep on the job."

"You're not mad?" I slipped out of bed and looked around to see if I had left any evidence of our Klinefeld Group investigation in there. We'd moved the whole setup to Nicolai Bled's office. It had more space and nobody had used it since he died.

"Why would I be mad? I've been waiting for this since your third day of Kindergarten." He shooed me into the closet with his fedora.

"That's oddly specific," I said, grabbing a pair of jeans and a sweatshirt.

"I picked you up from school and—"

"*You* picked me up from school?" I asked.

"I picked you up sometimes."

My father did not pick me up from school. Most of the time he didn't know what grade I was in. Number and depth of stab wounds on a decapitated corpse found in Maplewood at five in the morning by a paperboy named Jimmy Johnson in 1985 was the kind of thing my father remembered. True story.

"Alright." I got dressed and finger combed my hair. "What happened on my third day of Kindergarten?"

"You found Ellen's box of crayons."

"That's worth remembering." I came out and Dad shook his head. "No, Mercy. You are a professional. Dress like a professional."

I went back in the closet and looked for something professional. It was slim pickings. I was a nurse. Scrubs I had. The only suit was the Valentino The Girls bought me for Cousin Dorothy's funeral, and, while it did impress, it wasn't a detecting suit. "Why did you care about crayons?"

"You found them," said Dad. "Your teacher, Miss Mabel, was astonished. You did interviews, you traced her last steps, you did a methodical search in a grid pattern and finally found Ellen's brand new box of crayons in some grubby kid's coat pocket."

"Willy Frank!"

"Willy Frank!" exclaimed Dad. "What happened to that little dirt ball?"

"He married money and got tagged for insurance fraud last year."

"And you were the first to pinch him."

I picked out a white tailored shirt that was mostly clean and kept the jeans. "I was five, Dad."

"You were four. The youngest in your class." There was pride in my dad's voice. At least I think it was. I wasn't very familiar with the sound.

I came out and asked, "You really picked me up?"

"I did," he said. "And here you are finally. Taking your first paying case as a licensed investigator. I never thought it would happen."

Neither did I.

"So why are you here exactly?"

Dad handed me a little box with a bow on top. "To give you this."

I opened the box and found a slender red wallet inside. "Um..."

"Open it."

Inside was my Missouri PI license with my number and expiration date. It was official and kind of depressing. Nursing seemed farther away than ever.

"Thanks, Dad."

"Put your license to carry in there and take the Mauser with you. Do you have a shoulder holster?"

"I have a purse," I said.

Dad grinned at me, dimples popping out and all. "That works."

"I thought you'd be upset about this. The guys were not fans of me even meeting Thooft's sister."

He put on his hat and bent the brim down in a rakish way. He looked like a PI straight out of Raymond Chandler, if you ignored the red hair and gangliness. "I wasn't either, but a paying gig is another thing altogether."

"Is it though?"

"Look, my girl," Dad gave me a hug and held me back by the shoulders, "we're rebuilding our brand here."

The Watts brand, of course.

He tweaked my chin. "Don't frown at me. You're not satisfied with what Campbell and Rich came up with. Neither am I. Neither is the Thooft family. If they're willing to pay you to find out what really happened, I'm all for it. Between you and me, we need the money."

"What do I do?"

Dad let go and went for the door. "Do what you normally do." He grinned at me and the Watts charm shone like a sunlamp. "It's been working for you so far."

"Yeah, but I don't usually get paid. Aren't there contracts involved?"

"All done. Claire emailed the contract to the Thooft family, they signed, and we're all set. They are expecting you at eight."

"In Whiskey Ridge?"

"Where else?" Dad asked.

"I don't even know where they live," I said.

"Oh, right." Dad pulled a packet of papers out of his breast pocket. "That Spidermonkey's efficient and he hasn't cursed at me yet."

"That's a nice change."

"You've used him a few times." Dad's blue eyes bored into me.

I looked right back. "I have. He's super-fast and doesn't yell or hang up."

"He likes you quite a lot."

"Did he say so?" I asked.

The focus was getting uncomfortable. Dad was watching my every reaction. "He didn't have to."

Ah, that's why you're here. You have a feeling.

I smiled and thrust out a hip. "I do have that Watts charm."

"On the phone?"

Not falling for it.

"Especially on the phone."

Dad's focus dropped. He wasn't getting anything and he knew it. Something about Spidermonkey made Dad's hackles go up. That was so not good for me. The last thing I wanted was Tommy Watts sniffing around my life.

"Are you giving me that or what?" I asked.

"It's background on Thooft and the family."

I held out my hand. "Great."

Dad didn't hand it over. "It was very fast. Like he'd already done it."

"So?"

"Why would a hacker waste his time doing background that he hadn't been hired to do?"

"Maybe he figured you'd want it or Chuck. He's not an idiot."

"Maybe he thought you'd want it."

"I didn't, but I do now." I took the papers from him. "Anything interesting?"

"I wish," he said, his eyes still narrowed. "Run of the mill American family."

"They're not so run of the mill now."

"No, they're not," Dad said with warmth. "You can put yourself aside in this, can't you?"

"What choice do I have?" I asked.

"Leo and Avery can do it, if you prefer." That's what Dad said, but his eyes said he wanted me to do it. It was a big deal to him. He could've done it, if it were him, so I would, too.

"No. I want to do it. Like Kimberly said, nobody's going to care as much as me."

"Smart lady." Dad pulled another box out of his pocket and tossed it to me. "I almost forgot. Stick some in your wallet." He touched the brim of his hat and left.

I opened the box and my heart sank. Business cards with my name on it. Nothing was more official than that, not even the license.

I sank down on the bed and my phone started ringing on the nightstand.

"Aren't I the popular one this morning?" I picked it up and it was Mom. "Hey, why are you awake?"

"Is your father still there?"

"Yeah."

"Tell him he forgot to eat again and give him a granola bar or something."

I ran out my door and down the hall to yell over the bannister at Dad who was at the front door, "Mom says you have to eat!"

"I'm fine!"

"You're going to get osteoporosis like Grandad!"

Dad whipped open the front door and said, "That's not going to happen," and out he went.

"Did he say no?" said Mom, still on the phone.

"He said no."

I commiserated with my long-suffering mother for a minute and then went to wash my face and apply the spackle Fats gave me. The look wasn't great, but I no longer looked like a topographical map so there was that. Then I called Fats to see if she was both conscious and available.

"I'm here," she said.

"Where's here?"

"The kitchen. Joy's giving me ginger ale and saltines for the road."

"Well, alright then."

I found some riding boots that looked sort of professional and grabbed a blazer that Mom gave me because she thought it would disguise my chest. It didn't, but it did have a professional-type vibe to it. A last mirror check said I was not too bad. Me, but grown up like a big girl with a job.

"What are you doing?" Fats lounged in the doorway wearing nothing that could be remotely mistaken for professional. She had on a one-piece pink and black leopard bodysuit, turquoise sneakers with thick soles that gave her four more inches in height, and an electric blue men's parka with a fur-lined hood.

"Seeing if I look professional," I said.

"You look boring."

"Nailed it."

"Ready?" she asked.

"Did...my dad call you?" I asked.

She smoothed her slicked back ponytail. "He did. Why?"

I don't think Dad thought this through.

"No reason. I guess he still hasn't put you together with Calpurnia yet." I got the Mauser out from under my sweaters and stuck it in my purse with the new wallet and business cards. If I was going to do it, I was going to do it right.

She snorted and did a squat. "Oh, he knows. He's just decided not to know, ya know."

"What makes you say that?"

"When we were waiting for you in the ER, he asked how Uncle Moe was doing." A toothpick popped out onto her lip and dangled there, attached by the thick coating of lip gloss.

"He knows your Uncle Moe?"

"Turns out he arrested him for racketeering about twenty years ago," Fats said with a wicked grin. "Small world."

"Too small," I said, getting a little weak in the knees. "Does he know about Calpurnia?"

"His lawyer was Joey the seal Farina."

"And?"

"The Fibonaccis were his only clients."

"Why 'the seal'?"

The grin grew larger. "He was slick. The charges were dropped on a technicality."

My stomach tried to tie itself into an extra knot. "I don't know what to do."

She checked her phone. "We're due in Whisky Ridge at eight. This is cutting it close."

"My dad thinks something's going on with Spidermonkey."

Fats came out of her squat and ran a hand over her growing bump. "It had to happen."

"Why?"

She came to the mirror and admired her sideview. The bodysuit was from her pro wrestling days and did a great job of accentuating her new curve. "It's Tommy Watts. You thought he'd talk to Spidermonkey and not get the gist that you two know each other very well?"

"They're just emailing and texting."

"You're hopeless."

"I'm getting that way and you're saying he knows I'm involved with Calpurnia Fibonacci," I said.

"He knows I am and so what? My sheet's cleaner than yours."

And that's not suspicious at all.

"True," I said.

"It's also true that we're going to be late. Do you want to be late? I don't want to be late," said Fats.

"I don't want to be late."

"Get the dog and let's go."

"We're taking Pick?" I asked.

Fats tapped her wrist pointedly, so I got the dog, and we went. We were not late. We were early because when you travel with a nauseated Fats Licata nothing takes very long.

The Thooft family had gathered on the family farm just outside Whiskey Ridge and were waiting for us there en masse. I want to say I wasn't nervous, but that'd be a big fat lie. Kimberly had been lovely, but that didn't mean her parents would be.

"Breathe," said Fats.

"Same to you."

"I'm breathing." She wasn't breathing. She was panting and gripping the steering wheel like it was a safety line on Mount Everest.

"I could've driven," I said as we went down into another gully and Fats gulped. "I can drive now. Pull over."

"No. I just have to get through this," she said through gritted teeth.

"This is not a workout. You don't have to power through."

"I can do this thing."

"There's no thing and nobody wants you to do it." We came out of the gully and into another. "Tiny doesn't want you to."

There was a big bump in the gravel road and she made a noise halfway between a burp and a croak. "What did he say?"

You can do it. She probably won't kill you.

"That you are losing weight," I said.

"A couple of pounds."

"And," *Somebody pray for me,* "losing muscle mass."

Fats slammed on the brakes. "He would not say that."

I plastered myself against the door and Pick climbed onto the center console, barking. I pulled the hair ball into my lap and peeked at her from around his panting muzzle. "He did say it. He's worried. And...and...your bodysuit is getting loose."

It wasn't, but if she didn't keep some food down the baby was going to be in trouble, so I decided to risk a pounding.

"You're lucky this is a paying gig," said Fats.

"Oh, yeah?"

"I need the money."

"For the baby?" I asked.

"For everything. Calpurnia's going to put me out to pasture."

Fats had been over at the Fibonacci compound, gotten dizzy, and proceeded to vomit in a fern right in front of Calpurnia. A leave of absence was mentioned.

"Maybe she won't."

"I get one more chance and then I'm out like some geriatric loser that can't hold his water."

I'm not sure what that means, but okay.

"You'll just have to rock the last chance."

She slammed her hands on the steering wheel and I think it may have bent a little. "I will do it." She hit the gas and we careened up over a hill, catching some air, before landing with a thump. Fats didn't throw up, but I nearly did.

Then we cleared the woods and drove past multiple barns, a couple of tractors, and a smell invaded the cabin of Fat's truck. The Thoofts were hog farmers of the industrial type and although the scenery was beautiful, the smell wasn't. Their farmhouse sat on a hill overlooking the working property. It was large, white, and square with a deep wrap-around porch and had an American flag blowing in the breeze off one of the slender columns. The house had been built in 1900 and the current Thoofts were the fourth generation to live in it. Kimberly's middle brother Gregory and his wife took over the farm when her parents retired and they lived in the big house, taking care of the elderly Thoofts.

Another house, modern with tons of window, sat on another hill not far away with a sign pointing down the gravel road to it *Stackhouse Veterinary Services*. That was where Kimberly and her husband lived. People thought I lived too close for comfort to my parents on Hawthorne Avenue, but, at least, I couldn't see in their windows and vice versa.

But, according to Spidermonkey, the Thooft family didn't seem to mind the closeness. He included every detail that he could find in the information packet he made me mostly, I suspect, because there wasn't much to say. No criminal history. No divorces. Profitable working farm with low debt. Personal debt was low, too. To top it off, they were devout Evangelicals with a history of community service. I hoped they didn't look too hard at me. Those DBD covers weren't going to put me in a favorable light.

Fats parked in line on the circle drive behind three trucks and a couple of Camrys. "So what are you looking for?"

"No idea."

"Why don't you ever have a solid plan?" she asked. "These people are grieving and flipping freaked."

"They aren't the only ones."

Fats popped a couple Altoids in her mouth and chewed them. Altoids! They were white pellets of fire.

"I know," she said, drumming her fingers on the steering wheel. "We'll find out why their son turned out to be a woman-hating psycho nut job and then we'll go to lunch."

Not at Crabapples.

She grinned at me. "At Crabapples."

Dammit. Where's the nausea when you need it.

"I thought you were sick," I said.

"And now I'm hungry." She got out and opened the back door to retrieve Moe, who'd been snoozing on her special donut in the backseat, nice and calm. Pick was anything but calm. We got out and he went batshit crazy. So many sniffs to sniff. I doubt the poodle had ever been on a farm and it was going to his head.

"Oh, I'm glad you brought him," said Kimberly from the porch.

"You're the only one," I said as Pick yanked me around the trucks.

"Chase!" yelled Kimberly. "Come out here and bring Justin!"

Two dark-haired teenage boys in crisp polo shirts and denim jackets came out to stare at me stumbling around. Until, that is, they caught sight of Fats, who came out from behind the trucks with a yipping Moe. The mini mutt had on a doggy puffer coat that matched Fats' and words cannot express what those two looked like standing next to a mud splattered farm truck. Did I mention that Fats' shoulder holster was clearly visible?

"Wow," said the boys in unison.

I think Kimberly would've reprimanded them for being rude, but she was staring, too.

"This is my associate, Mary Elizabeth Licata. She helps me on cases."

"How much can you bench?" asked one of the boys.

Kimberly woke up. "Chase, for goodness sake."

"It's alright," said Fats. "All men want to know."

The boys fluffed up at the word "men" and grinned shyly at us. Kimberly came down the steps and shook both our hands, trying not to stare at Fats. "I told the kids that you had an adorable giant poodle, but they didn't believe me."

"Why not?" I asked the boys.

"Detectives have Rottweilers," said Chase.

"Or German Shepherds," said Justin.

"I agree those would be more logical choices. This is Pickpocket and he's actually my boyfriend's dog."

"Is he a hairdresser?" asked Chase.

Fats quaked with suppressed laughter.

"He's a cop, but I'll tell him you asked that question." I was so going to enjoy Chuck's reaction. Hairdresser. He might have to show me how fast he can break down and rebuild his service revolver again.

Pick yanked me toward the boys, yipping and wagging his stumpy tail. Moe woke up and joined in.

"What kind of dog is that?" Justin asked.

"Nobody knows," I said.

Kimberly suggested the boys take the dogs for a walk around the farm and I happily agreed. Fats had to give them a lecture on the delicacy of Moe's paws, which the boys were good about, but I could sense the inner eye rolls.

"Are you...ready to come in?" Kimberly asked once the boys were out of sight.

"If they're ready for me."

"Ready as they'll ever be."

We walked up the stairs and Kimberly opened the door for us. In the small foyer next to the well-worn staircase were Kimberly's surviving brothers. Spidermonkey had included pictures in my packets, but I was still surprised. They looked almost identical to their brother. Big, heavy men with wispy blond hair and receding hairlines. The same bone structure and softening jawlines just at different ages. Gregory did have a mullet, so there was that.

Gregory and Kevin shook our hands, snuck peeks at Fats, and apologized to me before leading me into the living room where their parents, wives, and Kimberly's husband, Holt, sat on flowered overstuffed sofas with coffee mugs in their hands. Holt was instantly recognizable, not only because he wore a fleece vest stuffed with a stethoscope and who knows what else but also because, unlike the Thooft men, Holt was slender, dark-haired, and wore glasses on his calm, studious face.

Kimberly introduced us and there was more hand shaking. Fats sat down in a rocker recliner and I perched on the edge of a bentwood rocker that was probably a family heirloom. We exchanged pleasantries and eyes were averted. Fats, groping for something to say, informed them that she was expecting. After they got over the initial shock that, I suspect, she wasn't born a man, there were many congratulations and some discussion of morning sickness cures. Gregory's wife Heather got me some coffee and ginger tea for Fats. Then it was back to averted eyes and uncomfortable silence. It was up to me to open things up. I guess that makes sense, but I wasn't happy about it.

"I was surprised that you wanted to meet me, much less hire me," I said to no one in particular.

"Why?" Stephanie, Kevin's wife, asked. "Don't people make amends when they've hurt someone?"

"You didn't hurt me," I said.

"We did," whispered Ann Thooft, Anton's mother, from her corner. "We must have."

"It's not your fault."

Ann shook her head and tried to speak. Her round face crumpled and her faded blonde hair in a pixie cut waved around her head as she cried softly into a handkerchief.

Tearfully, her husband patted her back. Anthony was a large man without an ounce of fat on him. The boys got their bone structure from him. "Miss Watts, I don't know how to tell you how sorry we are. If we'd known what Anton was going to do, we'd have stopped him."

"I believe you," I said and I did. There was nothing but raw sincerity in his face. "But I'm going to have to ask questions and you might not like them."

They shook their heads in unison and waited.

"You had no hint that this was coming?" I asked.

The entire family agreed that they didn't and a picture emerged as they began to talk about Anton and it wasn't what you'd expect. I didn't hear about a loner, disconnected from his family, and angry. Quite the opposite. He called his mother and sister twice a week. He visited. He joined in on the farm.

They told stories about growing up, school, church and Scouts.

Photo albums came out and we poured through dozens of photos of a perfect family.

Anthony showed me his favorite photo, a shot taken on a beach with the four kids making sandcastles and grinning so wide it made you feel a little bit happy just seeing the joy.

"It was a perfect day with my family, all of us together," he said. "I always wanted four."

"Four troublemakers," said Kimberly. "Or maybe three."

Her surviving brothers groaned and the meeting became like a memorial service where you remember the good and forget the bad. I listened and flipped back and forth through photos of a young Anton and the older Anton. There was something. I felt it. There were always smiles, but something else, too. Something with Anton. I just couldn't quite get it. Same boy, same smile, but what was it? Something behind the eyes as he got older. He was gay in a family where that wasn't ideal. Maybe that was it.

In the middle of the discussion, Anthony, Anton's father, went out and returned with a box.

"Ah, Dad," said Kevin. "Miss Watts doesn't need to see that stuff."

"She should have the complete picture, if she's going to understand," said Anthony and he gave me the box.

"I can't believe you have all that stuff," said Gregory.

"We wouldn't throw it away," said Ann. "We have all your things, too."

"And mine?" Kimberly asked.

The men groaned and the wives laughed.

"Mom would run into a burning barn to save your third-grade report card," said Kevin.

"I would not," said Ann, but her loving gaze on Kimberly belied her words.

Everyone began to tease about Kimberly being the favorite, the much loved fourth child and only girl. It was good-natured and I sat back to watch the interplay in a large family. I'd never had that and I missed it sometimes. There's a lot of focus that comes with being the only, but watching Kimberly defend herself against her loving brothers,

I guessed that being an only daughter with brothers came with its own pressures.

Fats watched, too, her face inscrutable. I didn't know much about her family, just the little I picked up here and there. I got the feeling she was not the daughter that her mother expected.

"Alright. Alright. Alright," said Kimberly with her hands up. "This is not about me."

"It's always about you," said Gregory laughing.

"No kidding," said Kevin.

"Boys. Boys," objected Ann, wiping her eyes in both grief and laughter.

"Miss Watts," Kimberly said. "Please open that box and prove to my brothers that Anton's stuff got saved just as much as mine."

They started in about how many boxes Kimberly had to Anton's one, but I ignored that and unfolded the cardboard flaps. It was a pretty big box, the size of a laundry basket and it weighed a good amount, too.

There might've been a lot of different things in that box and my mind pictured the bad options, which looking back was ridiculous. Ann and Anthony kept that box. It wasn't going to have violent porn, dead cats, or graphic depictions of the girls he wanted to dismember, namely me. The box had what normal people would've thought of. Memories (good ones), mementoes (ones you could show your grandma) and awards. So many awards.

"He was such a good speller," said Anthony.

I pulled out medal after medal for spelling, heavy ones with ribbons

"I don't know where he got it." Gregory gently elbowed his dad. "How many is that, Miss Watts?"

"Eight," said Ann. "He won eight. Now I ask you does a boy who wins the spelling bee for his grade eight years in a row do what Anton did?"

Not gonna answer that.

Instead, I kept digging past bundles of report cards, stacks of art projects, two baseball gloves, baby clothes, some lop-sided pottery, Hot Wheels cars, and a Dukes of Hazzard racing set to find more awards in tennis, theatre, debate, and chess, all from eighth grade and below. Anton had almost nothing from high school except report cards and academic awards.

"He was a renaissance man," I said as a dug through to double check Anton's high school activities or lack thereof.

"Anton was good at everything," said Anthony.

So why did he stop doing anything, except school?

I looked around and saw no disagreement in that room. What happened? Something happened.

"He could've done anything," said Ann, "but he decided on teaching."

"I thought it was going to be politics," said Gregory.

Heather shifted in her seat, turning to him. "Really. He was quiet."

"Not when he was younger."

"It looks like he stopped doing a lot of activities in high school," I said.

"He had different priorities." Ann focused on me, her liver-spotted hands trembling slightly. "But Anton was very popular and outgoing. He wasn't one of those oddballs that hide in their parents' basements playing Atari by themselves like Shifty Scott."

Everyone nodded. Anton was not Shifty Scott. Kimberly went pale and got up, just to sit down again. Her husband, Holt, frowned at her, confused, before offering to get her more coffee that she didn't want.

"What happened to Shifty Scott?" Fats asked, speaking up for the first time.

"We really shouldn't say," whispered Ann and I figured it must've been something really awful since Ann's son was thought to be a woman-hating kidnapper and wannabe murderer.

"Oh, go on, Mom," said Kevin. "It's not that bad. I'd rather that than—" He turned red and clamped his mouth shut. It had slipped, the façade that everything was fine.

"Spill it," I said. "With a name like Shifty it's bound to be interesting."

It wasn't that interesting. Shifty Scott was the son of friends from church. I got the feeling that Ann had spent plenty of time consoling Jackie Scott over her weird kid while feeling wholly superior. Shifty didn't win anything. He was the friendless boy with pimples and awkward interactions. Everyone thought he'd stay in that basement forever, but he didn't. Shifty, out of nowhere, went to UMKC to study costume design, came out as gay, and now owned a drag club in LA. He was married and had twin boys from a surrogate.

"He was just quiet," said Gregory. "He never did anything…bad."

Ann made a sniffing noise and said, "He didn't stay with the church's teachings."

"He's happy, Mom," said Kevin. "Jackie loves those twins."

"I'm going to lie down now." Ann wobbled to her feet and Kevin quickly took her arm to take her out. "I just have one request," she said to me.

"Name it," I said.

"I want you to promise not to do any interviews about us. No articles or TV interviews."

"What else could they possibly say?" Gregory asked. "They've said everything bad that anyone could think of."

Ann Thooft's gaze got hard and focused and I could see the strong matriarch in her still. "The point is I want no publicity whatsoever again. No pictures in the paper. Nothing about us. Can you do that, Miss Watts?"

"I can't promise that," I said with all sincerity. "The media has a mind of its own, especially when it comes to me."

"Then we will call it a day. Thank you for making this long drive for nothing—"

"Hold on, Mom," said Kimberly, jumping to her feet. "You agreed. We all agreed."

"It's different now," said Ann. "We've already had reporters following us around town. She could make it worse. Find someone else."

"There's no one else," said Anthony. "Miss Watts has agreed and they've signed the contract. Thoofts don't go back on our word."

Ann gritted her teeth and walked out.

"We're still on?" I asked.

"Yes," said Kimberly. "She'll come around. It's just been so hard."

I looked around the room and the faces told me that Ann Thooft wasn't in the habit of coming around, but they also hadn't changed their minds. I still had a job, so I packed everything back in Anton's box, skimming some notebooks and taking note of dates. When I looked up, Kimberly's eyes were on me and she was biting her lower lip again. I gave her what I hoped was a reassuring look. I wasn't going to out her brother, although I couldn't imagine that could be worse than what had already happened.

"So when Detective Rich told me that he was closing the case, he said that Anton had a lot of female friends at the school. Other teachers."

Kimberly blew out a breath and said, "He did. He always had female friends."

Anthony showed me photos of Anton's friends, Karen and Laurie. They were in school together all the way from kindergarten to senior year. Looking at those pictures, if I hadn't known Anton was supposed to hate women, I'd never have guessed it. I would have guessed he was gay though. A farm boy who wore ties to school, never dated, and who has girls for best friends. Come on.

"He was always very protective of the girls," said Gregory.

"Yeah, he went to parties just so he made sure they got home safe." Kevin turned to Kimberly. "You know how he was."

She smiled. "Not really. When Anton was in high school, I was watching Smurfs." She looked at me. "He was fourteen years older."

I knew that, but I kept forgetting. Kimberly was a late in life baby. Ann got her in right under the wire at forty-two. "You said he was very good with you."

"He was," said Anthony. "He really was. Anton babysat, changed diapers, played with her for hours on end."

"Did you ever cry when he went to college," said Kevin, rolling his eyes. "I never thought you'd stop bawling."

"We were close," objected Kimberly. "That's why this is so hard, Miss Watts. I knew him best, except for Mom. We did everything together when he was home."

Anthony reached over and gently touched her shoulder. "You three were quite a team."

"Mom, Kimberly, and Anton," said Gregory. "Couldn't pry you apart."

Kimberly nodded. "That's why I know that what happened wasn't just out of character, it was impossible, unless something happened to him."

They all nodded and agreed that it was out of character, all except one. Stephanie Thooft frowned and looked away as the Thoofts all started regaling me with stories of how protective Anton was to women. Always kind. Never a nasty word. Never a complaint or a problem. Anton liked women. Stephanie didn't say a thing. She only nodded when someone asked her to agree. She did agree, but her silence said a lot.

"Anton didn't say anything about coming back to the States?" I asked when the insisting was done.

"No," said Anthony. "We would've picked him up. We always picked him up."

I had to ask. I'd been putting it off, but it had to be done. "What about me? Did he ever mention me?"

There were loud protestations at that, including Stephanie. Anton never mentioned me or my dad or anything to do with us. He wasn't a fan of DBD, preferring jazz to rock, and he didn't spend any time in St. Louis. Never went to school there and had no friends in the city.

"Well, I'm stumped," said Fats, surprising everyone. "He couldn't have done it, but he did it."

They nodded and Anthony said, "That's about the size of it."

"Is there anything else you want to ask?" Gregory asked.

I couldn't think of a thing. "I think that's it for now."

"What will you do next?" Kevin asked.

"Are those friends still around? Karen and Laurie?"

Anthony looked at his kids. "Didn't Laurie move?"

"Chicago for grad school," said Gregory. "She never came back. We might be able to find her address from someone at church."

"Don't worry about it," I said. "We'll find her if we need to. It's what we do."

"Karen lives in St. Seb," said Anthony. "You know St. Seb, of course."

I smiled. "I do more than I ever expected to."

A head poked through the door to the hall. "Was that nun's ghost really in the basement of the high school?" asked Chase.

"Chase!" exclaimed Kimberly.

I stood up and put the photo albums back on the coffee table. "Chase, you wouldn't believe the things I've seen."

Justin's head poked in. "The floating eyeballs. I bet you saw those eyeballs at Miss Elizabeth's."

"She certainly did not," said Anthony. "That's just a rumor."

I winked at the boys when I walked into the hall and they high-fived each other. Pick and Moe were dancing around with muddy feet and happy smiles.

"How were they?" I asked. "Not too crazy?"

"Totally crazy," said Justin. "Your poodle thinks he can herd."

"He can," said Chase.

The boys started bickering about the herding of pigs, which wasn't a thing but still happened when there was a poodle involved.

I took Pick's leash and Fats picked up Moe, trying not to frown at her muddy paws.

"Here you go," said Gregory, handing me a sticky note. "Karen's number and address. She brought us a casserole the other day and she doesn't believe it either. I texted her to say you're here."

Nobody believed it and I had to admit I was having a harder and harder time, too. Who was Anton Thooft?

"Did she say if she's available today?" I asked.

"She's at work, but you can go there."

"Where's there?"

"She's a waitress at"—*Do not say it*—"Crabapples in St. Seb," said Gregory.

Crap and double crap.

"Oh, well, we wouldn't want to disturb her at work," I said.

"I'll disturb her," said Fats. "I'll disturb the heck out of her. I'm starving."

Kimberly gave me directions and she looked like she wanted to hug me, but I wasn't there yet. I might never be there.

We walked out of the Thooft house into the smell of hogs and impending snow. Fats closed the door and we walked down the wide steps in silence. After we got all the paws cleaned with Fats' emergency paw cleaning kit in the back of the truck, we got in and she said, "Did you see that sister-in-law?"

"Oh, I saw her," I said.

"She's got a story to tell and I bet there aren't any medals involved."

"Will she tell it though?"

Fats cracked her knuckles. "Oh, she'll tell it. Don't worry about that."

"We're not threatening our clients," I said.

"Not threatening. Encouraging." A toothpick popped out and she gnawed on it.

"You're feeling better."

"Hog stink doesn't make me sick. Who'd a thought?"

"Is there any chance that mung beans and tofu make you yark?"

"None."

Swell.

"It's too early for lunch," I said, throwing out my last hope.

"I'm pregnant and losing weight. It's not too early."

"You've got me there."

"To St. Seb," said Fats, "and we get to interview a Karen. I've got fifty bucks that says she'll have the haircut."

"She's not going to have that blonde bob," I said. "But I think she'll call the manager at some point."

"This Karen works there," said Fats. "She's not going to call her own manager."

"Wait and see, my friend, wait and see."

CHAPTER SEVEN

Crabapples sat on Main Street, occupying a storefront that would've looked at home in Deadwood with a high false front to make it look impressive and a crusty wooden cornice and door. The picture window proclaimed it to be the only vegan restaurant within fifty miles. Shocking.

Fats parked in front and said, "It looks fantastic."

"It looks like we should be wearing holsters and ready to kick some butt at a drop of the Stetson."

"I am."

"They don't allow dogs," I said, not knowing what the dog policy was. If you advertise cauliflower steaks as better than beef on your sandwich board, who knows what you believe about dogs.

She whipped open the back door and said, "I don't know why you even try that anymore."

"Desperate?"

"I was going with stupid, but okay."

"Hey!"

"You've eaten with Moe at California Pizza Kitchen next to a table with cops and health inspectors, why would you ever bring up anyone's dog policy?"

"I have a head injury."

"How long are you going to use that?"

"Until the next head injury," I said as I reluctantly got out. Pick climbed over my seat to jump out my door and clamped his jaws on my ankle, chewing like a nut.

"What's he doing?" Fats asked with her weirdo tucked under her arm and, for once, Moe looked like the superior animal.

"He chews on me sometimes."

She snapped her fingers. "Stop that."

Pick jerked away and sat. If I didn't know better, I'd have thought he was embarrassed.

"I think you missed your calling," I said.

"My calling is—" She dashed into Crabapples, banging the door so hard I was afraid she cracked the glass.

It was now ten thirty, but there was a decent crowd, sipping soy lattes in front of laptops and stacks of books and folders. Everyone looked up as Fats frantically scanned the restaurant.

"Bathroom?" I called out. "It's an emergency!"

A woman with a Karen haircut pointed at a hall in the back and Fats shoved Moe in my arms before barreling through tables and spilling more than a few lattes. A door slammed and I took a breath.

"She's pregnant and having some wicked morning sickness. Sorry about that," I said to the room. Everyone nodded in sympathy and started mopping up the mess.

The haircut came over and said, "You can't have dogs in here."

"They're service animals," I said. "I have the vests and paperwork in the truck, if you need it."

"Well…"

Please don't ask to see the nonexistent paperwork.

"She's just so sick and she loves vegan food, I didn't grab it," I said quickly.

She looked me over, recognizing me easily and threw up her hands. "Oh, it's fine. I'll just put you in the back."

We walked to a back booth and she leaned over to me, "Besides, I'm afraid your friend might pound me if I say no."

"She gets that a lot." I put Pick on my side and Moe on Fats.

"Morning sickness is rough. Are you eating? We're starting lunch."

"She'll try."

"We have an amazing alfredo with cashew cream and lots of Meyer lemon and ginger. A bunch of our pregos swear by it for the nausea."

"Sounds great," I said.

"You're not vegan, are you? I can always tell."

"Not even close."

She leaned over. "Me, either, but Yuki does a mushroom burger with Asian slaw that'll knock your socks off."

"Let's knock off the socks then," I said. "Actually, we're also looking for someone. Is Karen here?"

Her smile melted. "Is it the hair? Everyone assumes I'm Karen." She patted her asymmetrical blonde bob.

"I'm not assuming." I kinda was. "I was told she was working and open to being interviewed for the Thooft case."

"That's you? I thought you were…"

"The victim?"

She sat down next to Moe and typed in our order on her electronic thingamajiggy. "I didn't think *you'd* be investigating. That's unusual, isn't it?"

"Very, but that's how I roll," I said. "Are you Karen?"

Say no.

"Yes," she said.

Fifty bucks down the drain.

"Do you mind answering some questions about Anton?" I asked.

"Not a bit." Karen was touching her bob again. "Do you think I should change my hair? I got yelled at this morning at Schnucks. I didn't say anything to anybody."

She was such a Karen. The right age. The right makeup. "I have to say I would."

Karen sighed. "My husband offered to pay me to change it. I guess I will."

Fats came out of the bathroom and lurched over. Karen barely got out of the way as she fell into the booth. I'm surprised nobody yelled, "Timber!" It was that kind of slow fall.

"I've got a ginger spritzer," said Karen. "How about that?"

Fats gulped and nodded. Karen headed off into the back and returned immediately with two ginger spritzers. They had decorative orange and lemon slices with paper umbrellas.

"I brought you one, too, since head injuries have nausea, don't they?"

"They do." I took a sip. "That's really good."

Fats took a fearful sip and said, "Oh, thank God."

"What was it this time?"

"I got out of the truck too fast."

Karen and I winced, waiting to say anything else until she got a little more down.

"So this is Karen," I said.

A smile flickered on Fats' lips, but she continued to clutch her spritzer. Karen pulled up a chair and asked, "What do you want to know?"

"About Anton, your relationship with him, his demeanor, anything."

"Let me just say that I know he did it, but the Anton I know couldn't have. Never in a million years."

"That's what we're hearing from pretty much everyone," I said. "You never saw him be violent or angry with women?"

"Never. He was so sweet. He looked after me. Anton vetted my boyfriends. A couple weren't very nice and he told them off." She got out her phone and showed us pictures from Anton's last visit home. I'd seen plenty of pictures out at the farm, but somehow Karen's pictures were different. It was a Christmas party and there Anton was, smiling and holding up a beer, arms around Karen and other ladies. In one shot, Karen and another lady were kissing Anton's cheeks as he beamed with happiness. I had to look away. I couldn't see that face anymore. He came at me. His hand on my face, pressing that sopping cloth over my airways. How was that the same guy?

Pick pressed against me and gave me a little kiss on the cheek. I put my arm around him and let his heartbeat soothe me.

"I'm sorry," said Karen, her eyes filling with tears. "I thought it would help you understand where I'm coming from."

"It does," I said. "I just don't know what to do with it."

Fats finished her Spritzer and gave Moe a scratch saying, "Let me see those again."

Karen gave her the phone and Fats flipped through the photos shaking her head. "It's almost like we're tracking the wrong dude."

"I know you're not, but that's what I'm saying," said Karen. "Anton was great with women. If he had a problem, I would've known."

You didn't know something.

"Think back," I said. "Was there anything, even in high school?"

She smiled and dabbed at her eyes with a tissue, careful not to dislodge the heavy eyeliner. "Absolutely nothing. Anton was always popular with the ladies." Her smile turned coquettish. "Half my friends were in love with him."

"Were they?" Fats had a wry twist to her lips and Karen frowned slightly.

"Yes," she said, firmly, "and he was pretty into them, too."

"Really?" I asked, trying to keep the disbelief out of my voice and failing.

"You know!" she exclaimed and I think she surprised herself with the ferocity of her own words.

I'd promised Kimberly so I merely said, "What do I know?"

"You know and now you know that I know, but nobody else knows, so we should stay quiet about what we know."

"Well, that's clear as mud," said Fats. "How about you order me another spritzer to wash it clean?"

Karen put in the order and gathered her thoughts before saying, "I should've known you'd figure it out. I mean it's what you do."

"What did I figure out?" I asked.

She leaned over, looked around, and whispered, "That Anton was gay."

"Well, that wasn't hard at all."

"Yes, it was. Nobody knows. How did you figure out?"

"I'd like to think I'd have put it together, but I was actually told," I said.

"You're saying...somebody else does know?"

Fats and I exchanged a look and she lifted a shoulder. I felt weird about letting Kimberly's secret out but couldn't think why I shouldn't.

"Kimberly told her," said Fats, taking that decision right off my plate and I was grateful.

"Thanks," I said.

"And thank you for my fifty bucks."

"Fifty bucks?" asked Karen. "Were you betting on whether I knew or not?"

"Nope. Not that," I said. "You didn't know that Kimberly knew?"

"No. I can't believe it. Anton told me I was the only one he could trust."

I wonder what else he lied about.

"Did Laurie know?" I asked.

Karen laughed. "Absolutely not. She was completely in love with him."

Her order thingy dinged and she dashed into the back to get our lunches and Fats said, "How much do you want to bet that Laurie knew?"

"The farm."

"This has got to be the worst kept secret in St. Seb."

"Or the best," I said.

She gave me the side eye as Karen came out with a laden tray. I have to admit the burger looked and smelled fantastic. Fats' cashew pasta thing was a little on the green side for me, but she took a bite and groaned with pleasure. "I think I can keep it down."

Karen didn't look thrilled, but I said, "High praise, trust me."

"I'll take your word for it. Is there anything else you want to know about Anton? I can't think of anything that would make this thing he did make sense."

I glanced around at the other diners. "Anybody else here know him?"

"I'll call my manager," said Karen.

I stifled a laugh and Fats gagged on a noodle.

"What? She knew Anton. He took a painting class with her, I think."

"It's nothing," I said. "I'm amazed at how many people knew him."

"Well, Whiskey Ridge is tiny. The only restaurant they have is

Subway." She made a face. "Everyone comes into St. Seb for everything."

We nodded and she went into the back.

"So you owe me fifty," I said.

"Does that count?" Fats asked.

"Did Karen say she was going to call the manager?"

Fats gritted her teeth and the muscles in her cheek rippled. "She did. I cannot believe I lost that bet."

"Now we're even. You know, sometimes I'm right," I said.

"Eh."

"I am."

"Mercy!" a voice rang out across the restaurant and I nearly dropped my burger. Carrie Norton ran across the room, wearing an astonishing outfit of a holey black crocheted floor-length dress with green pleather unitard underneath and a pair of cowboy boots topped off with her curly purple hair in pigtails. She wrapped her arms around me and kissed my cheek. I'd met Carrie on my last trip to St. Seb and she never failed to make an impression. "I'm so glad to see you two. How are you, Mercy?"

"Fine. Well, mostly fine."

Carrie plopped down in Karen's seat. "Well, I don't believe that for minute. How could you be?"

"It's what I'm supposed to say," I said.

"Not to me," she said with conviction. "With me you can always say the absolute truth."

Let's see about that.

"I'm investigating Anton Thooft."

"I know. Karen told me. Excellent idea in my opinion."

Fats' eyebrows shot up and I gagged on a marinated cucumber slice. "Really?"

"Of course, who would investigate him like you? No one, that's who. It's not just a job, is it?"

"No, it isn't," I said, swallowing hard. "So you knew him?"

"I did and quite well in fact," she said conspiratorially.

I picked up my burger and asked, "Did you see this coming?"

She waved that idea away with both hands. "No. I would've said it was impossible. It wasn't in him."

"It was," said Fats rather harshly.

Carrie nodded and her pigtails bounced around wildly. "I know, but I'm telling you right now something terrible must've happened to make Anton do that to you."

I took a bite and the burger did knock off the socks. Not meat, but dang good. "The cops think he was going to rape and murder me."

"I can't speak to the murder thing, but rape? Nope. Would never happen."

Fats and I hid our smiles behind our food and waited for the inevitable as Carrie lowered her voice and looked around to see if anyone was listening. "Anton was gay."

"We know," I said.

She jerked back astonished. "You know? How?"

We went through the Kimberly revelation and Carrie reacted with suitable shock and I said, "I'm more interested in how you knew."

She laughed and stole a fry off my plate. "Look at me. Do you seriously think I don't know a gay man when I see one?"

"You never know."

"Well, I guess that's true, given recent events in my fair town, but I *did* know. It wasn't hard to put together. Plus, a friend of mine knows Jamie, they dated for years."

My ears perked up. This was the first boyfriend, someone who reasonably knew Anton better than anyone. "Jamie who?"

"Jamie Koplar. He works at Black Heart Books down in your neck of the woods."

A St. Louis connection!

"So did Anton know the Central West End?" I asked.

"Sure. He and Jamie still talked. It wasn't a bad breakup, just sad."

"Why sad?" Fats asked.

Carrie sighed and told us how Jamie and Anton really loved each other, but after they graduated from college, Jamie was ready to come out. He wanted to live together as a real couple, buy a house, and have a family. Anton wouldn't do it. He downright refused to even contemplate cracking open the closet door. Jamie came out and broke up with

Anton, who took a teaching job in Wentzville where no one knew them, continuing on as a straight man who hadn't found the right girl yet.

"My friend said it broke Jamie's heart," said Carrie. "But in a way he understood with the Thoofts being how they are."

Fats polished off her pasta and asked, "How are they?"

"Very religious. Evangelical. Didn't you know that?"

"I did," I said. "But how did they never figure it out? It sounds pretty obvious."

Carrie shrugged. "They saw what they wanted to see and Anton put on a good show."

"How? I thought he didn't date women."

"Oh, he didn't, but in high school he always had a date for Homecoming, Prom, Sadie Hawkins. They just never went anywhere."

"What did he say to you about it, being gay and his family?"

"Nothing. Nobody knew and I couldn't tell anyone. Top secret."

"And you didn't tell anyone?" Fats looked doubtful and I have to admit I was, too.

"Well, Yuki knows," she said. "But he's my husband. I couldn't lie to him when he asked."

"Yuki asked?"

She laughed and stole another fry. "Come on, Mercy. A man in his fifties, never married, never lived with a woman, paints, enjoys ballroom dance, and adores his mother? Come on."

"I see your point," I said. "Do you think staying in the closet was about Ann?"

"Yes, yes, and more yes. He was devoted to her. Last time he was home, last Christmas, he came in for a painting class with her and Kimberly. They were quite the trio. Very close. Did everything together."

Just those three.

"It's a big family," I said. "We just came from the farm. They all seemed very close."

"They are and nice people, too, but Ann, Kimberly, and Anton, they were kind of their own unit."

"Interesting."

"Is it?" Fats asked.

"Yes."

"Why?" Carrie asked. "Gay men love their mothers. It's a thing."

It was a thing, a stereotype, but for a reason. The gay men I knew did love their mothers a lot, but none of them were lying to their mothers. Carrie was describing a trio where everybody was lying to each other. Well, Kimberly and Anton were lying to Ann. He was lying to Kimberly about nobody else knowing his status. What was Ann lying about? Did Kimberly lie to Anton? Dad always said that lies were like cockroaches. If you find one, you can bet there are ten more you haven't found yet. This was the tip of the iceberg. I had a feeling.

"I don't know yet, but I think we're on to something," I said.

"Like what?" Carrie asked. "So he was in the closet? So what?"

"He was going to Incel websites."

Carrie crossed her arms. "No."

"The cops found evidence," said Fats. "Rape, kidnapping threads."

"I don't care what they found. Anton did not look at that stuff."

"What do you think he was planning on doing with Mercy after he got her in that trunk?" Fats wasn't angry. She was thinking, calculating. I could see it on her face. She knew criminals. Heck, she was one and her experience was going to work for me.

"He wasn't going to rape her," said Carrie. "I would bet my life on it."

Fats tilted her head. "Would you bet your daughter's life though?"

"Yes." No hesitation. None.

"Alright," I said. "I believe you."

"Good. Because the sooner you get off that hating women BS the better."

"There had to be a reason."

Carrie stood up. "Unless he had a psychotic break, I can't think of anything that would make him do that."

"I think we can rule out psychotic break," I said.

"What's left?"

"Money," said Fats. "And love."

"Speaking of money," said Carrie. "Lunch is on the house."

We thanked her and finished. When we got up to leave, Karen

came out with treat bags for the dogs and a to go cup with another spritzer for Fats' stomach.

Snow was beginning to fall as we stepped out into the increasing cold. After loading the dogs, they got treats and Fats asked, "Where to now?"

"Let's see if Tank Tancredi is in at the Sentinel," I said.

"He probably knows Anton was gay, too."

"Probably."

She fired up the truck and eased into the noontime traffic, which was considerable for such a small town. "Want to let me in on how Anton's sexual orientation was a best kept secret? We've got four people so far that knew and you're barely trying."

"It's about what they believed about someone they knew well. Three people, not counting Yuki, that knew, didn't tell, and believed completely that only they could be trusted. Think of how convincing Anton had to be, how secretive, how manipulative. If we keep going, we'll find more and they'll all be the same. Who does that? How does it start?"

"Some people compartmentalize their lives," said Fats. "I had a boyfriend like that. He acted like his childhood was on lockdown. I couldn't get near it. His family never knew about me. I showed up at his work once and they were shocked. Everyone thought he was gay because he wouldn't say anything about anything."

"Did you ever find out why?" I asked.

"No, I dumped him. I'm either in your life, all your life, or I'm out," she said, popping out a toothpick and splintering it to bits. "I didn't know that guy. I was sleeping with him, but I didn't know him. He didn't want me to."

"I wonder how well they really knew Anton."

"I don't think they knew him at all," said Fats.

I zipped up my coat and wrapped my arms around myself. "And when we find out why, we'll know why I ended up in that trunk."

CHAPTER EIGHT

We found Tank Tancredi standing in the doorway of the Great Missouri Shoe Factory, wearing a fat stocking cap and an orange camo hunting jacket, which was both hideous and probably oddly effective. He held a steaming mug of coffee as he watched us pull into the parking lot with a knowing smile and some sympathy as Fats drove over enormous ruts and a couple flattened trash cans. Since the Sentinel's bombing, thanks to Bertram Stott, he'd had to relocate the paper's operation. Tank called the long defunct factory an urban renewal project. Everyone else called it a dump.

The most amazing thing about the shoe factory was that it still existed. Built in stages from 1900 to the thirties, it was a hodgepodge of different styles, but all brick and pretty sturdy, considering it'd been abandoned in the eighties. About ninety percent of the windows had been broken out and looked about as haunted as a place can look.

"Took you long enough," said Tank.

"You've been expecting us?" I asked with a smile.

"Only a matter of time."

"Nice place you got here," said Fats. "Did it come with ghosts or did you have to import?"

"Fully stocked." He opened the door and stepped aside. "Welcome to the new Sentinel."

Pick dragged me over the threshold and yipped at a couple guys working on the light fixtures. I was expecting scary, cold, and uncomfortable. Wrong on all counts. There were desks, new linoleum, and lots of filing cabinets. A couple staff members waved and got back to their computers, typing madly.

"This isn't bad at all," I said.

"It's the accounting section," he said, like that meant something.

"All the windows are intact and you've got heat."

Tank laughed. "Nobody comes in here."

I frowned. "We're in here."

"But we're not trying to wreck the place, are we?"

"I don't know what that means," I said.

"Don't worry about it," he said.

"Too late."

Tank laughed, hugged me, and stepped back. "How are you? How's the head?"

"Not bad, considering."

We turned to Fats and found her just inside the door, pale and sweaty.

"What's wrong?" Tank asked. "They're not here right now."

"Is that…Italian beef?" she asked.

"Yeah, Mallory made it. Are you hungry? I thought—"

Fats put down Moe and ran out, letting a blast of cold air in. Tank ran over and grabbed the door. "Where's she going?"

"Probably to throw up," I said.

"Still?"

"It's getting worse."

He frowned out the door. "Should we go after her?"

"It's best to let her be. She gets…angry."

Tank closed the door and said, "Well, I'm not brave enough to make Fats Licata angry. My office?"

"You have an office and everything?"

"Impressed?"

"Very. Hasn't been long," I said.

"Feels long," he said. "You can leave the dogs here."

I unclipped the leashes and Moe led Pick on a merry chase around the desks. Coffee would be spilled, but Tank wasn't concerned. He led me out of the main room into a corridor to a plywood door with his name hand painted on it. "We did that Go Fund Me thing and the Bleds gave us a grant. We're doing pretty good. Bought the whole factory."

I walked into a cushy office with carpet, an IKEA desk, and a bunch of filing cabinets that looked original to the property. "What are you going to do with it?"

"Apartments and an upscale coffee shop. The industrial vibe is in and the interest in St. Seb, thanks to you, is huge. We've got loans and a decent contractor. We start the renovation in January."

"Congratulations," I said. "That's pretty cool."

He offered me a chair and a cup of coffee. I accepted and he turned up the space heater to take the chill off. "So Anton Thooft."

"Yep. Anton Thooft."

The veteran newsman steepled his fingers, his thin face barely concealing the glee of having a scoop. "So tell me what you've got so far."

"For starters, Anton was gay." I got the joy of watching Tank shocked and then a little peeved.

"How did you know?" His chin jutted out. So disappointed.

"I don't think that's as secret as advertised," I said.

"Nobody knows that. The cops don't know it."

"You know it."

"That's different," he said.

It wasn't different. Tank's wife Mallory was on the town fair's board of directors with Anton back when he was still in the States. They'd become good friends and he'd followed a familiar pattern. He confided and swore Mallory to secrecy because nobody else knew. She believed him without reservation as everyone did. She told Tank because married people do that and Tank seemed to think Anton should've known that, but I doubted he did.

"How well did you know him?" I asked.

"Barely at all. I tried to interview him once." He poured himself more coffee and I could see the wheels turning.

"You tried?"

"Yeah, it was after he went off to teach in Germany. He came home for a visit after a year and his sister, Kimberly, got this idea about having me interview him. He knew Mallory. Mallory's my wife. You know how it is."

"The interview was about the job in Germany?" I asked confused.

"In a way. Sort of a hometown boy has an interesting life, oh and by the way, his family owns the Heritage Hog Farm. They'd just gone organic and had added some heritage breeds. Nothing like a little free advertising."

"It didn't go well?"

"It barely went at all," said Tank. "Mr. Thooft and Kimberly frog-marched him in and he gave me the worst interview of my career. I've interviewed people just out of comas, so that's saying something."

Mr. Thooft and Kimberly. Mr. Thooft and Kimberly.

"What did he say?" I asked.

"Monosyllabic answers. Yes, he liked Germany. No, he wasn't returning anytime soon. That kind of thing."

"Were Mr. Thooft and Kimberly in the room?"

"You bet and they were embarrassed. Ten minutes in, Anton stood up, announced he was done and that I should go with another story. He wasn't interesting and neither was hog farming."

"Holy crap," I said. "Were they pissed?"

"Stunned more like. He walked out and they fell all over themselves apologizing. Mr. Thooft said that Anton was extremely shy and had trouble with public speaking. Kimberly begged me to forget all about the article, which I did."

"A teacher that can't speak in public? Get real," I said. "Teachers have an audience every damn day."

Tank cocked a finger at me and fired. "Exactly my thought so I went down into the archive and spent a little time looking up the very shy Mr. Anton Thooft."

"You are a reporter."

"I am and guess what I found out?" he asked.

"Anton was a spelling bee champion and rocked debate."

Tank threw back his head. "Son of a bitch. Why are you even here?"

I batted my eyes. "To get your help naturally."

"Do you need it?"

"Of course. When did Mallory tell you Anton's so-called secret?"

"After the interview. I told her how he was and she told me he was very private and never liked to be the focus of anything. I told her about the debates and spelling bees. She was floored. On the board, he insisted on doing only behind the scenes work, none of the showy stuff like interviews or being on TV. He didn't even want his name on the website."

"Any idea why?" I asked.

"None at all. Mallory chalked it up to being gay and keeping that secret from everyone."

"Except a lot of people knew. We're up to six and I've been on this for two and a half hours."

Tank pushed a manila folder over to me. "When it happened, I pulled all the articles I could find on Anton. I thought the cops would come calling."

"But they didn't?" I asked.

"Not a peep, but I knew you'd show up eventually."

I opened the folder and found a series of articles on Anton covering all the stuff I'd found in his box at the farm. There were pictures, too. Anton Thooft as a proud boy with an eager smile. "Nothing after eighth grade."

Tank grinned so wide it looked like it hurt. "I wondered if you'd notice that."

"Gimme some credit," I said, returning the grin.

"Oh, I do and that's why I'd like an interview after you figure it out."

"Figure out what?"

"The connection between what happened to radically change Anton Thooft between eighth grade and high school and what he did to you," said Tank.

"You're sure there's a connection?"

"I feel it and so do you. That kid was the golden boy up until high school. Whatever he tried, he won. Afterwards nada."

"I noticed that," I said. "Even in the family albums, he sort of disappears. Family says he was going into politics and then the big switch to teaching. A distinct change. Was there anything going on at that time in Whiskey Ridge or here in St. Seb?"

"Like a child molester or some such?"

"Yeah."

"Not that I saw, but we're still reassembling our files."

I sat there, a little worry lighting up in my chest. "You don't think Anton had any contact with Bertram Stott or the Sniders?"

"I thought about that, but Stott was in prison at that time," said Tank softly.

"Right. Of course. He was just such a nightmare," I said. "No connection to the Sniders?"

"No. I doubt it. Anton graduated high school in 1984 well before Robert Junior."

"So something else was going on. Have you got anything interesting on the family?" I asked.

"Nope. Quiet, conservative, very religious. Nobody had a bad word to say before it happened. Mallory was gobsmacked. She doesn't believe for a minute that he'd do what the cops said he was going to do."

"That seems to be the consensus."

Mr. Thooft and Kimberly. Mr. Thooft and Kimberly.

"Mrs. Thooft wasn't there on the day of the interview?" I asked.

Tank shook his head. "No. Why?"

I rolled the coffee mug between my hands. "It's odd, isn't it?"

He tilted his head at me. "Is it?"

"Sounds like it was always the mother, Kimberly, and Anton. A trio. But she didn't come."

"Maybe she was sick."

"Maybe," I said.

"What are you thinking?"

"I don't know, but it's off. It's weird."

Tank chuckled. "I think you're nuts, but you're pretty freaking good at this, so what's next?"

"I guess I'll wander over to the cop shop and see if Stratton's got anything," I said.

Tank laughed. "You think she'll know? That attic's still a wreck."

The St. Sebastian police department had some serious issues with both flooding and leadership. The former chief threw everything willy nilly into the attic after a flood, including old files and evidence, and forgot about it. If a crime happened before computers, you'd have to dig, literally.

"I'm not interested in what the Thoofts were up to in 1960."

"You never know."

"Don't go there."

Tank stood up and said, "I'm not the one going, but I'll be happy to report on your trip."

"I didn't agree to an interview," I said.

He grinned. "I heard you did."

"Mrs. Thooft is against any interviews. Period."

"I get it, but if you find something that mitigates what her son did, I'm sure she'll change her mind."

I agreed and we went back to the accounting section to find Fats sitting in a chair with her head propped on a desk above a trash can.

"That can't be comfortable," I said.

"It's not," she said. "But I don't want to go outside again."

"I've got some weird mints from Germany," said Tank.

"I'll try anything," said Fats, taking a mint.

Except meds.

"Did you keep anything down?"

"Maybe." Fats stood up and staggered to the left until Tank grabbed her a second before she hit a space heater.

"We've got a couple of good obstetricians in town. Jolie is a friend of Mallory's. I'm sure she'll see you immediately."

Fats shook her head. "No, it's over. I'm fine."

The entire room tilted their heads in doubt, but Fats ignored the obvious. She snapped her fingers expectantly, but nothing happened.

"What are you waiting for?" Tank asked.

"The dogs."

One of the staff waved and pointed at the corner by the coat rack. "Good luck. I don't think they're going anywhere."

We walked over and found Pick curled up on a pile of coats that I'm sure he pulled off their hangers 'cause that was the kind of thing he did. He was a poodle with a brain and an eye for comfort. So was Moe, but with less brain. She was curled up on top of Pick's own fuzzy coat and very slowly sliding off the big dog.

Fats snapped again and both dogs closed their eyes tighter.

"Eh," said Tank. "Just leave them. They're happy."

"I guess we can," she said.

I went and got the leashes. "Nope."

"Why not?" Tank asked. "I doubt we'll be firebombed ever again."

"It's not that," I said. "The last time I left Pick for convenience, I got stuffed in a trunk."

"Good point." He reached for his glow in the dark jacket. "I can walk you over. It's only four blocks."

Fats waved him off. "No need. I've got this." And she sounded steady. She didn't burp or stagger at all. "You *can* tell me where you got that jacket."

"I don't know. Mallory got it for me. She's afraid I'll get shot when I turkey hunt."

"Can you ask her?"

"Sure," he said slowly. "Why?"

"I need a bigger coat and that makes a statement." Fats shrugged on her purple puffer and looked at us straight-faced.

"It says I'm not a turkey," I said. "Don't shoot me."

"Exactly."

With that, we left a confused Tank and his staff to walk over to the police station. I wanted to drive, but Fats overruled me, saying she needed the fresh air. It was a decision with unintended consequences that for once worked out well for me.

Chief Candace Stratton looked the part more than her predecessor, Will Gates, ever had. She was pressed and polished with clear eyes and no hint of booze. That was all good. Her expression on seeing me was less so.

She sat at her big desk with stacks of paperwork framing her and she sighed when I walked in with a poodle and an apology. "'I always knew some day you'd come walking back through my door. I never doubted that. Something made it inevitable.'"

"'Hello, Marion,'" I said with a grin.

Fats sashayed in with Moe under her arm and dropped into a chair that protested with all its might. "So if you're Marion and Mercy's Indiana Jones, who am I in this scenario? Don't say Sallah. I can and will punch you."

"You're not Sallah." *He's a big sweetheart.* "You're more like…"

"Well, you're not Brody," said Stratton.

"Satipo?" I asked.

Fats scowled and Moe growled. "He gets killed five seconds in."

"Belloq?" suggested Stratton.

"Toht?" I asked.

"Dietrich?"

She cracked her knuckles. "Stop suggesting the evil ones."

I had a brainstorm and said, "The mechanic."

Fats gave me a look that made every hair on my body go rigid.

"The one that was evil *and* stupid?" she asked.

He was enormous.

"No, no," I said quickly under her withering gaze. "There's that other guy. I can't remember his name. He was cool and definitely not evil." My eyes pleaded with Stratton, but she only shrugged.

Patton walked in, just as polished as her new boss with her blue eyes as wide as ever and said, "Are you talking about *Indiana Jones?*"

"Yes," I said. "Who was that cool guy that wasn't evil?"

"The hot captain?"

Stratton and I pointed at each other. "Captain Katanga."

Fats smoothed her ponytail, for once it needed it, and said, "It's a small part, but I'll take it. He was kickass."

"Now that that critical fact is established," said Stratton. "What are you doing here?"

"I have fresh coffee." Patton raised a full pot.

"Hit me."

Patton filled the chief's mug and got me a polka-dotted chipped one. She asked Fats if she wanted some.

"Not unless you want me to throw up on this shiny floor," said Fats.

"I don't," said Patton.

"Then let's go with no."

Patton scurried out and Stratton said, "I don't know what to hope for. That it's about Anton Thooft or something else entirely."

"At least you know about Thooft," I said.

"Then please let it be Thooft then."

"It's Thooft."

"Thank goodness," she said. "Are you alright?"

I shrugged. "As well as can be expected."

"So crappy?"

"Medium crappy," I said. "What have you got on Anton Thooft?"

"Not a damn thing and when I say not a damn thing, I mean it."

Fats leaned forward and I noticed beads of sweat breaking out on her forehead. "Have you rooted around in that disaster area upstairs?"

Stratton rolled her head around on her shoulders and we got to listen to all her vertebra crack. "I have not."

"Why not?"

"'Cause I don't have the time and that guy never did a crime. Until he went all in and nabbed Mercy," she said. "Please tell me that had nothing to do with us."

"Well..." I said.

Stratton put her head on the desk. "Fantastic. It's been all out nuts here since the Bertram Stott story broke."

"What happened?" Fats asked swaying slightly in her seat.

"Did you see all those people in the lobby?" Stratton asked.

I had. The area inside the front door of the station had about twenty people milling around with little numbered tickets in their hands, like it was a bakery or something. It turned out they were in line to ask about old crimes, accidents, and what have you. They were coming out of the woodwork and Stratton had to hire a couple of new deputies to deal with the deluge.

"How many old crimes do you have?"

"Not that many in the city limits, but we've got quite a few in the surrounding area."

"What do they expect you to do?"

The chief laughed. "Call you."

"Please, don't," I said.

"Somebody obviously already did."

I slumped down. "Yeah."

Dallas Mosbach walked in and gave me a friendly grin. "Hey, Mercy. Can't believe you're back so quick."

"Me either," I said.

"What is it, Dallas?" Stratton asked.

The young cop made a face. "*Nightline* called again."

The chief groaned. "What do they want?"

"They heard *Dateline* was here."

"Did you tell them they're not?"

"Yeah, they don't believe me. They're sending a crew."

"God dammit. Why?"

"I'm not sure."

Dallas crossed paths with another cop I didn't know and he was so distracted by the sight of Fats, he forgot to speak.

"What is it, Kreidt?" Stratton asked.

"Oh, uh..."

"Kreidt, focus," she commanded.

"Right, chief," he said quickly. "Number Seven wants to see you personally."

"What for?"

Number Seven drove in all the way from Ohio to demand that her mother's slip and fall be reinvestigated. She wasn't satisfied with seeing the report or talking with the cop that wrote it. From Stratton's expression, I got the impression that nobody was satisfied with anything lately.

The chief took a big drink of coffee to fortify herself and asked, "When did it happen?"

"1982." He winced when he said it.

"Why on Earth would she come here *now* about *that*? It's not even a murder."

"She saw *The Staircase* on Netflix."

Stratton cracked her neck again. "Awesome."

"Should I take a look for the evidence box?"

"Are we sure there is a box?"

"No."

"God help me," she said.

"Sorry, Chief," said Kreidt.

"Not your fault. Go ahead and see if you can find it on that inventory list Dallas found last week." Then Stratton looked at me.

"Don't even," I said.

"I'm not, but let's face it, if these nutballs find out you're here, they're going to be even more excited, if that's possible. Did they recognize you?"

"I had my hood up."

She turned to Fats. "Tell me you didn't drive."

Fats swallowed hard and sweat sparkled on her upper lip. "I did."

"Damn."

"You got a problem with my truck?"

Stratton turned her screen to us. It showed a bizarre website with vehicles and alerts. "People are waiting for you two to show up."

"Is that a reporting system for us?" I asked.

"It sure is." She pointed at Fats' truck. "So you are marked at the Sentinel. I'm surprised it hasn't been updated."

"We didn't drive over."

Stratton raised her palms to heaven. "Thank you. The last thing I need is anyone thinking you're on a case here."

"What have you got?" I asked. "Anything interesting?"

"Everything from murdered mistresses to adoption scams."

"St. Seb is getting more exciting by the moment," I said.

"It isn't. The mistress wasn't murdered by the wife. She got drunk as a skunk and fell off a boulder at Johnson Shut-ins in front of about 800 witnesses on the Fourth of July."

"That's not even your jurisdiction."

"I'm glad you picked up on that," said Stratton. "The woman's daughter can't wrap her head around it. As far as she's concerned, her mother lived on High Street, so it's our rodeo."

"Nightmare."

"You said it." She looked puzzled. "Why are you here again?"

"Anton Thooft," Fats and I said together.

"Oh, right," she said. "I think I'm losing it. This used to be a sleepy jurisdiction. Now I'm working fourteen hours a day and getting hassled by old ladies who are sure I'm not telling them something about a purse that got snatched in 1952. God help me." She turned to her computer and started typing. "No. No. Nothing."

"The whole Thooft family?" I asked. "They're all clean?"

"As a whistle," she said. "As you know something could've gone on before we got computers, but unless you want to dig…"

"I do not."

Fats stood up. "Bathroom?"

The chief pointed and she ran for it.

"She's not looking good," said Stratton.

"If you like me at all, don't mention it to her," I said.

"No problem." She leaned back and eyed me. "So you're really working your own case?"

"I am."

"I can see it, but it might not be the best thing for you."

"The best thing is to find out why."

She nodded. "I hope you can. Have you tried Tank yet?"

"I did. He's got nothing really. What about you? Do you know Thooft or the family?"

"Not really. Like I said, they're squeaky clean so our paths never crossed."

I sipped the coffee and it wasn't horrible. Another vast improvement under Stratton. "I have to say I liked them. Nice people. Close family."

"So you've met them?" Stratton asked and there was something about the way she said it that made a tiny little hint of a feeling bloom in my chest.

"What?" I asked.

"You met all of them?"

"I think so."

"Including the mother, Ann?"

"Yes," I said. "Why her in particular? You don't like her?"

The chief shook her head. "I don't believe I've ever met the woman."

"What's the deal then?"

Stratton told me a secondhand story she had from her sister, Amber, who was in the same class as Kimberly. The girls knew each other and were friends, although not close friends. Sophomore year Kimberly decided to try out for the school musical, *Guys and Dolls*. She came in and sang "I Dreamed a Dream" from *Les Misérables*, knocking everyone's socks off.

"Amber said she was unbelievably good and she got the lead," said Stratton.

"What's the problem?" I asked. "That sounds like a good thing."

"It was. Kimberly could do everything, act, dance, and sing. My sister was so jealous. I remember the complaining about how she practiced and practiced and couldn't do anything half as well as Kimberly, who didn't seem to work at it at all."

"And..."

"And one day about two weeks before the opening, Mrs. Thooft shows up in the middle of a rehearsal, drags Kimberly off stage, and says no daughter of hers was going to perform like some showoff. Sister Joseph tried to intervene. She told Mrs. Thooft how truly great and talented Kimberly was. She said Kimberly could be famous. She could be on Broadway. It was a knife to my sister's heart, but what are you going to do. Kimberly had it."

"What did Mrs. Thooft say?" I asked astonished with my mind pinging around.

"She didn't care. Kimberly wasn't going to be in the show. Sister Angela begged her to reconsider, but she wouldn't hear it. Kimberly wasn't allowed to be in anything, choir, plays, nothing."

"And Kimberly just went along with it."

"I guess so. Amber said she sobbed and ran out, but she never tried out for anything again and when Amber asked her about it, she just said her mother didn't want her to."

"That's really weird."

"What kind of a crap mother does that?" Stratton asked. "What's wrong with theater?"

"Nothing," I said, "if you're Anton."

"Huh?"

I told her about Anton's plays, bees, and whatnot. "Could be a male female thing," I said.

"Did you get that vibe from the family?" Stratton asked.

"I didn't, but we weren't talking about gender politics either." I finished my coffee. "Kimberly and Ann seemed close. The family acknowledged her preference for the daughter."

"What does Kimberly do? Vet tech?"

I nodded. "She works in her husband's practice."

"Oh, right. Dr. Stackhouse."

"Do you know him?" I asked.

"No. He's more of a large animal vet," she said. "I'm telling you that family isn't interesting."

On purpose.

"We'll see about that," I said.

"Why me?" Stratton groaned.

"It's St. Seb."

Dallas walked back in and said nervously, "*48 Hours* called. They think *Nightline* has something on Anton Thooft."

"I can't believe I'm bothering to ask, but," said the chief, "why?"

"Because *Dateline* is here."

"For the love of God. Nobody is here. What is wrong with these people?"

Dallas looked at me and I said, "Should I sneak out the back?"

"Would you?" Stratton asked.

I flipped up my hood. "Sure. I think I kind of owe you."

"You don't, but I appreciate it." She eyed Pick who was sniffing around the flag stands in the corner. "You're taking that fuzzy pee pot, right?"

"I have to. He's my protection."

"A poodle?"

Pick went up on his hind paws, danced like a bear at the circus, and then proceeded to come over and gnaw on my knee.

"You should rethink that plan," said Stratton.

"I am. Constantly." I headed out into the lobby with the dogs, keeping my head down and skirted the group of cranky ticket holders, looking for Fats. I didn't have to go far. She came out of the bathroom and lurched toward me like Godzilla in Tokyo. Ticket holders went down, pins in a bowling alley, and Patton's podium with its little red ticket dispenser tipped over when Fats grabbed it to steady herself. Patton shrieked and Dallas panicked. The dogs barked and I went to Fats. It was one of those slow motion moments you see in the movies. Fats going over. Me diving to stop her while yelling, "Noooo."

Real life is nothing like the movies. Instead of stopping Fats, I got flattened. Now I know what a fly feels like under a swatter.

"Help," I said into the purple puffer over my face.

Nobody heard me. That was impossible, but Fats did roll off and looked at me with surprise.

"What are you doing?" She staggered to her feet and tried to assume an air of dignity. Impossible. She had mysterious stains down her front and her ponytail had migrated to the side of her head.

"What am I doing?" My ribs were killing me. Oh, the burning. "Getting a collapsed lung or two."

"Is that..." a woman asked.

"It is."

"Mercy Watts!"

"What case are you on?"

"My father was killed by a drunk driver six years ago. But it wasn't an accident."

"My adoption was a scam."

"I'm suing the department."

"Are you here on my case? I emailed *Dateline*."

They came at me hard and fast. Anton Thooft had nothing on those nuts. Patton grabbed me and we went through the throng, batting away files and ignoring the so-called facts being hurled at me.

"Holy crap!" yelled Stratton, rushing out from behind her desk. "How did it go wrong that fast?"

Fats staggered in behind me, supported by Kreidt and Dallas. "Nothing happened. I don't need any help."

I dropped back into my chair. "You need professional help."

She laid down on the floor and put an arm over her face. "Just give me a minute. I'm fine."

Stratton closed her door against the horde trying to get in and said, "Go to the hospital."

"No."

"Mercy," said Stratton. "Do something. Look at her. This can't be morning sickness."

I felt my ribs, all were intact, more or less. "It is, just supersized."

"Take her to the hospital."

"No hospital. I can take it," said Fats.

"Nobody else can," said Patton, peeking out the door. "We've got bloody noses and one's still down."

"Go," said Stratton. "Everybody go."

The cops rushed out to triage Fats' collateral damage and Stratton and I stared at Fats lying on the floor. We couldn't get her up if she didn't want to go.

"You have to be reasonable," I said.

"Why start now?" she asked.

"There's a baby involved."

"It's supposed to pass."

I nudged her with my foot. "It's not passing."

"Five minutes," she croaked. "I'll get the truck in five minutes."

"Forget that," said Stratton. "You have to get out of here. I wouldn't be surprised if there wasn't a news crew en route right now."

I stood up. "I'll get the truck."

"No."

"I've got Pick," I said. "What's the worst that can happen?"

Word to the wise. Never say that.

With the help of Stratton, I snuck out the back of the station through an emergency door that she helpfully disabled the alarm on.

"I still say we call an ambulance and let the hospital deal with her," said the chief.

"Don't you like your EMTs?" I asked.

"They could sedate her."

"With what? A tranquilizer gun?"

She frowned. "You got a better idea?"

"As a matter of fact, I do," I said. "Keep her quiet until I get back."

"How do you suggest I do that?"

I bit my lip.

"That's what I thought," said Stratton. "Get outta here."

Pick and I ran around the building, slipping on the icy sidewalk and ducking between cars in the parking lot. Tank sent me a text saying that a news crew from Channel Five was headed to St. Seb to cover whatever I was doing. Swell.

"I'm coming back," I texted as we walked onto the street. Halfway across, Pick saw his mortal enemy. A squirrel. He took off like his tail was on fire, nearly yanking me off my feet.

I felt the car go past rather than saw it as I stumbled onto the sidewalk. Pick dragged me to an ancient oak, barking his fool head off and I looked back to see a Hyundai do a three sixty and then slide into the intersection to get hit head-on by FedEx truck. Three other cars piled up and the sound of crunching metal and blasting horns echoed through the buildings to surprise me with the intensity. It was the slowest crash I'd ever seen. I doubt anyone was going faster than twenty, but the damage belied that.

"Come on!" I yanked on Pick's leash, but he wasn't having it. The squirrel was chattering at him from a branch not five feet over his head and the poodle was losing it big time.

"I'm going to leave you!"

The dog did not care and I dropped his leash to run toward the accident. I say run, but it was more an ungainly jog. Even though everything had been salted, it was hardly safe to all out run.

People and cops swarmed out of the police station and surrounding buildings. I was halfway there when Stratton appeared in my face. "Nope. Not today." She grabbed me and spun me around. "Go."

"I'm a nurse!"

"I don't care if you're the Queen of Sheba."

"That doesn't even make any sense."

Stratton shoved me toward Pick and the squirrel. "I've got enough problems without you being in the middle of this. Go."

"I can't just go. Look." I pointed at the Hyundai. A woman with a steel grey bob struggled with her deployed airbag and a guy was trying to keep her from getting out.

"I already had an ambulance on the way for Fats' debacle. It's fine. Hear that siren?"

I heard it, but I wasn't happy. It was my duty to go and help, but Stratton pushed me off the street as the ambulance arrived. "Beat it," she hissed, "and I'll see what else I can dig up on the Thoofts. Somebody has to know something."

I watched as the EMTs rushed over to a Hyundai and reluctantly agreed. "Fine, but I'm taking you seriously on that."

Stratton gave me a thumbs-up and slid her way to the accident. I tromped over to Pick, who was trying to run up the tree and had lost three booties in the process.

People were starting to look in my direction, so I grabbed the booties and ran for it. I fell three times, but we made it back to the Great Missouri Shoe Company in record time and found Fats standing—or swaying, if you prefer—at the station's emergency exit five minutes later. She climbed in with Moe, who couldn't get away from her spattered front fast enough, and we got out of St. Seb with minimal damage, to us anyway.

Fats insisted she was fine and made me pull over in Eureka. I made her put her parka in the back because the smell was getting to me. Recycled cashew cream is not a good thing. Neither was Fats' expression.

"What do you think this means?" she asked.

"Um...are we talking about the Thoofts or your condition?"

"My baby doesn't like anything that I do."

Get used to it.

"Pregnancies are different for everyone," I said lamely because what could I say. The only pregnancies I saw up close and personal where Ellen's. Compared to Fats, she was downright boring. Never threw up once.

Fats banged on the wheel. "I try to feed her the healthiest food. I throw up. I lift. I throw up. I run. I throw up."

"It's not personal," I said.

She yanked out her hair tie and shook out her frazzled locks. "What am I going to do?"

"Stop running, for starters."

"That is not an option. Look at me. Can you imagine how much weight I'd gain? Before the morning sickness, I was a house."

A brick house.

I shifted in my seat to look at her. "You're pregnant. The baby doesn't like running, so you don't get to run until she does." *If ever.*

Fats grimaced and gripped the steering wheel. "I'm in charge of my own body. I decide what happens."

"Not while you have a roommate," I said. "She gets a vote."

"Does this mean something?"

"Like what?"

"That...she doesn't like fitness or my food."

"She's a fetus. Her likes and dislikes are limited to calories and belly poking."

"I don't know. My mother knew about me early. I was very active. She has a video of me doing sit-ups in utero."

Super weird.

"That's...unusual. She can show it at the shower."

"Shower?" Fats asked.

"Your baby shower," I said.

"Somebody's throwing me a shower?"

I assume so.

"Everybody gets a shower."

Fats looked at me and beamed. Okay, so she had stuff crusted on her chin, but she still looked pretty happy.

I'm throwing a shower.

I pointed at her. "It's not going to be fitness themed, so don't get any bright ideas."

"Vegan?"

"I can't hear you."

"Cashew cheese is fantastic."

I crossed my arms. "Maybe not everyone gets a shower."

Fats laughed until she got nauseated again. It was going to be a long pregnancy.

CHAPTER NINE

Pick and Moe raced into the Bled Mansion, over the Turkish rug, and onto the highly polished wood floor. Because they never learn, they immediately lost control and wiped out, running into a wall and rattling the many framed photos overhead before disappearing around a corner, only to hit another wall.

"Mercy!" called out Millicent. "We're in the kitchen."

"Coming!" I turned to Fats, who was leaning on the doorframe to the breakfast room. "You don't have to stay. I'm in for the day."

"Yeah, right." She went toward the kitchen with her dignity more or less intact. I followed at a distance. I'd set my getting flattened limit to once a day and Fats wasn't looking so steady.

"You coming?" The unmistakable voice of my father rang out from the kitchen and I groaned. It'd been a long day already and, if Dad was there, it was bound to get a whole lot longer.

I trudged in behind Fats and found my dad leaning on the marble pastry counter drinking a Bled beer out of the bottle. I stopped at the door and considered turning around. Dad had that look, the look I'd hated since I was deemed old enough to help with his cases. I was about to have a pain in my butt.

"What happened to you two?" Dad asked as Myrtle and Millicent rushed over to sit Fats down in Lester's chair, tuck a blanket over her lap, and push a cup of peppermint tea into her hands.

"Pregnancy complications," I said.

He raised an eyebrow, but asked, "How'd it go?"

"It went. How was Greta?"

"Walk with me." Dad left the kitchen by the other door without checking to see if I agreed to follow. I didn't agree and I didn't follow.

"We made Ghirardelli," said Myrtle.

"With double cream," said Millicent. "I didn't over whip it this time."

Fats and I exchanged a look. This was not a good sign.

"What happened?" I asked. "Do the turtles need to be moved again?"

Myrtle poured a mug of hot chocolate and Millicent scooped a blob of stiff cream on the top. "Nothing's happened, dear. You just deserve a treat."

"Oh, yeah?"

"Of course." Millicent gave me the mug, shooed me out of the kitchen, and firmly closed the door behind me. No going back apparently.

I wandered around the house, looking for Dad and finally located him through my exceptional sense of smell. Dad was smoking. It didn't happen very often and that alone would've been enough to give me pause. I followed the whiff of pipe I caught by the staircase through the house to Nicolai Bled's smoking room. That's right. He had an entire room dedicated to smoking. That's when you know you're well and truly loaded. And it wasn't just any old smoking room—if there is such a thing—Nicolai's was designed to look as though you'd stepped into an English manor house. There was nothing of the mansion's Art Deco sensibilities. No potted palms, geometric shapes, and definitely nothing Egyptian. Nicolai filled his room with dark wood paneling, reclaimed from a renaissance palace, stained glass, and fat sofas with tufted red leather. I rarely went in there, but I liked its cozy, masculine vibe, so different from the rest of the house. The only thing I didn't like was the blue haze that hung around my father's head like a thunder cloud.

"That took a while," said Dad from a spot next to a fire that was just coming to life.

"I didn't expect you to be smoking."

"Neither did I. Life's full of surprises." He pointed to the sofa opposite and I sat down obediently, mostly because my ribs hurt and I didn't have the energy to run for it.

"How bad is it?" I asked, hoping Dad hadn't gotten into Nicolai's office and seen my Klinefeld Group stuff, because bad wouldn't cover it. Catastrophic came close.

"I found out why Greta wanted me at her hearing," he said.

"Is she okay?"

"She's fine. Well, as fine as she gets."

"Not getting out then," I said.

"No. This is about who was trying to get in," said Dad.

"Into...Hunt?"

Dad nodded and told me just about the last thing I expected. I'd like to say it didn't knock me on my ass, but it kinda did. Greta had been doing better and, in an effort, to stabilize her condition, the staff decided to give her more time out of her cell. She got to be in the staff break room, wander the halls unsupervised, stuff like that. It cannot be stressed enough that this was against the rules, all the rules. Greta had been judged criminally insane. You don't let criminally insane people walk around with access to other criminally insane people. That's... insane. But it's also what happened.

To be fair, Greta was about the sanest insane person you could ever meet and I didn't think for a minute that she would walk down the hall and let Harvey the Head Case out of his cell. But I also wouldn't have let her go free range. But since the staff did, Greta got to pick up some interesting tidbits. Wilson Cleves, the director of Hunt, had an affair with a twenty-year-old Golden Corral waitress, who kept trying to ineptly blackmail him with obviously doctored photos. One of the guards had a fight with his wife, got locked out of the house, and broke a leg while climbing a ladder to a second floor window. He'd hidden the injury until he got to Hunt and was now filing for Worker's Comp. A secretary had diabetes but hadn't told her husband because she loved M&Ms. A janitor was transgender and thought no one knew, but everyone did and were politely waiting for her to mention it.

And most interesting—for me, anyway—was Kent Blankenship's visitor list. Kent Blankenship was a mass murderer who had a fondness for me and serial killers. The last time I'd seen him, he'd bitten me on the face. I kept hoping he'd die choking on his own tongue, but it hadn't happened yet.

About a week before I was attacked, a man named Thomas Smith had shown up and requested a visit with Blankenship. He claimed he was a relative of one of the victims in the Tulio shooting and his paperwork was in order. Blankenship's privileges were severely restricted after he bit me and they weren't lax before that either, but it really didn't matter. People weren't exactly lining up to see that dirtbag and he refused everyone who did want in, except me. Thomas Smith wasn't any exception. Blankenship refused him and we never would've heard about it, if it weren't for Greta. She was in the staff break room at the time and it had a big bank of windows overlooking the parking lot. She saw Thomas Smith come in the visitor's center and leave fifteen minutes later. Later, some staff came in and mentioned it while they ate lunch. Nobody paid Greta any mind and they discussed Blankenship's visitor. She only noted it because of me and Blankenship's visitors being so rare.

Then my attack happened. Greta found out about it two days ago when she walked by a security guard station and heard my name on the guard's TV. Right there on the screen was the man she'd seen walking out of the visitor's center and, low and behold, the car he got into was the very same silver Ford Taurus he used in the kidnapping.

Greta didn't tell anyone. She was afraid they'd ignore her and cut off her privileges. Instead, she requested Dad speak at her hearing. She figured, given his fondness for her, that he'd show up and he did.

"You don't think she was imagining it?" I asked.

"Always a possibility given her condition, but no. After the hearing, I went directly to Wilson at Hunt. We looked at the security footage and it was Anton Thooft alright."

I sat back on the sofa with my mug growing cold in my hands. "When did he go to Hunt?"

"The day after landing at Lambert," said Dad.

"So he had a plan."

"It seems so."

"But...have you heard of any connection to Blankenship?"

Dad puffed on his curvy Calabash pipe, doing his best to look like Sherlock Holmes. He had the Basil Rathbone intensity down, but the red hair ruined it. Dad always looked slightly goofy with that pipe, not that anyone was going to mention it. "Think, Mercy."

"I am," I said, but I wasn't. I was panicking. Not this crap again. I was not going to Hunt to talk to Blankenship. My face couldn't take it.

"You're the connection," said Dad.

"I don't suppose I can ignore this."

"It's your case."

Has to be a trick.

"Oh, really? You're not going to make me go out to Hunt to get molested by that lunatic?"

Dad grinned at me, his dimples popped out and made him seem more handsome than he actually was. "I am not."

"So I can just *not* do anything about it?"

"Yes."

I gave my father the stink eye I learned so well from Aunt Miriam. "I can ignore this info and go on like it never happened?"

"Up to you," he said.

"What's the catch?" I asked.

"No catch," he said.

We eyed each other for a minute until Dad asked, "When do you plan on telling Detective Rich?"

"About five seconds after you leave," I said. "Anything to say about that?"

He thought about it for a second and then asked, "Good job?"

"Are you asking me?"

"I don't know. This is new."

"I'm not going to Hunt," I said.

"Fine with me," said Dad.

"I'm going to tell Mom you were smoking."

He shrugged. "She'll smell it on me anyway."

"What's the advice?" I asked.

Dad blew out a series of smoke rings and then said, "I got nothing."

"Are you going to call your buds at the FBI?"

"I have no buds since they pulled that crap with your mother," he said. "I wouldn't call them if a tsunami were about to hit Quantico and they were unaware."

Hard to believe.

"I thought you were back in," I said.

"Thanks to you, I am. That doesn't mean they're back in with me."

"I'm surprised," I said and I was. Actually, more like astonished. My father was holding out on the FBI. How the tide had turned.

"So am I," he said.

"You...seem relaxed." Relaxed was not a word anyone associated with my father. Even saying it was weird.

"I think I am. That's also new." He glanced at the bookshelf behind. "Anything good on there?"

"To read?" I asked.

"I'm not thinking of turning it into papier-mâché," said Dad, grinning again.

I got up and looked at Nicolai's personal collection of books, something I'd never done before. "There's a lot of poetry."

"Figures. The Bleds love poetry. What's he got?"

"The usual Pound, Poe, Keats, Eliot, Shakespeare, Wilde, Emerson," I said.

"Any Missourians?"

"Well, Eliot."

"Langston Hughes?"

"Him, too."

Dad held up a hand and I put *Shakespeare in Harlem* in his palm. He opened it and began reading like I wasn't there. He looked okay, but he might've been having a stroke.

"Are we done?" I asked.

"I am."

"With what?"

Dad flicked a glance at me and smiled. "Giving you the information I had."

"What do *you* think is going to happen?" I asked because my father without an opinion on my impending crappiness wasn't my father.

"I think you're going to find out all of Anton Thooft's secrets, solve the case, collect a hefty fee, and get us back in the news as the tremendously successful firm we always were."

"Um...what are you going to do?"

"I'm going to read this book and then take your mother out to dinner, if she's up to it," he said.

"Nothing else?"

"Nothing else."

"I hope you're not having a stroke."

"I'm not having a stroke."

I slipped out the door and leaned on it. A calm Tommy Watts and no stroke. Something didn't add up.

"Saddle up," I said as I hurried into the kitchen.

Myrtle, Millicent, and Joy all whispered, "No."

I skidded to a halt. "What?"

"Mercy dear, Fats is not going anywhere," said Millicent. "She needs her rest."

"It's decided," said Myrtle and Joy nodded, fiercely.

"Okay. Okay," I said it like I was acquiescing when I had no choice. Fats was out cold in Lester's chair with a dripping popsicle in her hand. I went to take it and got a bunch of nos in the form of wild gesticulations.

I shrugged and said, "Well, I'm off then."

"Not so fast," said Myrtle.

"You want me to wake her?"

If looks could kill, I would've been dead meat. Millicent went to the intercom and pressed a button. "Rocco, are you busy?"

"No, ma'am. I'm just cleaning your father's Chapuis Savana. The firing mechanism is a little sticky. Where would you like to go?" Rocco asked over the crackly antiquated system.

"I'm not sure yet. Which of the cars hasn't been out in a while?"

"The Isabella could use a run," he said.

"Excellent," said Millicent and she turned to me. "Will you need weaponry?"

I wrinkled my nose. "I hope not."

"Best to be on the safe side." She pressed the button. "Rocco, could you arm yourself for this trip?"

"So I'm taking Mercy." He laughed and said he'd be there.

"I don't need the cavalry," I said.

"You don't know what you need until you need it," said Myrtle. "Where are you going?"

"Thooft's old school district."

She took my mug and looked terribly disappointed. "You didn't drink it."

"Dad was weird. I got distracted."

Millicent steered me out into the breakfast room and gave out a low whistle. Pick and Moe came running, slipping and banging into the back door. That did not affect the wagging that was full on.

"How did you do that?" I asked.

"Fats taught me." She gave me my coat and a kiss on the cheek. "You will be careful, won't you?"

"I will." I clipped on Pick's leash and waved off Moe. "My dad's weird, right?"

"Oh, yes. Definitely. If I didn't know better, I'd have thought he hit his head."

Concerning.

"Does Mom know?" I asked.

"I believe so." She hugged me and went back in the kitchen to make a Greek lemon orzo soup for Fats' nausea.

Rocco came down the hall dressed like he was setting off with Shackleton to explore Antarctica.

"Where do you think we're going?" I asked, pointing at his full Gore-Tex getup.

"With you, ya never know," he said and pulled on a full-face black balaclava.

"Take that off," I said. "We're not robbing a bank. We're going to Liberty High."

He opened the door. "I should've brought another piece."

"You're insane." I headed out to the stable/garage, said hello to the workmen working on the apartments, and got into the 1954 Borgwald Isabella. It wasn't the most impressive car in the stable but certainly the most adorable. Rocco opened the garage, still full arctic, and got in after sticking Pick in the back with his service dog vest. "So where are we really going?"

"Liberty High in Wentzville."

"Come on, Mercy. Nobody's listening. I'll take you anywhere you want to go."

"Take me to Wentzville," I said.

"Ah, shit. Really?"

"Really."

Rocco wasn't happy, but he got over it once we were on the road. Such was his love for vintage automobiles. I got out my phone and considered the options.

"Detective Dustin Rich," said an irritated voice on the phone and I thought maybe I chose unwisely.

"It's Mercy Watts," I said with confidence I didn't feel. "Got a minute?"

"Yeah, hold on." The detective left wherever he was and came back a bit breathless. "Sorry. At a crime scene."

"I can call back."

"Screw that. It's a 7/11. What's up?"

I told him about Blankenship. He whistled and said, "Well, that's not good."

"Did his friends in Germany say anything about Blankenship?" I asked.

"They didn't, but they were in shock and we only asked about you. Was he obsessive? Did he talk about you? The answers were all no."

"Swell."

"In my defense," he said, "the guy was dead. We were dotting the Is and crossing the Ts."

"Nobody mentioned Hunt or the Tulio shooting?"

"Absolutely not. If they had, we'd have been on it."

We went back and forth about the Thooft family and then he went quiet. "What are you holding back?"

"Nothing," I lied but it didn't come off well.

Rich snorted. "Why'd you let Kimberly Thooft hire you?"

"Who's going to care about this more than me?" I asked.

"That's not enough. That family's looking for mitigating circumstances for the guy that was going to rape and murder you."

"I'm following your feeling," I said.

"Flattering but no."

"Anton Thooft was gay."

Rocco chuckled and said, "That'll do it," and Rich began cussing and, I suspect, punching the air.

"Are you done?" I asked.

"We interviewed every member of his family, his former boss, his current boss, friends, past and present, and nada. How'd you get it?"

I told him how, but it only made him more mad. "I could've kept the case going."

"You can't reopen it now?" I didn't want him to reopen. It was mine.

"I'd need a compelling reason."

"That's not?"

"He still kidnapped you. He's still dead."

"Did you hear any hints of childhood issues?" I asked and Rocco gave me the side eye, making him look a whole lot like his sister.

Rich didn't have anything unusual on Anton's childhood. It all came across as perfectly normal, but again he wasn't looking that far back, so he didn't ask. Thooft showed no signs of what was coming. Campbell and Rich had asked about that repeatedly. Interest in Blankenship and Hunt would've been a big sign, but nobody knew about that.

"I'll go back through the notes and see if anything sticks out, but don't hold your breath," he said. "What's all this got to do with the sister getting booted from a crappy high school play?"

"I don't know, but I'm about to ask her about it," I said.

"Keep me in the loop, will ya?" Rich asked.

"I will and I've already asked my guy to look into your uncle's death."

"I don't know if it's necessary." He'd gotten the death certificate from his mother and talked to the doctor at the ER. A coronary sounded like a sure thing.

"Maybe, but I've got a bit of a feeling myself," I said.

"Mercy..." Rich trailed off and then said abruptly, "Never mind. I've got to get back in. Good luck and I'll check those notes."

We hung up and Rocco said, "You got a thing with that guy?"

"A thing?"

He waggled his brows at me.

"No, idiot. He was the detective on my case," I said.

"Which is closed."

"Not so much anymore."

"You sure you don't have a thing with that guy?" Rocco asked.

I punched his arm and called Kimberly. She was at the grocery store and it didn't seem like a good time, but she was anxious to talk.

"What did you find out?" she asked as breathless as Rich.

"A few things, but mostly I have a question." I asked her about her brother's interview with Tank Tancredi and it was fair to say she was completely caught off guard.

"I'd forgotten all about that. It was years ago," she said. "Why on Earth would you care?"

"I never know what's important," I said.

Kimberly related the story much the same way Tank had and it wasn't enlightening by a long shot.

"Why wasn't your mother there?"

"Mom? Oh, well, gosh, why do you ask?"

"People seem to think you three were a trio, doing a lot together. I thought it was odd that she wasn't there and your father was."

Kimberly chuckled sadly. "We were, but Mom didn't like the idea."

"Why specifically?"

"My mother's old school. She thinks that kind of thing is uncouth or bragging or something. Dad and I thought it was a good chance for some exposure. We'd sunk a lot of money into going organic and it would've helped get the word out."

"Your mother didn't want the word out?" I asked.

"Mom is very private. She hates that kind of stuff. So did Anton.

We shouldn't have tried it. He was too shy."

I agreed and told her I'd keep her up to date as the investigation went on and hung up. Too shy. That kept coming up. Anton wasn't too shy. He couldn't have been, but she sounded completely genuine. She believed it, even though it made no sense.

"So how come you didn't ask her about that play?" Rocco asked he pulled off the highway in Wentzville.

"Too personal," I said. "She'd have known I was looking at her."

"That's bad? Shake her up. She knows something."

I shook my head. "I don't think she does."

We arrived at Liberty High, a fairly new complex in tan and blue. Once Rocco truly believed the high school was my goal, he lost the arctic wear and the weaponry. The weaponry with reluctance. The Licatas were a family that felt most comfortable when armed, but we were going into a school. Weapons couldn't happen. I put my Mauser into the glove box.

"Who are we here for?" he asked, opening the door for me.

"Whoever will talk to us," I said.

"So you've got no plan."

"That's a plan."

He rolled his eyes and sidled up to the desk with a school resource officer eying us with us so much suspicion I expected to be strip searched.

"No dogs," he barked.

I dangled the service vest.

"Bullshit. I know who you are, Mercy Watts."

Rocco kicked his desk and said in a low, incredibly threatening voice, "Then you know she's a victim with a head injury. You want to deny a victim her support animal? Is that the way you want to play it?"

That took him back, but only for a second. "Who are you?"

"Rocco Licata, the chauffeur."

The officer blinked for a minute at that and then asked me, "You have a chauffeur?"

"'Cause of the head," said Rocco. "You want Miss Migraine driving around endangering children?"

"No. I...uh...Rocco Licata?"

"That's right," said Rocco and he popped out a toothpick that dangled off his lip for a second before he used it to pick his molars. What was with that family and toothpicks? "Check me out. I got no issue with that."

The officer looked at me and I got to see the situation dawn on him. He wasn't wrong about Rocco, but he also wasn't going to get anywhere with it.

"Who do you want to see?" he asked me.

"The principal would be great," I said cheerfully. "Thanks."

He lowered his voice. "It's about that guy?"

"It is."

"The detectives were here and they interviewed everybody and their brother."

"I know. Detective Rich told me. I have different questions," I said.

The officer took our IDs, wrote down the important info, and gave us a couple of visitor passes. "I don't think you'll find anything new."

"I already have," I said.

"You don't say?"

"I do. Did you know Thooft?"

He shook his head and said, "Before my time." Then he gave us directions to the office and watched us walk away. He still wanted to do a strip search, but now it was just me.

Inside the office, after a bit of confusion, we were ushered into the principal's office and he was none too happy to see me or Pickpocket, who started spinning in a circle for no reason.

"What can I do for you?"

"You can tell me what you know about Anton Thooft," I said pleasantly.

"I've been all over this with the police."

"Then it won't be hard to recall."

Dr. Conway did find it hard to recall, because he didn't want to. Having the police and the press showing up because he was once the boss of a would-be murderer wasn't ideal for him or the school.

"Perhaps you could go out the fire exit by the gym," he said, "since we're done."

"We're not done," I said.

"I don't know anything," he said.

"Sure you do. What was Thooft's demeanor? Was he open, cheerful, friendly with staff? How did he interact with the community?"

He held up his palms. "How would I know? That was years ago."

"Five years." Rocco positioned his toothpick vertically and then crushed it.

Dr. Conway stared at him with something between fear and disgust.

I slapped my hand on his desk to get his attention back. "Did Thooft do well with the community? Open door policy? Closed door?"

His eyes flicked back and forth between me and Rocco. "He was a teacher."

"That's not helpful," I said.

"I don't know what you want me to say."

"What was he like?"

"It was five years ago. What difference does it make?"

"I don't know. That's what I'm trying to figure out, Dr. Conway," I said. "The cops think he was going to rape and kill me. Call me crazy, but I'd like to know why."

The principal wrenched his eyes off Rocco, who was sucking toothpick splinters from between his teeth. "He was...normal. Average guy. Nothing stood out, but I was just his boss, not his friend."

"Who was his friend?" I asked.

"I can't have you walking around the school bothering my staff," he said.

I smiled and sat back. "Let's hope I don't have to."

"I won't allow that."

"Do you know her at all?" Rocco asked and cracked his knuckles. "She uncovers serial killers and interviews murderers at Hunt. You think she can't get to every goddamn person in this joint?"

"Evan Price."

Rocco winked at me and I asked, "Good friend of Thooft?"

"Yes and head of our counseling department."

Ding. Ding. Ding.

"Available now?"

He glanced at the clock and stood up. "Should be. Third door on your left."

Rocco and I stood up.

"Thank you," I said.

"Miss Watts, can you please stay out of sight? Our students are just starting to settle down."

I flipped up my hood and he gave me a wan smile. "Good luck. I do hope you find what you need."

"And hopefully it has nothing to do with your school," I said.

"From your lips to God's ears."

Rocco and I slipped out past some students. I kept my head down so no one noticed me, but they sure noticed Rocco.

"Stop flirting with teenagers, Captain Creepy," I hissed.

"They're flirting with me," he said with a laugh. "My mother taught me to be polite to girls."

"Well, stop smiling."

"How do you know I'm smiling?"

"I can feel it."

He laughed and grabbed my shoulder. "You passed it, Super Sleuth."

I glanced up at the door and the name tag. Dr. Evan Price. A male friend for Anton. Score. Rocco started to knock, but I grabbed his hand.

"You stay out here," I said.

"Why? You'd let Fatasaurus Rex in," Rocco said.

"She's in the contract for this job. I shouldn't have had you in with Conway."

"He didn't say crap."

"I know, but he could have. I'm supposed to be keeping this close to the vest. You already know too much," I said.

"It doesn't matter. I can't say anything." He raised his hand again and I grabbed it.

"I can add you to the contract, but for now you should stay out here."

Rocco shook his head. "Naw. I'm watching you. The Baroness of Barf will have my ass if anything happens to you. Besides, I *can't* say anything about you."

I peeked up at him from under my fur-lined hood. "What do you mean you can't?"

"The NDA. You're covered. Let's do this thing."

"NDA?"

"Hello. The nondisclosure agreement I signed."

A couple of girls walked by and whispered, "You're hot." When Rocco got done smiling or whatever, I asked, "What NDA?"

"For The Girls. I signed it when I came on board. We all have them."

"I don't."

He rolled his eyes at me. "Are you an employee?"

"I don't understand. The Girls had you sign an NDA."

They did and all the personal employees of the Bleds had them, including Joy, Rocco, and my cousin, Tiny. According to Rocco, the intent was privacy and protection. No giving out family info on location, money, visitors, or art. Rocco couldn't give interviews about the family. He couldn't write a book or a blog. It all made sense, except for the fact that I was included on the NDA.

"Tiny never told me any of this," I said.

"He probably didn't read the whole thing."

"But you read it?"

"Hell, yeah. I don't sign a damn thing without reading it," said Rocco. "Tiny's got trust in his heart. I don't."

"How long was it?"

"Six pages of legalese. Lawyers love to use a lot of words to say very little," he said. "Can we go in?"

"Who was the lawyer?" I asked. "Big Steve?"

"No. Some corporate guy from the brewery. Total douchebag. He kept asking if The Girls really wanted to hire me, like I was tainted or something."

I can't imagine why.

"I was on the NDA? You're sure?"

"Sure I'm sure. It surprised the douchebag, but The Girls said it was standard."

"What did it say?"

Rocco thought for a second and said in a monotone, "All Bled family members by blood or marriage to include Carolina Watts also known as Mercy Watts."

"Just me, not my parents?"

Rocco gave me the list. Grandad, uncles and cousins, Weepy, Snot, and Spoiled Rotten were in his NDA. Not my parents. The two people The Girls absolutely adored didn't make the list.

"So you can write a blog about my dad, but not me?"

"Get real," Rocco scoffed. "That dude wouldn't say anything revealing around me."

Or me.

"Do you have a copy of your NDA?" I asked.

"Sure. You wanna see it?"

"I would, yeah."

"Nope."

"Huh?"

"I'm not supposed to show it to anyone, unless part of a legal action," said Rocco.

"But you can tell me about it?"

He lifted a shoulder. "No, but it's you so screw it. Why can't I tell you about how you're protected?"

Good question.

"Well, I guess we can go in," I said.

"Finally." He knocked and we got a quick, "Come in."

I expected to see a man behind the desk and hopefully one with some insight into Anton Thooft. Instead, I got a petite woman with two-inch long hair that was dyed purple.

"Evan Price?" I asked.

She gaped at me and then said, "Well, holy crap, I won."

"Are you Evan?" Rocco asked.

She stood up quickly and slammed her chair against her bookcase. "I am. I...my parents thought naming a girl Evan was somehow edgy. Instead, it's just confusing." She stuck out a hand and we shook. Rocco held her hand a little too long making her blush and stammer. She covered by loving up the poodle.

We sat down in her institutional chairs that may as well have been rocks for all the comfort they provided.

"So what did you win?" I asked.

"My staff and I bet against the Science department that you'd come here about what happened and here you are."

Rocco sat back and smiled. "There's no science that explains Mercy or my sister, for that matter."

"Who's your sister?" Dr. Price asked.

He showed her a picture on his phone and her eyes went wide. "I can see your point."

"She's a freak and so's this one." He jerked a thumb at me. "You should always bet on Mercy."

Ah, thanks.

"She's kinda random, but it always works out," he said.

Bastard.

Dr. Price smiled at him with big dopey eyes. "I'll remember that."

I doubt she remembered I was in the room and my name? Forget it.

"Hello?" I waved a hand between them.

"Oh, yes," said Dr. Price. "What can I do for you?"

"The principal said you were good friends with Anton Thooft. Would you be willing to talk to us about him?"

"I already told the police everything I know."

I smiled at her. "I bet you didn't."

"I assure you, I did."

Rocco slipped off his hoodie and flexed. The guy might've been tiny compared to Fats, but he was built and Dr. Price noticed. A lot. "Did you tell the cops he was gay?"

Her mouth dropped open and then she shook her head. "No, I didn't and I'm very surprised that you know about that."

I looked over at the diplomas on the wall. She was all about social work and psychology and from some kicking schools, too. Truman, SLU, and Wash U. "Look, I know. He knows. Anton's sister knew. At least one friend growing up knew and quite a few others. You have a doctorate in psychology. What do you make of that, Dr. Price?"

"Call me Evan."

"I'll call you cheesecake if it'll get you to level with me."

Evan took a deep breath and relaxed in her chair. "I'll tell you everything I know, but I warn you, it's limited."

"You were close friends?"

"Still were until the day...it happened," she said. "But I'm not sure I should say close. That's not really an accurate description."

"'Cause you didn't see him throwing Mercy in a trunk?" Rocco asked.

"I didn't, but that's not why." She reached down into a drawer and pulled out a framed photo. It was of her and Anton raising a glass under a banner saying "Congratulations, Dr. Price."

"Did you have a thing with him?" Rocco asked after glancing at the photo.

"Anton was gay."

He shrugged. "It happens. My cousin's gay. She had a couple boyfriends back in the day."

"I suppose it could happen, but it didn't." She told us the same old story about being the only one to know, sworn to secrecy, the whole spiel Anton always used. The difference was Evan didn't buy it. She didn't think she was the only one to know. His lines were too practiced and his pleas down too pat. Evan took her field seriously and she smelled a rat.

"That was it?" I asked. "Just the delivery?"

"That and Anton was great. I loved him a lot, but you couldn't get close to him. He told me about being gay, but oddly everything else was off limits."

"Like what?"

"His family, his favorite food. You name it, it was held close to the vest."

"But not being gay?"

"No and wouldn't you think tacos or burritos would be less of a big deal than being gay?"

"I would. So you'd say he was secretive?"

"Incredibly so and very good at it," said Evan. "If you go down to the English department and ask Libby Mueller, she'd say he was the most open person she ever met. So would Jena Richards and Mary Johnston."

"How does that happen?" Rocco asked.

"Anton was very good at asking you questions, so it seemed like you were bonding, sharing, but it was really only you sharing and Anton didn't say a thing."

Rocco nodded. "Slick."

"Very," she said. "I did like Anton a lot, but I didn't know him."

I leaned forward. "Any hint of what was up with that?"

"I figured abuse of some kind, but I couldn't get within a mile of it. Before you ask, no, I didn't think he would hurt anyone, particularly a woman. He was always kind and generous with female staff. He preferred us to the men."

"But he was gay," said Rocco.

"He didn't dislike the men. He just didn't seek them out. He preferred female friends."

"Anything else strike you as odd?" I asked.

"Well, like you said, plenty of people knew," said Evan. "After his death, I started asking around. Five other members of staff knew."

"They all thought they were the only ones?" I asked.

She smiled. "Yes, they did and I've tried to work that out. Why he compartmentalized us, I mean."

"And?"

Evan took the photo back and looked down at her friend. "There was this strange kind of atmosphere about Anton, like he yearned to be known and free, but had silence imposed on him."

"He came from a very religious family," I said.

She shook her head. "No, that's not it. He had faith, but it didn't appear to rule him. It was something else. He was hiding, but he didn't like it."

"Hiding?" Rocco asked. "From who?"

"I don't know, but he didn't want his picture in the yearbook. He was nominated for Teacher of the Year and he withdrew his name from consideration. Dr. Conway wanted him in the paper for an interview to tout his AP methods. Anton had a pass rate of seventy-five percent for AP Government. The average is something like fifty-seven percent."

"He wouldn't do the interview?"

"He wouldn't even consider it," she said. "He said the work was its own reward, but that wasn't the point. It was to highlight the school. We need funding like everyone else. If you've got a stellar teacher, you put them out front."

"How hard did Dr. Conway push?" I asked.

"Pretty hard. He was frustrated. Anton was a great teacher. The kind that kids come back from college to visit and he wasn't shy. I don't know what the problem was."

"He said he was shy?"

"He did and it was bull. Anton could talk to anyone about anything," said Evan.

"Was anything else happening? Something Anton fought?"

She smiled. "You know there was. Our media kids wanted him to do a kind of Khan Academy for AP Gov, but he refused. You know how kids are. They saw right through the bull and didn't buy the shy or work/reward thing."

"Kids don't give a crap," said Rocco. "They'll get right in your face."

"I bet you did," I said.

"You know it." He looked at Evan. "So what happened?"

"They got a petition going. Pretty much the whole school signed and then the PTA got in on the act."

Wait for it.

"Right after the PTA made a formal request, Anton announced his retirement and he took a job in Germany," said Evan with a flourish.

"And that was the end of that," I said.

"It was."

"This weirdo moved to Germany so he wouldn't have to teach a friggin' class online?" Rocco asked. "He was a teacher."

"I know. It was very strange. Nobody understood it, but Anton was absolutely opposed to getting out there."

"And being known," I said.

"He'd have moved to a desert island to avoid it," said Evan.

"The question is why."

"I wish I could tell you."

Me, too.

With the help of a granola bar from Evan, we got Pick in the back of the Isabella. He spun round fifteen thousand times before curling up on his cushion and yipped for another bar.

"None for you," I said. "Chuck will say I'm making you fat."

Yip.

Rocco snapped his fingers and Pick hid his eyes under a paw. "Where to now?"

"I was going to say home, but let's try Black Heart Books," I said.

"That's practically home."

"So it works out." I started digging in my purse for a Hersey's Kiss or something. I needed chocolate and there was bound to be something in the depths.

Rocco started the Isabella and waved to his fan club that had gathered on the sidewalk to watch us leave. "Are you looking for Investigations for Dummies in that purse?"

"I will kill you."

"I'd like to see you try," he said.

"It'd be a good fight," I insisted and held up a wonky Kiss covered in lint.

"If by good you mean incredibly short, I agree."

I ate my Kiss and said, "You and Fats are so much alike."

"Take that back," said Rocco with a grimace.

"It's true."

"Do I look like I stepped out of a comic book?"

I shifted in my seat. "In a weird way, yeah, you do."

"Freaking how?"

"You've got a super villain thing going on. People tend to look at you, not me. I dig that about you."

Rocco grinned. "Chicks do like a bad boy and I'm all boy."

"And plenty bad."

"That's how I come across anyway." He popped out a toothpick. "It's working for me."

"And me," I said.

"What's at the bookstore?"

"A boyfriend."

"Chuck know?"

I laughed. "Anton Thooft's boyfriend from college."

"Is it Jamie?"

"You know him?"

"He helped me find some knitting manuals. I'm moving on to socks."

I cannot see that.

"In the meantime, let's talk about Fats," I said.

"Yeah, let's do that." Rocco eyed me. "When are you gonna take care of that BS?"

"If you're talking about the morning sickness, I'm thinking you should take care of it."

Rocco merged onto the highway and made a face. "What am I gonna do? I haven't been able to take her since we were in grade school."

"I heard you could never take her," I said.

"Drop dead. I pounded her a couple times and she remembers it, believe me."

"Whatever. You're her brother. Talk to her. She loves you."

"She likes me enough not to kill me and hide the body."

"That's something. You have to try."

"You're the nurse."

"I tried. She's freaked out about medication hurting the baby," I said.

He nodded. "She's not going to take meds."

"I think she has to."

"She wouldn't take painkillers after some dipstick dropped a weight on her foot and broke six bones. It might've kept her out of competition. She's not doping up her kid. It ain't happening."

"Wow," I said.

"That sums up my sister," said Rocco. "Wow."

"What about your mother?"

He looked at me puzzled. "What about her?"

"Has she tried to talk to Fats?"

"I doubt it."

I watched his face for a hint of what was going on, but he was blank. "Could you ask her to talk to Fats?"

"What would she say?" he asked.

Do I have to spell this out?

"Um...to take the meds so the baby can have calories," I said.

"Yeah, no. She's not going to do that."

"Why not?"

"They fight."

"Define fight."

Rocco looked at me and I got the picture.

Enough about that.

"Who else has influence?" I asked.

"You."

"I don't have any influence."

We drove in silence and I wanted to ask about other female friends, but Fats already said I was the first. Sister Clarence was in there, but she was the original soft touch. I don't think she could make Fats drink a glass of milk.

"What about guys?" I asked.

"Tiny's trying. He practically begged her the other night, but it's a no go."

"What is up with that? This is an approved medication. A doctor prescribes it."

Rocco's jaw tightened and the muscles danced underneath the taut skin just like Fats.

Enough about that.

"What about other guys? Friend guys."

"Guys aren't my sister's friends. She didn't know that for a long time. They either want to dominate or do her."

"For crying out loud, this is depressing," I said. "Suddenly, I want to call my mom."

"And you can," said Rocco. "Get it?"

I got it and this was going to be harder than I expected. I didn't want to appeal to Calpurnia and owe yet another favor, but I might have to.

"She's such a pain in my ass."

Rocco nodded. "Welcome to my world."

CHAPTER TEN

Black Heart Books was in the heart of the Central West End and fairly busy, considering it was a Friday afternoon and bookstores weren't exactly the rage anymore. Black Heart was the bookstore of my childhood. We couldn't afford a lot of books—we used the heck out of the library—but every once in a while The Girls and I went. I'd pick out a book of my very own and they'd order Italian espresso and scones with lemon curd while I shopped, settling in on the big comfy sofa in the back because it was going to take me a while.

"Mercy!" Jerry Edwards waved at me from behind the cash register and the entire shop looked at me.

"Way to keep it on the down low," said Rocco.

"I was never keeping this on the down low." I waved back and came over as Jerry apologized to his customer and came out to hug me. Then he squatted down to give Pick a biscuit and a good scratch. The poodle got all nutty and Rocco had to calm him down with a well-placed snap.

"How are you?" Jerry asked, standing up and touching my face with both hands. "It's not bad this time. Carolina said you were barely leaving the house, but it's just like a crusty beard."

I do not feel better about myself.

"I was staying in, but I've got things to do."

Jerry leaned over to me. He was an old hippy and the smell of patchouli wafted over me, comforting and taking me back to afternoons of deciding between a book on horses or a new *Magic Treehouse.* "Are you looking for Jamie?"

I smiled and he hugged me again. "Do I know you or what?"

"You know me."

"He's back in Children's restocking. Go easy on him, please, Mercy," said Jerry.

I said I would and he returned to his customer who'd been listening to every word we said, so it was good we said almost nothing. I headed to Children's and Rocco did a fantastic job of keeping people away. He may have smacked some phones down, but I'd never swear to it.

We found Jamie in my favorite childhood section, mystery, next to the Nancy Drews and Hardy Boys. That was before crime became a part of my real life. Vintage mystery was empty and it could've been because Jamie Koplar was standing in the aisle, listlessly staring at nothing. I'd seen him before. In fact, he'd helped me pick out Christmas gifts a few times. He was excellent with biography and crime. I knew his name was Jamie, but I hadn't put it together.

He looked the same as I remembered, about five six, thin, light brown hair and a scraggly beard. I'm pretty sure I'd never seen him without a sweater vest, even in summer, and, as it was winter, he had both a sweater vest and a cardigan on.

"Jamie?" I said softly.

He slowly turned to me with red-rimmed eyes and a slack expression. "Jerry said you'd come."

"He knows me."

"I know you, too," said Jamie. "Do you remember me?"

"Of course. *Devil in the White City* was a hit. My grandad loved it," I said.

"I'm glad. It was meticulously researched."

"So I've heard." I came closer. Slowly because I had the strange feeling I might spook him. "Can I ask you a few questions?"

Jamie wiped a tear off his cheek and nodded. I took the stack of books out of his hands, thinking we'd go back to the sofa, but he just stood there, lost.

"Hey, Rocco," I said. "Can you get us some coffees or whatever Jamie likes?"

Rocco surprised me by saying nothing. He just nodded and went. Jamie didn't react and I put Pick in front of him. The poodle wagged and pawed his shin for attention. Nothing lightens the mood like a goofy poodle in desperate need of a haircut.

Jamie smiled and tentatively lifted the poof of hair sagging over his eyes. "He's adorable, like a black sheep."

"He's a black sheep all right, but we like him when he's not stealing food or turning on the news."

"The news?"

"Yeah, he always finds one of the twenty-four hour channels and they make him bark for some reason. He tries to attack the talking heads and nearly cracked the screen the other day."

"That's odd."

"Tell me about it," I said. "Can we sit down?"

He led me to The Girls' sofa, still black and still comfy. Pick jumped up and climbed into Jamie's lap, knocking him back and bringing a smile to his face.

"He's a sweetheart," said Jamie.

And he knows sad when he sees it.

"He is." I scratched Pick's chin after he got himself situated and then quietly asked, "So Anton?"

"I don't know what I can tell you. He was—I hope this is okay to say—a lovely person," said Jamie.

I saw Anton coming at me, a blur of dark, but I shook it off. "It's okay."

He touched my hand. "I'm so sorry."

I swallowed hard and we sat in silence for a minute before Jamie began to talk. He'd been with Anton for longer than Karen said, nearly seven years. Their relationship had a lot of the hallmarks of a great one, mutual interests, laughter, conversation, and trust. But it wasn't perfect. Jamie came out, not as Karen thought at the end of their relationship, but in the middle, at the end of their senior year of college. Jamie's parents didn't blink. They'd figured it out long ago and welcomed Anton into the fold quite happily. On the other hand, Anton didn't come out and insisted on hiding their relationship, but still it went on. Jamie never met his family and was sure they didn't know of his existence.

"Why did you put up with it?" I asked.

He raised his eyes from Pick and said simply, "I loved him."

The past tense wasn't appropriate. Jamie still loved Anton. They'd been broken up for decades, but nothing had changed for the man quietly weeping in front of me.

"Did you still see each other?" I asked.

"Occasionally, but it wasn't like before. We didn't date or anything." That was said with such pain, it hurt me to look at him and I felt like blubbering myself.

"Have you had another partner?"

"A few, but no one like Anton," said Jamie.

"He was the love of your life."

He nodded and Rocco came back with two mugs and a box of tissues. "Mulled cider. Jerry says it's your favorite."

Jamie managed to get out a strangled, "Yes," and Rocco surprised me again by saying, "I'm going to check out the knitting section."

He took off into the stacks and Jamie watched him, puzzled. "He really knits?"

"He does. I guess it helps with anxiety."

"You never know about people, do you?" Jamie looked at me and reddened. "I'm so sorry."

"You don't need to apologize. You didn't do it," I said.

"I feel like I should've known."

"When was the last time you saw Anton?"

He took a breath and picked up his steaming mug. "Last Christmas. He came in to Christmas shop."

"Anything unusual at that time?" I asked.

"No, nothing. We text occasionally. The last time was almost two months ago. Nothing odd then either. He wanted a recommendation for a book."

"What was the book?"

Jamie got out his phone and scrolled through. "It was several actually." He held up the screen for me to see. I don't know what I was expecting, maybe something on crime, kidnapping, or the FBI, but it wasn't even close. Anton wanted psychology or self-help books. *Influence: The Psychology of Persuasion, Getting to Yes: Negotiating Agreement without Giving in,* and *Toxic People.*

"Why did he want those?" I asked.

"He said he was having problems at work and needed to figure out how to deal with it," said Jamie. "I can forward you the text."

I gave him my number and he sent it. "Is this helpful?"

"Maybe. The cops said he was all good at work."

"The books might've done the trick. Anton liked to study." He smiled at the memory. "If he had a problem, he'd head to the bookstore and figure it out."

"He wouldn't ask you for help?"

"No. He might ask my opinion, but he usually went to an expert. Anton wouldn't believe anything unless you gave him two independent sources."

"It sounds like you two had a reasonably good breakup and remained friends."

He nodded and clutched Pick, who gave him a little lick.

"Was he involved with anyone recently?"

"We didn't talk about it. Honestly, I didn't want to know," he said. "I always thought that maybe..."

"You'd get back together?" I asked.

"Yes. I thought if enough time went by, he'd get over it."

I picked up my mug and breathed deep the spicy steam. "Get over what? Karen said you broke up over coming out. Anton didn't want to make it official or something."

Jamie frowned. "No, I mean, I wasn't happy that he hid me, but I would never have left him over it."

"You didn't break up with Anton?"

"Are you kidding?"

"That's what Karen said," I said.

"I don't know why she'd say that. Anton left me and it was my fault." Tears pooled in his eyes again. "I don't even understand why it was a deal breaker, but it was."

"What are you talking about?" I leaned forward and touched his knee. "Was it something to do with privacy or publicity?"

"Sort of, but it was...I was trying to do a nice thing."

Jamie was trying to do a nice thing and, boy, did it blow up in his face. Anton was devoted to Kimberly and talked about her all the time, how smart she was, how pretty, and, most importantly, how talented. She could sing. She could dance. There was nothing she couldn't do. Anton showed Jamie videos of Kimberly singing in the choir and her voice was amazing. Jamie thought she sounded like an untrained Lea Salonga and I pretended I knew who that was. Kimberly was also a performer. Anton had videos of her doing skits at home and she glowed, engaging everyone who looked her way and making them laugh. In Jamie's opinion, she was made for musical theatre, but Anton poo-pooed that idea, claiming she was shy and was only at home in front of a known audience. That sounded awfully familiar. Besides, Anton said, what chance did a farm girl have to make it to Broadway? None was his assessment and that was that.

Jamie agreed on the face of it, but he also had connections of a sort. His sister, Emily, worked on Broadway in costume. Jamie had offered many times to see if Emily could help, but Anton said no. But then Emily started talking about a production she'd been hired to design and there were children's roles. They were going to start auditioning girls ages nine to thirteen. Kimberly was eleven at the time. Jamie knew Anton would say no, not to get Kimberly's hopes up or something like that, so he got ahold of several of her videos and sent them to Emily. She showed them to the casting director and they went bonkers. Jamie's word, not mine. Bonkers. They wanted Kimberly to fly to New York with her parents. All expenses paid. The whole shebang, but according to Jamie, it was almost a formality. They wanted her. They loved her. They were going to make her a star.

"I bet Anton didn't like that," I said.

"He lost his mind. He screamed at me and Anton never even raised his voice before. He was almost hysterical. I had to call the whole thing off, demand all copies of the videos be destroyed, and he left me."

"Because people wanted to make Kimberly a star?"

"I betrayed him. I couldn't be trusted. I wanted to expose his sister," said Jamie. "I kept asking what he was afraid of. Kimberly was talented. She belonged on Broadway."

Expose.

"Did he ever say why he had that reaction? You obviously kept in contact."

Jamie hugged Pick tight and the poodle licked the tears off his cheek. "No. He never explained. We were over and our contact was limited after that. He never spoke about Kimberly again. He literally never spoke her name. If I asked about her, he would change the subject."

"Anton was very adverse to publicity," I said more to myself than Jamie.

"Who said that?"

I told him about the fair board and Tank's failed interview.

"I suppose he was. At the time, I thought it was because he was so far in the closet. It's hard keeping a secret like that, but you think there was something else going on?" Jamie asked.

"Being in the closet has nothing to do with Kimberly, but he and his mother were determined to keep her hidden, too." I told him about Kimberly's lost lead in *Guys and Dolls*.

"I don't get it," said Jamie, his face no longer sad but full of confusion. "If she were my daughter, I'd want her to shine."

Rocco sat next to me with a stack of knitting books and said, "Not all parents like shine, especially if it puts them in the shade."

I was pretty sure which parent Rocco was talking about, but I asked Jamie, "Do you think there was any jealousy going on?"

"No, not at all." He smiled. "It was a big joke how no one else in the family could carry a tune in a bucket. Sometimes they'd get up and sing with Kimberly and they'd all end up laughing at how bad they were. It was really sweet. I don't remember anyone looking upset or angry in those videos. Just happy and proud."

"Proud but she had to be hidden," I said. "Did Anton say anything about his mother?"

"He adored her," said Jamie. "She was the best cook. The best hugger. He often said she was his best friend. I'm close to my mother, but their relationship was much tighter."

"Anything weird about it?"

Jamie shrugged. "Not really. Before you told me about *Guys and Dolls,* I wouldn't have said she was controlling."

"Kimberly was her favorite?"

He laughed and wiped a few stray tears away. "Hands down, but according to Anton there weren't any problems. Nobody minded."

"There had to be some problem," said Rocco. "Nobody's that great and that crappy without a problem."

What's your mom's problem?

"I'll have to think about it," I said. "Thanks, Jamie. I know this was hard."

He looked at me smiling through tears. "In a way, I feel better. You're going to get to the bottom of it. That man that attacked you wasn't the man I loved."

Rocco glanced at me but held his tongue. He knew that Anton Thooft wasn't a man that anyone really knew.

CHAPTER ELEVEN

I love Laclede's Landing in the morning. Busy, but not too busy. No tourists. No parents. The air was crisp. The sidewalks were salted and, most importantly, I was alone.

If you don't count Pickpocket, that is. The poodle was prancing beside me in his brand new coat and booties, proud as all get out. They were Black Watch tartan, imported all the way from Scotland and made of the finest wool. Not my idea. I'm pretty sure the booties cost more than my entire outfit, which I got on Black Friday at the Gap. The Girls bought the tartan and it was definitely not on sale. Millicent said that if Pick was going to be my protection, he should look the part. Personally, I thought the plaid could not begin to make up for the enormous topknot on the poodle's head. It had a large bow.

The dog stylist came to the mansion the night before and gave Pickpocket a trim. I thought when she asked me what we wanted and I said, "Something sensible and low maintenance," she would, ya know, give him something sensible and low maintenance. Instead, he looked like we were headed to the Westminster Kennel Club for the big win.

When I squawked about the goofy cuffs and whatnot, Angela was aghast. This was a modified show cut. Did I really want Pickpocket to go out like he was an ordinary dog and not a poodle?

Yes. The answer was yes. But...The Girls thought he was adorable and that's when they broke out the tartan. If Pick scared away so much as a purse snatcher, I'd be shocked.

I couldn't imagine what Spidermonkey was going to say. We were meeting at Café Déjeuner and he, like everyone else, was on about my safety. He didn't want to meet at all, but, since we were keeping the liquor cabinet off all devices, there was no other way to discuss it.

"Sit," I said to Pickpocket when we arrived at the café door.

He didn't sit. He never sat unless there were treats involved. That poodle was too smart for my good and he made life hard. It was getting pretty old having to bungie cord the fridge closed and hide the remotes because he knew how to turn on the TV and liked the volume on max.

"Sit."

Nope. Not gonna do it. Pick wagged his stumpy tail at me and tilted his head. I think he felt sorry for me that I was so dumb.

"Fine," I said. "Treat."

His rump dropped so hard I heard it hit the sidewalk.

"You're a bad boy, you know that?"

He knew and he was proud. I pulled out his therapy dog vest and opened the door. Sally the usual barista glanced up from her phone. I waved the vest and she rolled her eyes. Pick dashed in and danced in circles as Sally admired his duds.

"I have to take him in the back," she said. "He's adorable."

"Go for it."

"What'll you have?"

"Latte and a cinnamon roll," I said.

She grinned. "Help yourself," before taking Pick off to be loved up by the baker.

I went behind the counter to make my own latte and I waved at a firefighter I knew. Cory and his friends were drinking protein power smoothies and discussing their abs. Chuck should've been there. Cory looked like Shy Baldwin on *Mrs. Maisel* if he were a lumberjack. On second thought, Chuck would probably start drinking that stuff and it smelled funny even from a distance. I had enough stink to deal with as it was. Boiled eggs were the bane of my nighttime existence.

Spidermonkey smiled at me from his usual seat by the fire. He set aside his Wall Street Journal and adjusted the plaid cuffs under his lavender cashmere sweater, every inch the successful grandfather and not a bit the incorrigible hacker that knew the ins and outs of every sleazy enterprise in our fair city.

I poured perfect foam into my cup and ignored his darkening expression as he kept glancing at the door. The microwave dinged and I carried my ginormous cinnamon roll over and sat down with my nose in the air, waiting for the inevitable dressing down.

"Where is Fats?" he asked.

"Bevo Mill 7-11," I said.

"What is she doing in Bevo Mill? She's supposed to be with you."

I took a swipe of icing off my roll and taste tested it. Oh, so good. "She didn't make it."

"Mercy, what is Fats doing?"

"You know what? I don't like to ask, but I'm thinking debt collection. Early morning. They're in bed. Easy pickings."

"At the 7-11?"

"Oh, no. She was done with whatever she was doing at seven in the morning on a Saturday and now she's barfing in the 7-11 parking lot."

"Why didn't you wait?"

"I'm perfectly capable of driving ten minutes and I've got Pick," I said.

"Oh, yeah. He's very intimidating with that ball of fuzz on his head."

"He's got huge teeth."

"You'd never know it."

I shrugged. "Well, I'm here now. Are we doing this or what?"

My super hacker grumbled, but he pulled out a file from a leather attaché case. "I normally would've emailed this to you, but, to be on the safe side, I went old school."

"On everything?"

"I feel the need to keep you dark for now."

"Alright." I took the file and read Rich's Uncle Orson's death certificate, chart from the ER, and police report. Pretty straight forward. Elderly. Heart attack. Found on kitchen floor by housekeeper. No sign of foul play. No autopsy.

Then Spidermonkey handed over Rich's record. He was a good cop with an unblemished record except for an excessive force complaint from a drug addict that attacked him with an ice pick. I was inclined to dismiss that and I focused on his write-ups. Excellent all-around. Top detective in his department. His instincts were mentioned more than once.

"So Rich has the goods," I said.

"If he doesn't like how Thooft looks for this, I'd be inclined to listen," said Spidermonkey.

"I'm more than inclined." I told him about my meeting with Kimberly and my day in St. Seb.

He tapped his long fingers on his files. "I wasn't sure about that, but you're obviously onto something."

"Were you able to dig anything up on Anton?" I asked.

"I want to show you this before we get to him." He gave me another file. I wasn't exactly sure what it was telling me. Electronic data. My phone. My laptop.

I held up my palms. "Want to give me a clue?"

"Someone has been trying to breach your communications hard during the three months before your attack. Three weeks before, the attempts doubled."

"Anton?"

"In my opinion, no," said Spidermonkey. "He had a six-year-old Dell with out of date virus and malware protection."

"He wasn't a hacker," I said.

"Not even close, but I took a better look at whether your phone had been breached. Thooft wasn't a computer guy, but one is easily hired"—he winked at me—"and while I was looking, I got to thinking."

"About what?"

"You have a tight group of family and friends and it's well-known."

"So what?" I asked.

"So if someone wanted to know your whereabouts and they couldn't get at you directly, maybe they'd try your boyfriend or your mother."

"Did they?"

"Yes, but only certain people in your life had an uptick in attempts."

"Which ones?" I asked.

"Those of us that know about your interest in The Klinefeld Group and Stella."

I ate some cinnamon roll while he got out another file, this time with color-coded graphs for the nimrods like me. There were plenty of attempts going on, efforts to get into all our accounts, email, banking, etc.

"People are trying to hack The Girls?"

"They're fabulously wealthy and elderly. Their accounts are under assault constantly. Can you imagine the payday if someone got into their checking account?"

"Cha-ching," I said.

"To put it mildly," said Spidermonkey, "but that's not the concern here. You are always under assault from whatever obsessed man has decided you're his type. Carolina has some of the same issues, but not nearly so much, unless you're making headlines, then her attempts go up. Your dad has issues, but those are generally ex-cons trying to screw him over."

"Chuck's all," I said, looking at his charts, "communications, not banking."

Spidermonkey smiled at me. "Glad you saw that because that's what made me dig. Take a look."

I leafed through the pages. He had Aunt Tenne in there, Grandad and Grandma J, my grandparents in New Orleans, Claire, himself, Uncle Morty, Joy and all the academics we had working on the Stella inquiry. Basically, anybody close to me. Everyone looked steady for the last year, except me, Chuck, Fats, Mom, and The Girls.

"Attempts on our email and texts are way up in the last four weeks," I said.

"Yes, but I have to say I didn't think much of it. There were spikes in that data before when Lester died and when you were attacked in New Orleans. They also went high after Carolina had her stroke, too. St. Seb was predictable."

"My head hurts," I said.

"Drink your coffee," he said, "and take a look at the communications tries. Pretty steady and didn't change after the attack."

"If it was Anton, they should've."

"Unless he had a partner, yes."

"So have you taken a hard look at Anton?" I asked.

"I have and so far what I've found matches his sister's account of him."

Behind me the café door banged open and Fats staggered in with Moe under her arm and sweat on her brow despite the icy fog hanging around outside.

"Mercy...I told you...to...wait," she gasped.

"I decided against it," I said. "You should go home. You don't look so good."

She took a deep breath and drew up to her full size, which seemed bigger than normal given the parka she was wearing. "I promised Chuck I'd stick with you." She paused. "Is that coffee?"

"It's a coffee house," I said.

"Oh, God." She dropped Moe and dashed to the back, yelling for the bathroom and startling the firefighters. A door slammed and Sally came running out with Pick.

"What the hell was that?"

"My friend," I said. "Coffee makes her sick."

"Pregnant?"

"Very."

"Poor thing." Sally lit a couple candy-striped Christmas candles and started brewing peppermint tea. Pickpocket and Moe had a good sniff and started tussling on the rug.

"So," I said, "where were we?"

"Thooft," said Spidermonkey. "Totally normal until six weeks ago like the cops said and then obsessed with you."

"I don't buy it."

"Neither do I and I've reached out to Novak in Paris. His network is top notch with the sex trade."

"I don't like where this is going," I said. "What are you hoping to find?"

"What was going on in those Incel sites with regards to you. I can see that Anton was on several boards, but there's more to it than what I'm seeing. He was also on 4chan, but the discussions he was in have been deleted. Novak says he can get them back, but it'll take a day or so. He's busy just now."

"You think there are more where Anton came from?" I asked, my stomach in a knot. "Could he have been kidnapping me for the sex trade?"

Spidermonkey reached out and patted my shoulder. "That's a possibility. You wouldn't believe what goes on in those groups these days."

Yes, I would.

"Did Thooft need money? Presumably he wasn't kidnapping me for his own pleasure."

"I haven't found any money issues, but that doesn't mean he didn't have them. I'll keep hunting, but you have to keep Fats with you."

I glanced back toward the bathroom. "I'll try, but it's not looking good."

"I'm sure Calpurnia would give you someone else, if you asked," he said.

"She's not going to ask." Fats walked, dignity intact and looking like, *Vomit? What vomit?*

"I'm on it," she said.

Sally gave her a cup of peppermint tea and came out to play tug of war with the dogs. "I won't brew any more coffee."

"Thanks, but that's not necessary," said Fats. "I'm fine. It was a temporary situation."

Sally wrinkled her nose but, wisely, didn't counter that. Spidermonkey said, "Well, I should probably go, ladies. Have a nice trip."

"Trip?" I asked.

"To St. Sebastian. I hear they have a nice police chief down there."

Fats gulped her tea, but sweat appeared on her brow again. "I'll be ready...in a minute."

Sally came over when I finished my latte and gathered up our debris.

"Thanks, Sally," I said.

"No problem. Say hi to your mom," she said. "Everybody still worries about her. People ask about her since she comes in with you."

"That's so nice." I smiled, but that didn't last long. Fats bent over doing what sounded like Lamaze breathing, including the hehehe. Sally ran away and Pick hid under my chair.

"What's happening?" I asked. "Are you going to throw up again?"

"There's nothing left," she croaked.

"Can't you do something?" Spidermonkey asked. "Isn't there a pill?"

"There is and she won't take it," I said.

"The baby isn't getting any drugs." Fats straightened up. "I'm better."

We looked sideways at her, but she was armed and, ya know, her, so I moved on. "Do you think The Klinefeld Group is behind the communications attempts?"

"I would think so, but they haven't broken through so I can't imagine why they'd be after your mother's communication. There's no reason to think she knows anything about what you're doing. We may have another bad actor."

"What's going on?" Fats asked.

I gave her a quick rundown and she asked, "Could Thooft have anything to do with The Klinefeld Group?"

Spidermonkey shook his head. "No. I don't think so. No connection to money, art, and his attempt was amateur hour. The way they went after the Bled Mansion and Lester, that was pretty slick, so I don't see it."

"He lived in Germany," said Fats.

"With few connections to Germans. He was a teacher. His friends and life centered around the school," said Spidermonkey. "Since Thooft tried to access Blankenship at Hunt, he could be connected to Kansas through someone he met on the Incel sites. I'm tracking where the attempts came from, but I'm not there yet."

"What about his family?" I asked.

"There's nothing to connect them to Blankenship, Kansas or The Klinefeld Group, but I'll continue to look," Spidermonkey said.

Fats breathed deep her tea and asked, "Did you tell him about the weird personality change and Kimberly?"

"I was getting to that." I told Spidermonkey all my new info. "You're a father. How weird is it that Ann didn't want Kimberly to perform?"

"You're sure she was talented?"

"It sounds like it, but I can dig."

Spidermonkey steepled his fingers. "You should because it's hard to say. My oldest thought for certain he was the next Tiger Woods, but he was only ever slightly better than average. My daughter was gifted with math like me but decided that literature was her thing. She was going to be a novelist."

Fats got sharp-eyed. "What did you want her to be?"

"A physicist."

"What is she?"

He laughed. "A physicist."

Fats gritted her teeth. "You made her?"

"We didn't make her get a PhD in physics. She came to it on her own."

I forced myself not to lick the remaining icing off my plate. "Oh, yeah? Like how I'm a private investigator. They didn't make me, but here I am."

"I made her take math. All the math and she excelled, despite doing her level best to fight us every step of the way," said Spidermonkey.

"Is your son a golfer?" Fats asked.

"He is, but it's not his day job."

"Because you didn't support him?" she asked.

I don't think we're talking about Kimberly anymore.

"So...parents do what they think is best?" I asked. "Maybe Ann didn't think Kimberly was any good."

"I'd go to the school and talk to the teacher. But all these little things may not mean anything. Kimberly not going to Broadway is hardly unusual. Every little town has a kid that looks like they've got the X factor. Lots of people don't want to do interviews and be in the press."

There it was, a little feeling. Something wasn't right. Those little things, as Spidermonkey called them, were important. We were missing something. "It can't be a coincidence, can it?"

"Life is full of coincidences."

I nodded, but my gut said no. And not just no, hell no.

After Fats finished her tea, Spidermonkey paid the bill and my body-guard sprang to her feet. "Where to next?"

"Are you okay?" I asked.

"Never better." She gave a thumbs-up to Sally behind the counter. "Those peppermint candles are the bomb."

Sally held out a particularly pretty candy-striped candle. "Take it."

"How much do I owe you?" she asked.

Sally winked. "On the house."

Fats took the glass mason jar and happily carried it, still lit, to the door. "Let's hit it."

"Aren't you going to blow that out?" I asked.

"Why?"

I walked out onto the street and blew out a frosty breath while Pick selected a parking meter to pee on. It was a hard decision. So many choices. "You can't have an open flame in the truck."

"Says who?" Fats asked.

"Common sense."

"People smoke in cars and somebody I know puts on mascara while driving."

"That's you," I said.

"There's no law against it," she said as Pick stretched out his lead to a Porsche, bypassing a battered Hyundai, to pee on the upscale meter. The poodle was a snob.

"There should be," I said. "Speaking of the law, what was that wink about?"

"Do you really want to know?" Fats asked.

I pursed my lips.

"I didn't think so."

Spidermonkey came out and we hugged. He gave Fats a particularly good one and said, "I can't wait for the baby to move."

"She already has," said Fats. "Three days ago."

"Really. That's unusual, isn't it, Mercy?" he asked.

"For a first pregnancy, but it happens."

Fats grinned like the Cheshire Cat. "She's an overachiever already." *God help her if she's not.*

"Were you poking her?" I asked.

Fats' eyes shifted to the left and Spidermonkey laughed. "First time moms are always—"

Above us was a slam and a harsh scrape of metal against wood. We looked to see the window air conditioner on the second floor above us slide out of the window and hang by its accordion side panel. Fats shoved Spidermonkey out of the way, he hit me, and we both rammed into the Hyundai. The AC unit crashed onto the sidewalk, exploding into a million pieces and a woman above us shrieked.

"That almost hit you," I said to Spidermonkey and he sagged on the Hyundai clutching his heart, nodding.

Sally ran out with a cup of coffee in her hand. "What the hell was that?"

"Air conditioner," said Fats.

"I told Lenny to replace that thing," she said. "Are you okay?"

We nodded and she banged back inside yelling for Lenny, whoever that was.

"Oh, my God," Spidermonkey said. "What are the odds?"

"Not good." I took his wrist and checked his pulse.

"And it's my second time."

"It can't be," said Fats.

He nodded gulping for air. "My uncle's house in 1962. That one grazed me on the shoulder."

"Holy crap." His pulse was up there, but that was hardly surprising. "I'm calling Loretta."

"No, don't. She gets upset," he said.

"I don't blame her. I'm upset," I said.

Fats cracked her knuckles and said, "I'm going to have a little talk with Lenny."

"Who's Lenny?"

"He owns the building. That's an Airbnb up there. Dirtbag obviously did it on the cheap. Look at that window casing. It's falling apart."

We looked up and I became aware of muffled crying. "I'm going to check that out."

I went in and saw Cory and his friends going up the back stairs.

"The guys have got it," said Sally. "Don't worry about it, Mercy."

A man yelled down, "She won't open the door."

"She has to open the door!" she yelled back.

"She's naked!"

Sally slapped her forehead. "It's always something."

"It really is," I said. "But she's crying. You've got to call 911."

She slumped. "Alright. Geez, it's not even Friday the thirteenth." She started to call the cops, but just then a police cruiser wailed to a halt in front of the café. A couple of uniforms stopped to talk to Fats and Spidermonkey before rushing in.

"Ah crap!" said Parker. "It's you."

I met Parker when I was investigating Gavin Flouder's murder and he was not a fan. I admit the feeling was mutual. Parker was just as disheveled, cranky, and bleary-eyed as I remembered, but the look of disgust he gave me was worse.

"I didn't do it," I said.

"That's what they all say."

"Who's this mysterious *they*?"

Cory came pounding down the stairs. "We need the EMTs and a key."

"What happened?" Sally asked, digging around in drawers.

"Your guest fell and she won't let us in," said Cory. "I told her we were firefighters."

"She's naked," said Sally.

"That doesn't matter."

It kinda did. Cory was one of those guys that even sounded hot. Unless I was spurting from a carotid I wouldn't let him in to see me all messed up on the floor. A girl needed good lighting, preferably candles, to be seen naked by Cory. He was on the St. Louis firefighter calendar and it left little to the imagination.

Sally held up a janky old key. "I found it."

The other cop said, "EMS en route. ETA in two."

"She's going to freak. She doesn't want help." Cory shook his head and sighed, making him both hot and adorable. "She said she'll kill herself if we come in."

Parker jerked a thumb at me. "Send up the wiener threader."

I thrust out a hip and stuck my nose in the air. "I'll have you know I don't thread wieners anymore."

"Wieners?" Cory asked.

"Oh, that's right," said Parker. "You got fired from that stellar job. I wonder why."

"It wasn't a wiener problem. I'm good with wieners."

"That's what they all say."

I threw up my hands. "*They* again."

"I bet you miss them wieners," said Parker.

Cory frowned. "What are we talking about? Hot dogs?"

Parker glared at him. "For God's sake, go flex outside. You're giving me acid reflux."

"But what's Mercy threading?"

"Penises, ya showboat," barked Parker. "Get out."

The firefighter drew back. "Huh?"

"Is it penises?" Sally asked. "That sounds wrong."

"Penai?" suggested Cory.

The other cop stepped up. "Penes."

"I like penai," said Sally. "Mercy?"

"I don't know. Penises, I guess," I said. "The point is I don't thread them anymore."

"Why would you?" Cory asked and gave me a look that you never want to get from a superhot firefighter or any hot guy really.

"I was a nurse," I said. "Catheters."

"Oh." Cory's faced scrunched up. "Ew."

Parker glared at me. "What do you mean 'used to be'?"

"I'm a private investigator now," I said with pride. I don't know where it came from. Maybe just a desire to bother Parker.

"Oh, hell. That's just what this friggin' state needs, more weird shit happening," he said. "I'm gonna retire and move to Florida."

"'Cause there's no weird stuff going down in the Sunshine State," I said.

"You're not there, so it's a start."

Sally waved the key at me. "Are you going up or what?"

My phone buzzed and I checked the screen. Kimberly. Problem with my contract. Awesome. I pocketed my phone and reached for the key, but Parker snatched it away. "Get lost. You're not a nurse anymore."

"I'm still a licensed BSN," I said.

"I rethought it," said Parker with a sneer. "The last thing a naked middle-aged woman wants is *you* walking in."

"You don't know," I said. "And what's middle-aged got to do with it."

Parker tossed his hat on a table. "Everything. I've got a wife and I know."

"She might not be middle-aged."

"Pretty sure she is," said Cory. "Maybe even older."

"Not helping," I said.

"But he has a point," said Sally. "I'm not sure I'd want you to see me naked."

Cory turned to her and winked. "What about me?"

"For you I'd make an exception." Sally winked back.

"I'm going to vomit," said Parker.

I crossed my arms. "I'd enjoy that."

Fats opened the door. "Ambulance is here. Mercy, Spi— he's trying to drive."

I hated to let that douchebag Parker win, but the EMT squeezing past Fats cinched it. Parker waggled his fingers at me and I ducked out. Spidermonkey was trying to book it to his Mercedes and we chased him down.

"Hey," he said as Fats pinned him to his door. "Let go. I'm fine."

"Loretta will be the judge of that," said Fats.

"This isn't my first rodeo."

"Well, your last one was a long time ago, so deal with it," I said.

Loretta was speedy. She showed ten minutes later with one and a half hands manicured. "Another air conditioner? What are the odds?"

"Third time could be the charm," he said.

"That's not funny." Loretta hugged him and gave her husband the once over. "You seem okay, but I'll drive and the boys can get the car."

"Loretta—"

She stuck her finger in his face. "This is not a discussion."

"It could be a negotiation," he said, oozing charm.

"Not if you want to be able to find your golf clubs tomorrow."

Spidermonkey sighed and said, "I won't forget this."

"Nobody will. It's too weird," I said. "Speaking of weird, Loretta, can I ask you a question?"

Loretta flipped an untamed curl out of her face and said, "It makes me nervous when you say things like that, but yes, you may."

"If you had a kid that was so talented that when she tried out for the school musical the choir teacher said she could be on Broadway, would you freak and pull her out of any school musical stuff?"

Loretta pulled back and made a face. "No, what kind of parent do you think I am?"

"So that's weird?"

"Absolutely. We supported our son's pro golfing dream until reality winnowed him out. That's what you do."

"Even if you were very private and didn't like publicity."

"Well, it wouldn't be my publicity, would it? If the child wants it, they deserve a chance, regardless of the parent's issues," said Loretta and Fats gave her a bear hug that literally took Loretta off her feet.

When Fats put her down, Loretta asked, "What's that for?"

"Proving me right," said Fats and she pointed me toward her truck.

"Is this a case?"

"It is," said Spidermonkey with a nod at me. "I'll explain in the car."

I waved and we got in Fats' truck. Pick decided today was the day he was going to ride in the front seat and I battled him as my phone buzzed again. Kimberly. Not a good sign.

"What does she want?" Fats asked.

"Something about our contract."

"Do you think she's changed her mind?"

"Maybe, but, if she has, I'm sure her mother's behind it."

"I'm liking Ann less and less," said Fats.

I pushed Pick back in his seat with Moe and threatened no biscuits for a month. He knew I was lying. You have to give giant poodles biscuits. You have to. There's no choice involved.

"Your phone's going again," said Fats.

I put my arm up, blocking another attempt by Pick, and answered with the other hand, "Hi, Kimberly."

"It's Chief Stratton down in St. Seb."

I checked the screen. Sure enough. It was Stratton and I liked that a whole lot better. If Kimberly was going to fire me, I'd rather do it later than sooner. "What's up?"

"I've got another tidbit for you," she said. "I don't know if it's relevant, but I thought I'd give you a buzz."

"On Anton or Kimberly?" I asked.

"Kimberly."

Stratton and her sister had gone out to dinner at Crabapples last night and got to talking with Karen and Carrie. It turned out both of the ladies were involved with the town fair in different capacities. They remembered when Anton left and his seat went vacant. There was a big meeting and they decided to offer the slot to Kimberly. It was kind of a tradition to keep seats in the same family and the general feeling was that Kimberly was the right choice. She did a ton of volunteering at the fair and had since she was a kid. She was social and knew everyone. They thought she'd be willing to do more promoting and interviews than Anton ever did. As expected, she was delighted and accepted.

"Let me guess," I said. "She changed her mind."

"Yes, she did. The day after, she called up and said she was too busy with the vet practice and her kids."

"Did they give it to Gregory or Kevin?"

"I think the board was a little pissed and the seat went to Sheila Molina. She's great and it worked out," said Stratton.

"You think it was Ann getting in the way again?"

"That's the consensus."

"What is her problem? Is she just a jealous, crappy mom or what?"

Fats glanced over and said, "That gets my vote."

"It doesn't play that way, but it's hard to say what goes on when nobody's looking."

"Ain't that the truth," I said.

"And one more thing," said Stratton.

"I can't imagine what's next."

Fats raised a brow and I shrugged.

"Now this isn't exactly a fact, more like a curiosity."

"Hit me."

Stratton told me about a fair tradition that went back to the beginning. Every year a local girl was named the St. Sebastian Town and Country Fair Queen and it was a big deal. The girls would be sponsored by a local business and do all kinds of activities to promote the fair before competing on stage in a Miss America-type deal. It sounded like a nightmare to me—your whole town judging you like cattle—I got that on a regular basis, so forget it, but most girls in St. Seb wanted to compete. There were good scholarships involved and some notoriety, if you were up for that. Kimberly was a beautiful, outgoing, and popular girl. Everyone expected her to do it. Stratton's sister, Amber, did compete, coming in second, and she said she was relieved because she figured Kimberly would walk away with it. She was that kind of girl, but she didn't come to any of the preliminary meetings for information or anything.

"Did Amber ever ask her why?" I asked.

"She didn't really see her. The fair's at the end of the summer and there was all the college prep and they didn't really run around together."

"Probably Ann again," I said.

"That's what they all think," said Stratton.

"But they like Ann?"

"They do. She's a nice lady apparently."

I seriously doubt that.

CHAPTER TWELVE

The mansion was quiet with the faint smell of mulled wine wafting around from the kitchen. While I was gone, Christmas decorating had happened. The florist and maids had come and gone, leaving the library dust-free and filled with pots of poinsettias and a beautifully decorated blue spruce covered in literary-type ornaments. I found my Thooft contract on Millicent's desk next to her Christmas cactus, just brought out into the light so it could start blooming.

Fats set her still-lit candle on the fireplace mantel and started doing squat thrusts combined with Judo or maybe it was Jiu-Jitsu. There was rolling on the rug. That's all I know.

"What does it say?" she asked between grunts.

I leafed through the contract. I'd seen a billion of Dad's contracts and it seemed standard. "They can shut me down."

Fats snorted.

"They just have to pay for the time we've already spent," I said.

She did a high-flying kick, barely missing the brand-new Christmas tree in the corner, and sending Pickpocket running for cover when she scurried to the fireplace in a crouch.

"You're not going to be able to do that for much longer."

"Wanna bet?" She went into a full split on one foot.

I spun around on the ancient desk chair and said, "Yes, I do."

"You do?" she asked. "You realize that candle worked."

"*You* realize that baby's going to get a heck of a lot bigger?"

She assumed a fighting position and punched the air. "I better get while the getting is good."

"You should eat," I said, looking at the contract again and nothing jumped out, but I felt like something should have.

"I ate."

"A protein shake that you threw up?"

Silence.

I took out my phone. "I'm going to call Claire. She'll know if anything's weird."

The super organized Claire answered on the first ring. "Watts Premier Investigations. Claire speaking."

"It's Mercy. Do you have a minute?" I asked. "I'm looking at the Thooft contract."

"Is there a problem?"

"You can't tell my dad."

She groaned. "Why? What did you do now? He's so happy."

Wait. What?

"Dad's happy? Why?" I winced while waiting for both shoes to drop.

"You haven't seen the news?" Claire asked.

"No. Oh, is it the air conditioner? That wasn't my fault. I had nothing to do with it."

"Air conditioner?"

"There was an air conditioner. Never mind. Did something else happen?" I asked.

"We are getting flooded with calls about St. Seb and it's a great picture, too. Pickpocket really makes you seem normal," said Claire.

"I am normal," I said.

Fats snorted again.

"I am. What picture are you talking about?" I asked.

"You outside the St. Seb police station with Pickpocket. It's all over the news."

"There's a story about me walking a poodle?"

"The story's about you investigating Anton Thooft," said Claire.

"Ah, crap."

"Want the headline?"

Brace yourself.

"Let me have it," I said.

"'Bombshell beauty joins forces with perps' parents to find the truth.'"

"That's not too bad." I leaned back and breathed deep the smell of mulled wine and...chocolate. Aaron appeared in the door with a pot.

"How'd you get in?" I asked him.

"I'm in the office at the house," said Claire with a touch of worry. "How are you feeling?"

"Fine. Aaron just walked in."

"Oh, he has the codes now. Anything else?"

"Yeah, the Thooft contract. Is there anything different about it?"

"Let me pull it and see," said Claire.

Aaron gave me a mug and then stared over Fats' head until she accepted hers.

"Did you put alcohol in this?" she asked after giving it a good sniff.

"Candy cane," he said. "The baby likes it."

"No, thanks. I'm trying to be sugar free."

He didn't move and it was a standoff. A very quiet one.

"Mercy?" Claire came back on the line.

"Got something?"

"No, it's standard. None of the language was changed for this particular job. Boiler plate, basically, but I didn't realize that that headline in the paper was wrong."

"Wrong?" I wasn't crazy about being called a bombshell, but it wasn't up to me.

"You're not working with the parents," said Claire.

"I am. I met with them yesterday."

"Okay. Fine." Her eyes were rolling. I could tell. "You're not working *for* the parents."

I flipped to the first page and it said rather enigmatically that my contract was with the Thooft family. When I turned to the signature page, I found who I was actually working for Kimberly, Gregory, and Kevin, not their parents, Ann and Anthony.

"So it's just the kids who really wanted an investigation," I said, "but Anthony said they'd given their word. He was okay with it. Ann not so much."

"Is that what you're looking for?" she asked.

"I think so. Thanks." I hung up and looked at the standoff still in progress. "Just drink it. The baby wants it."

"My baby is going to be sugar free and low carb," said Fats.

"Did your OB tell you to do that?"

She growled. "She told me to eat as much as I can because I have no fat layer. I need a new OB recommendation."

"Every doctor will be the same. You don't have a fat layer and the baby needs fat," I said. "Aaron, tell her."

"Drink it," he said. "The baby likes it."

"One sip," she said and she did it. "Oh, no. That's a lot of fat. What did you make this with?"

"Double cream."

"My baby will have diabetes."

"Drink it."

The world's most boring argument commenced and I decided to call Kimberly. Unless I missed my guess, she was firing me at the behest of her mother. Not gonna happen. Not this time, Ann.

"Hello. This is Mercy Watts," I said, very businesslike and I was pretty proud of me.

"Oh, Mercy." Kimberly sounded dismayed. Maybe she hoped I'd never call back and just, ya know, wander off or something.

"So you're calling to fire me because your mother saw the news and we're all over it."

A whoosh of breath went out of her and I heard a sofa creak in distress. "How...how did you know?"

"I'm a speedboat, Kimberly, not a pontoon."

"Of course not. I just...I'm so sorry. Mom decided to fire you and that's how it is."

I took a big drink of my hot chocolate that, thankfully, wasn't made with double cream—I was now educated enough to know—and said, "She can't."

"What?" Kimberly asked.

"Fire me."

"But I think you're fired."

"By your mother?"

"Yes."

"No."

The chocolate hit me and my whole body relaxed. That candy cane was hitting the spot.

"I don't know what you're saying," said Kimberly.

"I'm saying your mother isn't in charge," I said.

She hesitated and I could tell she was absorbing that. It was a slow process. "Who is?"

"You, Gregory, and Kevin."

"Well, then we fire you. I'm so sorry. So so sorry."

I took another drink. "Put 'em on the phone then."

"Oh, they're not here," she said nervously.

"And they don't know a thing about this. Am I right?" I asked.

"Please don't make this difficult."

"It's about time somebody did."

"What do you mean?" Kimberly asked.

I'm fired. What can it hurt?

"Answer a few questions and I might let you fire me," I said.

"I don't think it works like that," she said.

"Let's call your brothers and see how they think it works."

She swallowed hard and I had to wait a long minute before she said, "Go ahead."

"Why did your mother make you drop out of the school musical when you were in high school?" I asked.

I'm going out on a limb, but I think the only time Kimberly Thooft Stackhouse was more astonished was when she found out her brother kidnapped me. She sputtered and stuttered, hemmed and hawed.

I waited and listened to Aaron and Fats discussing good fats and bad fats. He thought they were all good and she thought they were all bad. It was like listening to congress. They were that opposed and intractable.

"I'm waiting," I said at long last.

"She didn't," Kimberly said finally.

I made an annoying game show buzzer sound.

"I wasn't any good."

Another buzzer.

"I didn't want to be in the show."

Buzzer.

"It was just a crappy part."

I can't let that go.

"Oh, come on. You got the lead and you were flipping fantastic," I said.

"How...how do you know?"

"'Cause I know. Now why did your mother do the opposite of what every other mother I know would do?"

Fats gave me a funny look and then shockingly drank the hot chocolate. I gaped at her while trying to focus on what Kimberly was saying. "My mother is a wonderful mother. The best mother."

"Who made you sob and quit the lead for no good reason."

"She had a reason. I wasn't that good. She didn't want me to be disappointed when I didn't get anywhere."

Your mom sucks.

"So she didn't let you try for fear of failure?" I asked.

"Um...yes, that's it."

"So why couldn't you be in the Queen contest for the fair?" I gambled on that one, but I felt good about it and it payed off.

"I might not have won," she said.

She did stop you.

"And what about the fair board? She made you give up that seat. Were you going to fail at that, too?"

Fats stood up. "I want more hot chocolate. The baby does like it."

Aaron ran out of the room as fast as his little legs could carry him. I think I heard him chortling as he went.

"I wasn't going to fail." Kimberly's voice broke. "I would've been good at it."

It was my turn to take a breath. "That's what I heard."

"Did you?"

"Yes. Absolutely," I said. "Kimberly, why did you have to give it up? Why?"

"My mother said...oh, I don't know what she said. She just kept talking and talking and then I was agreeing. I don't know how it happened."

I knew the feeling. All those jobs I did for Dad, for free no less. I always said no and then I was sitting in a car at two in the morning with a full bladder and a camera, waiting for some jerk to leave his mistress' house.

"I get it," I said.

"You're still fired," she said with more composure.

"No. I'm not. You started this, Kimberly, because you wanted to know why."

"I did, but it's got nothing to do with me," she said.

I said nothing. I let it sit and this time it didn't take long. I think she already knew.

"You think it *does* have something to do with me."

"I do. Don't you?"

"I don't see how," she said and then blew her nose. "Anton and I were so different."

"Were you?" I asked. "He gave up a lot. A career in politics, public speaking. No interviews. No Jamie. Couldn't be on the fair website."

That woke her up. "Jamie? Who's Jamie?"

I was starting to think Anton lived his life like a big shell game, hiding his truths and switching them around so people couldn't see them.

"Jamie was his boyfriend for seven years. They were very much in love and Anton dumped him because of you." I wasn't harsh about it, but I was tired of being gentle. I needed more hot chocolate and I was close to getting fired from my first official PI job, like a loser.

Kimberly stammered something about Anton never being serious about anyone and playing the field. Maybe Anton was some kind of congenital liar. In any case, I was pretty sick of him and his crap.

"Do you want to hear what happened or do you want to keep living your life behind the curtain your mother and Anton kept putting in front of you?"

"I don't think they did that," she said angrily. "How dare you say—"

"You had a part on Broadway," I said.

Kimberly went silent and there was a shuffling of the phone.

"Who is this?" Kimberly's husband hadn't said much when I was at the farm, but I knew an angry husband when I heard one.

"Mercy Watts. You don't want me to be fired."

"Who's firing you?" Holt went from angry to what-the-hell in a blink of an eye.

"Your mother-in-law," I said. "But whether the family pays me or not, this is happening. Anton came after me and I'm just about to find out why."

"Are you?" Holt turned to Kimberly and started pelting her with questions that she cried through. "What's this about Broadway?"

I gave him a quick rundown, ending with Jamie and the Broadway breakup. Holt was quiet throughout, a good listener and I suspected he was thinking hard about what I was saying.

"You believe that?" he asked when I was done.

"I do. Jamie lost the love of his life over it. I can't imagine why he'd lie. He still loves Anton and, for the most part, he only had good things to say."

"It's always been like that," said Holt quietly.

"What has?" I asked.

"Ann and Anton, keeping control of my wife." He said something to Kimberly, who was trying to shush him.

"Would you be willing to talk to me about it?"

Holt cleared his throat and I pictured him thinking about his family, his wife and how much trouble this was going to cause him. "What do you want to know?"

I didn't know what I wanted to know. That was the problem.

"I wish I could tell you, but I'm coming back out to St. Seb. Can you meet me?"

"Hold on."

I heard him go out a door and then he said, "She can't hear me now. What do you need? I'll give you anything you want."

"Really?" I expected a lot more resistance, if not an outright no.

"Look. I love this family, but if Ann's trying to shut you down, there's something we have to know. She's been weird with Kim forever. She loves her but she...throttles her is the best way to put it and now she's doing it with my kids. I'm not having it."

"What's Ann doing?" I asked.

"Our son Chase has an unbelievable voice. He wants to be a country music star and, believe me, he has the chops to do it. But Ann's telling him he can't. He isn't good enough. It's a pipe dream." Holt's voice got louder. "You know what? I don't care if it is. A kid should dream and every time she says that crap to him it's a cut on his soul, so whatever you want I'm going to give it to you. I want to know what is wrong with this family."

"Meet me at the Sentinel in a couple of hours?"

"I'll be there. What else?"

"Bring every family album you can lay your hands on," I said.

"Consider it done," said Holt.

"Good luck."

"I won't need it. This is happening."

Now that's a parent.

CHAPTER THIRTEEN

I tried to be fast, but Myrtle spotted us in the garage from the back of Nicolai Bled's 1921 Maybach as Rocco drove in.

So close.

My beloved godmother opened her door and got out, "Where do you think you're going alone?"

"I'm not alone," I said and pointed down. When I said *us,* I meant me and Pickpocket. For the first time in her life, Fats was slow, not to mention a little loopy from the double cream hot chocolate. We'd outrun her.

Myrtle wasn't satisfied and she asked again, "Where are you and Pick going?"

"St. Seb," I said. "I'm not fired yet."

She came over to kiss my cheek. "Fired? How ridiculous. Who would fire you?"

Ann, Shawna, my old temp firm, a couple of doctors' wives.

"Nobody today," I said. "So I have to, wait, what's happening?"

Rocco helped Millicent out of the car and grimaced at me. He usually loved driving the Maybach so something was up.

"Nothing, dear, just getting ready for the party," said Millicent.

Party?

"Oh, right," I said as Fats lurched into the garage.

"I'm ready. What are we waiting for?" she said.

Crap on a cracker.

"You, I guess," I said. "Are you okay? There wasn't alcohol in that hot chocolate, was there?"

"No, but I haven't had that much fat in one sitting in…ever."

The Girls went for Fats, trying to stand on their tiptoes to test her temperature and failing to reach the heights of her forehead.

"My dear, you don't look well at all," said Myrtle. "Come back in the house."

"I'm taking Mercy to St. Seb," said Fats, leaning down to have her head examined.

"No fever," announced Millicent. "But we're not taking any chances with that baby. Back in the house."

"I can't," she said.

The Girls tried to herd Fats toward the house, looking like a couple of sleek birds in their Chanel suits trying to move a building from the Las Vegas strip.

Rocco kept an eye on them as he began pulling packages out of the front seat of the Maybach and whispered to me, "We went shopping"—he had a wild look about him—"for crackers and cheese."

Well, there you go. The dreaded crackers and cheese.

I smiled at him and whispered, "Did you find what you were looking for?"

"Maybe. I don't know what it was," he said.

"Did you do olive oil and vinegar?"

"I tasted so much oil I feel slippery to the touch," he said. "Have you done this shopping trip?"

"So many times," I said, leaning over. "What party?"

"Christmas for the staff."

"Holy crap. I forgot. Enjoy the arranging."

"Arranging?" Rocco asked, his eyes wide.

"You have to figure out which oils go with which breads." I went for the exit, but he snagged me. "Hey, Millicent!"

"Yes, Rocco?" The Girls turned back and Fats attempted to dart around them, but Myrtle had a lot better reflexes than you'd think and blocked her.

"My sister looks like he— bad. I think I should go with Mercy and Fats should take it easy and do the arranging," he said, dripping with brotherly concern.

"Beat it, Skinny MacSwizzle Stick," said Fats. "That's my gig. This is yours."

"How are you going to protect Mercy? You can't even stand up straight."

"I'm standing up straight right now."

She wasn't. Fats was bent to the side like she was trying to form a question mark.

"No, you're not, dear," said Millicent. "Come inside."

"Mercy?" pleaded Fats. I'd never seen her at a loss before. It took little old ladies with netting on their hats to take her down. "You need me."

"I do, but"—I took a gamble—"Ernst is coming."

"Oh, yes," said Myrtle. "We have an hour."

"Ernst?" Fats asked like he might be another guy who would make her eat fat.

"Their manicurist," I said with a smile.

"Manicure you say?" Her eyebrows went up.

"And pedicures," said Millicent. "We haven't had them in a month."

The fight showed on Fats' face. She felt like hell as Rocco nearly said, but she'd never admit it and she'd never give in, unless...

"Do you think Ernst could bring Tammy with him?" I asked.

"She doesn't do manicures or pedicures," said Myrtle and then her face lit up. "I'll call right now." She began patting Fats on the elbow. It was meant to be a smack to get her going, but it probably felt more like a feather duster.

"What a good idea," said Millicent. "It's all settled. Rocco will go to St. Seb with Mercy—oh, Mercy, what about you? We always do our prepary ritual together."

"I'm happy to have Fats enjoy it. She is a mother-to-be."

"Who's Tammy?" Rocco asked, looking as though a Tammy might be his style.

"She does prenatal massage and she's supposed to be great," I said. "She's been doing them for twenty-five years."

"Never mind," he said.

"I thought so."

"I've never had a prenatal massage," said Fats.

Success!

"I have to go." I waved. "Have fun."

I grabbed Rocco.

"What about the cheese?" he asked.

"Joy'll get it."

And we were out, ready to drive to St. Seb barf-stop free.

"Thanks for this," said Rocco. "I owe you."

"Really?" I asked.

"Sure. I love The Girls and this is the best job ever, but the shopping? Man, that's rough."

"You didn't bring your knitting then?"

"I did," he patted the pocket of his coat, "but I couldn't get a moment. I tried so much blue cheese and it all tastes bad."

We laughed until we got to Fats' truck.

"I forgot," I said. "We need the keys."

Rocco dangled a set in front of my face. "Amateur."

"I'm a professional now, I'll have you know."

"Not pro enough to copy Fats' keys, just in case," he said.

"Your family is really weird."

"I'll tell you about it sometime," said Rocco. "Looks like we've got company."

I looked around the truck and saw no one.

"Inside. For crying out loud, you're the great detective? I don't think so."

I still didn't see him until I got to the passenger side. Aaron, in the back seat, scribbling on a little notebook he kept for recipe ideas.

"I thought you were in the kitchen," I said, getting in.

"Yeah."

"How'd you get in Fats' truck? I know she locked it."

Nothing. Typical.

Rocco fired up the truck and changed the radio from Fats' chosen rap to country.

"You're full of surprises," I said.

"It relaxes me. My dad likes show tunes."

"Do you know who Lea Salonga is?"

He grinned at me. "*Miss Saigon.*"

"Oh, well, then Kimberly must've been amazing," I said.

"She probably still is."

A dad kind of feeling came over me, not the usual something wasn't right feeling, but more of something's going to happen and I hoped Holt was ready for it.

The drive went fast and I hung up with Spidermonkey just as we pulled into the Great Missouri Shoe Company parking lot, but instead of Tank waiting, it was his wife, Mallory. Not a lot of people scare me, but Mallory Tancredi was one of the few. She was a tiny redhead who did not give half a crap. She went after her own brother, the former St. Seb police chief, and he's lucky she didn't beat him to death over his part in letting a serial killer slide and nearly getting her husband killed.

"Are you sure this is it?" Rocco asked.

"Their old building blew up," I said.

"Looks like this one did, too."

"The accounting section's okay."

"Why does that make me nervous?" he asked.

"I don't know, but it makes me nervous, too."

Mallory waved and pointed at a spot with less rubbish than the rest of the parking lot and by that, I mean it only had beer cans and a dead rat.

"Who's the redhead?" Rocco asked.

"Tank's wife," I said. "Don't piss her off."

"Don't worry. I know my way around a redhead even when they're fake."

"How many redheads do you know?" I asked.

"Three and they are feisty. When Fats went red, it was rough."

We got out. Aaron looked confused when I grabbed Pick off the back seat. I hadn't thought to put on his booties yet and I didn't want to risk his pads getting cut up. "Fats was a redhead? I can't see it."

"She did it to look like our mom. Talk about a wrong turn."

"What happened?"

"Two fakes don't make something real," said Rocco.

Two fakes. Real. Hmm.

Before I could respond, Mallory got to me, giving both Pick and I a big hug. "How are you? Don't tell me. You have a headache. I have Tylenol, Motrin, Advil, and some of the hard stuff, if you need it."

Moms. They come packing a pharmacy.

"Advil will do it," I said. "This is Rocco, Fats' brother. He's filling in."

"Another Licata. How many of you are there? I feel I need to be aware. Your sister is a lot," said Mallory.

"Only two."

"I bet that's plenty."

He grinned at her. "More than enough."

"Speaking of siblings," I said, "how's Will?"

"Still in rehab. I'm amazed that he stayed, but his kids told him if he didn't, they wouldn't come for the summer, so there's hope for him yet."

"I'm glad some good's coming out of that debacle."

Mallory opened the door for me. "A lot of good came out of it, a lot of truth anyway. Tank said you're coming to look into the Thoofts."

"I am."

Aaron trotted in past Mallory and disappeared into the depths of the abandoned shoe factory.

"Where's Aaron going?" Mallory asked.

"To the kitchen," I said.

"We don't have one."

"Then your guess is as good as mine."

We walked into the accounting section and it was empty. "Where is everyone?"

"They already put tomorrow's edition to bed." Tank came in,

wearing his usual two flannel shirts, but holding two puppies. "It's all ours."

Pick lost his mind and I dropped his giant butt. The poodle dashed over to Tank, yipping and wagging.

"We thought you might like to meet our new family members," said Mallory, getting a little tearful. What Bertram Stott did to her dogs years ago was still at the forefront.

"I didn't think you were ready."

"We had to move on. I wasn't going to let that bastard keep winning in our house."

Tank fended off Pick by turning a hip to him. "Do you think I can put them down?"

"If you don't mind him licking them to death," I said.

Tank put the pups down and a chase ensued, sort of. Pick didn't know what to make of those puppies. They were adorable, but not a breed you see every day.

"What are they?" Rocco asked.

"We've decided on long-haired American goofballs," said Tank.

That fit them to a tee, but they were probably corgis mixed with some kind of Shepherd. They had long bodies and short legs with a Shepherd's face and ears. I want one.

"Chuck would fall in love," I said.

"Everyone does," said Mallory fondly, "and we got them at the Humane Society. Abandoned at a truck stop, if you can believe it."

"People continue to surprise me," I said, looking at Rocco, who sat down and pulled out a couple of yarn balls and four knitting needles.

Mallory stretched and asked, "I helped recover the files from the old basement after it got bombed, so tell me what you're looking for and I'll tell you if I've seen it."

I had no plan as usual, but what popped out of my mouth sounded like I did. "Advertising."

"I didn't expect that," said Tank.

"What did you expect?" I asked.

"With you, who knows. Certainly nothing so prosaic."

"Hey!"

They laughed and Rocco smiled up from the beginnings of what I assumed was going to be baby booties.

"You all suck," I said with a pout. "I'm good at this, you know."

"We'll see," said Tank.

"You sound like my father."

"I'll take that as a compliment."

"Don't. He's a pain."

"Alright. Alright," said Mallory and she went to pour us some coffee. "What kind of advertising?"

"The Thoofts kind," I said. "They do advertise with you, don't they?"

They did. Tank pulled out the latest edition and showed me Heritage Hog Farm's ad on the third page. A standard ad, saying who they were, where, and how to buy direct. The Thoofts had deals with several grocery store chains and those were listed as well.

Mallory assessed an ad and said, "Pretty boring copy. Does it work?"

Tank shrugged. "They keep running it, so I assume so. Why do we care?"

"We don't," I said. "But my computer guy just told me that Heritage Hog used to be Thooft Family Farm."

"So?"

"So they changed the name in the summer between Anton's eighth grade and freshman year. Why'd they change it?"

"You could ask Holt," said Rocco from his spot, clicking away.

"I will, but I'm guessing he won't have a clue."

"Holt's coming?" Mallory asked with a frown. "Not Kimberly?"

I told them about our conversation and Tank nodded, "I'm with Holt. Nobody controls my wife, except me."

Mallory snorted. "Good luck with that."

"I dare to dream, my dear," he said with a laugh. "But seriously, what is up with Ann?"

"I don't know, but I'd like to see if there were any interviews with the family prior to that summer, too."

Mallory started yanking open filing cabinets. Tank was a modern guy, but only to a point. The summer of 1980 was past that point. He and Rocco pulled out an eight-foot folding table and we started arranging copy on it, starting when the Sentinel went digital and going back. No interviews and the ad copy were basically the same.

"Anything before 1985 is probably in the second storage room," said Mallory.

"Please don't say on Microfiche," I said.

"Sorry."

Dammit.

I winced. "Is it better organized now?"

"By organized do you mean in piles on the floor?" Tank asked.

"Why is this my life?"

"The eternal question," said Mallory.

The outside door opened and Aaron came in, loaded down with two boxes and bags emblazoned with St. Sebastian Family Market.

"When did you leave?" I asked.

"I left."

"That's been established."

"Table."

Tank and Rocco found another eight-foot table and set it up as directed next to a bank of outlets.

"You hungry?" Aaron asked. "I'm making Mallory's Italian beef dogs."

"Um...I could eat," I said.

Nothing.

"I'm starving."

The little guy turned around and started unpacking. There was a meat grinder.

"So about that microfiche?" I asked.

"Yeah...about that," said Tank.

"What?"

"That area's not part of accounting."

"Super. Let's go."

Tank and Mallory stood there and their mouths sort of twisted to the right.

"Oh," I said. "Fine. Who's in there? The ghost of a fired cobbler?"

"It's more like a what," said Mallory.

I tried to think of something totally off the wall. "A floating severed ear?"

"Not bad," said Tank. "But that's at The Landing Bar and Grill and it doesn't float. It just kinda lies there."

Rocco made a gagging sound and I said, "Ew. Are you serious?"

"We had a town drunk back in the day. He was in love with a waitress, who he insisted was a prostitute because she brought him beer and he was a big fan of Gauguin. You do the math."

"You mean Van Gogh?" I asked.

"We're talking about the town drunk."

"Oh," I said. "So there's an ear at the bar and there's something else in your storage room?"

"You still want to go?" Tank asked.

No.

"Are you going to do the microfiche?" I asked hopefully.

"We got new machines." He grinned at me. "I'll take one. You can have the other."

I looked at Rocco and he shook his head. "I deal with the living. For the dead, you want my Uncle Tuna."

"Er...priest?" I asked.

"Mortician."

We all waited, but no other information was forthcoming about the mortician named Tuna.

"Alright then," I said. "Mallory?"

"It doesn't like me," she said. "I'll call around and see if anyone remembers that summer as unusual."

Swell.

I would've asked Aaron. I was that desperate, but he was grinding meat and sautéing veggies, so no help there. "Lead on."

Tank led me into the depths of the shoe factory, entering a huge open area with broken down machinery. We skirted the main floor, going all the way around to a rusty door on the other side.

"Couldn't we just cut straight through?" I asked.

"I don't feel like dealing with it." Tank didn't elaborate and I was kinda glad. The ear was enough. "Here we go." He opened the door and a stench rolled out and I mean that. It rolled out like a heavy fog and it was green. I swear to God. Green fog.

"What the crap is that?" I backed up and ran into an iron pillar supporting the roof.

"We're not sure. There was a gas leak in 1912 and it was a bad scene. Lost fifteen workers on the night shift. Or it could be related to a fire in 1949. Lost three in that."

"This place was a death trap," I said.

"Don't get me started on the lost limbs."

"I won't."

Tank waved at the fog, but it didn't move. You could see through it, but it seemed solid. "It's fine. It won't hurt you."

"It doesn't like Mallory," I pointed out.

"Oh, that's not the fog," he said. "Come on. We'll know in a minute."

Tank went and switched on the light. I had no choice but to follow him into a room that could've been easily mistaken for the old Sentinel basement, only without the shelving.

"Wow," I said.

"Remember, we've only been here for a few weeks." He squatted by a stack of microfiche boxes and started going through them. "Come on. I don't want the fog to get worse."

It was pretty bad, but I could see the labels on the boxes. That was the only upside to the situation. We were in there for a half hour before finding the eighties and another fifteen before 1980 was discovered under a pile of debris someone inexplicably brought over from the blown-up basement. I took June and Tank took July and August.

The microfiche movement made me sick as expected, but I hit pay dirt immediately. "Can I print?"

"Sure." He reached out and pressed a couple of keys. "What'd you find?"

"Ads."

"Me, too, and an interview with the parents," he said.

"Really?"

"They sponsored a fair queen contestant and had a prize pig at the Kansas fair. August was a busy month."

"Please print that," I requested.

"I'm printing everything." He grinned at me. "Gotta earn that interview."

I rolled my eyes and we worked our way through the rest of the summer months' papers. There really wasn't a need to go onto October, so we went back to May, April, and March. There was a lot happening in little St. Seb in the spring, but, after we got done, I had a pretty good handle on the situation. The Thooft ads changed between July and August. Whatever happened happened in July. The Thooft Family Farm Queen contestant, Lisa Larrabie, won the big prize in August. There were pictures of the other winners and their sponsors, second, third, and Miss Congeniality, but Queen Lisa stood alone with her fabulous feathered hair and a slightly confused smile on her super shiny lips.

Tank's phone buzzed and he took it off the clip on his belt. "Holt's here and he's alone."

"Are you surprised?"

"I am a bit," he said. "I've asked around. The Thoofts are tight, unusually tight."

"People think they're weird?" I asked.

"They didn't until Anton pitched you into his trunk. Now all bets are off. Every little thing is getting magnified."

I stood up and retrieved a stack of paper from the brand new printer and asked, "Like what?"

"Like how Kimberly and Holt live on the farm instead of having their own land. Kimberly doesn't really do anything with people outside the family. Gregory and Kevin do, but not Kimberly. She and Ann are always together."

"What are people making of that?"

"They don't know. It was accepted before. Good church-going family. No problems, but now they're weird. Irene and Lefty know them. Irene says Ann was stuck to that child like glue."

"Not the boys?"

"No, not the boys, but Irene always thought it was because she was a girl. Favorite child and all that. Now she worries that Ann was afraid for Kimberly to be alone. With what Anton did, maybe he hurt her or something."

I shook my head. "I don't get that vibe at all."

"I hope you're right and we didn't have a pedophile running around Whiskey Ridge."

"Let's see what Holt has to say," I said.

Tank turned off the machines and said, "Success. It likes you."

"And what would've happened if it didn't?"

He hustled out and threw over his shoulder, "A little mild shock."

I chased him around the big floor. "It would've electrocuted me?"

"Just a little. Mallory's fine. I suspect it doesn't like redheads."

"Finally, being a blonde pays off."

Tank snorted. "Like that's the first time. Please, Mercy, give me a break."

"You don't know," I said in a huff.

"Everybody knows."

We went back into the accounting section to the fab smell of frying meat and Holt Stackhouse staring at Aaron like he was an exhibit at the zoo. He was frying flatbread, stuffing more sausages, frying sausages, chopping veggies, frying veggies, and making what looked like his gourmet ketchup all at the same time. There was also a drinks table with punch. In a punchbowl. Who knows where that came from.

"Hi, Holt," I said. "Thanks for coming."

"Did you bring a caterer?"

"I didn't bring him. He just came."

With that, Aaron trotted over. He gave Holt a plate and instructions on how to properly eat a Mallory Italian beef hotdog with sautéed onions and peppers because there's a wrong way, I guess.

Holt stood there in astonishment. "Should I eat it?"

"I would, unless you want him to bother you senseless."

"Eat it," said Mallory talking with her mouth full and she was not a mouth full kind of girl. "It's amazing."

Rocco didn't say anything. He'd abandoned his knitting to double fist hotdogs. His face was not remotely clean.

Holt took a tentative bite. "Oh, my...wow."

Aaron ran over with a plate for me and I had to taste it in front of him. "Unbelievable, Aaron, really. The best." I felt a whole lot better about almost getting shocked and that green fog. Nothing seems quite so bad when you've got delicious spicy grease running down your arm.

Holt finished his plate in record time and pointed at a stack of albums on the table next to our pseudo timeline. "What are you doing with the ads?"

"We've figured out that something happened with Anton between eighth grade and his freshman year. There weren't any crimes and the family didn't mention anything," I said. "I think whatever that was is connected to why he kidnapped me."

"Why?" he asked.

"It stands out. Anton was one person and suddenly he was another. Very similar to what happened with me. Everyone thought he was great and then he attacked me. Anton wasn't born a murderer. He was made and I think he was made in the summer of 1980."

"So what happened?" Mallory asked.

"Let's see."

I laid out the ad copy from 1980, June, July, and August. In June and July, the ads were for Thooft Family Farm and the ad was a homespun one. A photo of the family, Anthony, Ann, Anthony's parents, Maude and Marvin, and the young boys, Anton, Gregory, and Kevin. It was lovely, a bunch of smiling blonds in front of a barn, wholesome, happy. If I was going to buy half a hog, I'd totally buy it from them.

The ad in August lost all that. The name changed to Heritage Hog Farm, no picture, and a rather cold, businesslike description.

"Why'd they change the name?" I asked.

Holt shook his head. "I didn't know they did. It's always been Heritage or, at least, I thought it was."

I pointed at the picture. "Anything strike you?"

"No, but I've seen this picture a million times. It's in the hallway at the house."

Tank said between mouthfuls of hotdog, "When was it taken? The boys are pretty young."

He was right about that. Ann had Farrah Fawcett hair and the boys wore plaid flared pants. "Has to be earlier. In the mid-seventies maybe."

Mallory leaned over. "Where's Kimberly?"

"She wasn't born yet."

Ding. Ding. Ding.

"When was she born?" I asked, already knowing the answer.

"1980," said Holt slowly. "July seventeenth."

"You shoulda caught that," said Rocco through a mouthful of peppers.

"I did catch it." I pounced on the stack of papers. "Birth announcements. I saw birth announcements."

Mallory and I shuffled through what we had and found six total, two girls and three boys, none were Kimberly.

"We have to look for her announcement," I said.

"Why?" Holt asked. "Kim couldn't have done anything to Anton. She was a newborn, for crying out loud."

"That's it," I said. "It has to be."

Holt looked at me like I had a big loose screw hanging out of the side of my head and said slowly, "It can't be."

"Oh, that's it," said Tank, taking off with a dog in hand. "I'll get that announcement."

"Thank goodness," said Mallory. "I thought he was going to ask me to do it."

"Nobody wants you electrocuted," I said.

"Electrocuted?" Rocco asked.

"Yeah, storage room two zaps me," said Mallory.

"A ghost zaps you?"

"No. Just the room."

Rocco set aside his knitting and cracked his knuckles. "No dead people?"

"Just fog and electrocution," said Mallory.

"I gotta check that out." He took off and Holt watched in confusion.

"Who is that guy?" he asked. "He looks like he should be an extra in *The Godfather*."

"He's my bodyguard's brother," I said, looking through the stack of paper to find the fair sponsor interview.

"The giant girl?"

"The one and only," I said. "Here it is."

The three of us bent over and read the interview with Ann and Anthony on July 1, 1980. It was pretty average when I compared it to the other interviews on the page. All the queen contestant sponsors did an interview on who they were, why they sponsored, and who they chose. Ann and Anthony owned Thooft Family Farm, specializing in hogs, and had sponsored contestants since the very first queen contest. They were expecting their fourth child, a girl, and very much hoped she would be healthy and happy. A girl was very important for the Thoofts, much as it was for Fats. The accompanying picture showed a very pregnant Ann and joyful Anthony with their contestant Lisa in front of the farm's sign.

"Does the family still do the queen thing?" I asked Holt.

"No." Holt had read the article and gotten quiet.

Mallory put a gentle hand on his arm. "What? Did you think of something?"

"No, not really," he said. "It's just that I suggested sponsoring and I was shot down pretty hard."

"Who shot you down?" I asked.

"I almost said the whole family, but now that I think about it..."

"Mainly Ann?"

"And Anton," he said. "It was at Christmas a few years ago. Kim was all for it and I think Kim's brothers liked the idea. Anthony was going to say something, but Ann talked over him about what a lot of trouble it was and Anton said it sexualized women. He thought it was debasing and the fair committee should dump the contest altogether."

"Interesting considering he was supposed to have been on Incel sites and they are all about debasing women," I said.

"We all think that's BS. It wasn't Anton," said Holt. "Maybe the cops planted that stuff."

"I'm looking into it." I turned to Mallory, but she was already calling Tank and asking him to look up the queen sponsors for 1981. I seriously doubted the Thoofts sponsored again, but it was good to double check.

Holt pulled up a chair and accepted a cup of punch from Aaron, who didn't spike it but should have. Holt needed a shot of something. The earth was moving beneath his feet and we still didn't know why.

"This is crazy. Kim was born and they didn't sponsor fair queens again. What in the world would those two things have to do with each other?"

I found the photo spread of Queen Lisa Larrabie standing alone and handed it to him. "Check that out."

Holt tossed the photo back on the table. "She's pretty. So what?"

I gave him the spread again. "The other sponsors took photos with their winners. The runners-up and Miss Congeniality." I pointed at Mallory.

"On it," she said.

"What?" Holt asked.

"Me again," said Mallory into her phone. "Can you check and see if the Thoofts had any other fair queen winners before 1980?"

She told him where she thought the early seventies microfiche boxes were and I grabbed some paper, writing, "Kimberly born July 17, 1980" in big black letters.

"I don't get it," said Holt. "I just don't."

"Where was Kimberly born?" I asked.

"Same as everyone else. Right here in St. Seb at the hospital."

"She was okay?"

"Sure," he said. "Doesn't she seem okay?"

I softened my tone. This was hard and it was going to get harder. That much I knew. "She seems great. I liked her immediately and that's saying something considering what her brother put me through."

Holt blinked rapidly. "She was so relieved. She thought you'd yell or blame her, but you didn't. You were kind. I'm grateful for that. You didn't have to be."

"It's not her fault. It was Anton's, although I'm starting to question that," I said and Holt looked startled. "He did it. I don't mean the facts are changing, but the circumstances might be."

"Because of Kim?"

"Yes. Were there any stories about her birth?"

"Like what?" he asked.

"Complications maybe. Was Kimberly premature? Or did Ann have a hard time with healing?"

"She was a preemie," said Holt, "but she was fine."

"How early?" Mallory asked.

"Two weeks. Ann doesn't like to talk about it."

Mallory and I exchanged a look. One thing moms like to do is tell their birth stories, easy, hard, terrifying, they can't wait to share. Sometimes they overshare. Moms were always trying to convince me I should have lots and lots of babies. I get hung up on the "lots" part and when they see I'm not convinced they think it's about birth and proceed to tell me their story. If I had to hear one more "I pooped on the table story" I'd seriously consider getting my tubes tied.

"Why not?" Mallory asked. "Having my kids were the best days of my life."

"I think because Kim was so small. Ann was thrilled to have a girl, but she was terrified of losing her."

So small?

"Two weeks isn't that early," I said. "Thirty-eight weeks isn't even considered preterm. How big was she?"

"I don't remember," said Holt. "Anthony talks about how Kim could fit in the palm of his hand."

Mallory looked at me, her freckled forehead wrinkling. "That doesn't sound like thirty-eight weeks."

"No, it doesn't," I said, but I wasn't willing to say what I really thought with Holt sitting there hanging onto the arms of his chair like he might float off it, "but sometimes they get the due date wrong. Women often don't know when they conceived and ultrasounds aren't perfect. It depends on who's doing the scan and the equipment."

Holt took a breath. "Oh, right. Of course."

I went over to Aaron to refill my punch and Mallory followed me. "Palm of the hand isn't a couple of weeks off," she whispered.

"No, but there's no use in upsetting him until we know more."

Mallory bit her lip and then said, "You think Ann might've..."

"Fudged the date to match when she should've gotten pregnant?" I shrugged.

"And Anton knew."

It made a bit of sense. Anton knew his sister was his half-sister and the secret changed who he was, but it just didn't feel right. It wasn't enough to put me in that trunk so many years later. Why would it?

"What are you two talking about?" Holt asked with an edge to his voice.

"The albums," I said. "Let's take a look and see how small Kimberly was. Anthony's a big man."

Holt relaxed and said, "Yes, he is. When he was younger, farmers used to ask him to come over to pull a calf. Didn't need a calf puller, just Anthony."

We went back to the table and started going through the albums. Holt had managed to nab six from his in-laws, including one that was from the early eighties. We found the Fourth of July easily enough. There was Ann, pregnant and wearing what I would describe as a flowered tent. Maternity clothes had come a long way, thank goodness. The enormous white sailor collar looked like she thought she needed a bib. Nightmare.

The rest of the family looked happy and normal. Anton was beaming, right out front in every picture he was in, and there were a lot of pictures. The Thoofts had a big party on the farm with fireworks and a suckling pig on a spit. I kept scanning those photos for some hint of something, but I found nothing unusual. Smiling. Burgers. Fireworks. It was every American Fourth, including mine.

"Let's find Kim's birth photos," said Mallory.

I flipped the page and said, "Wait a minute. When was this taken?"

The photo was a typical first day of school shot. The three boys were lined up next to a station wagon with faux wood on the side. The younger ones, Gregory and Kevin, were grinning from ear to ear and holding up brand new lunchboxes with pride, *Dukes of Hazzard* and *Pac-Man*. Anton wasn't smiling. He held a book bag in front of his chest like a shield and stared glumly at the camera.

"Must be first day of school," said Mallory. "We always started the week before Labor Day."

"I'm from St. Clair," said Holt. "We started on the Tuesday after Labor Day."

"That makes more sense. I hated going for three days and then having a three day weekend."

"That would suck. You couldn't take a long trip or anything," said Holt.

"We went camping, but for only two days."

"What's the point? You get there, set up, and then have to break down again."

Mallory put her hands on her hips. "I know, right?"

I waved a hand between them. "Focus, people."

"We're focused," said Mallory with an adorable pout.

"Oh, really? Where's Kimberly?" I asked. "They had a baby and no pictures?"

"Right," said Holt. "That pisses Kim off something fierce. Fourth kid. There's almost no photos of her."

"No hospital picture?" Mallory asked.

"Oh, yeah, but it's up on the wall at the house."

I need to see that picture.

I turned the page again and there Kimberly was swaddled on Anthony's lap at another barbecue, asleep and sucking on a pacifier. After that shot, there were more, mostly of Anton holding Kimberly, but there weren't a lot.

"You'd think with the only girl there'd be a ton of pictures," I said.

"Well, they had four kids and a farm," said Holt. "They were pretty busy. Gregory and Heather have hardly any of their second and third."

"They managed to go to Kansas for a pig contest." I held up the pig article. "You'd think they could take a picture of Kimberly."

"That's business," said Mallory. "Farmers have to prioritize and Holt's right. You take less pictures the more kids you have."

I put the pig winner with the fair queen stuff and went through the albums, noting all the kid pictures. They were right. Anton got a ridiculous amount of photos. Four whole pages were dedicated to his first birthday. Gregory got two. Kevin got one page and poor Kimberly got five pictures total. She was adorable, dressed up in a frilly dress and bonnet, grinning toothless at the camera. Kimberly looked normal although on the small side. She was standing in one picture, clinging to Ann's leg for support and smiling up at her mother. Ann was tenderly touching her head and it was the sweetest photo.

Did it make sense? Maybe I wasn't a good judge. I was an only child. Mom documented me like I might need an alibi later. Everything was labeled and preserved for the future generations I was supposed to provide.

I went back to that first picture of Kimberly with Anthony and popped the photo out of its black triangle holders. The back was annotated. "Anthony and Kimmy Labor Day 1980."

Labor Day.

"She was six weeks old here," I said with a glance at Mallory who attempted to look guileless but she knew. That was one small baby girl. I wondered what was going on in late 1979, because Kimberly wasn't thirty-eight weeks. She couldn't have been. I turned to Anton's photos, since there were so many. "Here's Anton at six weeks."

"What a porker," laughed Holt, missing the point entirely.

"Those boys were big and fat," said Mallory.

And full term.

"I love a fat baby." I checked the other two boys and they were also porkers. Anton, who was also born in the summer spent a lot of time in only his diaper, so we got a good view of his plump arms and rounded belly on his first Labor Day. Whereas Kimberly was bundled up in what looked like two receiving blankets.

"Our boys were fat ones, too," said Holt. "They could not stop eating. They'd squawk if you slowed down the food."

"Who was a fat kid?" Tank asked as he and Rocco came in. Aaron raised his hand and then ate his fourth dog. Not a shock there.

"Not me," I said. "Too busy screaming to eat. My dad could only say 'have mercy' hence the name."

They laughed and Rocco said, "Fat boy here, but Mom started me on rice cereal on day three, so it's no wonder."

That prompted a discussion of infant feeding that I had to interrupt, "Did you find it?"

"Yeah, we did. That fog is insane," said Rocco. "There's no source. I looked."

"Of course there's no source," I said. "It's St. Seb. Do you have the birth announcement and whatnot?"

Tank triumphantly slapped a slim sheath of paper down and plucked a single sheet out. "Here you go."

Kimberly's announcement wasn't in the paper until August fifth and it was pretty plain Jane. Proud to announce blah blah blah, but no picture. I went and found the other baby announcements. Four had photos. Two didn't.

"I'm way ahead of you," said Tank and he gave me Anton's, Gregory's, and Kevin's announcements. All three had photos of wrinkly newborns and were in the paper five days after birth.

"Do people usually do photos?" I asked.

"They do now, but back then, I'd say fifty-fifty. But since the Thoofts did it the first three times around, I'd say it's unusual."

Holt was on guard again and said, "They were busy. Four kids and a farm."

Tank started to say something and I gave him a look. He instantly agreed and gave me four other sheets. "The Thoofts had other winners at the fair. Four in the seventies, two queens and two first runners-up."

And they all had pictures in the Sentinel smiling with their sponsors, Ann and Anthony. Holt took the photos and peered at them in consternation. "It is weird that they didn't take a photo with the 1980 winner, but if Kim was more of a preemie than we thought, maybe they weren't up to going. She might've been too delicate to leave."

"That's true," said Mallory, giving Tank her own look. "I wouldn't want to leave a newborn preemie for a picture."

Rocco had gone back to his knitting, but had been waylaid by Aaron, who wanted him to taste test a new sausage, one with a core of onions and peppers. He dutifully tried the dog but kept his eyes on us. Like Fats, he didn't miss much.

"Any other queen contestants after 1980?" I asked.

"Nope. They never participated again."

We looked at Holt and his worried look intensified. "I don't know what to say. Should I ask Ann and Anthony about the fair queens?"

"No," I said. "Don't ask Ann anything. Will Anthony talk to you alone?"

"Sure, but he'll tell Ann. They tell each other everything."

Not everything.

"Alright. Will Gregory and Kevin tell their parents, if you ask them questions?"

Holt laughed. "I doubt it. There's still plenty of push and pull going on with the farm. They don't say much for fear of kicking something up."

"I thought Kevin and Stephanie were pharmacists," said Tank. "They work on the farm?"

"Stephanie doesn't. She's a townie, but Kevin's out a lot, especially during breeding season."

"What about Kimberly?" I asked.

"She'd try to stay quiet but keeping things from her mother isn't her style."

Tank made a face. "I wouldn't like that."

"Kimberly was worth it and I got used to their relationship." He went to his coat on the rack and dug something out of his pocket. "You got a computer I can use?"

Tank took him to one of the reporters' desks and he plugged in a thumb drive.

"We had all the home movies transferred to digital for Ann a couple of years ago." Holt clicked through a couple screens and then selected Kimmy Singing. An eleven-year-old Kimberly filled the screen. She was a pretty child with her dark hair back in a French braid, giggling and then asking, "Are you ready, Anton? I'm not waiting all day." It could've been petulant or whiny, but when Kimberly said it, you smiled.

"Alright, fancy pants," said a deep adult voice and my chest got tight. His voice. Anton's. I'd have known it anywhere. His few words of anger and frustration were imprinted on me forever.

Mallory put an arm around me and squeezed.

Breathe. He can't hurt you. It's over.

Then Kimberly struck a pose and sunk to the floor. What came out of that child was beyond compare. She sang "I Dreamed a Dream" with such beauty and despair tears came to my eyes. Mallory quaked beside me and Rocco came up and whispered, "Wow."

The last note hung in the air with Kimberly's face pained yet wistful as a tear rolled down her cheek. The video cut out and I breathed again.

Ann, how could you?

CHAPTER FOURTEEN

We were silent on the way back to the Central West End. Rocco drove at top speed and I held the albums to my chest. I could still hear Kimberly's voice, sometimes alone, sometimes mixed with Anton's. Watching us watch Kimberly sing got Holt so upset he had to leave, but not before he told me he'd pay me even if Ann got me fired. The way he said it made me worry about what he'd do if she tried it.

I had another thumb drive in my hand that Holt had given me. It had his son Chase on it, singing, as his father put it "his goddamn heart out". He thought, I guess, that I might need inspiration to see this through after I heard Anton's voice. I didn't. Kimberly was enough. I'd watch Chase at some point, but just then I had a party to get to, not to mention a long-delayed mission at my parents' house.

Hawthorne Avenue was quiet when we pulled in a mere hour before show time, but the mansion was hopping. Rocco had to park two houses away behind the glassware guy, wine guy, the caterer, and I don't know who all. Any party at the mansion was a production that included extra security and so much food you'd be lucky if you got out only five pounds heavier.

The second we parked, Aaron was out and gone, jogging down the alley in the direction of Kronos with a pan of Mallory's Italian beef hotdogs which were to be tried out on customers who would be grilled on how much they liked it. I, for one, was running out of adjectives, but Aaron didn't seem to mind.

Pick climbed over the seat and we got out. I was about to close the door until I saw Rocco just sitting in the driver's seat. "Are you coming? It's your Christmas party."

"Yeah, I'm just thinking," he said.

"About Kimberly?"

"About mothers."

I smiled a little. "And brothers, I would think."

"I wouldn't do that to Fats," he said. "I wanted her to succeed."

What about your mother?

I didn't ask the question. I didn't know him well enough.

Rocco turned to me. "Do you think I would?"

"Not for a second. First of all, she'd pound you to dust, and second, you're a good brother," I said.

"You think *he* wasn't a good brother?"

"If I didn't know about her voice and the chance he took from her, I'd say yes, no hesitation."

"Her mother did it, too. She's probably why he did it."

"Probably."

"I feel bad for Kimberly," he said. "Do you think Holt will tell her about what we found out?"

"Yes, but not today," I said. "Come on. You have martinis to drink."

Rocco got out and absentmindedly said, "That's not my drink."

"What is?"

"I like a good Rusty Nail."

Of course, you do.

"I'll stick with red wine," I said, hurrying down the alley between guys carrying racks of stemware and whole legs of prosciutto with Pickpocket desperately trying to leap up and get a taste.

Rocco caught up and helped me pull Pick off a guy carrying a rack of sausages. "You need to branch out. The Girls have a couple of bartenders coming in. I'll get you a Negroni."

"I don't like Campari."

"You haven't had good Campari then," he said hustling me into the garage and yelling at two guys with racks of booze. "Get away from that Maybach. Are you friggin' insane?"

They dashed out into the rose garden ahead of us and I said, "I had it in Florence and I don't like it."

"Florence," he scoffed. "You have to go to Rome for the best Negroni in Italy."

"Have you been to Rome?" I asked.

"Yes, I've been to Rome. I'm Italian."

"So what? My grandad's Irish. He's never been to Ireland."

"Take him. Maybe he'll eat something," said Rocco.

It wasn't the worst idea I'd heard, but I didn't have much time to devote to it. We got into the house and it was insane as all parties were right before liftoff. So many people going so many places. I don't know what they were all doing and I question whether they did either. Rocco was gone with Pickpocket and I was spinning in a circle.

"Mercy!" called out Millicent. "Where have you been?"

I couldn't see her. It sounded like she might be in the dining room, but I didn't find her there. Circling around, I finally located both of The Girls directing traffic at the front door. They were dressed in winter white and were incredibly elegant. I suddenly felt grubby and underdressed, which I certainly was.

They kissed my cheeks anyway, flushed with excitement.

"I think this will be the best party yet," said Myrtle. She said that every year and she was always right.

"It will."

"Can you check the cheese?" Millicent asked. "I question our pairing of the Rogue Blue. Poor Fats couldn't help. She got so sick."

"The brie is much looser than we expected," said Myrtle.

"The Manchego is a bit on the tangy side, too."

I nodded and assured them that I would check the cheese. As I went back into the fray, Millicent called out, "Don't forget to change, dear!"

Into a pumpkin.

I always felt overwhelmed at The Girls' parties. They didn't have many, the Christmas one and the occasional funeral, but they were all out affairs. My family's idea of a party was a potluck and The Girls always came bearing their casseroles and never batting an eye at the lack of crudité or the tubs of beer. It was one of the best things about them. They'd hobnob with Dad's cop friends or Mom's from when she was working at Big Steve's law firm and even though they'd be wearing Dior, nobody had a hint that they were Bleds. They came off as just a couple of lovely old ladies who knew their way around a casserole.

"What in the holy hell is this?" Rocco asked, finding me at the cheese display ten minutes later.

"This is a party," I said.

"And I thought Calpurnia was elaborate. This is over the top. Did you see the champagne?"

"I didn't." I saw the cheese, a whole lot of cheese. "Okay. You're going to help me make sure this is right."

Rocco looked at the spread with his hands in his pockets. "How could it be wrong? Booze. Check. Cheese. Check. Crackers. Check."

"We have to decide if this goes with this." I made him a cracker with the Rogue Blue and a smidge of fig compote. "Eat this and then drink this." I gave him a glass of German Gewurztraminer.

He did as he was instructed and then nodded, but said, "Needs honey."

"Really? Not too sweet?"

He made me a cracker and I tried it. He was right.

"You can be on cheese patrol from now on," I said.

"Oh, no," he said. "That's all you."

Myrtle rushed in past a frantic florist. "Mercy, dear, how is the blue?"

"Excellent." I winked at the chauffeur. "Rocco knows his way around cheese pairing. He should take over—"

She turned Rocco toward the door. "No, no, dear, Rocco is a guest. He'll go change and relax. You finish the cheese. Do check the brie with the pear. I'm just not sure."

I'm sure I don't want to.

"I will, Myrtle," I said. "It'll be perfect."

She bustled off and tossed over her shoulder. "Come along, Rocco. You're a guest."

He smirked at me. "Sucks to be you."

"Most days."

"Bullshit. I don't envy that rash, but being you is pretty rocking."

I touched my chin. Still bumpy. "It's better."

"Better than Impetigo."

"I hope Fats does kill you and hides the body. I'll even help."

He laughed. "I grew up with Princess Porks-alot. I don't respond to threats."

"I'm good with a weapon."

"I'm better," he said. "I'll tell you what. I'll try the brie as a gesture of good will."

I eyed him with suspicion. "What's the catch?"

"No catch. I like brie."

"Well, I hate it, so go crazy."

Rocco tried the brie, gave the pairing a thumbs-up, and went up to his room in the attic servants' quarters. Myrtle and Millicent had persuaded him to live-in and he'd made a nest, like a rat as Fats described it, but The Girls were very happy to have a man about the house twenty-four-seven.

I went on to try a few other pairings. I'd like to say I made adjustments. I didn't. Cheese, wine, fruit, whatever. It all tasted fine to me. Plus, I got a little tipsy from the alcohol. I have no tolerance and now I wanted a nap.

But there was no nap in my future. I ran around, directing this and moving that. And then, like magic, the house cleared. It happened every year, but it always astonished me. One minute a madhouse and the next quiet and calm. Well, the house was calm. I was not, but, at least, Chuck answered on the first ring when I called him.

"Chuck Watts, where are you?" I demanded as I raced up the stairs. "It's twenty to seven."

"I know what time it is," he said loudly over the noise of a crowded bar.

"How long will it take you to get here?"

"Where?"

"Here. The house," I said, dashing into my room and scaring the holy crap out of the poodle and cat curled up on my pillows. Skanky arched up and hissed and Pickpocket yipped and ran over to gnaw on my leg.

"No, stop it." I pried the poodle off my leg.

"What happened?" Chuck asked.

"Your dog uses me as a chew toy. How long?"

"For what?"

"To. Get. Here."

I stripped in the closet and then ran into the bathroom to turn on the shower. That funky fog left a hint of something on me and I smelled like a combo of burning rubber and corpse.

"Do you need something?" he asked.

"You." I looked in the mirror. Was I a tiny bit green?

"Isn't that staff party tonight?"

"Exactly. Hurry up."

"Let me step outside," he said. "I'm with the guys at a brewpub."

I checked the water. Boiling. "You're supposed to be here."

"I'm not an employee."

Is this hard and I don't know?

"You're my person," I said.

"Yes, I am. Are you coming down? The guys would love to see you. That stuff on your face is a lot better."

Thanks for reminding me.

"We're hosting."

"Who is?" he asked.

"We are."

He went quiet for a minute. "You and me?"

"Yes, for crying out loud, and it starts in fifteen minutes."

"I don't understand why I have to be there. Hell, why do you?"

I tucked my hair up in a towel and stuck a foot in the shower. "I do this every year."

"But why?" he asked.

"Because I do. The Girls will be upset if you're not here. You're part of me now. We're going to live together in the stable that they're renovating to the tune of God knows what."

"What do I wear?"

"Do that sport coat and vest. Hurry, please!" I hung up and jumped in the shower, almost falling and killing myself.

Five minutes later, I was out and discernibly hot pink, not green. I slapped on some makeup that would make Fats sad in both its application and palette and ran back in the closet to dig around. There had to be something in the range of this-is-special-but-nobody's-getting-married. In the back, I found a dress that wasn't mine, but had my mother written all over it. A forties-style dress, dark green with a keyhole and a high waist. It emphasized the chest, but nothing to be done about that. I pinned back my hair into a kind of forties roll and found some shoes that sort of matched before I gave Pickpocket a quick brushing.

"Ready?" I asked the poodle.

Bark.

I pointed at Skanky. "You stay here."

The cat stuck a hind leg in the air and cleaned his butt. He wasn't going anywhere.

I dashed out with Pick, locked the door in case anyone got nosy, and ran down the stairs, not as my mother had taught me with grace and a cool demeanor. Think lumberjack in heels.

I got to the front door as The Girls converged with two waiters carrying champagne flutes to greet the first guests. Undoubtedly, the first tram would be driving up the avenue at that very moment, bringing people from a nearby parking lot because everyone on Hawthorne Avenue would freak if we filled the street with Camrys or, gasp, Fords.

"You look just like Betty Grable," said Millicent.

"That's a nice change," I said.

"Lovely dress," said Myrtle. "Carolina's, I believe."

"It is." *Please don't ask about Chuck.*

"Where's Chuck?" Millicent asked.

Dammit!

"He got hung up, but he's on his way."

"Dear boy, he works so hard."

I gritted my teeth and nodded.

There was a slam and pounding that echoed through the house.

Chuck raced into the hall sliding on a rug with his tie askew. "I'm here. I made it."

"You did," said Millicent, pleased as punch even though he was red-faced and sweaty. She and Myrtle fixed his tie, straightened his jacket, and dabbed at his forehead with a handkerchief. Then they put him next to me and Pick before assuming their spots.

"What are we doing?" he whispered.

"The receiving line," I said.

"What do I say?"

"The usual stuff."

"Er...what's that?" Chuck asked.

Hopeless.

"Merry Christmas. Welcome. Have a lovely time."

"Men don't say lovely."

I rolled my eyes. "Whatever."

"They don't know who I am and they'll think I'm weird."

"First of all, you are weird and second, they know who you are," I hissed. "Smile. Tonight you're a Bled."

He bent over to me. "You're one every night."

I elbowed him as the doorbell rang. Millicent opened the door and the surge began. We welcomed every personal staff member of the Bled family from maids to accountants to Dr. Fisher who did the art restoration. And when I say every Bled staff member, I mean it. The staff from Prie Dieu came. The cousins' maids. Veronique's personal trainer. Everybody and that included my parents. Dad was The Girls security consultant and he handled it for the entire family. Uncle Morty was always invited, but he never came since he thought The Girls were creepy old bats and they weren't crazy about him either. Tiny came with Fats, since he also handled security and was their chauffeur for a time. He looked fantastic in a natty black suit with a silver vest and Fats was wearing black spandex and a white fur bolero jacket. She looked surprisingly formal, but maybe that was just because I was used to the neon cheetah prints.

It took forty-five minutes for every guest and their family to arrive. When the door closed, the real work began. The Girls nodded at me and went off to begin the mingling and making people happy. The mingling was hard, at least for me, the happy was a cinch. If you got to come to that party, you were flipping happy. The absolute best of everything for five hours.

Chuck went over to sag against the newel post. "What now? I'm exhausted."

"Mix and mingle," I said, waving to one of the kids who was peeking at me from behind a potted palm.

"By that, do you mean nap?"

"I do not." I took his arm. "Let's do this thing."

"Something smells good."

"It'll be totally worth it."

It was worth it. I fed him award-winning cheese and booze. We had Brazilian barbecue and to his surprise everyone knew him. He got into intense discussions with people about my truck's restoration at Egon's Cherry Pit. He talked poodles, weather, my misadventures, serial killers, and a host of other things.

At some point we got separated and I found Fats, who was rocking it and only intermittently ill. Several people asked her about her mother being excited about being a grandmother. Everyone in that crowd thought a baby was the best of news. Fats' face hinted at something else. I helped her steer the conversation into safe waters but wondered why. Presumably, my parents would be thrilled if I had a baby. Mom often said, "when you have my grand babies..." Dad never said anything to that, but he would get a calculating look. I couldn't tell if it was over how long I wouldn't be able to work for him while on maternity leave or at what age he could enlist my kid in tailing suspects. Probably both. But they'd be happy. I felt safe in that assumption, but I was guessing Fats' parents weren't. Rocco was. He was currently in the library, knitting pink booties and discussing yarn with a couple of elderly cooks who also brought their needles.

Curious and on a mission, I excused myself and went in search of Chuck and Tiny. They were nowhere to be found. I started getting a little worried that they'd bolted when I went in the kitchen and happened to catch voices in the pantry.

I whipped open the door and found them sitting on the floor with plates of meat in their laps. "What are you doing?" I asked.

"Eating," said Chuck, his blue eyes trying to be guileless but failing miserably.

"In the pantry. On the floor."

"Baby, I needed a break."

Tiny nodded. "Me, too. That's a lot of people and they're so happy for me. They all want to tell me about babies. I'm starting to get freaked out. Did you know that women in labor"—he lowered his voice—"sometimes poop?"

"I did know that," I said.

He drew back and a flush came over his brown cheeks. "So it's true."

"It's true."

"I didn't need to know that. I'd rather be surprised."

Chuck was so horrified that a piece of steak fell out of his mouth. Attractive. "That's going to...you're going to..."

"No," I said. "There are techniques to employ during labor."

It was the stupidest lie, but they totally bought it. Now Tiny would be surprised. My gift to him.

"Thank God," said Chuck.

"You said it," said Tiny. "I do not want to deal with my Fats if that happens. She will not like it."

She won't care.

"Speaking of Fats, what is up with her mother?" I asked.

Tiny's flush got a lot redder. "What do you mean?"

"That's what I mean. What's up?"

"Is she sick again?" He got to his feet, so tall his head nearly brushed the low ceiling.

"Not at the moment," I said and I told him about the hints I was picking up from Fats and Rocco. "Is she unhappy about the baby?"

"Not unhappy exactly," said Tiny. "She's just...her."

"And what's that?"

He was cagey and said, "You know."

"I don't. That's the point. Everyone wants me to get Fats meds. She's acting super weird about it and Rocco says their mom isn't going to help. I need her help. She's the grandmother."

"Fats didn't tell you?" Tiny asked. "You're her maid of honor."

"We have an unconventional friendship."

The big man grimaced. "I don't want to tell you. Fats, she's a little off her nut right now. She's so sick and pretending she's not."

"She's not pretending all that well. Everyone knows," I said.

My cousin gave me a look and I knew that I didn't know.

"How bad is it?"

Tiny told me that Fats had taken to sleeping upright since lying down made her throw up. She hardly slept. Calpurnia was on the verge of sacking her, but Fats wouldn't budge on the med question. She'd passed out a couple of times and had sworn him to secrecy.

I smacked his arm so hard I think they heard it in the library. "Are you crazy? You have to tell her doctor."

"I tried. She's out of her mind. She's locked me out of the office and she had her Python."

"Is there such a thing as prepartum psychosis?" Chuck asked.

"No." I smacked Tiny again. "Tell me what's going on."

He told me and I wasn't happy. Fats' mom was an addict. She'd been addicted to something in some manner or other their entire lives. Fats would never touch any medication, alcohol, or street drug for fear of going down that road.

"If she's that aware, she wouldn't have an issue," I said. "The nausea drugs aren't addictive anyway."

"I know. She's so afraid she'll do to our kid what her mom did to her and Rocco. She wants to be a great mother."

"There's no reason to think she won't be. The food thing is a little crazy though."

Tiny swallowed. "She's just like her mom and she knows it. The food. The exercise. That's her drug. Mercy, you have to do something. I can't get through."

"I will."

"Thank God," he said. "This thing with her mother..."

"She's not her mother," I said. "I'm not mine and look at me."

"Have you seen Gloria?"

"No."

Tiny got out his phone and opened an album. "This is Gloria. Tell me that's not a sign."

"Whoa," said Chuck.

Whoa didn't cover it. I looked like my mother to an unnatural degree, but Fats and her mother, it was just weird. They had the same size and shape, but Fats was a larger version of Gloria.

I took the phone and scrolled through Fats' life. It was much as I expected, a whole lot of gyms and no friends. But it was her mother that caught my eye, specifically a family photo from when Fats was about fourteen. Gloria and Fats both had red hair. Fats went with copper and Gloria a little darker. I thought they were carbon copies until that picture. With the red hair, I could see her father in her. She and Rocco both had his skin tone and eyes.

"What's wrong?" Chuck asked.

"I don't know. Something about them. Their faces. She and Rocco. They look more alike than I thought."

"They're striking," said Tiny. "Tony gave her those eyes, but most of her comes from Gloria and that scares Fats to death."

"I get that," I said, staring at the photo. "I've never been able to measure up to my mom."

Tiny squeezed over to me and put a big arm over my shoulders. "You measure up. You're just different than Carolina and she doesn't care what you do, not really. Now Gloria, she cares."

"That Fats isn't like her? She's pretty like her," said Chuck.

"That she's better," said Tiny. "Fats did everything Gloria couldn't. She's jealous."

The pantry door opened and Millicent looked in. "Someone's lost the plot, I see."

We stared at her and I admit I had a moment of intense worry, thinking she'd had a stroke, but she squeezed in the pantry with us and smiled.

"It's like our playhouse when we were young. We'd stuff ourselves in with Patrick and Maggie." Her eyes got moist, but the tears stayed where she wanted them. "Hardly an inch to spare, but we didn't care."

"The playhouse up in storage?" I asked.

"The very one. Rocco's going to repair it for the baby." She patted Tiny's enormous forearm. "For when she comes to visit."

Then Tiny's eyes got moist. "She'll love it."

"I do hope so," said Millicent. "Did you catch my use of slang? Wilfred taught me."

"Who?" Chuck asked.

"Wilfred Wallingford, dear. The architectural historian. Lovely man. He's teaching me some British slang like 'lost the plot' for when someone gets confused or forgets what they're supposed to be doing."

The three of us said in chorus, "Oh."

"You've got things to do or have you given up?" she asked.

"The boys were having a break. We'll come right back out."

"You *have* lost the plot." She smiled happily. "What are you supposed to be doing?"

"Er..."

"Your parents are singing carols, Mercy. They won't be home for hours."

Crap on a cracker!

"How do we get out?" I asked.

"Out?" Tiny asked. "You're not leaving."

Millicent opened the pantry door and said, "They most certainly are."

"But—"

She took his hand and led him away saying, "They'll be back. Just a little errand for me."

Tiny glanced over his shoulder at us, but he kept on walking. That was the power of The Girls. You often found yourself doing things that you hadn't intended to do. They were so lovely and generous it was impossible to say no.

"Back door?" Chuck asked.

We weaved our way through the kitchen and the morning room, but the back door had a steady stream of people going in and out to a marquee set up in the garden with fires in little braziers and cozy chairs with furry lap blankets. If we went out the back, we'd be noticed in a big way.

"Conservatory." I took his hand and we went through the house, smiling and chatting. *Not up to anything. Not leaving.*

The right conservatory had plenty of people in it, too, due to the surprising addition of a badminton court. The potted palms, banana trees, ferns, and flowers had been moved to make way. Rocco was in an intense match with Cornelius Bled's chef, Avril, and they had quite a crowd cheering for them. Rocco never looked more like Fats. He was an animal with blood running down his legs from diving for the save and that intensity? I knew that look. Avril had no hope.

We got around the crowd and found the side access door, the one my father considered a problematic entry point, because it was original to the house and The Girls would not allow him to replace it with something more secure. It was wired up. Chuck and I had to put in five codes to get it to open. If you wanted to break in, it would be a lot easier just to go through the glass.

Chuck put all the codes back in when we got outside and the light went back to blinking red.

"Everything has to be difficult," I said with a shiver.

"We should've gotten you a coat," said Chuck, taking off his jacket for me.

"That wouldn't have been suspicious at all."

He turned up the collar on his jacket and kissed me. "We're going to get in that liquor cabinet tonight."

I smiled, but I didn't feel good about it. I didn't feel good at all.

We stopped short at the side of the conservatory and stared up in awe. A series of fireworks went off over our heads in a dazzling display of Christmas colors.

"Is that new?" Chuck asked.

"It's not us." I pointed across the street. The Klemps' front yard was full of people cheering at the sky. Cars lined the avenue and children ran by with sparklers, screeching with delight. Music blared out of the front foyer of the enormous Queen Anne Victorian that managed to match the Bled Mansion in size, if not in style.

"Is that allowed?"

"Are you kidding?" I asked as we dashed around to the front gate. "The avenue was mad at all the emergency vehicles and crime scene tape after my mom's attack. This is a declaration of war."

"Who are they?" Chuck held the gate open for me and was nearly run over by a kid pulling a sled.

"I haven't met them yet, but Rocco says they have six kids and a distillery in the formal dining room," I said.

"Check out Mrs. Haas," whispered Chuck as we crossed the street.

The Girls' next door neighbor was standing in her front door, arms crossed, scowling, and, unless I miss my guess, plotting. She didn't like The Girls having parties and they were quiet, silent in comparison to the ruckus the Klemps wrought. If she found out about the distillery, she might have a conniption.

"I think I'm going to like them," said Chuck.

"Rocco does."

Chuck took my hand and we hurried past the main crowd. I saw things I never expected to see on the avenue. Mrs. Haas wasn't alone in her displeasure. A few mansions had angry occupants glaring out of their windows and a couple took it a step further. The McCallisters and the Rosecrans had deployed and armed their butlers. The super snotty Palfry, who I'd still like to beat to a pulp after what he said about my family, stood out front with a pistol held awkwardly in his pudgy palms and Loftis was across the street, peeking out from behind the Rosecrans' gate, with a handgun he clearly had never held before in his life. I think he pointed it at his own head at one point. That was totally going to end well.

I squeezed Chuck's arm. "Did you see—"

He yanked me out of the way when a car suddenly backed up. Several people were trying to turn around and got pinned between parked cars and each other. More fireworks went off in a colorful barrage overhead. Kids were directing traffic and we were just trying to get to my parents' house without getting hit by a bottle rocket. It wasn't looking good.

Our end of the avenue was completely parked up, too. I mean bumper to bumper. Chuck and I couldn't find a way between cars. It was that tight.

A boy about fourteen emerged from a truck bed and yelled, "I found a bat!"

The kid struck a batter's pose and the snowballs started flying. We ducked as he took out two in a row. Chuck grinned. "Let's play."

"You play. I'm wearing stilettos." I turned sideways between two vans.

"Chuck Watts!" yelled a man in front of our neighbor Sandy's house. "How's it hanging?"

"Terry! I heard you retired!" Chuck went to Terry, a retired firefighter who was dating Sandy. It was an interesting match and one that nobody saw coming. She was a solitary artist and I'd thought she might be gay until Terry started barbecuing in her backyard. They met at the time of Mom's attack and it was instant love. Dad was campaigning for Terry to move in so he could have a regular guy in the neighborhood instead of hedge fund managers, trust fund layabouts, and, of course, lawyers, but from the look of the Klemp mansion there was a dude in residence already. I spotted some kegs on the porch.

Terry lifted an overflowing mug and yelled, "The neighborhood finally got fun! Come on over! I've got the whole crew here!"

"The *whole* crew?" yelled Chuck.

"Fireball!"

Chuck pounded a fist. Fireball was a game invented to maim the players. You drank Fireball whiskey and played darts with a moving target.

"I'm going in," I said.

"Be right there."

"If you get another dart in the hand, don't come crying to me."

Chuck saluted and ran up the walk to the cheering firefighters. So much for the liquor cabinet. It was times like that that made me wonder if my guy might have a touch of ADD.

I hurried down the sidewalk past a van and another fireworks display went off overhead. The kid with the bat ran past me, being chased by another kid wearing a Santa hat. He had a Roman candle and was trying to hit bat boy with the blasts coming out of the end. Complete insanity. I pulled out my phone and dialed 911, before taking off running to get out of the way and then Santa hat was on our lawn screaming. The Roman candle kept firing, hitting a car and setting off the alarm which seemed to trigger a cascade effect. Alarms went off up and down the entire street. I kicked off my heels and dashed to the boy, who was screaming. The Roman candle kept firing in the snow next to him. I grabbed it and jammed it into the snow, pointing it toward our alley.

"My leg! My leg!" he screamed, clutching his right thigh. There was blood everywhere and other people screaming. I took off Chuck's jacket and pressed it to the boy's leg. Someone staggered onto our lawn screeching and clutching their head.

"Chuck!" I screamed and he was there. Terry and his crew were right behind. The person with the head injury ran past me and Terry chased them.

The boy with the bat dropped down next to me. "What happened?"

"I don't know." I grabbed my phone from where I'd dropped it and yelled, "Multiple injuries on Hawthorne Avenue in the Central West End. Fireworks."

"Mercy?" said the dispatcher.

I recognized the voice. "Yeah, but I didn't do it."

"What happened?"

"Fireworks. Uncontrolled."

"Oh! I'm sending units. How many injuries?"

"Two so far. One head injury and a white male about fourteen with a leg injury. Considerable bleeding."

"Two units en route."

"The street is blocked with cars. They'll have access on foot." I gave her my parents' address and said I didn't know where the other victim went. Then Chuck was there.

"Son of a bitch," he said, taking the phone from me. "That went south with a quickness."

Thankfully, the car alarms got shut off as Chuck updated the dispatcher and I ripped open the boy's jeans. He had a three-inch laceration on his thigh. No major vessels were hit, but the bleeding was tremendous. I put compression back on the wound.

"That's not from fireworks," said Chuck.

"No," I said.

He walked away so the boy couldn't hear him, which was a good thing since the kid was not exactly stoic.

"I'm going to die," he wailed.

"You're not dying," I said.

His friend, if you want to call him that, got out his phone and started taking video. "I'm going to do a TikTok."

The victim stopped wailing and said, "Get the boobs."

I slapped down the phone, but it was back up and recording a second later. Good reflexes. One of the firefighters ran over and grabbed it, calling the kid a creep and setting off a tirade of recriminations about rights and the constitution. I grabbed the little twerp by the coat and yelled in his face. "You do not have the right to video my breasts during an emergency!"

He went pale and the crazed look vanished from his eyes. "Shit! I'm sorry. I was just..."

"Never mind that," I said. "Did you see what happened?"

He shook his head. "Tyler was chasing me and when I looked back, he was on the ground. What happened?"

"I don't know." That's what I said, but I did know. Tyler had a gunshot wound. A .22 by the look of it. "Give me your hand."

The boy drew back. "Why?"

"I want you to put pressure on Tyler's wound."

"You do it."

"I need to check out the other injuries," I said.

He bit his lip and shook his head.

"You suck, man," said Tyler and I concurred.

Chuck came back over. "They're apprised of the situation."

"Check out Palfry at the McCallisters and Loftis at the Rosecrans," I told him.

"Yeah?"

I nodded and gave him a look.

"I'm on it." Chuck took off and then came back to ask, "You okay here?"

I said I was, although I was using okay very loosely, since I was flipping frozen and my knees had dug into the snow and what I could feel wasn't remotely pleasant.

But it didn't matter, thirty seconds later, the EMTs arrived. A guy hauled me out of the way since my legs weren't cooperating and then Mom was there, hugging me and putting a blanket around my shoulders.

"What in the world?" she yelled as the car alarms started going off one by one again.

"Complete madness," I yelled back. I didn't have to, but somehow I couldn't stop yelling.

More fireworks went off overhead and people ran around shutting down their car alarms again. My dad came through the chaos and ambled up, cool and calm as could be. "Situation's under control." He eyed me. "What are you doing out here?"

Mom clutched me tighter. She knew exactly why I was there.

"I—"

"She was getting my pills," said Mom stoutly. Now my mother is not a born liar. It's hard for her and she hates doing it, but I have to say she totally pulled it off. My dad, the human BS detector, totally bought it.

"I told you to take them," he said.

"Yes, I know, but I got distracted." Mom looked down as if she was embarrassed.

"You need an alarm on your phone or something."

She nodded emphatically. "I'll do that. It's a good idea."

The EMTs loaded the once again wailing Tyler onto a gurney and rolled him off the lawn. We looked down at the blood and then back at the avenue. There was car damage, kids wailing, cops, EMTs treating multiple injuries, firefighters putting out a fire in a trash can, and sirens, so many sirens, surrounding us on the other swanky Central West End streets.

I started smiling. I couldn't help it.

"Mercy," Mom scolded me. "This isn't funny."

"But it's worse than anything we ever did."

Mom bent her head to mine and I know she was smiling.

Merry Christmas, Hawthorne Avenue.

CHAPTER FIFTEEN

We didn't get to bed until four in the morning. Four. It took that long for all the witness interviews to be done and the street to be cleared so the trams could get back in to retrieve The Girls' guests. The hospital confirmed that Santa hat had been shot and he wasn't the only one. Palfry panicked and fired warning shots that were less of a warning and more of an assault with a deadly weapon. It was just dumb luck that he only hit two partiers and neither were seriously injured. He said he didn't hit the boy, but I'm not sure if he'd know that for a fact. Loftis admitted to firing his weapon but didn't think he hit anyone until the enraged firefighter he winged limped up and punched him in the nose.

Considering the night's insane events, I have to say everyone took it well, except for me perhaps. I had road rash on my knees from kneeling on the icy snow and it suggested things that I'd rather not have suggested. And people could not stop suggesting it. Everyone thought it was hilarious. And, yes, I changed out of my dress into knee-concealing sweats, but the damage was done. There were photos and bat boy did manage to get enough footage of my chest that I was once again trending on Twitter.

Mickey Stix called at three and wanted me in that dress for the next DBD album cover. The angle in the photo made me look...unnatural, and he was all about it. On the upside, I used the dress as a bargaining chip to get Dr. Halifax the swag she wanted for keeping my turtle transgression under wraps. Mickey agreed to send everything she wanted and then some. It meant I'd be on the next cover, but I'd pretty much accepted that already. Mickey's daughter, Peek-a-boo, was upset that we hadn't gone to Greece and he was sort of blackmailing me over it. I wasn't against going to Greece, but things happened. Things were constantly happening. Waking up that morning to Chuck's tremendous snoring and gas was a case in point. I needed sleep, but it wasn't happening next to the smelly grizzly bear with congestion, so I rolled out of bed at seven-thirty, threw on a robe, and hobbled down the stairs on my sore knees, not expecting anyone else to be conscious.

I was right, but someone was up. Sort of. Rocco was conked out in the kitchen on Lester's chair, fully clothed and drooling. He had on clean clothes, so he'd gone to bed. I couldn't imagine why he'd be up. The Girls weren't going anywhere. They'd stay in bed until the afternoon.

I tiptoed across the kitchen and turned on the espresso maker. If I couldn't sleep I had to be caffeinated. There was a job to be done and I was a Watts. We did not kick up our heels, even on Sundays, as Dad reminded me on his way out.

The case. I'd dreamt about it. Disjointed dreams with faces appearing and disappearing. Kimberly singing. Anton coming at me. Baby pictures. Green fog. Dad lecturing. Ann frowning.

I pushed the button for a latte, holding my breath as the beans were ground and tamped down. Rocco was still dead to the world and I went searching for something to eat. The kitchen was a wreck. A contracted cleaning crew would show up at noon so Joy or the maids wouldn't have to do anything, but I wasn't sure I could stand it. I'm no neat freak but seeing the counters would be nice.

My latte finished and I found some bread to gnaw on. Normally, there would be lots of food left over, but since everyone stayed hours longer than expected I was lucky to find a crust.

I was considering calling Aaron and begging for sustenance when Rocco said, "Where'd you find that?"

"Under a chafing dish," I said. "Why are you up?"

He yawned and stretched. "It's Sunday."

"Yeah. So?"

"Hello," he said. "Mass at eight."

"Hello," I said. "Mass at five."

Rocco smacked his forehead so hard he fell back in the chair. "I friggin' forgot. Jesus H. Christ. I'm an idiot."

I looked at him piously. "And on a Sunday, too."

"Bite me, blondie." He got up and snatched the bread out of my hand.

"Hey!"

"Whatever." He split it and gave me half before finding The Girls' little Moka pot for a real espresso. "Why are you up?"

"Chuck smells and snores. Plus, I still have a job to do," I said.

"Yeah, I heard your dad. He's not intense at all."

"Speaking of intense, I think Fats was a little better last night."

The kettle started whistling and Rocco assembled the pot mindlessly as he thought about what I said. With the pot on the burner, he turned around and said, "No. She's not."

I raised an eyebrow. "No?"

"She's my sister. I know when she's putting on a show. She felt terrible. I don't think she kept anything down. We have to figure something out."

I thought about what to say and how much. Tiny had told me about their mom, Gloria, but I wasn't sure how that was going to go over with Rocco.

"What?" he asked.

"I'm working on it," I said.

"My mom isn't going to do anything."

"Yeah, I got that." *Here goes.* "Tiny clued me in."

The pot started gurgling and Rocco took it to the sink to run the bottom under cold water. "Did he?"

"I won't mention it to Fats," I said.

He nodded and poured himself a perfect espresso. "This is going to get worse."

"The morning sickness? It might not."

"She's going to have to give birth eventually."

I frowned. The point was eluding me completely. "That's the plan."

"You haven't thought about that?" he asked.

"Er...not really. I'm doing the baby shower, but that's as far ahead as I've gotten."

"What are the chances that she doesn't have a C-section?" Rocco asked, totally astonishing me. Here was a character who looked questionable at best, drinking espresso and thinking not about a future bank heist, but his sister's birth plan.

"I haven't given it an ounce of thought."

"She has and she's freaked," he said. "Tiny was a whopper. Fourteen pounds. His mom had a C-section. So did my mom. Those two didn't exactly get off to a good start."

"That's hardly Fats' fault."

"Tell that to my mother."

I didn't know what to say. When in doubt, pivot. "C-sections aren't that bad these days. Minimal scarring and excellent pain control."

Rocco put his finger on the side of his nose.

"No," I said.

"She's scared to death of taking anything. Didn't Tiny tell you that?"

I pounded my latte and went for another. "She'll have to. It's surgery."

"It's Fats," said Rocco. "*Have to* isn't in her vocabulary."

"Well, maybe it won't happen," I said. "How big was she?"

"Twelve pounds a week early. And we're talking the baby of Fats and Tiny. She's going to be bigger. She has to be."

"Maybe not. How big were you?" I asked.

"Seven and a half."

"There you go."

Rocco stared at me with half-lidded eyes, disappointment radiating off him.

"I know. I know. But the scans will tell us more and we can plan," I said.

"You've noticed planning and Fats work out, have you?"

"No, she just does her thing."

He sighed. "And she's been doing her thing since day one. That comes from being a macro in a world of micros."

"What was it like to be her brother?" I'd been wanting to ask that for a while.

He pulled out his wallet. "I'll show you." He slid out a picture and handed it to me.

"Holy crap!" I looked down at a photo of Fats and Rocco and it was hard to believe what I was seeing.

"I'm two and a half there," he said. "She's six months."

They say a picture says a thousand words and does it ever. The photo he gave me was a studio shot with Rocco and Fats posed together in a typical way. Big brother behind little sister, holding her. That's where the normality ended.

Rocco was a typical two and a half year old. I'd have guessed him at fifty percent on the height and weight charts. Fats, on the other hand, was off the chart. He was holding her, but, at six months, she was bigger than him. The oddest thing was that she wasn't really fat. She was just massive.

"She walked at eight months and beat me up at ten," he said.

"Why?"

"I took her bear. She kept me in a headlock until Dad pried her off me."

I looked back at the picture. Both kids were smiling. There was genuine love in Rocco's eyes. Of course, Fats hadn't beat him up yet.

"You look happy and very cute."

He grinned at me. "We were good looking. Thank God. Can you imagine if Fats had been ugly?"

I shuddered. It would've been bad. "Both your parents are good looking. The odds were in your favor."

"Have you seen Uncle Moe?" he asked.

"I take it back. You dodged a bullet." I handed the photo back and he looked down with both fondness and dismay.

"When I was a kid, I kept praying that God would switch us."

"Huh?"

"It was like I got her size and she got mine. I was a boy. I wanted to be the big one and we were so alike. I mean, I look more like Dad and she's more like Mom but—"

"Let me see that." I held out my hand.

Rocco made a face and handed over the photo. "Why?"

"Hold on." I examined the photo, my mind pinging around wildly. Once I got past the size difference, I saw Fats and Rocco. I saw Gloria and Tony. Of course, I'd seen it in the family photos that Tiny had shown me, but the photo in my hand was pure. No makeup. No hair gel. Just them. Brother and sister. Fats had her mother's tremendous size and bone structure. That overshadowed everything else it was so pronounced, but when you got down to it, Fats Licata looked like her Dad and brother, too. And they looked like her.

I dashed out of the kitchen.

"Where are you going?" Rocco yelled after me. "That's the only one we've got!"

I ran through the house, dodging balloons and drinks tables, to dart into the library. It was pretty normal in there, except for the piles of wrapping paper from the children's gifts. Every child at the party got three gifts, a savings bond, a book, and a toy, lovingly selected by The Girls. I waded through the paper, bows, and ribbons to the shelf where I'd stashed the Thooft albums.

Rocco plowed into the mess and demanded, "I want my picture back."

"Don't have a conniption. I need it for just a second."

"For what?" he asked. "We've got nothing to do with the Thoofts."

"But you can prove something for me," I said. "Help me clear an area."

Rocco and I stuffed the mess in a corner and I got down, rather painfully, onto my knees. He stood there, watching in confusion.

"Come on." I waved him down and he knelt beside me.

"What are we doing?"

"You'll see." I flipped through the eighties album until I found Kimberly. The photo of Anthony holding her was useless, but the one of her holding onto Ann's leg was good. I slipped it out of its spot and laid it on the floor. "Help me find similar pictures of Anton, Gregory, and Kevin."

We set to work and found them in short order, laying out the photos in a four square.

"Do you see it?" I asked.

"I see some kids," said Rocco. "What of it?"

"Look closer."

He bent over and eyed the photos. "They're cute, healthy, and normal. The clothes are terrible. Is that polyester?"

"Oh, for crying out loud." I pointed at the photos again.

"What am I looking for?"

I gave him the picture of him and Fats. "Look at the two of you and now look at them."

He did as I asked and then sat up, frowning. "Yeah, but you know genetics isn't an exact science."

I smacked his arm. "Yes, it is."

"So she doesn't look like her brothers. So what? It's a fluke or...like we were talking about yesterday." He winked at me. "Mom had a little visit from the milkman."

I rolled my eyes. "I'm calling Holt."

"It's Sunday," he said. "Church."

"I'll leave a message."

I dialed and Rocco looked again. He came up less convinced. "You're going to need more than that. Look at you, for instance. Are you a gangly anorexic-looking redhead? I don't think so."

"You're missing the point," I said.

"Are you sure you have a point?"

I was about to smack him down with a stinging retort that I hadn't quite thought of yet, but someone answered the phone. I was all ready with my message and I was at a loss when Holt said, "Mercy?"

"Oh, I...uh."

"Are you okay?"

"I thought you'd be at church," I said.

"I would normally, but we had a bit of a blowout last night and I'm not welcome," said Holt, sounding tired but not exactly unhappy about it.

"Did they find out about the albums and our meeting?"

"Did they ever."

Apparently, Ann had a few informants in town and one called her to say that she'd seen Holt going into the shoe company carrying albums. A huge blowout ensued when Holt got back to the farm. Ann demanded to know what had happened. He refused to tell her. She wanted me fired and Kimberly agreed, but Holt said that was only because that's what Kim did, she agreed with Ann. Gregory and Kevin were taken off guard and didn't want me fired. They didn't see the problem at all and neither did Anthony. Everyone wanted to know what we talked about, but Holt wouldn't give an inch on that. I gathered there were threats from Ann and then Anthony, mainly because he wanted the yelling to stop.

"So am I fired?" I asked.

"I don't know. Ann threatened to kick my practice off the farm and I walked out. Kim wouldn't talk to me and cried all night. This morning she said it was best if I stayed home, so I did."

"I'm sorry," I said.

"Don't be," he said. "All Ann's yelling did was make me sure we were on the right track. I'm not stopping. I'll pay you myself, especially after Stephanie."

"What about Stephanie?"

"Didn't I mention that?"

"Nope."

"I don't know where my head is," he said. "She followed me out last night when I left. I don't think they know though."

"Anton did something to her, didn't he?" I asked.

"How did you know?"

"I could tell when I was at the farm."

Holt was surprised I knew. He hadn't detected anything in Stephanie's manner that raised a red flag and was completely taken aback when she chased him down with her information. She'd wanted to tell me but couldn't bring herself to go against Ann. Stephanie and Kevin got married in October of 2002. Kevin always said his sister was his favorite singer even though she hardly ever sang, so Stephanie asked Kimberly to sing their first dance song as a surprise. Kimberly sang "Vision of Love" by Mariah Carey and she blew the roof off. Kevin was thrilled. The wedding band wanted to hire her. The guests went wild with the glaring exceptions of Ann and Anton.

Later, Stephanie was in the ladies' room and heard Ann haranguing Kimberly about showing off and not being a lady. She said she'd made other guests feel bad and that she shouldn't have sang and left it to the professionals that were hired to do a job. It was a combination of accusations and compliments that made Stephanie think something weird was going on. She caught up with Kimberly later and found her in tears. To comfort her she told her that she should go on *American Idol*. The first season had just finished a month before and people were still talking about it. The women discussed the idea, how she would get there, what it would be like, but unfortunately Anton heard them. Later, he grabbed Stephanie, still in her wedding dress, and dragged her outside into the alley. He shoved her against the wall and threatened her. He said that if he found out that she ever tried to get his sister on *American Idol* or any other show, she'd be sorry. When she protested, he smacked her and went back inside. Stephanie was stunned and terrified. When she went inside, there was Anton laughing and talking like nothing happened. She decided he must be crazy and kept it to herself.

"She didn't tell Kevin?" I asked.

"No, but she told her family and her friends," said Holt. "She says they will back her up if you want to talk to them."

"Well, I already knew he didn't have a problem beating up a woman. This just backs that up."

"I thought you'd want to know," he said. "I wish she'd told Kevin. Maybe they could've done something about Anton."

"I doubt it would've made any difference," I said. "Is everyone at church?"

"As far as I know. They'd have to be on their deathbeds to miss it."

"Can you get into the house?"

Holt hesitated, but he said, "What do you need?"

"A picture of Kimberly's baby picture."

Rocco snorted and said, "All babies look alike."

I pointed at Fats.

"Almost all."

"I can do that," said Holt with a worried tone. "Are you still thinking that Ann...ya know?"

"No, I'm not." I waited to see if he'd get it, but all he said was, "Thank goodness. If you showed up here, saying Ann had an affair, I don't like your chances."

"I can take care of myself," I said.

Rocco snorted again and I wanted to bite him.

"I'm walking over now," said Holt. "Give me five minutes."

He hung up and I started through the albums again. "Not all babies look alike."

"You were blonde and plump with a rosy cheeks and a button nose, I bet," he said.

"You weren't," I said.

Rocco shrugged. "I said most."

"Explain this." I laid out first grade school pictures. Three blonds and Kimberly, the lone brunette.

"She had an Italian grandmother. That would account for the good looks." He grinned at me.

"If you'd look you'd see it." I got a little evil. "Fats would see it."

He gritted his teeth and stood up. "I'm getting coffee. Don't ask me. I'm not getting anything for you."

"You know I'm right," I called after him.

My phone dinged and there it was. Not a great shot since Kimberly's baby photo had been framed forty years ago, but, to my dismay, Rocco was right. She was a generic baby and wearing one of those newborn stocking caps so that I couldn't even see her hair. The photo was faded enough that her eyebrows were an indistinct color. She was tiny. I'd have guessed thirty-three or thirty-four weeks. So much for something obvious. Rocco would never let me forget it.

"What are you right about?" Fats walked in, wearing lime green workout wear stretched to the limit over her belly and a white fur jacket that had no hope of closing.

"Where's Moe?" I asked automatically. That dog was practically an appendage.

"She's working the old folks home with Uncle Moe."

Working?

"Oh, okay," I said.

"Back to my question, what are you right about?" Fats asked.

"That you would see what I'm getting at," I said.

"Rocco's not the brightest bulb." She took off her abominable snow coat and tossed it on the love seat. "What am I looking for?"

I pointed at the photos and printed Kimberly's baby pic on Myrtle's photo printer. I slapped it down next to the others and Fats raised an eyebrow. I smiled. "I knew it."

My phone rang and it was Holt. "Anything else?"

"This is a little off the wall, but are there other albums, ones from Anthony's and Ann's childhoods?"

"Not that I've seen, but I'll look in the cupboard." He shuffled around. Doors opened and closed. "Sorry, no. Why do you want those?"

"I have an idea," I said. "Are there any family photos from back in the day?"

"A few on the wall. They're not all great quality," said Holt.

"That'll work," I said.

Holt sent me four photos, but I only needed one. Ann at about twelve, all dressed up with perfect blonde curls and wearing a lovely cardigan and pleated skirt. I printed it and the others for good measure.

"That's all I need," I said. "You better get out of there before you get caught."

"I'm already out," said Holt. "They'll be back any minute. What has this got to do with Kim's singing and Anton?"

"I'm working that out. I'll let you know as soon as I have the definitive answer."

Holt wasn't happy, but he let me go with that promise. I would tell him, but the pictures weren't enough.

Rocco came in with the Moka pot and groaned, "Shouldn't you be home heaving?"

"Nice," said Fats. "I hear you can't put two and two together as usual."

"Look, Fatzilla," said Rocco. "I got it, but a bunch of pictures doesn't prove that Ann was messing around. She might have an Italian grandmother. Who knows."

I handed him one of the latest photos, Ann and Anthony's wedding, and Rocco cocked his head to the side. "That's a whole lot of blonds."

The two other photos were family reunions. Rocco tilted his head to the side. "Okay. It doesn't look good. What's the theory? Ann cheated and Kimberly's somebody else's kid and that made Anton nuts 'cause he knew? That's stupid. So what? It happens. If Mom hadn't been Paul Bunyan, I'd have thought you were Bad Sampson's kid."

"Bad Sampson?" Fats asked.

"That enormous dude that lived on the corner, used to throw things at us," said Rocco.

"That guy? You would've thought Mom did that guy? He got beat with an ugly stick."

"He was a prize fighter."

"Not a good one."

"That's not the point," said Rocco. "You didn't look like Dad."

"Yes, I do." Fats pointed between her eyes and Rocco's. "We've got the same eyes, dipstick."

"That's the point," I said. "Kimberly hasn't got anyone's eyes or chin or hair or skin."

Rocco dropped down and looked at the photos again. "She has to. It's just not obvious."

"It's not obvious because it's not there," said Fats. "What made you think of it?"

"You and Rocco," I said. "Your mom. Your dad. They're in you. I saw that and I didn't see it when I was at the farm. But I didn't dwell on it because it's crazy."

"Yes, it is," said Rocco. "What makes you so certain now?"

"Because Ann lied," I said, "and Kimberly told me that the very first time I met her."

Rocco and Fats both said a simultaneous, "Huh?"

I held up the picture of Ann. "Ann told Kimberly that she was a bottle blonde and Kimberly dyed hers to look like her mother. She believes they're both natural brunettes. The evidence that her mother was lying to her was right in front of her the whole time."

"I copied my mom when she dyed her hair red," said Fats softly. "It made things worse."

"In this case, it made things better," I said, flipping to the page in the album when Kimberly became blonde at about fourteen. "She doesn't stand out anymore."

"She's not their kid," said Rocco.

"No," I said, "and Anton was the only one who knew it."

Spidermonkey was at brunch when I called him and one of his buddies was telling a story about golf. Spidermonkey loved golf. He didn't love hearing about golf.

"Saved by the Mercy," he said. "Tell me there's an emergency."

"Well…"

"There's an emergency. Irwin has been in that sand trap for a half hour."

"Change the subject," I suggested.

"Impossible. He loves a captive audience," he said. "Did you think about what I said?"

When did you say what?

"Sure. Of course. I'm mulling it over."

"I'm so disappointed. You're a better liar than that," said Spidermonkey.

"Sorry. I didn't get a lot of sleep," I said.

"I'm surprised you're up."

"Me, too."

"Snoring?"

"Yep," I said. "We talked last night, didn't we?"

"We did. After the shootings. Before the interviews."

I'd forgotten in the adrenaline rush and chaos. "Remind me of the gist."

The gist was pretty good and I had to be seriously frazzled to forget it. Novak in Paris had gotten back with his deep dive into Anton's online activities or rather what was made to look like Anton's activities. On the surface, it appeared that Anton had gone to Incel and 4chan sites to look at discussions and photos of violence against women, but Novak concluded that he hadn't. The evidence was planted and they didn't do a great job if you thought about it and Novak was great at thinking. The history showed Anton going to pages, but he never clicked on anything. He stayed on the first page of every discussion. He didn't scroll. He didn't go into discussions that branched off from the original.

To make sure this was abnormal behavior for the kind of guys that visited the sites, Novak's data guys did what they did best. Data. The behavior Anton was supposed to have done wasn't just odd, it downright never happened. Incels loved to look, scroll, and talk. They couldn't shut up. Anton never made a single comment. He didn't dive into the depths of any site. It was all superficial. When Novak looked at the photos found on his computer, although they were tagged from certain sites at the time of download, he found all kinds of discrepancies. Anton downloaded photos from sites before they were on the sites. Photos had identifiers that were wrong and, most interestingly, Anton had never looked at them. They were simply put on the computer and left there. Not typical Incel behavior at all. If they downloaded a photo, they looked at it. A lot. Novak would eventually unravel where the plants had come from, but it would take a day or so.

Spidermonkey had been busy, too. He'd taken Anton's finances back to the studs, looking for unusual patterns or abrupt changes in the weeks before he came back to the States. After hours of pinpointing transactions, he finally found what he was looking for. A change. Two months before my abduction, Anton started taking money out of an ATM in Sindelfingen. It wasn't near where he lived and he didn't appear to be a shopping kind of guy. At first, it was small amounts. A hundred euros here and there. Then, two days after I found the evidence about the liquor cabinet, the amount went way up to 300 euros and he started taking it out every couple of days. He took cash out of other ATMs, too. There was no evidence that he was buying anything. He didn't talk about it on Facebook or texts. In fact, during the short period before he came to the States, he stopped texting friends almost completely and when he did, he was perfunctory.

"He was being blackmailed," I said.

"I don't see what else it could be, but what could they have on a middle-aged high school teacher?" Spidermonkey asked.

"Well," I said, "let me tell you."

Spidermonkey typed as I told him what I'd put together and was quiet when I finished. Fats and Rocco watched me with identical stubborn looks on their faces. I would never tell them how much they looked alike when they did that and it made me all the more confident in my conclusion.

"Are you not buying it?" I asked. "I can send you the photos. We can do facial analysis, if you like."

"No need. You're right. Everything points to it."

Fats mouthed, "What?"

I shrugged and asked, "Okay, so what's the problem? Other than proving it, I mean. There's DNA. I'm sure I can swing that with Holt's help."

"Yes, I think that is fairly simple," said Spidermonkey.

"But..."

He took a breath and said, "I'm a father, Mercy. I love my children beyond what I can express."

"I know," I said confused.

"What happened to Ann's baby?" he said and my whole body went cold. I hadn't thought of that. "And where did she get a baby at precisely the right time that she needed it?"

I took a breath and told Fats and Rocco what he said. Fats touched her belly tenderly and Rocco went red in the face.

"Maybe there wasn't a baby," I said. "Women have been known to fake it."

"One can hope."

"We need that birth certificate," I said.

"I'm working on it," he said.

"Don't bother," I said. "I'll get Holt to find it. Can you get into the hospital in St. Seb and look for records on Kimberly's birth?"

"Sorry, no. They're not required to keep anything past ten years and a birth record from 1980? Forget it."

"There has to be something to show if she had a baby or not," I said.

Rocco grinned at me. "Insurance."

"You're not as dumb as you look," said Fats.

"If you weren't pregnant."

"What?" she asked. "You'd get pounded faster."

The siblings began bickering and I left the library. I had to think and rivalry wasn't good for that.

"Insurance," I said.

"I'm accessing their financials and I'll find Ann's current doctor. Something may turn up," said Spidermonkey, "and, Mercy, we need to think about who was blackmailing Anton."

"I'm thinking about it." I went up the stairs slowly with my mind going in ten different directions. "What did Anton's phone show?"

"Nothing of significance."

"Can you look again?"

"Of course," he said. "What for specifically?"

I explained that if we were right and someone had sent Anton on a mission to nab me, then they were unlikely to stay out of touch. They'd want updates on his progress. I'd expect him to contact them asap when he'd gotten me in that trunk.

"Got it," said Spidermonkey. "I'll look for a false front."

"Eh?"

"An app that's disguised as something else to hide what the user's really doing."

"Like texting their blackmailer," I said.

"Exactly."

We hung up and I snuck into my room to find Chuck doing his version of da Vinci's Vitruvian Man. Yes, he was buck naked on top of the covers and still snoring and off gassing old eggs. Under his arms were Pickpocket and Skanky, curled up tight and apparently unbothered by the tremendous racket coming out of Chuck's face.

I hurried into the closet and threw on jeans and one of Chuck's flannels. He'd worn it into supreme softness and I'd been eying it for a while. This was my first chance to steal it. It was his own fault for making it so comfy and leaving it unguarded in my closet. At least, that would be my defense when he caught me wearing it.

I yanked on some boots and scooted to the door. Who was there waiting? The poodle. I didn't know Pick had a look that said, "Ha, I caught you," but he did.

"I'm not going anywhere," I whispered, trying to push him out of the way, but he latched onto my wrist and I was forced to drag him into the hall.

"What are you doing?" Fats asked with her hands on her hips.

"Trying to go to St. Seb," I said.

"Without the dog?"

"That was the hope."

"You promised to take him everywhere," she said as she checked her Python for flaws and then stuck it back in her holster.

"But hear me out, I don't want to," I said.

Fats turned around and did her muscle bound sashay to the stairs. "Give that a try and see how it works out."

"You could help me."

"I am."

I dragged Pick to the stairs and pulled out my phone to call Holt, who was oddly breathless.

"I got it," he said.

"What?" I asked.

"I'm freaking out here. I went back to the house and I looked and I see it now. I don't know what to do. They just got back. They're at the house."

I pinned the phone between my head and shoulder and tried to pry Pick's jaws off my wrist. "Get off," I hissed.

"What?" Holt asked, panic rising in his voice.

"Not you. Hold on." I shook my arm and told Pick, "Fine. You can go, you big worthless fuzzball."

The poodle did let go, but he gave me a hurt look. Dogs.

"Okay, Holt," I said. "What happened?"

"I see it, but it can't be," he whispered.

"Are you alone?" I asked.

"Yes."

"Why are you whispering?"

He paused and then said, "I don't know."

"Alright then." I went down the stairs behind Fats, who may or may not have been doing a prego thing by going down a little sideways. I wasn't about to ask. "What are you talking about?"

"You think Kimberly isn't a Thooft," he said.

"So do you."

"I don't. It can't be. It's crazy."

"Be that as it may," I said as I slipped on my coat and dug around in the enormous closet for a hat that would make me look cute and not chubby-cheeked.

"How would that even happen?" he asked. "The hospital accidentally switched babies and Ann ended up with somebody else's kid?"

"I don't think so."

"Why not?"

"Because it wasn't an accident," I said. "They knew she wasn't a Thooft and they were working to hide that fact."

"They?" he asked softly. "You mean Ann."

"And Anton. He knew."

"It can't be. There has to be another explanation," said Holt. "We could be wrong."

"You're a vet. Do a couple of German Shepherds pop out a Corgi? I don't think so."

"No, but humans are not dogs. Our genetics are complicated."

Are they? Really?

"I called for a reason. I need you to find Kimberly's birth certificate."

He surprised me by laughing. "You think Ann put the real parents on there? Give me a break."

"No, but there might be something off about it."

"What makes you think that?"

"Well, it's fake for starters," I said.

Holt swallowed hard. "It should be in the office. Kim used it to get her passport a couple of years ago."

I told him to text me and promptly ran into Rocco, who didn't look at all happy.

"This isn't a good idea," he said. "Wait for me."

"You're not going," said Fats.

"Oh, yeah?"

"Yeah."

"I think I am. We just found out that Mercy was targeted by someone other than Anton Thooft. Ya think that guy's gonna say, 'Oh, well, shit. I guess I give up'?"

Fats grabbed her beloved brother by the throat. "I'm locked and loaded. Mercy doesn't need protection from a 140 pound knitter."

"180 pounds." Rocco didn't blink and I considered that a bit of a feat since she had him up like a ballet dancer. En point. "What are you going to do? Hurl on the next guy?"

"I'll take care of business," Fats said so intensely that I took a step back.

"Look," I said. "I doubt any—"

"Quiet," they both said.

"Fine." I turned on my heels and booked it down the hall. I don't know where I thought I was going. My truck was still at Egon's, I didn't have a loaner anymore, and even if I was good at hot-wiring cars (I wasn't) I wouldn't dare try it on Fats' truck. She probably wouldn't kill me, but she would hurt me and I was against that.

I flung open the door and stomped out into a snowstorm. Of course. Why wouldn't it snow? Pick raced past me and dashed out, jumping and biting the fat flakes as they floated down.

Rodney has a car. It's gross, but it moves.

I stomped down the snow-covered walk and my phone dinged. There it was, Kimberly's birth certificate in all its fake glory. I let myself into the garage/stable and tried to figure out how to get Rodney to give up the keys to the world's rustiest, smelliest Camaro while squinting at the print on the birth certificate.

I barely made it to the other door when the Licatas got me, both of them. They had me off my feet and away from the door like I weighed nothing, which I clearly did not.

"Look, you," said Fats. "We're going to do this right."

"Who's we?" I asked.

"Us. We."

Rocco nodded. "We came to an understanding. I go and have my baby sister's back and yours."

"In exchange for what?" I asked.

"I don't tell Calpurnia how much she's really vomiting." He pointed at Fats' belly. "And I'm the baby's godfather."

"You have to drive The Girls to mass."

"We'll be back by then," he said. "I'm going to check the alley. Wait here."

Rocco went outside, hand inside his jacket on his weapon, just in case, and the door slammed shut behind him.

"He was always going to be her godfather, right?" I asked.

"I love him," Fats said, "but he's not the brightest."

"And Calpurnia already knows?"

Fats sighed. "You think I can hide it from her? Not possible."

"Then why is Rocco going?" I asked.

She smiled and a toothpick popped out on her lip. "He's my brother and he wants to protect me."

I wrinkled my nose.

"I know, but I gotta throw him a bone every once in a while. He is a man and this stuff's important to them."

Rocco came back and declared the alley clear of predators. I thought it was kinda stupid, but I did feel better. If The Klinefeld Group was behind Anton's efforts, I could use all the protection I could get.

CHAPTER SIXTEEN

I fell asleep fifteen minutes into the drive to St. Sebastian. Okay. I'm lying. It was five minutes. The buzzing of my phone woke me as Fats exited the highway on the road to town.

"Nice nap, Duchess Drool," said Rocco and he handed me a drive-thru coffee and a sausage biscuit. I must've really been out to miss a drive-thru.

I wiped the drool off my chin, thankful that nobody in that truck would've taken a picture for Instagram and posted it with a snarky comment. My breasts were blowing up all over social media as it was.

"Thanks," I said and checked the phone. It was Spidermonkey and it wasn't the first time. "Why didn't you wake me up? I've gotten like five calls."

"That dingus thought you needed your rest," said Fats.

"She did," said Rocco. "Besides, Kimberly wasn't born yesterday. Nothing was gonna change in the last forty-five minutes."

I wanted to argue with that, but the coffee hadn't hit yet.

"Where are we going?" Fats asked.

"The Sentinel until I get a plan," I said.

"A plan," scoffed Rocco and he turned to his sister. "She's not getting a plan."

"She never does. Out her ass. One hundred percent."

The siblings went back and forth, finally agreeing on something. Unfortunately, it was my incompetence.

"Hey, it's me," I said to Spidermonkey. "Sorry. I was asleep."

"I thought so," he said. "I've got some information."

"Lay it on me."

Spidermonkey gave me the names of the two obstetricians that were in St. Sebastian in 1980, Dr. Harvey McBride and Dr. George Burke. McBride died in 1984 at the age of seventy, so he may not have been practicing anymore. Burke was alive but at an assisted living facility in Florida. Spidermonkey had the Thooft insurance, which was, predictably, Farmers. They didn't have any of Ann's old records in the computer but did show that she'd had a hysterectomy ten years ago and the record claimed that she had four live births and three miscarriages. Her current GP had the same notes in his file.

"So miscarriages," I said. "She could've lost the baby in question and replaced it with an adoption."

"Possible," said Spidermonkey.

"But you don't think so," I said.

"Do you?"

I had a feeling that something wasn't right about that idea, but it was certainly possible. Women did try that kind of thing. Nutballs, but still they tried. Presumably some got away with it.

"Kind of," I said. "Would Anton really kidnap me to hide it? That's pretty extreme."

"If I found out Loretta had me raising a baby that wasn't mine, we wouldn't be married for much longer," he said.

It still didn't feel like enough, but I said, "I guess so. If Anthony wasn't in on it, he's not going to be happy."

Fats glanced back. "How didn't he know? When I go to the hospital, Tiny would notice if I didn't have a baby. Anthony didn't seem like an idiot."

No, he didn't.

"I'll call you back," I said to Spidermonkey.

I refocused on the birth certificate and blew up the image,

searching for some kind of something. The date was right. Ann and Anthony were on there.

"We're here." Rocco got out and took a chain down that was in front of the entrance to the Great Missouri Shoe Company parking lot. If I'd been thinking, I'd have questioned why that chain was up, but I wasn't thinking and I didn't.

Rocco jumped back in and Fats turned into the crusty parking lot.

"I will totally do the microfiche again," Rocco's voice went really deep, unnaturally so.

"Don't be a hero," said Fats, her voice had an edge I'd never heard before.

"I'll take one for the team."

"What team?"

"Us," said Rocco. "We're a team."

"Mercy and I are a team. You are an appendage that I can cut off."

"Try it Porky Boy!" Rocco yelled at her.

"What did you say, asshat?" Fats screamed.

Rocco turned in his seat, his handsome face twisted in rage. "You're fat and people think you're a man!"

The obscenities that came out of them were scorching. I never heard anything more hateful in my life, not even when I was tossed in a trunk.

I scrambled for the door handle. Fats slammed on the brakes and went for Rocco. I was not a hero, nor was I taking one for any team. I jumped out with Pick and ran for the Sentinel door. I grabbed the knob and nearly ripped my fingernails off when I tried to yank it open. Locked. The town newspaper was closed in the middle of the day. Did that happen? Was that a thing?

I turned around, hoping to spot some kind of sanity, only to see the Licatas having an all-out slap fight in the front seat while the truck slowly rolled toward the building and a bank of half-broken windows.

Son of a bitch!

"Stop!" I went for the truck, but the poodle didn't. He went the other way, yanking my recently-healed arm nearly out of its socket and getting me off balance. I slipped on a discarded hubcap and fell onto iced-over dirt. Pick pranced around me, whining and tucking his tail.

"What the—" I spun around. "Holy crap!"

Four jagged pieces of metal moved in front of the truck's wheels. There was a series of bangs as the truck ran over the metal. Then a whooshing sound and I swear, just for an instant, I saw a bunch of people in the parking lot. Like twenty or thirty and could smell rancid male sweat and something like hot grease or machinery oil. Then they were gone and Fats was staring straight ahead with her hands at ten and two. Pick's tail untucked and he danced around in the debris of the parking lot.

I jumped up, at least I remember it that way, and ran for the truck, whipping open the door. "Are you alright?"

Fats stared straight ahead with a blooming black eye and a bloody lip and Rocco said, "I need to knit." I think that's what he said. It was hard to understand him. His jaw looked like it was dislocated.

"What happened," I asked. "Why did you do that?"

Fats still didn't move. No blinking. No nothing. I didn't really want to touch Fats Licata, especially after I just heard her tell her brother that she was going to rip out his left eyeball and eat it on toast, but I put out a tentative finger and gave her a poke.

Please don't kill me.

Nothing.

"Fats?" I poked a second time, a little harder as I was starting to worry that she'd popped a vessel.

"That happened," she said.

"Yeah."

"You saw them?"

"I did."

"I think my truck's wrecked," she said.

"Little bit," I said and pulled out my phone. Neither Licata was moving and it was creeping me out, not as much as seeing translucent dudes in a parking lot in broad daylight, but it was up there in the creep factor.

I texted Tank. "Where are you?"

Thirty long seconds later, he texted back. "Church. Where are you?"

"Your parking lot."

"Right now?"

"Yes."

"Get out. Something might happen," he texted.

"Too late," I wrote.

"On my way."

I tugged on Fats' sleeve. "Tank said we have to get out of the parking lot."

"I'm not moving." The instant she said that, she was moving. The truck started rolling backward. Fats was not doing it. The truck was in drive.

"Get out!" I tried to unclip her seatbelt and pull her from the vehicle, but it was like a flea trying to move a dog. No effect whatsoever.

Someone yelled behind me. "Are you crazy? Get out of there!"

I turned around and saw a young couple on the porch of a little Craftsman-style house, waving frantically at us. More neighbors came out to watch and began to shout. I yanked on Fats, but she was clamped onto that steering wheel like her hands were vise grips. I ran to the other side and opened Rocco's door. He sat there with his hands limp on his lap. I climbed in to undo his seat belt, but then I was out of the truck skittering across the parking lot on my rear. Yes, it was painful. Very.

"Run!" People were screaming. I was freaking. Pick was gone. The truck was rolling on completely flat tires and there was some kind of horrible metal breaking sound coming from the undercarriage.

"Get up!" a woman at the edge of the parking lot screamed at me, but I couldn't move. I could only stare as the truck rolled toward the street. It reached the entrance and the front end lifted up. Then the truck got flipped ass over tea kettle by nobody. Nothing. Then it started going again.

Another truck screamed to a halt in the street. Tank jumped out and ran over. He got me under the arms and started dragging me backward to the street. Fats' truck flipped up right side up and damned if it didn't tip up again.

Tank got me out of the parking lot and the instant we were on the sidewalk the truck dropped back onto its four flat tires with a tremendous crash. He dropped me and ran for the truck. "Call 911! Call 911!"

People converged on the truck and I staggered to my feet, dazed and tingly. A woman was with me. "They're coming. Don't move."

I was moving. I was flipping moving.

"She's pregnant." I careened toward the truck as sirens started sounding in the distance. People grabbed at me. I may have smacked them. I don't know and I don't care. "Get out of the way."

"Mercy"—Tank was with me—"she's talking. She's okay."

"I don't think so," I said. "Bleeding."

"Yes, but the belly's okay."

Tiny. I have to tell Tiny.

I hurled on the sidewalk and a cruiser careened to a halt, siren wailing. Dallas Mosbach ran up to me. "Mercy! What happened?"

"They went in the parking lot," said Tank.

"Why? My God why?"

Tank looked at me. "What are you doing here?"

"I figured it out," I said weakly.

"What?"

I stared at them and told the absolute truth. "I don't know."

An hour later, Fats and Rocco were in the ER having every test known to doctor-kind run on them, despite their angry objections, and I was sneaking out the back. The baby was fine. Heartbeat fine. No abruption. No bleeding. But neither Fats nor Rocco were getting out of there anytime soon. They'd been so bleary when they were brought in, they made the mistake of telling the staff that they'd seen ghosts in the Sentinel parking lot. You'd think in St. Sebastian General Hospital of all places that wouldn't be a sign of insanity or head injury, but apparently it was. They had a Confederate regiment roaming the halls on occasion, for crying out loud, but they were keeping my bodyguards overnight.

I didn't say anything about ghosts or smells or the Licatas beating the crap out of each other. I went with, "I don't remember." I remembered and they knew I remembered, but it wasn't in the chart so they couldn't say I was nuts. I checked out fine. By fine, I mean I had shards of metal and glass pulled out of my butt, a rope burn from Pick's leash, and a shoulder that burned like someone had injected me with acid. Otherwise, I was good to go, but I had once again been forced to shop at the hospital giftshop, which, I decided, was staffed by the colorblind and chronically incompetent. The clerk sadly told me they were all out of bubblegum pink, but they had mint green and naturally only in men's extra-extra large. I could've fit my whole body in one leg and, to make matters worse my coat was a dark chocolatey brown. I know you're thinking that I had bigger problems like bandages all over my butt, but I'm vain. I spend a lot of my life trying not to look stupid and failing. When I went in to tell Fats I was leaving I opened with, "At least I'm not a marshmallow peep." She said, "You're grasshopper pie." This was not an improvement. It might've even been a downgrade.

"I'm going to have Aaron cater your shower with meat, lard, and sugar."

She bared her teeth at me, but then said, "I'll just barf it up anyway."

"Didn't the doc give you anything? You were vomiting on the way in."

Fats crossed her arms and her biceps bulged to an amazing degree. "I declined his suggestion."

For some reason, I thought being in the hospital might have an effect. Dr. Crocker talked to me. She was worried. Fats' blood chemistry was all wacky and she was afraid that the baby was in danger.

"Don't you understand the situation?" I asked.

"*You* don't understand the situation." Fats rolled over and faced the window. "I can do this. I will do this."

Fats' will had never failed her before. I had every faith that she could do anything, but this wasn't a matter of personal strength and it was time—past time really—to pull out the big guns. I fought every instinct I had, then stepped out into the hall and called Aunt Miriam. Asking her for help was to open yourself up to guilt and quid pro quos. I would have to watch horror movies. It was happening.

After throwing myself on the not so tender mercies of my delighted Aunt Miriam, I went for the front door of the hospital, but when I turned the corner, I saw no less than three news crews angling to get inside and only being held off by a couple of elderly security guards who had no clue why they were there. I did an about-face and went through the ER and radiology to an out-of-the-way exit I'd discovered on my last visit to St. Seb.

"Are you serious?" Chief Candace Stratton yelled down the hall at me as I pushed open the door.

So close.

I went out the door and pulled out my phone. Did St. Seb have Uber?

Stratton came out to find me hobbling across the parking lot, looking for the closest driver. Thirty minutes. Awesome.

"Where are you going?" Stratton fell in slow step beside me. "We found the poodle. He's fine."

"I know." I held up a key. "I hear the red door in the west section is safe. They don't mind that."

"Where did you get that key?" Stratton asked.

"I may have liberated it from Tank during the excitement," I said.

"Why on Earth would you do that?"

"Tank said the place was off limits, considering the situation, but I thought I might need to get in." I grinned at her. "And I need to get in."

"I will kill him," Stratton said.

"Don't bother. Mallory's on it."

"He didn't tell you about the situation? It's unpredictable. The Licatas obviously triggered something."

"Do you think we would've driven into that parking lot if we knew?" I asked.

Stratton screwed up her mouth and said, "Maybe. It's you."

"That's fair, but I like to think I'd have avoided rioting ghosts from 1933."

"I can't believe he didn't tell you."

"He forgot," I said.

She gave me a look and I can't blame her. Normally, a riot that turned deadly in 1933 wouldn't be cause for concern, but we were talking St. Seb, home of floating eyeballs and a nun that looked after students fifty years after her murder.

"To be fair," she said, "it's only two Sundays in December."

"Of course, I would hit one."

"I knew we were in for it when you turned up again," said Stratton. "Now why do you have to get into the Sentinel?"

"I figured it out," I said.

"And you remember?" The chief dripped with sarcasm.

I turned up my nose. "Do you want me to tell you or not?"

Stratton considered it for longer than I expected and I thought for a moment she might go against me. "How much trouble is this going to cause me?"

"Hard to say," I said cheerfully. "Since I just got attacked in a parking lot, but I'm not going to sue anyone or make a fuss, I'd think you might give me a break."

She groaned. "Come on. I'll give you a lift."

"To the Sentinel?"

"To the station. Your poodle is there and he isn't happy. He keeps gnawing on people."

"That's not unusual. That's Pickpocket," I said.

"He's not my problem and your bodyguards say you're not supposed to be without him."

Swell.

She waved me over to her truck and helped me get in. I sat—I use the term loosely—by wedging my feet on the floor and my back pressing against the seat back so my rear wouldn't touch the seat.

Stratton got in and eyed me. "You want to lie face down in the bed?"

"If it requires moving, no," I said.

"Have it your own way." She started the truck and carefully drove out of the back lot avoiding as many bumps as she could.

"You think this is my way?" I asked. "My butt is torn up and swollen to epic proportions."

"Big butts are in," she said in a motherly way that was meant to be comforting.

"Lumpy butts aren't."

Stratton screwed up her mouth to hold back a laugh. My life. So funny. Ha. Ha.

"Kimberly was adopted and it was illegal," I said and I got the gasp I craved. I might have a rash and a lumpy ass, but I could figure things out.

"No way." Stratton set her jaw and then looked over at me. When she saw my expression, her eyes went wide. "You think that has something to do with Anton kidnapping you."

"We think he was being blackmailed," I said.

"What is it with you?"

"It'd be better to ask what's wrong with your town."

"The Thoofts live in Whiskey Ridge."

"Kimberly was born, supposedly, in St. Seb."

Stratton pulled into a back lot behind the station and parked right next to an emergency exit door. She radioed Dallas to open it for us and then said, "Supposedly?"

"If Ann gave birth here, it wasn't to Kimberly."

The chief rubbed her eyes, spreading chips of mascara across her cheeks. "We have a missing baby?"

"Maybe."

"Great. Fantastic."

"Do you wish I still didn't remember?"

"A little bit." Stratton got out and came over to help Dallas hoist me out of the truck.

"How bad does it hurt?" the young cop asked with a grimace.

"Medium pain with a side of sting," I said.

"I can't believe Tank didn't tell you."

"You and the entire world."

We went into the station and young Patton glanced back with a pained expression on her face. There was a crowd around her with their numbers and they weren't looking very happy.

"They're worse on the weekends," said Stratton as she helped me up on the first stair.

A man yelled, "Look here, girl. I'm taking time outta my busy life to come down here to this podunk town to do your job for you. The least you could do is get me a cup of coffee."

"Can she shoot him?" I asked.

"I wish."

"It's not your turn," said a woman. "I'm twenty. You're twenty-five."

"I'm sick of waiting. Mine is a murder case," he bellowed.

"Your father had a heart attack."

"He was fifty. They have something up in that attic and I want to know what it is."

"My father's just as important," said the woman, "as yours."

"Go to that doctor and ask him."

"He's dead."

"Then there's no hurry."

Another man said, "I've got a current case. That's the most important."

"Mr. Curran," said Patton. "Please, I told you Pacific isn't our jurisdiction and it happened a year ago."

"You've had snatchings. I've heard about it. There might be a connection. My wife's arm was pulled right out of the socket."

"I need a vacation," said Stratton.

"I need a drink," said Dallas.

"Don't you start. Will was bad enough."

We made it up the back stairs to Stratton's office and closed the door on the clamor downstairs.

Pickpocket leapt at me and tried to choke himself to death. He was tied to the desk and he'd just about chewed his leash in two. Stratton untied him and he acted like he hadn't seen me for a year.

"Calm down, meathead," I said and gave his puffy head a scratch. He started to gnaw on my leg and Dallas hauled him off me and found a coat in the lost and found for him to curl up on. Stratton offered me a chair, but I chose leaning on the wall as a safer bet.

"So let's have it." Stratton braced herself and I flatter myself to think she wasn't disappointed. "You have the birth certificate?"

"I do, but it's hard to look at on a phone. Can we print?"

"Sure."

She printed Kimberly's birth certificate and the three of us leaned over her desk looking for discrepancies. She and I saw it at the same time.

"Ha! It's not my town," she crowed.

The chief was right. It wasn't her town. Kimberly's birth certificate said she was born in Whiskey Ridge, not St. Seb.

"Was there a birthing center in Whiskey Ridge?" Dallas asked. "It's kinda a one-horse town."

Stratton shook her head. "No. Maybe she was born at home."

"She wasn't," I said. "Holt said she was born at the hospital here in St. Seb."

"Well, he's wrong obviously."

I kept looking at that certificate. Holt wasn't wrong. That was the story, emphasis on story. "Ann lied. Again."

Stratton leaned back and crossed her arms. "You're assuming that."

"I'm not. Holt said she was born two weeks early at the hospital and Ann didn't like to talk about it because Kimberly was so little, she was afraid of losing her." I rolled my eyes. "It was traumatic or so the family story goes."

"Look," said Dallas, "how could she lie about it? People know where you had your kid."

There was something...right there. I could almost remember it.

I called Holt and he answered with a whisper, "Are you okay?"

"Mostly," I said. "I want to double check something with you."

"Okay."

"Where was Kimberly born?"

"How the hell should I know?" Holt's voice rose dramatically and then he went back to a whisper. "I don't know anything. I don't know who she is."

"I meant to ask where does Ann say she was born?"

"I told you St. Seb. Why?"

"You're sure?"

"Absolutely. When Kim went to have our boys, she and Ann were talking about it."

"What did Ann say?" I asked.

"You know, about how Kim was giving birth in the same hospital where she was born. Yada. Yada. Ann said it might even be in the same room."

"Thanks. That's a big help."

"It feels like nothing's going to help."

"I know, but I'm going to find out what happened and you can go from there."

Holt agreed, but he sounded pretty glum. Kimberly wasn't speaking to him. Her father and brothers were bewildered and Ann was enraged.

"She was born at the hospital here in St. Seb," I said. "Ann said it in front of Holt. No mistake."

"Maybe the certificate's wrong?" suggested Dallas.

"I might think so, if it weren't for the length and weight." I pointed at Kimberly's stats. She was seventeen inches long and weighed a mere four pounds and three ounces.

"Whoa," said Dallas. "I didn't notice that. She was teeny."

Stratton went and sat down heavily in her swivel chair. "She wasn't thirty-eights weeks. That's for sure."

"How long would a baby like that stay in the hospital?" Dallas asked.

"It depends on her condition," I said. "A few days to weeks."

Stratton relaxed a bit. "Kimberly had to be in the hospital then. You must be wrong."

I could've called Holt back to check, but he would've mentioned talk of Kimberly being in the NICU. And why would she be? She was supposed to be thirty-eight weeks. Those babies have very few complications. No. There would've been too many questions in the hospital. Like Dallas said people notice.

I am an idiot. So obvious.

"She wasn't in the hospital. At least not St. Seb's hospital."

"How do you figure?" Stratton asked.

"This is a small town. Kimberly isn't a Thooft. People would notice if a preemie girl was born here and went home with Ann."

Dallas threw up his hands. "Dads aren't dumb. We know where our kids are born. Where was Mr. Thooft? Under a rock while his wife is adopting some random kid from who knows where?"

There it is.

"Yes."

Stratton gave me the side eye. "Anthony Thooft was under a rock and had no clue?"

"No to the rock and yes to the clue." I hobbled for the door. "Come on."

"Where are we going?" Dallas asked, taking up Pick's leash.

"To the Sentinel. I have to check something."

"The old Sentinel?" he asked hopefully.

I would've rolled my eyes at him, but I would've had to turn around and it wasn't worth the effort.

"Do we have to?" he asked the chief.

"I hope not," she said. "What's at the Sentinel?"

"An article. Anthony won some kind of prize pig contest." I got to the stairs and took a breath. *I can do it. It won't hurt that bad.*

"So what?" Stratton asked.

"It was in August," I said. "The article."

"That's a month late." Dallas jogged down the stairs being dragged by the poodle, who was always ready for a trip.

I went down four steps.

Fire butt.

"It'll be worth it," I said.

"I don't know about that," said Stratton. "You look like you're going to pass out.

"No passing out." I did go down the rest of the stairs under my own power, but Stratton went on ahead since toddlers could've outrun me. Sundays were not a day of rest in St. Sebastian. I couldn't see the crowd of complainers from the back stairs, but I could hear them. The same woman was raising her voice but pleading at the same time.

"It can't be a coincidence. Mrs. Tishell sent me. You know Mrs. Tishell, don't you?"

Patton groaned. "She's always stirring the pot. There's absolutely no proof."

"That's why I'm here," said the woman. "You people turned my dad away ten years ago. You said that all the records were destroyed, but they weren't."

"We're working on it," said Patton. "Please give us a chance to reorganize."

I got to the bottom of the stairs and a man said, "Enough of that.

My grandmother's car was stolen and I want to know who the suspects are."

"We haven't had any stolen cars recently," said Patton.

"Well, it happened in 1998."

"What the!"

"It was a cherry '68 Mustang. She says you knew who stole it and you wouldn't do anything about it. We're going to sue."

"That's a car," said the woman. "My father wants to know who he is."

"Do you know how much a—"

"Listen here," said another woman. "I've got number twenty-eight and these two have been yammering on for—"

"Yammering?" the man yelled. "We've been waiting for forty years for answers."

"You can't even count."

The door closed behind me and, in a moment of weakness, I did lie sunny side down in the bed of Stratton's truck, which is totally illegal, but she was the chief and nobody cared.

In five minutes, we were at the red door at the west wing of the shoe factory and Tank was there to meet us. After hoisting me out and tactfully not commenting on the size of my butt and enormous sweatpants, unlike somebody I know—Dallas—Tank apologized profusely and let us into the silent factory.

"What are we here for?" Tank asked.

"You still have all the stuff we printed, right?"

He took me by the arm and helped me down the hall. "I kept it all. Did we miss something?"

"Maybe," I said. "Is it safe in here?"

"Safe as it ever is."

"That's not reassuring."

"I know, believe me." Tank led me into the main area. It looked exactly the same but smelled odd. I got a whiff of septic wound. In case you're wondering, that's bad. "Ignore that," said Tank.

"Easy for you to say," said Dallas.

"You get used to it."

"How in the world are you going to put apartments in this place?" I asked. "Who would live here?"

He gave my arm a squeeze. "Funny you should ask, our last five leases were signed while I was at the hospital."

"You've rented to a bunch of crazy people," said Stratton. "Just what we need."

"I've rented to a bunch of yuppies with more money than sense." Tank grinned down at me. "Your accident is all over the news."

"But they're saying it was a gas explosion," I said.

The trio of St. Sebastian natives laughed.

"Nobody believes that and it was all over social media until they removed it as fake news and disturbing," said Dallas. "You getting dragged across the parking lot is very popular."

"Lots of conspiracy theories," said Tank. "We've got a waiting list now. Thanks, Mercy."

"I hope Mallory beats you up," I said.

"She did and she will. No worries there."

They walked and I hobbled into the accounting section that was as calm and undisturbed as ever. Pick ran over to the puppies' big dog bed and made himself at home, rolling around and grunting. So not proper poodle behavior.

Our table was still up and I found the stack I needed easily. I flipped past the pages of fair queens and there was the Thoofts, smiling out of a grainy black and white photo. A Thooft Family Farm pink porker had won grand champion in some town in Kansas on Saturday, July 19, 1980. Anthony and an elderly man named as James Thooft smiled broadly behind the champion with their arms around Kevin and Gregory.

"He wasn't here," said Dallas. "He went to Kansas and she had the baby or whatever then."

"That can't be a coincidence," said Stratton.

"No," I said. "It can't."

Tank put his long finger on the photo. "And Anton isn't there."

"He was home taking care of his *pregnant* mother," said Stratton.

Dallas took a big sniff. "Something smells good. Did Aaron cook in here?"

I laughed and Tank got leftovers out of the fridge. They microwaved some dogs and I went through the papers again, in case I missed something. I *was* missing something. I felt it like something between my teeth. Right there, but I couldn't get at it.

Between bites, Dallas said, "Ya know, I don't get it."

"What's that?" Tank asked as he fired up his computer. "How she got away with it?"

"No, I get that. Who's gonna think their wife's passing off somebody else's kid as your own? I wouldn't."

I took a dog and leaned on the table. I wanted to sit so bad. "Why she did it?"

"Yeah," said Dallas. "She already had kids."

"She wanted a girl," said Tank. "She had three boys and she wanted a girl."

"You don't get to pick," said Stratton. "You get what you get and you don't throw a fit."

"Apparently, that doesn't apply to Ann Thooft," I said. "But why not just adopt in the open?"

Dallas nodded emphatically.

"Maybe the husband wasn't interested," said Stratton, "so she took matters into her own hands."

I chewed and thought it over. Ann took a pretty big risk. So many things could've gone wrong and how did she get a baby on exactly the right weekend? Adoptions for newborns don't go smooth like that. Was she just lucky? No. Ann Thooft left nothing to chance. Luck wasn't part of the equation.

"Too bad the doctor's not on there," said Dallas.

"My source says there were two obstetricians working in St. Seb at the time," I said. "Do you know anything about them? Harvey McBride and George Burke."

They all knew Dr. Burke or knew of him. He was sort of the Andy Griffith of town doctors, sweet and beloved. He delivered Tank's kids before he retired.

"We haven't had any problems with Burke," said Stratton. "I'd know."

"Good guy," said Tank. "He was great with Mallory and her pregnancies weren't easy."

"He delivered me," said Dallas. "My mom liked him."

People liked Anton Thooft, too.

"I'm not saying he did anything," I said. "But how did Ann come up with this idea. She didn't strike me as a criminal mastermind and it's not like she had the internet to help her out."

"So you think a doctor helped Ann fake her pregnancy?" Stratton asked.

"Somebody helped her. She didn't get Kimberly out of the cabbage patch," I said. "The town docs are a place to start."

Tank nodded. "We might've had midwives, too."

"I doubt it," said Dallas. "We don't have any now and they're kinda in style. Stacy wanted one, but we couldn't find any outside of St. Louis."

"Back then, it might've been different," said Stratton, picking up Kimberly's birth certificate. "The birth was registered here in town. Somebody likely knew something."

Tank stopped typing. "I've found nothing interesting on either doctor online. Looks like Burke graduated from medical school in 1972. I'm not seeing anything fishy in our database. He retired five years ago after a stroke. I remember that now. Poor guy. He wasn't ready to retire."

I went over to look at the screen. The Sentinel did a two-page spread of the town's beloved OB retiring and moving to Florida, loving tributes, the works.

"He certainly looks good," I said.

"He was good," said Tank. "I never heard a bad word."

Stratton and Dallas nodded.

"So let's start with the geezer," I said.

"To the microfiche!" Tank jolted up and grinned. "Your favorite."

I turned around and said, "Dallas, I'll pay you a hundred bucks to look for crap on Dr. McBride."

"Sold," he said.

"No," said Stratton. "You're on duty, dufus. You can't take a bribe."

"It's not a bribe."

I smiled. "A tip?"

"No tips," said Stratton. "You'll do it because we're investigating a possible crime."

Dallas sighed. "That could've been dinner out and a babysitter."

"Hey," I said, "doesn't your wife do facials and whatnot?"

"Yeah? So?"

"Could she maybe go to the hospital and do that for Fats?" I winked. "I'm sure she'd be very grateful and generous."

Dallas puffed up. "She will be happy to do that."

"I'm not hearing this," said Stratton.

"Hear what?" Tank asked, his long face blank. "She's just doing her job and if she happens to do a great job and get tipped, what's the harm."

"I give up." Stratton took out her phone. "I'll see if we have anything on Dr. Burke. Don't hold your breath, Mercy."

"I never do," I said, eying the table to see if I could lie down on it without collapsing the legs.

Tank and Dallas headed into the back and Stratton made coffee while talking to Kriedt back at the station. She had a hard time talking him into getting into their database to look for info on Dr. Burke. The line in the front of the house had grown angrier and the word *lawsuit* was being thrown around.

"Tell them to shove it," said Stratton. "No, no. Don't say that. I want to say that, but we can't. Call Watanabe and see if he can come in."

I climbed onto the table, facedown, and listened to the creaking complaints of the apparatus beneath me. Worrying but worth it. I was so flipping tired I put my head down on my hands and took a deep breath.

"Mercy," said Stratton. "You want some coffee?"

"No, thanks."

"You need to stay awake."

"I'm good."

"Your phone is blowing up," she said.

I couldn't think of a single reason to care, so I didn't.

CHAPTER SEVENTEEN

Tank woke me an hour later after I'd drooled through my sleeve and snored myself into a sore throat.

"Wake up," he insisted.

"No."

"Good. You *are* awake."

"No."

"Come here, Pickpocket," said Stratton.

The next thing I knew I had a poodle with bacon treat breath licking my hair. Ew.

"Alright. Alright," I said, propping myself up on my elbows. "What's so important?"

Tank spun me sideways on the table and pulled me back so I could stand. "Look at this," he said, putting a printout of Dr. McBride's obituary in my hands.

I read it and did not find it worth waking up for. "He died of a massive heart attack. Please don't tell me Ann killed him. I can't handle it."

"No. He was a seventy-year-old obese guy who decided to clean gutters. That's on him. Natural causes."

"Best news I've had all day. All week actually," I said. "Why are we interested?"

Dallas fairly vibrated with excitement and gave me another paper. "Because I found this."

The article Dallas found was about a lawsuit Dr. McBride's wife filed against the local pharmacist, blaming her for McBride's death. My old friend Barney Scheer wrote the article. He was the Sentinel editor that probably got his intern murdered because he told his WWII buddies what the kid was up to and then protected them. Scheer sucked as far as I was concerned and that article did nothing to change my mind. It was full of umbrage about how the doctor had been treated and more than a little sexism toward the pharmacist who had the temerity to be a woman and young. How dare she! The article didn't say anything about what the pharmacist had actually done. Not one single fact on that score. Eloise—yes, he used her first name, not her last, like she was a child—had both libeled and slandered Dr. McBride—described as an eminent doctor above reproach but didn't outline what Eloise had said or even bother to say that the doctor hadn't done whatever it was. Eloise killed Dr. McBride by saying things that nobody denied.

"That's super weird," I said. "What happened?"

Dallas gave me another article, if you could call it that. It was barely a paragraph buried in the middle of a Wednesday edition. Mrs. McBride dropped the lawsuit six weeks later after motions were filed. Then the wife up and moved to the south of France.

"Motions," I said.

Tank tapped the paper. "I bet this was about Discovery."

"Coffee. Need coffee."

Stratton put a cup in my hands and took a look at the articles. "I agree. I'm thinking Eloise had something solid on the doc and it was going to come out."

"Any idea how long records of old lawsuits are kept?" I asked.

"No idea," said Stratton.

Tank went to his computer. "I'll check in Westlaw, but I seriously doubt there's anything from a dropped suit. It sounds like it barely got off the ground."

I looked back at the initial article. "The wife is probably dead, but Eloise was young at the time. She might still be around. Anybody know a pharmacist named Eloise?"

"From 1984?" Stratton laughed. "No."

"We go to Walmart," said Dallas. "They're always different."

"You should go to St. Seb Wellness," said Tank. "Kevin and Stephanie will actually remember who you are and what your deal is."

Stephanie!

"Are they open today?" I asked.

Stratton checked her phone. "Kreidt says we have nothing on Dr. Burke. Totally clean."

"The pharmacy," I said, grabbing my coat, "is it open?"

Tank turned around. "They open at noon after church. We're not quite there yet. Why?"

"They're pharmacists. They know other pharmacists."

"Good point. By the way, Westlaw has nothing, but there might be something buried at the courthouse."

I groaned and they laughed.

"I'm glad I amuse you. How far is the pharmacy?"

"Six blocks, but I'll drive you over in fifteen. No use waiting in the cold," said Stratton.

"Thanks," I said. "I hope Stephanie is working. I don't know how—"

Stratton's radio crackled. "Chief, we got a 911," said Kreidt.

The chief looked at me. "At least I know it's not you for a change."

"Nice."

She clicked her radio. "What have we got?"

"Fire at 3131 Long Lake Terrance," said Kreidt.

Tank jumped to his feet. "That's my house. I have to go. I have to go."

"Who's home?" Stratton asked.

"The puppies!"

Stratton grabbed her coat and said, "Kreidt, are units responding?"

"En route," he said. "ETA six minutes."

"Dallas, take Tank! I'll be right behind you!"

Dallas grabbed his jacket and keys and ran out toward the storage rooms. Stratton slipped on her jacket, muttering, "This cannot be happening again."

She ran for the exit and I yelled after her, "Good luck! Save the pups!"

Stratton ran back in the door. "Shit! Come on! You're going!"

"Me?" I asked.

"I can't leave you alone!"

"I'm a big girl."

"You're a big problem!"

"Go!"

Stratton gritted her teeth and ran out. A couple of minutes later, a disappointed Dallas walked back in. "So much for that."

"Do you have to watch me?" I asked.

"Yeah."

A siren went past the factory and faded into the distance.

"Cheer up. You can come with me and break Kimberly's case wide open."

He cocked his head to the side and looked at me critically. "That *is* something."

"What do you want?" I asked with a sigh. "You weren't going to be climbing in a burning building to save the puppies anyway. You'd just be watching."

"That's true." Dallas scratched the scant bristles on his chin. "When you do that interview with Tank, could you mention me?"

"Sure. Weren't you in the paper last time?"

"No," he said sadly. "My parents were bummed. Patton got in, but not me."

"Well, you're my bodyguard for the moment. It's bound to get exciting," I said while fervently hoping it didn't. I could barely walk.

Dallas pumped his fist. "Alright. Let's hit that pharmacy."

I folded up the pertinent articles and stuck them in my purse. "Do we have the keys to lock up?"

"Gimme a break. Nobody wants to come in here."

No sooner had Dallas said those words than a resounding knock echoed through the accounting room from the front door. We looked at each other and neither of us moved.

"Do...*they* knock?" I whispered.

"Yeah, Mercy, rioters knock," said Dallas, sarcastic with me for the first time. I have to say it looked good on him.

"Well, then you better answer the door."

"Hell, no."

"Fine," I said. "I'll do it."

"We're not opening the door to that parking lot today."

Another knock rang out and I put my hands on my hips. "If it's not the 1933 guys then it's a real live person standing in that parking lot. Today." I pointed at my bulbous butt. "I hear that's bad."

"Ah, crap!" Dallas flung his hat away in a fit of temper, marched over to the door, and turned the key. He whipped open the door, ready to yell at whoever was moron enough to be in that parking lot, but he didn't get the chance. The second the door was open, two canisters were lobbed inside. They spewed double trails of red and blue smoke, filling the room with thick, gag-worthy color.

"Son of a bitch!" Dallas ran through the fog, picked up a can, and winged it out the door. "Where's the other one?" he yelled as it got too thick to see.

"I can't see it!" I yelled, getting knocked sideways by a panicked Pickpocket.

"Get out!" he yelled. "Get out!"

I went in the direction of the back door as fast as the pain would let me. "Pick, come!"

"Found it!" Dallas yelled.

I got a glimpse of him through the billowing colors as he ran to the front door. There was a thunk and a piercing scream. Then he was with me, grabbing me around the waist and dragging me to the door. Pickpocket streaked by us and then we were out in the hall and he slammed the door behind us. We bent over coughing, our eyes and noses running as we leaned on the wall.

Once I stopped hacking, I pulled a packet of tissues out of my purse and gave Dallas a couple. "What was that?"

"Smoke grenades," he said after blowing his nose straight through the tissues.

I gave him two more. "Like from a fireworks stand?"

"No." He had another fit of coughing and then wheezed out, "More like for effects, like photography or events."

"You better call it in."

Dallas nodded, and called in the smoke grenades, but it took a minute for Kreidt to believe him. "I can't send anyone," he said. "We've got calls all over town."

"For what?"

"Fires."

"I need somebody here now." Dallas started coughing again and I took his radio. "Kreidt, Mercy here," I said. "Your deputy is not doing great. We need somebody."

"You can't be on here," said Kreidt. "This is a police channel."

After coughing in his ear, I said, "So sue me. We need somebody now."

"It's just me and I've got a full lineup of people waiting."

"Kick them out," I said.

"They won't like that."

"Bummer. This is an emergency. Close the station."

Kreidt closed the station and said he'd come to the red door. We hung on to each other and made it to the main floor. We didn't make it any farther.

"Do you see that?" Dallas asked.

"Oh, I see it," I said.

"Maybe the grenades were filled with drugs."

"Not painkillers. I can tell you that."

"LSD?"

LSD sounded about right because Dallas and I were looking at the main factory floor as it was a hundred years ago and it was working. There were rows of odd upright sewing machines with big spindles of thread and cords hanging from the ceiling. Racks wheeled past us and enormous black machines thumped and rattled. We could smell the sweat, leather, and oil. And there were voices like birds twittering away just beyond our ability to understand them.

Then Kreidt was there with the poodle, who promptly latched onto my leg. "Come on, you two! What are you waiting for?"

We pointed and he grabbed us. "What a bunch of babies! Come on!"

Kreidt pried Pick off me and took us through the main floor. We didn't go around. I wanted to go around, but instead I got bumped into by things that weren't there. Somebody felt me up and I think I heard a catcall. A new low. I was being harassed by dead men. That crap never ended. Literally never.

We got out the back door and the icy air cleared my head, even as it made me cough more. Dallas was bent over double with drool hanging from his mouth.

"There really was a smoke grenade." Kreidt took off his hat and ran a hand through his grey hair.

"What was your first clue?" I asked.

"The multi-colored fog spewing from the door and in the parking lot," he said.

"Did you—" Dallas spasmed in another coughing fit.

Kreidt banged him on the back. "You guys have to go to the hospital."

Hard pass.

"I've got stuff to do." I spit into the gravel. I know, I know very ladylike. Mom would be disgusted with me and I could just hear her saying, "Mercy, you have tissues." I did have tissues, but I was saving them for whatever came next.

"It's not optional," said Kreidt.

"You'll find most things are optional if you're willing to bear the consequences, which I am," I said. "How about a ride?"

He stared at me and said, "To where? The nuthouse?"

"Hopefully, not, but it's not looking good." I leaned on his squad car and spit again. "St. Seb Wellness Pharmacy. I need some information."

"You need a therapist."

"Got one. You can drop me off at the pharmacy and then take Dallas to the hospital."

"No," croaked Dallas. "I'm sticking with you."

"You sound terrible," said Kreidt.

"Chief told me to stay with Mercy no matter what."

"I don't think she meant this."

Dallas nodded. "She did."

Kreidt sighed and settled his hat back on his head. "I can't take you to the pharmacy until you stop gagging. Tell me what happened."

We told him and he just kept shaking his head. "I guess it could be kids playing a prank."

"What kind of kids do you have in this town?" I asked. "They get blamed for everything."

"You got a better idea?"

I didn't, but the whole kids thing drove me up a wall.

"Did you see anyone?" Dallas asked as his coughing finally let up.

"No. Just the smoke. Nobody running and not a car on the street."

"I saw someone."

"In the smoke?" I asked.

"Yeah, when I was throwing out the second grenade I saw someone running at me. I think I hit them," said Dallas.

"You ran into them?" Kreidt asked.

"No. I hit them with the grenade when I threw it."

"I heard that," I said. "They screamed."

Kreidt looked at the sky. "I was supposed to be off today. I'm never trading shifts again." He called the hospital and gave them a heads up about what happened. If someone wandered in with an injury from a projectile, they should give him a call. They wanted us to come in, but that wasn't happening.

Kreidt's radio crackled and Stratton's voice came over, "All units, stand down. False alarm. Repeat false alarm."

Dallas grabbed his radio. "Chief. Mosbach. No fire?"

"Correct. No fire in any reported location," said Stratton. "All clear."

Kreidt heaved a sigh. "That's a relief."

Dallas and I looked at each other with furrowed brows.

"What?" Kreidt asked.

"Bit of a coincidence, don't you think?" I asked.

"That we got pranked after pissing off a bunch of people over old ass cases that probably aren't even real cases? No, not really."

"That all those calls came in and we got smoke bombed right after," I said.

He scratched his chin. "That is weird, but shit happens in this town. You saw the main floor, right? This is St. Seb."

"Somebody was trying to come in," said Dallas.

"To do what? Get smoked out like you two? Genius idea."

"Has to be an out-of-towner. Nobody local would set foot on that parking lot."

"Get in," said Kreidt, "and we'll take a look at those grenades."

I climbed in the back of his cruiser and lay face down on the back seat. It was comfortable until Dallas let Pick in and the giant poodle decided to sit on my back.

"Ow! Get him off."

"Can't put him in the front," said Kreidt. "It wouldn't be safe."

Pick spun around in a circle and then lay down on my shoulders.

"Help."

"Oh, you're fine," said Dallas. "It could be worse."

"How?" I croaked. "He's heavy and he has claws."

"He could've sat on your butt."

That didn't make me feel better, but it reminded me of how much my rear hurt. So it was a lose-lose situation.

Kreidt drove around the factory and stopped.

Dallas hacked for a minute and then said, "I can't see them well enough."

"Open the glove box. I've got binoculars."

Dallas got the binoculars and Kreidt said, "There you go. Says EG18 Smoke. We've got red, blue, and green."

"There were three?" I asked.

"Yes, ma'am. I guess the green one didn't make it inside."

I got out my phone and googled EG18 Smoke and found Dallas was right. They were smoke grenades from a company out of Nevada and were for use in stage shows, photography, and weddings. They even had baby reveal packs. The company claimed their dyes and chemicals were non-toxic, which was good news for our lungs.

"I still don't see a point to this," said Kreidt. "Other than pissing

Tank off. It made you cough, but it didn't incapacitate you, like tear gas."

"We have to canvas the neighbors," said Dallas. "Somebody might've seen something."

"Now or after the pharmacy?"

They decided that Dallas and I would get dropped at the pharmacy. Then Kreidt would fill in the chief, walk back to the factory, and canvas the neighborhood. He wasn't holding out much hope since nobody was on the street waving us down. Apparently, St. Sebastian residents were known for doing their civic duty. He and Dallas thought there was a good chance everyone was off gossiping about our earlier incident.

We rolled into the parking lot of St. Seb Wellness a few minutes later and Pick started jumping around, excited to get out.

"Open the door! Open the door!" I yelled.

The poodle ran over my head, which was better than my butt, I know, but I still got a couple of claws to the head. If he took a chunk of hair out, I really didn't want to know.

Kreidt and Dallas pulled me out by my arms. Totally elegant and still looking like grasshopper pie.

"Alright," I said, straightening myself up to look just as terrible as before. "They're open."

Dallas held an arm out. "After you."

"You just want to see if my butt got bigger."

"Maybe." He grinned at me and waited. My life is hell.

I walked into St. Sebastian Wellness Pharmacy with blood in my hair, a halting gait, and an unleashed giant black poodle. Nobody was glad to see me.

Kevin came out from an aisle and said, "Get that dog out."

"The dog stays," I said. "I have some questions for your wife."

"No. Don't even think about it."

"You hired me to think about it," I said, holding my arms wide, "and look what I have to show for it. I should charge you for my jeans and my butt, but I won't because this is St. Seb and I don't want to get into it."

"If my mother finds out I was—"

"Is your wife here?" I asked. "I came to talk to her, not you."

Kevin became even more wary. "Why?"

I hobbled to the counter in the back and leaned heavily on it before I pulled a script out of my pocket. "I wasn't going to fill this, but I changed my mind."

Kevin tried to pull me away from the counter and Pickpocket growled, showing off his very large teeth. "Go to Walmart." His grip tightened. Pick must've sensed it because he bumped Kevin with his snout, hard, above the kneecap. Kevin stumbled back, letting go, but he came back fast.

Dallas stepped in front of him, coughed for a minute, and then said, "Man, you do not want to do that."

"Officer, I'm not trying to make trouble," said Kevin with his hands up.

"Then don't. We've both had a hard day. Mercy, who you hired to do a job, is killing it and getting herself beat to hell in the process. How about you tell me where your wife is?"

"I'm right here." Stephanie came out from behind a partition. Her face was flushed and she kept brushing at the immaculate front of her white lab coat. "I knew you'd come."

"Come for what?" Kevin asked. "What have you got to do with anything?"

Stephanie bit her lip and I said, "Nothing. I wanted to ask her about a pharmacist from the eighties that I thought she might've heard of."

"You don't have to protect me," she said. "I'm going to tell him."

"Oh, well, that's up to you," I said. "About that pharmacist—"

"Tell me what?" Kevin asked. "Did you help Holt take Mom's photo albums?"

"No, and they're not your mother's albums. They're the family's."

The couple went back and forth until Dallas slammed his hand down on the counter. "She needs painkillers and I need a beer. Can we get a move on?"

Stephanie rushed over to take my script. "I heard about the shoe factory. I'm so sorry. It must hurt terribly."

"It's not great. Have you ever heard of a pharmacist named Eloise?"

Kevin went behind the counter and snatched my script away from Stephanie. "Tell me what you did."

"I didn't do it," she said.

"You said you did," said Kevin.

"I didn't."

"You said you were going to tell me what you did," said Kevin.

"I did not. I said I was going to tell you. Not that I did something."

"If you have to tell me something, you must've done something."

I slammed both hands down on the counter. "Your brother attacked and threatened your wife!"

Kevin's mouth dropped open and he stuttered, "Gregory hurt you?"

"Not Gregory, ya nut ball," I said. "Anton. Stephanie told Holt and he told me."

"But Anton wouldn't do that," said Kevin, showing every sign of not believing his wife. I might hurt him. No. I would hurt him.

"Enough of this Anton was a saint bullcrap," I said. "He kidnapped me. Violently. I was lucky to get out alive. Now somebody tell me who Eloise the pharmacist is."

Kevin balled up his fists and said, "You're fired."

"I'm so sick of your family trying to fire me."

"Tough shit."

"Right back at ya," I said. "I'm doing this whether you fire me or not. Now I'm looking for a pharmacist named Eloise."

Stephanie opened her mouth, but Kevin made a slashing motion at her. "No. We're not cooperating anymore."

"So you can hide how messed up your family is? Got it." I looked at Stephanie. "Does he get to decide? Is he in charge of your knowledge?"

She took a breath and her shoulders went back.

"Stephanie," said Kevin with a warning in his voice.

"Are you going to hit me, too?"

"Anton didn't hit you. Don't be an idiot."

Stephanie spun around, went into the depths of the pharmacy, and came out a minute later with a bottle in hand.

"Where are you going with that?" demanded Kevin.

She stepped out from behind the counter and handed me the bottle. "On the house."

"You can't do that! That's a controlled substance!"

"But it isn't when you hand them over like Tic Tacs to your mother?" Stephanie's voice was calm. She looked perfectly pleasant, but she gave me a chill. "I'm leaving. Do not follow me."

Stephanie marched out of the pharmacy and I followed. Dallas didn't.

"Come on," I said.

"Dude," Dallas said to Kevin, "I don't know how you make up for that. Your murderous brother over your wife? What the hell?"

"Dallas, we're going to lose her," I said.

The cop ran to open the door for me because sadly I hadn't actually made it to the front by the time he finished with Kevin.

"What is up with this family?" he asked me.

"We're about to find out."

Stephanie stood next to a minivan, sobbing with her head against the window. She had her hands on the door handle, but it appeared that she didn't have the strength to open the door.

I hobbled up behind her and tentatively put a hand on her back. "I'm sorry. I shouldn't have blurted it out like that."

Tears dripped down her nose and splattered on the packed snow. "It's not your fault. I should've come out with it the night it happened."

"Why didn't you?" Dallas asked as he put Pick in the cruiser.

"I knew what he would do and I didn't want to end my marriage before it started like a big fat loser."

"He might come around."

Stephanie straightened up, wiped her eyes, and turned to us. "He might, but I won't."

"You sound sure," I said.

"I am. It's been getting worse since you came to the farm. Kevin knows that Anton did it, but I think Ann's getting to him. What's going on? And does it have to do with Kimberly?"

"I'll tell you everything when I know everything," I said.

She blew her nose. "You think you'll find out?"

"If you tell me who Eloise is."

She put a palm to her forehead. "I don't even remember what you asked me. Eloise who?"

"A pharmacist. She worked here in the eighties. I got the impression that female pharmacists weren't a dime a dozen."

That got a smile. "We still aren't."

"Any ideas about Eloise?"

"You must be talking about Mrs. Tishell. She's the only female pharmacist I know before me. I don't know her first name. She retired in 2012 and we moved here to take over."

Tishell. I know that name.

"Do you know if she's alive?" I crossed my fingers.

"Of course, she's not that old, not even seventy, I don't think."

Dallas got out a phone. "Do you have an address?"

"Sorry, no," said Stephanie. "What in the world has Mrs. Tishell got to do with Anton?"

Tishell. Tishell. Tishell.

"What do you know about her?" I asked.

Stephanie blew her nose again and said, "I don't really know her, just enough to say hello, but I had a lot of people tell me I'm nicer than she was." Stephanie made a face. "She was bossy, opinionated, and stuck her oar in. That kind of thing."

"I'm guessing men said that," I said.

"Hey," said Dallas. "It might not be the men."

"It was the men," said Stephanie.

"Dammit."

I elbowed him. "Come on. Bossy? Opinionated? That's got sexist old dude written all over it."

Dallas sighed. "Yeah, I know. I'm just sick of those geezers giving us young guys a bad name."

"To be fair," said Stephanie, "some women said it, too."

"Ann?"

She nodded. "She hates Mrs. Tishell. Ann is a quiet person for the most part. She hardly ever says a bad word. Our church doesn't condone that. Love your neighbor. We believe that."

"Except for Mrs. Tishell?" Dallas asked.

She leaned against her van and crossed her arms. "I never thought about that before, but yes, you're right and she's been talking about her lately."

"Since when?"

"A few weeks ago, she came back from shopping and she was upset. Mrs. Tishell was getting people worked up. Outsiders and we didn't want people paying attention to St. Seb. Something like that."

"What happened?" I asked.

"I don't know. She was mad about Mrs. Tishell, but she blamed you, Mercy," said Stephanie.

"What does she say about me?" I asked.

"Do you really want to know?" Dallas asked.

"I do. I want to know how much I have in common with Mrs. Tishell."

"Now that you mention it, it was about the same," she said. "You were nosy, disrespectful, incompetent, and stupid."

"Your family hired her," Dallas gasped.

"Ann didn't want to. She was totally against it, but Kimberly insisted after we couldn't get anyone else interested in the case. Then she pretended like she was fine with it."

"So Mrs. Tishell and I are in the same category," I said. "Interesting."

"Aren't you pissed?" Dallas asked.

I smiled. "That isn't new. It's my basic Tuesday. Better actually. Usually, I get slut."

"She said that, too," said Stephanie. "I just didn't want to say it."

"Well, there you go," I said. "Can you tell me what Ann said about Kimberly's birth?"

That took her back a minute. She wasn't expecting it. "Nothing."

"Nothing? No birth story. I heard she was really tiny."

"She was. They talk about that. How little she ate compared to the boys. Her itty bitty clothes. Stuff like that."

"But not the birth?" I asked.

She frowned. "I don't think so."

"How about the other ones?"

"Sure. They were difficult. Big fat boys, you know."

"What about Kevin? Did he say anything about Kimberly's birth?"

"No, he was little. Eight, I think."

"He was in Kansas when she was born. Did he mention that?" I asked.

She threw up her hands. "That he talked about. He knew Ann was having a baby, but he was a boy and not paying much attention. He said they came home from a fair and Kimberly was there. Kevin described it as a kind of shock."

"She was home when they got there?"

"Yeah. Ann brought the boys in to see her in a little bassinet in her room. She was so small he thought she wasn't real."

"Never saw her at the hospital?"

"No. That's weird, isn't it? I never thought about that. Depending on where they were in Kansas, they could've gotten back for the birth or right after."

"Thanks, Stephanie. You've been a big help," I said.

"I wish I knew how."

"You will."

She opened her door and climbed in. "Well, I'm off to have the locks changed. Wish me luck."

"Really?" Dallas asked.

"It wasn't the first straw," said Stephanie, "but it's the last."

I closed her door and Dallas said, "Whoa, she is hard core. No second chances for Kevin."

"He took Anton's side and called her an idiot."

"Sucks to be him," said Dallas. "I guess we'll go to the station and see if we can find that pharmacist."

"Sounds like a plan." I hobbled to the cruiser and Pick went nuts leaping at the window and sticking his snout out the crack. We had a discussion about opening the door and not jumping on me. I opened the door. He jumped on me. I'm so good at dog parenting.

Dallas got me down in the back and seat belted Pick in the front with the promise of biscuits. We had no biscuits and I felt surprisingly bad about that. He was being a pretty good poodle.

"I hope those nuts aren't waiting at the door," said Dallas. "If I have to hear one more idiotic idea about how Aunt Tilly was murdered by so and so and they know because somebody had to stir the pot, I will lose my friggin' mind."

Stir the pot.

"Mrs. Tishell!" I burst out.

"Holy crap! Don't do that. I could've had an accident."

"That woman at the station," I said. "She was talking about Mrs. Tishell."

"Who?"

"One of the nutters."

"Oh, yeah. I remember something about that," said Dallas.

"What? What do you remember?" I asked.

"Er...that people are coming in and saying she sent them or something."

"About what?"

"Sorry. Patton's been on that. They're obnoxious. You heard them."

I did hear them. What did she say? Her father.

"Oh, my God," I said. "Hurry. She might still be there."

"Do we *really* want that?"

"Yes. That woman said that her father wants to know who he is."

Dallas sped up and did a hard turn. Pick yipped and I bonked my head on the door handle. It was worth it. "Two minutes," he said.

We squealed into the parking lot in record time and startled Stratton and Kreidt who were in the lot talking. They pulled me out and unclipped Pickpocket, who danced around in a circle, excited for impending treats.

"We just got a call from Kevin Thooft," said Stratton. "It seems you have a dangerous animal that must be destroyed."

"Good luck with that," I said. "Pick was protecting me."

"He bit Thooft," said Kreidt.

Dallas slammed the cruiser door so hard we all jumped. "He did not. Pick bumped him with his snout when he grabbed Mercy. I gotta tell you any other dog would've bit the crap outta that asshat."

"Chuck trained him," I said. "He doesn't bite without a command."

Stratton squatted down and gave the poodle all kinds of love. "Who's a good dog? Who doesn't bite asshats?"

"Are any of the nutters still here?" I asked.

"Nutters?" Kreidt asked.

"The people who want you to dig into cases that aren't cases."

Stratton stood up. "Don't tell me."

"Yeah," I said. "One of them's real."

She looked at the sky. "I knew it."

"Well, they're gone," said Kreidt. "I told them to beat it and it turns out they hit the road when you put them out in the cold."

"Do you have contact info?"

"Which one?" he asked.

Dallas and I smiled at them.

"Eloise is Mrs. Tishell," I said.

Stratton's and Kreidt's brows furrowed.

"Sounds familiar," said Kreidt. "I think there was a woman here today, asking about..."

"An adoption scheme," said Stratton. "Mrs. Tishell sent her."

"There were others," said Dallas.

Kreidt nodded. "Mrs. Tishell's been"—we all said it together—"stirring the pot."

Dallas and Kreidt got me under the arms and carried me in the station, where we found Patton in the conference room bent over a white board with a rough map of St. Seb drawn on it.

She looked up and said, "Five calls, Chief. Spread out all over town. Looks random, except given what happened at the factory, I think it was designed to get Tank out of there."

"Where'd the calls come from?" Stratton asked.

"Looks like a cellphone. We can get the closest towers. Might get lucky with surveillance footage from a house or business."

Kreidt stepped up and looked at the map. He'd gone door to door and hadn't gotten particularly lucky. The people that had been home at the time of our earlier incident weren't there anymore and the smoke grenades were quiet. A Mrs. Emil Kiel, ninety-three with coke bottle thick glasses, saw the colors and came out on her porch to watch. She thought it was more of the same and didn't call 911 because that young man deserved what he got going in the lot.

"A young man?" I asked.

"That's what Mrs. Kiel said, although I think they need to check the old girl's eyes. She said he had a fat head."

"Huh?"

"I don't know. The kid had a hood up and his head was big." He held out his hands. "Like wide."

"That has got to be the weirdest description I've ever heard," said Dallas. "Short, tall, thin, fat?"

"Small, dark clothes, fat head," said Kreidt. "That's what we've got. Oh, and he was driving a car."

Stratton sighed. "What kind?"

"Not a clue, but she knows it wasn't a truck or a minivan. A car."

"Color?"

"I'm sure it had one," said Kreidt.

That got a round of groans.

"Patton?" I waved.

"Hey, Mercy," she said. "Rough day."

"Tell me about it. Do you have a list of the people who came in asking about the old crimes?"

She rolled her eyes. "Yeah, I've got their names and info. They insisted. Lot of good it will do. I'm not contacting them."

"Actually, you are," said Stratton.

I asked her about the woman who was in that morning about her father and talking about Mrs. Tishell. Patton remembered her because she was very genuine and desperate to get some answers for her father who was dying of cancer. The details were sketchy. Her father was adopted in 1955, but he didn't know that until his mother confessed it on her deathbed. His birth certificate had his adoptive parents' names on it. Her father had tried to find an adoption agency, some kind of trail, but had come up empty.

"What sent her here?" I asked. "Mrs. Tishell?"

"There's a group of people who think there was an adoption scheme in the area. There's a Facebook group. I think she googled Whiskey Ridge and that's how she found it."

"Whiskey Ridge?" I asked. "Why Whiskey Ridge?"

"It's on his birth certificate," said Patton. "I told her that's wrong because Whiskey Ridge doesn't have a hospital or an orphanage."

Dallas grabbed a laptop and started typing. "I found it. Children of Whiskey Ridge."

We gathered behind him to look. It was a closed group, but it had nearly a hundred members. To join you had to answer questions and submit a photo of your birth certificate. If they stuck to that, we had 79 people with Whiskey Ridge as their birthplace.

"Who wants to go into the attic?" Stratton asked.

All hands went up and Pick barked.

"Alright, Patton," she said. "Find that woman's information and get her back here. Then see who else came in talking about this adoption thing."

"Do you want me to call them?" Patton asked. "I think there were four or five others."

"Not yet." Stratton looked at me. "You still got that hacker, right?"

I got out my phone and gave her a thumbs-up.

"Dallas, find Mrs. Tishell. With any luck she's in town."

"She is," said Patton. "That woman, I think her name was Patty, said someone had met Mrs. Tishell in Walmart and she told them that a local doctor was selling babies."

Selling. So much worse than a scheme.

"Did she give you that name?" I asked.

"You know, she might've." Patton flushed. "I was getting yelled at about murders and snatch and grabs, I wasn't on point."

"No matter. We'll get it." I looked down and paled. My phone *had* blown up. Mom. Dad. Tiny. Fats. Rocco. Spidermonkey. Chuck. Multiple texts and calls.

Stratton and Kreidt went up into the attic. Secretly, I was happy not to be going. I was totally willing to dig through that crap again, but the stairs were murder. Instead, I called Spidermonkey first, because he was less likely to yell than everyone else.

"Mercy, thank God," he said. "I was climbing out of my skin."

"Why? It's all good."

"Who's with you?"

"A bunch of cops," I said.

He blew out a breath. "Thank goodness. Chuck's driving down right now."

"What for?"

"You won't answer and he just heard that the Sentinel got hit with smoke bombs. The man is freaking out."

"No harm done," I said. "I need you to get into a Facebook group."

"You suspect the bomb thrower has a group?"

"Not that. I don't care about that. This is an adoption group called Children of Whiskey Ridge. A doctor was selling babies according to an old pharmacist."

He started typing and said, "What do the cops say about the smoke thing?"

"An old lady saw a kid. The description is basically useless."

I told him about the fat head and he said he'd see if he could access surveillance around the factory. He was hoping for some Nest cameras. Super easy to hack apparently.

"I'm in," he said.

"That was fast."

Spidermonkey snorted. "Please, Mercy. It's Facebook, not Zurick Cantonal."

"I don't know what that is, but I'm guessing they're secure," I said.

"It's a bank and they are."

Dallas and Patton looked at me with suspicion. Yeah, I'm planning some kind of heist in front of the cops. People give me zero credit. Zero.

"You can't get in them?"

"Oh, no, I've gotten in. It just takes a couple days," he said. "What do you want to know about these Whiskey Ridge people."

"Everything."

Everything was a very short list. They knew they were adopted. Their birth certificates said Whiskey Ridge. Their parents either never told them they were adopted or were very secretive about it, giving various stories about where they came from. Only one woman had gotten the name of the doctor out of her mother on threat of never speaking to her again. Dr. Harvey McBride. Mrs. Tishell wasn't a member of the group, but she'd run into a man at the Walmart, being friendly she asked him what brought him to town. He was wearing a NY firefighter tee and she was curious. She told him that a doctor was selling babies. Several members had tracked her down, but she had no information about any individual child. She told them to come to the station because she'd filed a complaint.

"Call up to the chief," I said to Patton. "Mrs. Tishell filed a complaint about Dr. McBride."

"When?"

"His wife claimed Mrs. Tishell killed him in 1984, so before that, but I'm guessing not long before or something would've happened to him."

Patton nodded and called.

"You're right on the money, Mercy," said Spidermonkey. "Eloise Reed graduated from Drake in 1980. She worked one year in Chicago, became Mrs. Tishell, and then moved to St. Seb."

"So it took her a while to put two and two together," I said. "I wonder what took so long."

"The question for me is *how did she* and why didn't anyone else," he said.

"Can you find out where Dr. McBride lived?" I asked.

"I'll call you back."

I went and got a cup of coffee, mulling those questions over, when my phone lit up. Tiny. He was a sweetheart. It wouldn't be too bad.

"Hey," I said. "Sorry I haven't been answering."

My cousin's voice exploded out of the phone. "Did you call Aunt Willasteen?"

I could've lied. Honestly, that was my go to, but in this case, I could split a hair, so I did.

"No, I didn't."

He took a deep breath and on a man as big as Tiny it sounded like fireplace bellows. "You didn't?"

"I didn't."

It was true. I did not call Tiny's Aunt Willasteen, the holy terror of New Orleans, 'cause she scared me. I called Aunt Miriam, who was equally scary, but I knew her moves. She might whack me with a cane, but I expected it. The devil you know and all that.

"She's coming up here right now," he said. "She's on a plane."

"Is your mom coming?" I liked Tiny's mom. She was nice and didn't look capable of putting a hex on me. Aunt Willasteen muttered things that made me think she could and would.

"No, she has to work," he said with incredible regret. "What did you do? I know you did somethin'."

"Well..."

"Mercy, gawdammit. You know she scares Fats. She doesn't need that. The woman is in the hospital throwing her guts up right the hell now."

"Did she take the meds for nausea?" I asked.

"You know she didn't. She won't. She's gonna power through."

"When does Aunt Willasteen get here?"

"She lands in a half hour and Sister Clarence is picking her up. How did—you told Clarence to call her and now she's coming up here to take care of us."

"I didn't call Clarence. She's a bonus. You can thank me later," I said.

Patton waved at me and I nodded. "I have to go."

"I'm not thanking you. Aunt Willasteen freaks Fats out. You know how tiny and relentless she is."

"Yes, I do. As a heads up, Aunt Miriam's coming, too."

Tiny cussed in the politest way possible and asked, "Are you crazy? Do you hate me?"

"I love you. I love Fats. But most of all, I love that baby."

"Oh...I know that," he said softly. "But then why?"

"Because I can't get her to take those meds. You can't. The doctors can't. Her mom's a drug addict. We gotta play the cards we're dealt. Aunt Willasteen combined with Aunt Miriam and sweet Clarence, that's a royal flush. Nothing beats that. You asked me to do something. I did."

"Mercy, I don't...there's gonna be hell to pay. You know she can take me, right?"

"I'm *so* not worried about that," I said. "Are we good?"

"I'm never asking you for anything again."

"Sold," I said. "Bye."

I hung up with an exaggerated sigh and Dallas asked, "What did you do?"

"Called in reinforcements."

"Will it work?"

"Yes. What do you have?"

Dallas had Mrs. Tishell and she was chatty. She couldn't drive because she'd just had cataract surgery and her husband was bowling, so he was going out to her house in Augusta to pick her up. Patton tracked down Patty Horowitz who had cried on the phone and was coming over from The Landing Hotel.

"Maybe we should go up and help search the attic," said Patton. "It's a huge mess. We tried to work on it, but so many people showed up, pummeling us for answers that it pretty much stopped our progress."

"Isn't that always the way," I said. "Yeah, let's go up."

"By the time you get up there," said Dallas, "it will be time to come down again."

I considered my painkillers and decided against it. The last thing I needed was to be muddled. I took a couple of Advil instead and said, "I'm good."

"That's not enough," said Patton. "You have stitches."

"I don't. I've got glue and butterflies."

They recoiled and I laughed. "It's fine." I hobbled toward the door, but only made it halfway there when someone pounded on the front door of the station.

"That was fast," said Dallas and then he looked at me with suspicion.

"You've been with me the whole time," I said. "What could I have done?"

"I wouldn't put anything past you."

He's catching on. Dammit.

"Well, I didn't do anything." I hobbled for the door, but Patton jetted by me to get it amid more pounding. Then a woman's voice, frantic and high-pitched, resounded off the walls of the St. Seb police station, "Did you change your mind? Please don't. Please."

Patton said something we couldn't make out and led a disheveled woman wearing workout gear and no coat into the conference room.

She laid eyes on me and burst into tears. "My dad said it would be you. He always knows."

Dallas got her a box of tissues and then left to pick up Mrs. Tishell. Patton sat Patty down and we listened to her story. Her father, Harold Horowitz, a construction manager, had always known something was off about his life. Not unlike Kimberly, he didn't look like anyone else in his family. He was shorter with heavy features and large blue eyes. His parents were professors at Northwestern, but he liked working with his hands. He rebuilt car engines for fun and was, in Patty's words, rotten at school, but it wasn't until Patty was in college that an idea sparked up. She decided to do a semester abroad in France and her mother, Shelly, was desperate to visit, so her parents got their first passports. That's when Shelly noticed that Harold was born in Whiskey Ridge, Missouri. Harold's dad had already passed away, but he asked his mother about his birthplace and she said something he would never forget, "Don't think about that. Have some brisket."

Harold came from a family of thinkers. Thinking was their favorite thing. He'd spent his life being encouraged to think. So he ate the brisket, but he didn't stop thinking. He started searching. Whiskey Ridge was a blank slate. He couldn't find any answers or interest. His mother said he was her son and got upset if he broached the subject. After ten years of trying, Harold Horowitz decided to stop. He was a Horowitz. But then he was diagnosed with cancer and a month ago, his mother went into congestive heart failure. As she lay dying, she confessed the truth. He was adopted out of Missouri. She couldn't have children and since his father had had chronic health problems his whole life, a regular adoption was out of the question. No one would approve them. So they saved up and bought him in March of 1955 from Dr. McBride of Whiskey Ridge. Harold Horowitz cost two thousand dollars and his adoptive mother said it was money well spent.

"That was a lot of money then, right?" Dallas asked.

"Over ten thousand dollars," said Patty, wiping her cheeks. "Dad thinks it was probably their life savings."

"What else did your grandmother say?" I asked. "Any specifics on his birth mother?"

"She said she heard about Dr. McBride through the grapevine from someone else that got a baby from him, but she didn't remember who that was."

"How did it work?" Patton asked. "They wrote him a check or what?"

"The doctor called and said he had a baby. They drove down and got him. It was cash."

"Where?" Patton asked. "Here in St. Seb? At the hospital?"

"She said out in the middle of nowhere," said Patty. "She was on painkillers and fading in and out. A big house she said."

"Did she meet the birth mother?" I asked.

Adele Horowitz said she had met the mother, but she was vague on the facts. Her name was Betty or Barbara. She didn't remember what she looked like other than she was very young. Adele was shocked that she was probably no older than fifteen, but she didn't ask her age because it didn't matter, other than it made her feel better about adopting Harold. She said that little girl couldn't take care of a baby.

"Did she want to give up the baby?" Patton asked.

Patty shrugged. "Adele seemed to think so. She agreed to put their names on the birth certificate instead of hers."

"What about the father?" Dallas asked.

"She didn't ask." A tear ran down Patty's cheek. "She said she was so happy to get my dad she didn't care about anything but getting him home and loving him. I want you to know my dad has had a great life. My grandparents loved him so much and they loved us. I remember her saying so many times that her life would be empty without us. My dad isn't mad. He forgave her on the spot. He just wants to know who he is before he dies."

"That's not too much to ask," I said. "Have you tried DNA on Ancestry?"

She nodded. "Dad was so excited. We were sure we'd get somewhere with DNA, but his closest matches were so removed, sixth cousins and they were nice but didn't have a clue who he might be. Other members of the group have tried that route, too. Some got closer matches, but people don't always want to talk to them. There's a lot of shame."

"Do you have your dad's birth certificate?"

Patty opened her enormous handbag, emphasis on bag, and pulled out a fat folder. "When I told the group I was coming, some of them gave me copies of their birth certificates."

She gave me the top one and it was pretty much identical to Kimberly's, except for the height and weight. Harold would have been full term at twenty-one inches and eight pounds. We laid out the other certificates, thirty-two in all, ranging from 1950 to 1982. Dr. McBride had been a busy boy. Assuming he charged the same for every baby— which he didn't—there was at least half a million dollars sitting on that table, considering inflation and whatnot. No wonder Mrs. McBride retired to Provence. She had the bucks to do it.

Only two of the certificates had prices attached, Cherylanne Stoltz in 1975 for 3000 and Nicolas Peterson in 1982 for a hefty 7000.

"What does this mean?" I asked, pointing at Nicolas' sticky note. "Special order?"

"Yeah, I know that's not a great way to put it, but it was the best way I could come up with."

"Enlighten me."

"Nick's parents were a bi-racial couple. They asked for a bi-racial boy and that cost extra." Patty looked a little sick. I certainly felt that way. A child to order was repugnant, but I had no doubt most of the kids on that table were the same. Ann certainly wanted a girl after three boys. I doubted she was alone in that desire.

"How did he find out?" Patton asked.

"A letter in his father's will. His mom had already died," said Patty. "It gave all the information they had."

I looked at the sticky note. "So not much."

"No. His birth mother was twenty-two, in college, and white. His father was twenty-five, in college, and black. Nick said college was important to his dad and he thinks that would've been part of the deal, even though the letter didn't say that."

"That the parents be smart?"

"He thinks so. Achievement was very important to his dad. He was a judge."

Nick's parents were older than most parents at the time of his birth and I supposed if they were going to have one egg in their basket they wanted some assurance it would be a good one. His father was fifty-seven and his mom forty-eight. I went through the certificates and found that to be a common trend. About seventy percent of the parents were over thirty-five. That doesn't sound so old, but even now the average is thirty-one. I knew that because Fats told me. She's competitive about everything. Average isn't her favorite.

More importantly, in 1982 the average parental age would've been a lot younger. Probably twenty-five or so. That made Nick's parents geezers. A lot of those parents were geezers and that made sense to me. My parents couldn't have afforded jack to buy a baby when they were young. Now, they could fork over plenty and Dr. McBride clearly wasn't running a charitable organization.

"Will this help?" Patty asked.

I couldn't lie. I really didn't know.

"I hope so." I looked over the table. So many babies. So many mothers. "Somebody had to know what was going on. This is a lot."

"We have more. 79 total."

"There's more than that," said Patton. "There has to be."

I nodded. "I'd guess at least double that."

"That's like five kids a year."

"That's what we've been saying," said Patty. "Somebody had to know."

Dallas walked in with an elderly woman wearing sunglasses and a huge smile. He guided her to the table by an elbow and she dropped a file box on the table. "Somebody did know."

CHAPTER EIGHTEEN

Eloise Tishell was exactly the kind of woman that men liked to call bossy and opinionated while secretly peeing their pants. It didn't take five minutes to know that. It didn't take five seconds. I loved her and there was a lot to love. Eloise was sixty-five, super smart, stylish as hell, and organized. It was hard to say which was my favorite, but I'm going with the style. Eloise wore a striped Breton top, ropes of pink pearls, artfully ripped jeans, black boots, and a red cape.

"Where do you want to start?" she asked after we finished introductions.

We looked at each other and I said, "The beginning."

So that's where my new style icon started. Her beginning in St. Sebastian in 1981. After a short internship in Chicago, Eloise decided small town life was for her. A professor at Drake recommended her to Bernard Stritch, the one and only pharmacist in St. Seb and the surrounding area. He was looking to retire but luring a new pharmacist to a ghost-ridden town in the back of beyond—that's how St. Seb was thought of in those days—wasn't easy. He'd got a couple men, but they didn't stay, scared off, either literally or by the total lack of Chinese food. That's why an eighty-two-year-old WWI veteran agreed, reluctantly, to take on Eloise, who was, as he put it, too pretty and smart for her own good.

Eloise was smart and she wasn't blind. After a while, she started noticing a certain doctor coming in for medications himself. Bernard always shooed Eloise away when Dr. McBride or his wife showed up. The pharmacist had a box ready for them and no money exchanged hands. When Eloise asked about that, her boss said he put it on the doctor's account. There were no accounts for anyone, except Dr. McBride, and she couldn't find any evidence of one for him either.

Small town life wasn't exactly a mile a minute so Eloise had time on her hands and Bernard napped. One day when the old man was asleep in his office, Eloise searched the pharmacy and found a box packed with birth supplies, Pitocin to cause contractions, Bupivacaine for a spinal block, painkillers, disposable pads, Vitamin K, Erythromycin, syringes, and IV supplies. Dr. McBride was an obstetrician, but supplies like that were at the hospital. It wasn't BYOB.

That afternoon Mrs. McBride came in, flushed and in a rush. She grabbed the box and ran out without saying anything. Bernard didn't look happy and refused to answer any questions. When Eloise got a chance, she started looking through their ordering files and found that Bernard routinely ordered those particular supplies and had been for years. He wasn't supplying the hospital. They did their own ordering, so Dr. McBride had to be doing home births.

"When was this?" I asked.

Eloise opened her box and dug through it, coming up with a file. "1983. I kept an eye on orders after the incident with Mrs. McBride and Bernard restocked. Not everything, so after a while I got so I could see the pattern. It looked like he kept enough on hand to handle three births at any one time. Here are all the orders from 1983. I think Dr. McBride delivered six babies that year."

I spread out the orders and it certainly looked like six to me. "Patty, grab me Nick's birth certificate, please."

Patty handed it to me and looked over my shoulder. "There he is. March tenth."

"Bernard restocked two days after," I said, drumming my fingers on the table.

Patty turned to Eloise. "My father was born in 1955. Do you have anything from back then?"

She smiled. "I do." She pulled out a fatter file and we went through it. Fifteen births in that year. A bumper crop and there was Patty's dad. Bernard resupplied right after his birth like clockwork.

"My dad will be so happy," said Patty. "He came down here ten years ago and the old police chief was nasty to him. He told him he was crazy. There were no adoptions. No nothing. He almost had my dad thinking that the birth certificate was wrong somehow."

"Our old chief had some issues," said Dallas. "I'm sorry about that."

"Thank you," she said. "I appreciate you saying that."

"But I don't know how these files can help you find your father's birth parents though," said Dallas. "It's just accounting and dates. No names."

Eloise put her hands on her hips. "And here I thought I had you convinced I was smart."

"I'm convinced," I said. "What else have you got?"

"Now this isn't for sure, so try not to get your hopes up too high."

Patty clasped her hands together. Hopes were definitely up. Mine were, too, because Eloise was nothing if not thorough. She noticed a young woman coming in a couple of days after a birth restock. She was sore and wearing very loose clothing. Eloise had recently given birth and she recognized the look. The girl had a prescription from Dr. McBride for antibiotics.

"What was it?" I asked.

Eloise got out another file, filled with copies of scripts. Not a lot, but they were usually for Amoxicillin, occasionally something stronger, or painkillers. She pulled out that girl's script. Her name was Julia Malone and she got her script on August 6, 1983.

"She probably had a perineal wound-related infection," I said.

"That was my guess and it got me thinking about other women coming in. So I kept track. It didn't happen a lot, but I copied the script when it did."

"Did you find prescriptions from 1955?" Patty asked.

"Honey, I didn't look. By that time, I was run ragged. I'd had my first and I was pregnant with my second. Bernard, well, he was a good pharmacist, but he was so old I had to do everything and fight with him to be allowed to do it. I was exhausted."

"Then you can't help my dad." Patty slumped. "So close."

"You might still be," said Eloise. "In the old days, everything was paper."

I grinned. "You kept them."

"It was routine," she said. "We bundled them and kept a log. Bernard's policy was ten years. He didn't have to do that for so long, but I think it made it easier to forget about them."

"He wanted to forget about what evidence he had?" Patton asked.

Eloise laughed. "Good God no. He just didn't want to clean."

"So it was all still there when you took over in 1984?" I asked.

"It was. I worried about what would happen when Bernard finally gave it up and left. He wasn't happy with me being nosy and asking questions about Dr. McBride. He said I should know my place."

"Sounds like you did."

"Exactly my response," she said. "He wasn't happy about that, I can tell you, and I thought that he might fire me at any time. That's why I kept all this stuff, just in case."

"But he didn't fire you?" Dallas asked.

"No, I really thought he would after he caught me copying scripts, but his wife liked me and I don't think she liked Dr. McBride. I don't know if Elizabeth could've saved my job. They were a very traditional couple. He wore the pants and all that. But Bernard's eyesight was going and he hit a pole in the Walmart parking lot and totaled the car. He was pretty banged up. Elizabeth told him he was retiring and leaving me alone. To my surprise, he did. Maybe he was in too much pain to fight. I don't know how she did it."

"Do you think the records still exist?" Patty asked.

"They did when I retired in 2012. They were in the attic. A fire hazard, but I told Stephanie Thooft that she ought to leave them be. They might come in handy one day."

"What did she say?" I asked.

"Stephanie was a busy young mother. I doubt she had any interest in clearing out that attic and her husband, Kevin, would never," said Eloise.

"Why not?" Patton asked. "Men can clean."

"Not Kevin Thooft. I doubt he'd recognize a toilet brush if you hit him in the face with one."

"Stephanie should try that," said Dallas. "He's a real douchebag."

We told Eloise and Patty about our encounter at the pharmacy and Eloise nodded. "Those Thoofts are clannish to say the least. They don't let anyone close."

"Now we know why," I said.

"I hope they'll let me in that attic," said Patty. "My dad's birth mother's name could be up there."

Eloise put an arm around her. "It could be. It very well could."

"Do you have a 1980 file?" I asked.

"I do." Eloise gave me the file and I laid out the orders. An order in July fit Kimberly's birth date. There were no corresponding scripts so her birth mother didn't have any trouble or didn't fill her prescription in St. Seb.

"Why did Mrs. McBride say you killed her husband?" I asked, staring down at Kimberly's birth certificate.

"Because I probably did," she said without a trace of give a crap, "in a way."

"Really?"

"Sure, but it was his own fault in the end."

Bernard the antique pharmacist was dragged out of work in June 1984 and upon leaving he told Eloise, "Just do as you're told. Dr. McBride's a good man and your husband is only a teacher."

"What does that mean?" Dallas asked. "He had something against teachers? What a dick."

"No." She laughed. "It meant my Tom didn't make a lot of money. I think that Dr. McBride made it worth Bernard's while to fill those boxes. He definitely lived better than we did and Elizabeth never worked."

"Would she have known where the money came from?" I asked.

"He gave her an allowance, so I seriously doubt it."

There was some jaw-dropping on that one and Eloise shook her head. "Yes, I know, but it wasn't that unusual for the old people. Elizabeth sometimes had to come in for money to have her hair done or for groceries. I was a shock to the system. One time Tom came in and asked me if we had enough money to buy a canoe. Bernard nearly passed out. He couldn't believe that I knew the money period, much less had a say in how it was spent."

"So what happened?" I asked. "Did Dr. McBride come in for another box?"

"He did and *that* was a shock to *his* system."

About a month after Bernard and Elizabeth boogied off on an around the world cruise, the doctor came in for a box. There was no box. Eloise had put the supplies back on the shelves. She didn't think Dr. McBride would come in and try it. He was no fan of hers and would literally leave and come back if she was alone in the pharmacy. That day he showed up asking for his box and she asked what those supplies were for. It got pretty heated when he wouldn't explain what he was going to do with them and Eloise wouldn't fill his request without an explanation as to what he was going to do with Pitocin and Bupivacaine outside a hospital. He stormed out, saying he'd take his business elsewhere, but he didn't. He came back the next day, red-faced, incredibly angry, and more than a little desperate. Eloise knew those supplies were for some poor girl probably already laboring, so she made a judgement call and gave him the supplies. Then she marched right over to the station and filled out a police report. She and Melanie Gates had a long talk and she thought Melanie took her seriously. A deputy copied everything Eloise had and started an investigation that included interviewing the doctor and his wife.

"When did he die?" I asked.

"Four days later, a coronary brought on by stress, not gutters," she said. "It was me and my nosy, interfering self that got him all worked up."

"And the fact that he was a criminal," said Patty.

"What happened afterwards?" Dallas asked.

"Nothing. He was dead. His darling wife sued me, but as soon as she saw the files, she dropped it and hit the road."

"Melanie didn't investigate?" Stratton walked in covered in dust and followed by a spastically sneezing Kreidt.

I gave the chief a quick rundown, Eloise shook her hand and

informed a surprised Kreidt that he needed a netty pot. "There wasn't a lot to investigate. I may have given you the impression that Dr. McBride wasn't well liked, but that isn't accurate. He was. People loved him. He delivered three-fourths of the babies in town and never lost a patient or a baby. Nobody would say a word against him. Melanie couldn't get an ounce of cooperation."

"He didn't deliver your babies though, I'm guessing," I said.

"No. I went with Dr. Burke. He joined McBride's practice about the time I came to town."

"Did he know?"

"Yes, absolutely," said Eloise, "but he was a young doctor looking to build a practice here. He wasn't going to go against his boss and I don't think he had anything to do with it. Dr. Burke never wrote any odd scripts or came in for boxes."

I looked at Stratton, who was lustily blowing her nose. Kreidt had gone to the locker room to find nose spray.

"Did you find anything?" I asked her.

"No. What a disaster. I think it got worse." She looked at the deputies. "What have you two been doing up there?"

"Looking for stuff," said Dallas.

"Using a leaf blower?"

Dallas and Patton hung their heads.

"But there was an investigation though?" I asked.

"Melanie did the best she could," said Eloise. "Her father and son weren't any good as you discovered, Mercy, but Melanie was. Another reason why McBride keeled over. The obesity didn't help either."

"What exactly did you accuse him of?" Stratton asked after finishing with another two tissues.

"Selling newborns," said Eloise, "but it took me awhile to get that. It wasn't until a couple showed up in May 1984 that I put it together. I was young and, in a way, innocent. The thought had simply not occurred to me. I thought it was some sort of home birth service that he was doing under the table. The hospital charges a boatload for a birth. He could just do it at home and get paid in cash for a lot cheaper. No insurance to deal with, etcetera. I wasn't even sure if it was illegal, but the way they were sneaking around made me nervous. That's why I started collecting evidence."

"What did the couple say?" I asked.

"Enough."

The couple was older, like a lot of the parents on the birth certificates. They asked Eloise about Dr. McBride, was he reliable, did he deliver healthy babies, would she trust him, that kind of thing. The woman was obviously past childbearing age and they were from Arizona. Even then she thought that they were asking for their daughter or someone. But about a week later, she saw them with an infant at a restaurant in town. The woman told the waitress that she'd had the baby herself.

"Then I knew. I asked around about Dr. McBride doing adoptions, but I was told to mind my business, that he was a good man and a good doctor. Bernard threatened to fire me, but then he had his accident. I took over, but then it was all moot because McBride was dead less than two months after I put it together. I told all this to Melanie."

Stratton looked through Eloise's orders. "That is a lot of babies. Where in the world did he find the mothers?"

Mothers.

I looked at the numbers. Some years were big. Fifteen or more. They declined over the years to four in 1984. Better birth control options and less stigma about out of wedlock pregnancies would probably account for that, but even four was still a lot for the St. Seb area.

Babies. Mothers. Meds. No hospital.

"Parents didn't talk about it," said Patty, "but from what my grandmother told my dad, I think it was word of mouth."

"I guess that kept it on the down low," said Patton.

"They'd have to," said Stratton. "This was highly illegal. Buying and selling children, that smacks of slavery, not to mention falsifying documents and safety concerns. It had to be as private as possible."

Private.

"Where did he do it?" I asked suddenly and everyone jumped.

"Good question," said Stratton and she looked to Eloise, who shrugged.

"I never had a clue on that," said Eloise. "Obviously it was in the St.

Seb area, but I never had pregnant girls coming in the pharmacy before giving birth. At least not ones that I didn't know and, in this town, we all know each other."

"What about his house?" Dallas asked. "That's private."

"Did he live in Whiskey Ridge?" I asked.

Eloise shook her head. "No. McBride lived here in town on Dogwood Lane."

"Which house?" Stratton asked with a sudden sharpness. "The French one?"

"No. The one that looks like a faux plantation house."

"Then he didn't do it there."

"Why not?" I asked. "It sounds like he had the room."

Eloise got out her phone but couldn't see it well enough through her sunglasses. "Here, Mercy. 698 Dogwood Lane."

I put the address into Zillow and had to agree when McBride's house came up. It was a statement house and meant to be seen with little in the way of obscuring trees or shrubs. It was even on a hill overlooking the town, easily visible pretty much everywhere. "You're right. That's not the place. As well-liked as he was, pregnant girls coming and going would make people talk."

"But people had to know," said Dallas. "Bernard knew. Eloise knew."

"And town hall," said Eloise.

"Right," said Stratton. "Somebody was registering the births."

Patton picked up a 1950 birth certificate. "What about a hotel? Did we have a hotel in 1950?"

"We're not that much of a backwater," said Eloise. "The Landing is a hotel, remember? They've been in business for eighty years."

"I'm staying there," said Patty. "It's right on the waterfront. Very public."

The St. Seb natives went round and around, naming hotels, inns, and motels. The more they talked the funnier I felt. All those mothers and babies. Something about the numbers, but I just couldn't quite get it.

"I don't like it," said Dallas. "The sheer numbers of pregos going in and out of a hotel would raise questions. Travelers passing through would notice. They'd have no loyalty to McBride or St. Seb."

Stratton slapped him on the back. "Good point. That's very true."

Not to be outdone, Patton quickly said, "But look, the births are spread out. It's not a tidal wave. It's a trickle."

"People would still notice a bunch of pregos going into a hotel."

"But it wasn't a bunch." Patton pointed at the table. "It was one at a time."

One at a time. One at a time.

"Where's Kimberly's birth certificate?" I asked. "And the meds."

Eloise bent over the table to point at the list next to Kimberly's birth certificate. We didn't have any other ones for that year, but there were five births. I took the list and Kimberly's certificate. There it was in black and white, but if it weren't for Eloise's records, I never would've seen it.

"Eloise, Dr. McBride always replaced his birth supplies after a birth?"

The elderly lady took off her glasses and squinted at paperwork. "I believe so, yes."

"Look at this medication," I said.

"Yes," she said. "Dr. McBride kept a stock of steroids and antibiotics."

"For preemies?"

"I think so. I suspected that he might have an incubator, but I never found evidence of that in our records. It would've come from a medical supply store."

I pointed at Dallas and Patton. "Find those meds on Eloise's other lists."

"It didn't happen very often," said Eloise.

"That's what I'm counting on," I said.

All in all, Dr. McBride ordered medications that would've been used on premature babies rarely. There were only two orders in Eloise's records.

"So he didn't have a bunch of preemies," said Dallas. "So what?"

I held up Kimberly's birth certificate. "So her birth date is wrong."

They all bent over Eloise's med orders for July 1980 and there were two. Notably for July eighteenth, which was the day after Kimberly's birth, supposedly. But that order was normal. No steroids. Nothing special. But three days earlier on July fifteenth, there'd been an order for the preemie meds.

Stratton put her finger on the order for July fifteenth. "We know Kimberly was a preemie, so she was born, at the latest, on the fourteenth, not the seventeenth."

Patton touched the July eighteenth order. "So then who's this?"

Eloise and I looked at each other and said, "Ann Thooft's real baby."

Chuck Watts walked into the St. Sebastian police station conference room and, without a greeting or any acknowledgment at all, began to whip off his scarf, hat, and coat while going off on me.

"I cannot believe you didn't call me. I had to hear you got smoke bombed from somebody else. You have stitches in your butt. Fats and Rocco are in the hospital. Tank got pranked and Fats' truck is totaled. Is that it? Am I up to date? Am I? Mercy? Hello?"

I was still off balance from realizing that Ann Thooft didn't fake a pregnancy. She ditched her own kid. I just...I couldn't.

"Mercy!"

Eloise, in all her glory, stalked over to my incensed boyfriend and proclaimed, "No, you are not." She stuck her hand out and said, "Eloise Tishell, former pharmacist and this case's linchpin. If you want to yell, you can hit the road."

After a long hesitation, Chuck shook her hand.

"Wise decision," said Eloise. "Do you have anything to offer?"

"I...uh...I'm a cop."

She sighed. "Yes, I know. I recognize the stance. Have you got any information for us?"

"Not really."

"Well, we've got information for you," said Eloise.

Chuck looked at me. The wind was out of his sails, but he was still butt hurt. Not as much as me, so I wasn't too worried.

"We know what Anton Thooft was being blackmailed with," I said.

"Yeah?"

I told him and he leaned over the table to look at our evidence, saying, "Well, that would do it. You think the real Thooft baby is alive?"

"There's nothing to say he isn't," I said.

"He?" Dallas asked.

"It had to be a boy. Otherwise, there was no point in the switch."

"Oh, right."

Patton went over and made a fresh pot of coffee. "How could she do it? Her own blood."

We all looked at Eloise and she said, "I didn't know her well and she never came into the pharmacy after the investigation. It was always Anthony and later the kids."

"Hold on," said Chuck. "There was an investigation?"

She told him how it went down in 1984 and Chuck grew more serious by the moment.

"Have you found the file?" he asked Stratton.

"No, not yet," she said. "You know what a mess it is."

"We have to find that file."

I frowned and took a cup of coffee from Patton. "Why? We probably know more than Melanie did."

"We need to know what she knew," said Chuck.

"Let's just ask her," said Dallas.

"She's no fan of mine," I said.

Eloise nodded. "I spoke to her last week. You really wreaked havoc on her world with her father and that murder, not to mention Will losing his job. I recommend we find the file."

"Why do we care?" Patton asked.

"Because someone sent Anton after Mercy," said Chuck. "How did they know about Ann and her baby? If that investigation is the source"—he gave me a hard look—"then we'll be closer to finding out who sent him."

The Klinefeld Group. They were in that attic.

"Could be a lot of people," I said.

"No, not a lot of people have access to our files," said Stratton. "It can't be a coincidence that Anton was sent right after you were here."

"That's the way I see it," said Chuck.

Stratton downed her coffee and said, "Let's go back up."

Kreidt walked in and groaned. His eyes were red and swollen and he had a wad of tissues clamped to his face. "I'll pay you to not make me go up there."

"Fine. You stay with the dog," said Stratton, "and start working on a press release."

"For what?"

"Dr. Harvey McBride's adoption ring."

"I hope you have it all figured out, because the news crews are at The Landing. Matt says they're arguing in the bar and pissed that we closed up shop," said Kreidt.

"Don't they care about what happened with Fats' truck?" I asked. "You'd think they'd be on that or, at least, the smoke grenades."

"Nope," he said. "They're interviewing the nuts we had in here this morning about how idiotic we are."

I looked at Patty to see how she felt about being called a nut, but she wasn't paying attention. She was looking at the med order for Ann Thooft's child.

"Patty?" I asked. "See something?"

She tapped the date on the preemie med order. "This seems familiar to me."

"What are you thinking?" Stratton asked.

"I don't really know," said Patty. "Do you mind if I start asking group members about it?"

"Not at all," I said. "Please do and we'll look for your dad's dates in the files."

She thanked us and I hobbled out of the room toward the stairs. The cops followed me, but Chuck stood there, watching.

"What's up?" I asked at the door.

He picked up my prescription. "You should take this."

"Later."

"How are you going to get up those stairs?"

I put my nose in the air. "The same as everyone else. I'll walk."

He plunked down the pills and came after me. "Get real. I'll carry you."

"Pass." I got up two stairs and got over it. Chuck got in front of me, I hooked my arms around his neck, then I had a childhood flashback of Dad, on one of the rare times he was around, carrying me through the zoo, dangling on his back.

Upstairs at the attic door, I dropped off Chuck's back, but I had to be persuaded. It was such a pleasant way to travel. I was totally overusing my legs for stairs.

"My throat," croaked Chunk as Stratton unlocked the attic.

Eloise gave him a throat lozenge and told him to suck it up. She had a bit of my dad in her.

Stratton opened the door and said, "Now don't judge us."

Oh, I judged her. I judged her hard. The attic was worse. Last time we were there I thought hurricane. This time tornado after a hurricane came through.

"For crying out loud," I said.

"Yeah. Cases keep getting requested." She jammed a thumb at Patton and Dallas. "And these two are like toddlers looking for a toy."

The deputies hung their heads but got to work. It took about thirty minutes before Patton's hand shot up. "I found a prescription slip."

Eloise took a look. "Yes, it's one of mine."

The cops converged on the area, but I held Chuck back. "That's where we found the plane crash stuff."

He kissed my forehead and went over to sift through evidence boxes and files. I followed, but my phone buzzed.

"Got something?" I asked.

"A little yes, but mostly no," said Spidermonkey.

"Bummer."

"Yes, it is."

My hacker hadn't been able to find any porch cameras around the factory. Apparently, porch pirates weren't a thing in St. Seb. He did catch a car speeding away from the area at the right time, but the license plate was obscured and the driver wasn't visible. They had a hood up and were hunched over.

"Did it look like a kid?" I asked.

"Maybe. Certainly on the small side and the car is crap. They're either broke or a kid. It's a Hyundai and at least ten years old."

"How about Anton's phone?" I asked. "Anything turn up?"

"Nothing, which might be something," he said.

"Come again?"

Spidermonkey had taken a second look at all the data from Anton's phone and there were no false fronts. No suspicious apps at all. It did ping the towers around the Central West End for several days before he nabbed me. Anton looked at restaurants and checked out Ode de Caffeine in our neighborhood. But that was it.

"How is this good news?"

"Well, I was thinking," said Spidermonkey, "that Thooft was taking you somewhere to meet up with whoever was blackmailing him."

"Right," I said.

"How'd he know where to go?"

"They told him."

"Thooft was like you, directionally challenged," said Spidermonkey.

"Thanks," I said.

He chuckled and said, "He used Google maps constantly in Germany, even around where he lived. If he was going any place new to him, he used it."

I smiled and nodded at Chuck, who looked worried. "He had a burner phone."

"I think so. He must've, but here's the thing."

"Where is it?" I asked.

"Not in evidence. A second phone wasn't logged."

"He ditched it when I got noticed in the trunk," I said. "I don't suppose you got the mile markers that correspond to the 911 calls."

"Yes, I do," he said and I could tell he was smiling.

"You are awesome."

"I agree one hundred percent," said Spidermonkey.

I told him what we were up to and said I had to go.

"Hold on. I'm not done."

"Something on Thooft or Ann?"

"I wish. McBride, but it's not what you're hoping for."

Spidermonkey had taken a look at Dr. McBride. He found the house on Dogwood Lane and agreed that wasn't a place to hide elicit adoptions. Unfortunately, he and the wife owned no other property. They had two sons, both of which lived out of state. Neither owned anything in St. Seb or the surrounding area.

"Nothing in Whiskey Ridge?" I asked. "I'm thinking it has to be Whiskey Ridge. People do things for a reason. He used Whiskey Ridge on the birth certificates the entire time. It has to mean something."

"I think you're right, but I've got nothing," he said.

I thanked him and hung up, craning my neck back to stretch before heading over to help.

Chuck and Stratton turned around with some files in hand.

"There's nothing new here," said Stratton.

"But you've got the investigation files?" I asked.

They did. Chief Melanie Gates had investigated. She'd gone through Eloise's information, making notes and a timeline. She'd talked to the prosecutor about subpoenas and gone into vital records to look at the birth certificates. They had her interviews with Dr. McBride and his wife, if you wanted to call them that. Mostly, the couple refused to say anything other than to attack her credibility and education.

"Anything on the Thoofts?" I asked.

"No, but there are files missing," said Patton. "Chief Gates numbered her folders. Six and seven are missing."

"She does reference the Thoofts the second time she talked to Dr. McBride," said Chuck.

"What did she say?"

"She asked if he knew them, but he started yelling and clutched at his chest. They called an ambulance and he was hospitalized until he died."

"That's a pretty extreme response," I said.

Chuck came over and hugged me. "I think so. She definitely hit a nerve."

"Any clue why she asked about them?"

The cops shook their heads and Stratton said, "We'll have to ask Melanie."

"I'll do it," I said. "How bad can it be? She's a florist now."

"She has black belts in Judo and Karate," said Dallas. "She can kick butt."

Patton nudged him. "You mean your butt."

"I'm not saying which butts. Just butts."

We left the attic and Chuck gave me a lift downstairs. At the bottom, Kreidt was waiting, looking better physically, but with a kind of astonished look on his face. "You're gonna want to hear this."

We went into the conference room and Patty was there, sitting on a chair and feeding Pickpocket beef jerky.

"Are you okay?" I asked.

"I found out about that date," she said.

Patty had started messaging the Facebook group about July 14, 1980. It took a while, but she finally found the right person to ask, a former administrator. It seemed a woman named Jessica Lutz had contacted the group a couple of years ago looking to join. She thought her husband was adopted out of Whiskey Ridge. His name was Christopher Lutz and he was not adopted according to his parents and neither were his two older sisters. Jessica had always thought the siblings looked nothing alike and didn't particularly resemble their parents, but it wasn't so obvious that she'd have brought it up. Three years ago, Christopher had a motorcycle accident, a bad one, and he lost a leg. He'd have died if he hadn't been wearing a helmet and he needed quite a bit of blood. Jessica wanted to feel like she was doing something, so she donated, but her blood type didn't match. His parents claimed they had a problem with needles and wouldn't consider donating or being typed. Jessica was out of her head upset, but his sisters came in and donated. One matched his type and her blood was used during one of his surgeries.

Christopher's parents were wonderful during the long hospital stay and his extensive rehab, but Jessica was curious about the blood. She was still thinking about that when her mother-in-law went into the hospital for a hysterectomy. The mother's blood type was right out in the open written on the whiteboard in the room. B. Christopher was an A. That meant his father had to be an A. She took a peek at his dog tags from Vietnam, proudly displayed with his multiple medals. B.

Christopher wasn't their son. She looked at his birth certificate and there was Whiskey Ridge, but Christopher wouldn't talk about it. He wouldn't join the Facebook group or question his parents, and he barred her from asking his sisters. That was the end of it.

"Okay," I said. "So that's why you don't have his birth certificate."

Patty nodded and Kreidt went over to the laptop. "I know the Thoofts. Not well, but I know them."

We waited and he turned the screen around to a Facebook page for Christopher Lutz, his profile pic front and center. "This is a Thooft."

CHAPTER NINETEEN

Melanie Gates stood on her front porch and it was a good thing. We had railing between us and although the tiny redhead looked completely capable of coming over it at me, I felt good about my chances given that Chuck was there and he had a gun.

"You have some nerve showing up here," she said, her green eyes glittering.

They'll put that on my tombstone. "She had some nerve." I'm good with it.

"I'm known for nerve," I said.

"And a lot of other things," said Melanie.

Chuck bristled beside me and I put a hand on his arm. "I don't deny it, but a lot of it isn't my fault."

"Yeah, right. I've seen the posters."

Mallory Tancredi stepped up beside her mother. "You said you'd be nice, Mom."

"I didn't say that. You said it."

Mallory looked to the heavens. "Mom, please, it's been a long day."

"Because of her," said Melanie.

"Me?" I asked.

The former police chief slammed her fist down on the railing. "You think those prank fire calls weren't about you?"

"They could've been about me," said Tank from his corner of the porch. "I've gotten some blowback from my coverage of Sister Maggie's murder and the rest of it."

"It's not you," Melanie hissed. "It's her. Look at us. Our town is now known for aiding and abetting a serial murderer."

"That's hardly Mercy's fault," said Stratton. "It had already happened. She just uncovered it."

"It should've stayed covered."

"Janet Lee Fine's parents didn't think so," I said.

Melanie's face got so pink that the freckles stood out like they were floating. "That wasn't my fault."

"Nobody said it was," said Stratton. "Just answer some questions and we're out of here."

"I don't see why I should. She'll just make me look like an idiot again and you'll probably get fired," said Melanie.

"Mom," Mallory raised her voice, which surprised her mother. "Getting fired was Will's fault. You knew he had a problem. We all did."

"I don't want to talk about that."

"Fine. Talk about Dr. McBride."

Melanie set her jaw and then spun around to go in the house.

"Sorry," said Mallory. "We tried."

"I'll leave!" I yelled just as Melanie went over the threshold and she yelled, "Good!" over her shoulder.

"Helpful," said Chuck.

"Hold on," I said and then yelled at the house, "I'll leave sooner rather than later!"

The door was almost closed, but then Melanie stopped and poked her head out. "What do you mean?"

"I'm staying until I find out what I want to know and I draw news crews like flies to a corpse."

"Ew," said Patton behind me. "Gross."

"But true," whispered Stratton.

"You want me out of here?" I asked. "Tell me about your investigation. From what I've seen it was thorough until Dr. McBride bit the dust."

"Tonight you'll leave?" Melanie asked. "And no interviews."

"Hey," said Tank. "She owes me one on this whole deal."

Melanie gritted her teeth, but said, "Fine. That interview and you don't say our town is a crappy load of crap."

"Never said that. Never will," I said.

She came back out on the porch, no more friendly than before. "What do you want to know? I didn't get far."

"Far enough that he had a heart attack," I said.

"Not my fault."

"I know that. What happened in that interview? What set him off?"

She leaned a hip against the railing and said, "I don't really know. I'd questioned him before about the medication records Eloise had. I wanted to know where the babies were and who the mothers were. He stayed cool and collected. Denied everything. No births outside of the hospital."

That was a jaw-dropper.

"Seriously?" I asked. "What about the meds?"

"He claimed he got them on discount and took them into the hospital."

Stratton snorted. "Give me a break. That's not how that works."

"Exactly what I said and I followed up with the hospital. They were reluctant to confirm what he claimed, but they did. He was popular."

I walked up closer, but Melanie didn't notice. The old chief was thinking about that day so long ago. "You went back and asked him about the Thoofts. That time he got really upset?"

She nodded. "He did, but I didn't know why. I still don't."

"Why did you bring them up?" Chuck asked.

"Because they owned the farm next door."

We all stopped moving and I could hardly breathe. "Next door to what?"

"The old holiday camp," she said. "It was the only place I knew of that you could possibly hide pregnant women without anyone being the wiser."

"Who owned it?" asked Stratton as breathless as me.

"Bernard Stritch's family."

We stayed quiet and Melanie warmed to her subject, forgetting who she was telling and remembering her old days of investigating. She was logical and she had an advantage on us and on Eloise back in the day. She'd grown up in St. Seb and knew about the old holiday camp in Whiskey Ridge because her mother worked there as a lot of the locals did before the war. It was a faux rustic camp with individual cabins laid out around a small lake. City slickers would come out and rough it by cooking over a fire, hiking, canoeing, and listening to nature talks. It was kind of like a low-rent Catskills, but WWII put an end to all that. Nobody was vacationing during the war years and when it was over the Stritches tried to reopen, but nobody was interested. They survived a world war. They wanted new and different. Modern and exciting. The Stritches tried to sell, but it wasn't prime farmland and too far from the city to feed the suburban building boom, so the holiday camp sat empty and still did. Being next to the Thoofts' industrial pig farm certainly didn't help. Smell and run off was a factor.

"So you went over to the Thoofts," I said. "What did they say?"

"It was just Anthony and I regretted that interview in more ways than one."

"Why?" Stratton asked.

"Ann and I were friends." Melanie's face changed and sadness crept in. "We were on the PTA and did things for the food drive at Thanksgiving. She was easy to talk to and I didn't know Anthony very well. He was sweet but always looked like he had a list a mile long and no time to spare."

"What did he say?" I asked.

Melanie looked at me directly and for the first time without anger. "Nothing and I'm serious when I say that. He didn't know anything about the camp or anything going on there. He thought Dr. McBride was a saint for bringing Kimberly into the world safely and didn't believe for a moment that he'd do anything underhanded or illegal."

"Why did that upset Dr. McBride?" Stratton asked. "That's a ringing endorsement."

"I never got to say any of that," she said. "I mentioned that I'd been out to the Thoofts' farm and talked to Anthony. I might've said something about going back out to interview Ann. I don't know. Something like that. Dr. McBride got red in the face, started clutching his chest, and yelling. Mrs. McBride kicked me out and I called the ambulance."

"That was it?" Chuck asked.

"He died not long after," said Melanie, "and once that happened forget it. He became a saint, more than he already was and that was considerable. I questioned people in Whiskey Ridge and, boy, did they clam up. The Stritches wouldn't let me on the camp and I had no cause for a search warrant. I didn't have any evidence that anything actually happened there and no victims, no mothers, babies, or adoptive parents."

Chuck crossed his arms. "You had nothing."

"Zippo."

"But you believed Eloise?" I asked.

She nodded. "Oh, yeah. No doubts. I just had nothing to go on and nobody to prosecute, except maybe an elderly widow. I'd have gotten drawn and quartered."

"But then the widow sued," said Stratton.

Melanie rolled her eyes. "She was not the brightest bulb. Eloise had all the records to back up her assertions. My investigation was justified."

"You weren't named in the suit," I said.

She laughed. "She couldn't name me. I'm from here, born and bred. Eloise was an outsider."

"What happened with Ann?" Stratton asked.

"I tried to talk to her, but she never spoke to me again. Don't get me wrong, a lot of people were mad about the investigation, but when Mrs. McBride dropped the suit and ran off to France, they got over it. There were whispers about the camp and I was off the hook."

"But no one came forward?" I asked.

"Nope and that's what I know," said Melanie. "How about you tell me why Dr. McBride had a heart attack over the Thoofts?"

Stratton and Chuck laid it out for her, but I stayed silent. We were missing something. If The Klinefeld Group found out about what

Ann did from those files, they must've been clairvoyant because Melanie—if I went by her reactions—didn't have a clue about Kimberly.

Melanie held up the photo we'd printed of Christopher Lutz and said, "I can't believe it."

"It's all true," said Stratton.

"I would've kept going, if he hadn't died. There would've been press. A spotlight right on the Thoofts as the neighbors to the camp and, Kimberly, she looks nothing like them."

"Only a matter of time. Can you imagine what would've happened when it came out that he took Anthony's son away and sold him without his knowledge," Stratton asked, "and that Ann had him do it?"

Melanie handed the photo back to me and said, "I can't. I really can't. No wonder McBride dropped dead." She looked at me. "So you're done then. You know why Anton did it. Someone threatened to expose his family's ugly secret."

"What was in your missing files?" I asked.

She frowned. "Missing files?"

Stratton told her about our search of the attic and the theory that the files were how someone found out.

"Dear lord. I don't know. We're talking 1984. What do you have? Maybe we can narrow it down," said Melanie.

Chuck got out his phone and listed everything that was in the other folders and it seemed complete. If it weren't for her numbering system, we'd never have known something was missing.

"Oh, that's easy," she said. "The witness list and my interview with Anthony is missing. I always kept separate folders for each interview subject."

"You had witnesses?" I asked. "Who?"

Melanie didn't have witnesses per se. She had people she wanted to talk to, but McBride died before she got to the majority of them. The Thoofts were on there, Ann in particular. People in Whiskey Ridge. Some different people who worked for Bernard Stritch and Dr. McBride, like maids and gardeners. Melanie wanted to talk to the meter reader and the electric company to see if power was being used at the camp. Her list was surprisingly extensive and I had no doubt that if she continued, she'd have gotten what she needed to make a case, but that didn't help us.

"You always have a witness list?" Chuck asked.

"Always," she said firmly.

"No exceptions?"

Stratton turned to him. "What are you getting at?"

"I didn't see a witness list for Mercy's great grandparents' crash," said Chuck. "But I wasn't in the attic. Was there one?"

The breath went out of my body and I wavered. He grabbed my arm and steadied me. No witness list. I hadn't noticed that. I hadn't been looking. What would they have witnessed anyway? A plane going down? An explosion?

"There wasn't a list that I saw," said Stratton. "Mercy?"

I shook my head.

"I can go back and look, but I'm pretty confident we have your report on the crash, coroner reports, and evidence list for the effects, but no witnesses," said Stratton.

"What's that crash got to do with anything?" Melanie asked. "It was years later."

"Were there witnesses?" Chuck asked.

"Yes, of course. People saw it go down and were at the crash site before me."

"Did you interview them?" Stratton asked.

"Yes, but I don't remember anything standing out. We thought it was an accident," said Melanie.

Two witness lists. Two missing witness lists.

"Who was on both lists?" I asked.

"I have no idea," she said. "You think that's the connection?"

Chuck and Stratton nodded and conferred with Melanie. My mind went to the memorial. It was out toward Whiskey Ridge. I got out my phone and pulled up a map. Agatha and Daniel's plane would've passed over Whiskey Ridge and they crashed within a few miles of the Thooft farm and the Stritch defunct holiday camp.

"You have the report back at the station?" Chuck asked.

"Of course," said Stratton. "It's in my office."

"We can go back and—"

"Who died?" I asked.

The cops looked at me like I might've finally lost it.

"Your great grandparents—"

I cut off Stratton. My mind simply would not be polite. "No who died right after Agatha and Daniel's crash?"

"A lot of people, I'm sure," said Melanie with some exasperation.

"Of your witnesses, who died unexpectedly right after?" I asked.

Melanie screwed up her face and asked, "What in the world makes you think someone died?"

"Because the people who brought down my great grandparents plane kill people. If a person did something to catch their eye and caused a problem then they'd get dead."

"No one was murdered," she said. "I'd remember that."

"Not murdered," I said. "Dead. Unexpectedly dead."

Melanie rubbed her forehead. "Just dead. Nothing suspicious?"

"No. There would've been no hint of foul play."

"I have to think about who was on the crash list. Not the Thoofts, I don't think."

Not just a witness. Has to be evidence.

"Someone who saw something at the crash site," I said. "They had something. A piece of evidence. Something odd about the plane."

Melanie clapped her hand over her mouth and Mallory touched her shoulder. "Mom?"

She dropped her hand slowly. "Joyce Franklin. She died, but it *was* an accident."

Chuck nodded. "It would be. What happened to her?"

"She died of carbon monoxide poisoning right after the crash."

"Did she live in St. Seb?" I asked.

"No. Whiskey Ridge," said Melanie. "She was a maid."

Stratton put her hands on her hips. "Let me guess. She worked for Dr. McBride."

Joyce Franklin worked for both Dr. McBride and the pharmacist, Bernard Stritch. Melanie described her as a sad case, one of those people whose life never quite got off the ground. She was fifty-four when she died, alone with her five cats. The body—or bodies, if you prefer—weren't found for eight days, and it was Melanie who showed up at her small bungalow between tiny Whiskey Ridge and St. Seb to follow up for her interview. Nobody locked their doors in those days and the smell of decay was apparent the second the door was cracked. Joyce and her cats appeared to be sleeping when they died and that led to the discovery of a carbon monoxide leak in her furnace. The body was badly decomposed and the family opted to skip the autopsy since the cause of death was obvious.

"She never made a statement?" Chuck asked and I could see the judgement in him, but he was trying to contain it.

Melanie saw it, too, and her eyes narrowed. "Joyce was driving into town when she saw the plane go down. She went to assist and she was the first one there. When I arrived, she was hysterical. We took her to the hospital. They tranquilized her and kept her overnight. The doctor said to let her calm down, so I did."

"Why was she hysterical?" Stratton asked, glancing at me. "It was awful, but was there something else?"

Something worth killing her for.

"Well..." said Melanie, "who knows. She wasn't a happy woman. Joyce had a history and people judged her harshly."

She didn't say anything else. She just stood there awkwardly and Melanie Gates was not an awkward woman. She was a woman holding something back.

I took a breath and said, "They weren't dead."

Chuck put an arm around my waist and said, "No, the report said 'died on impact'."

"Yes, it did." I watched Melanie and Mallory said, "Mom? Were they alive?"

Melanie looped arm around Mallory shoulders. "I don't know. I was there in less than fifteen minutes and they were dead, both of them. Joyce was screeching. I had to drag her away from them."

"Did she tell you anything?" Stratton asked.

"Candace, the woman had blood all over her. She was incoherent. When she went home from the hospital, I told her to come in when she was ready. I said a week. She said she would and her sister drove her home. I never saw her again. Nobody did."

Somebody did.

"No one went to check on her before you did?" I asked, feeling suddenly sad for a lonely woman I'd never known.

Guilt came over Melanie's face and she said, "She was a loner. Always had been and we didn't think anything about the crash. Jeff City took over and said pilot error immediately."

"Who else did Joyce work for?" I asked. "Why wasn't she missed?"

"I don't remember her working for anyone after Dr. McBride and Stritch left. She always just worked for them."

"Two housecleaning gigs supported her?" I asked.

The mood changed around me. Tank and Mallory exchanged a look and Stratton shifted her feet.

"She must have had other clients," Melanie said slowly. "Her family wasn't wealthy by any stretch."

I had a feeling. That old dad feeling that something wasn't right. A fifty-four-year-old former maid with no husband didn't need a job to feed those cats? I didn't think so.

"What was her history?" I asked, but I already knew. Fifty-four was the key.

Melanie was thinking hard and it took a second for her to refocus. "Oh, she was"—she shook her head—"I feel stupid saying it, but my mother called her a fallen woman."

And there it is.

"She had a baby out of wedlock," I said, "in, say, about 1950."

"There abouts."

"And who was the father?" Stratton asked, her voice tight. She knew, too.

Melanie bit her lip. It was so obvious. Necessity breeds invention as they say. How did McBride and Stritch come up with this idea for high dollar adoptions? They had a home grown problem and they solved it.

"It was McBride, wasn't it?" Eloise had gotten out of the cruiser and come up behind me to put her warm hand on my elbow. "That wife of his watched me like a hawk when I came to town. I thought it was funny. He was older than my father by ten years, but she was worried."

Melanie nodded. "That was the rumor, but there wasn't any proof.

Joyce got in trouble and she went away. That's what you did then. You went off, did what had to be done, and came back like nothing happened. I don't remember anyone saying they knew for sure. Just all that 'I heard that so and so said that so and so said she heard' and like that. There may never have been a baby."

"Oh, there was a baby," said Eloise. "Joyce came in once when another woman was there picking out formula and diapers. She wasn't very nice to Joyce, acting like she was a middle-aged loser who didn't know anything when she suggested a size up from the tiny newborn diapers she was buying. The hospital would give her some of the little ones. After she left Joyce said, 'I had a baby. I know something.'"

"What did you say?" Mallory asked.

"Bernard came out of the back and she ran out," said Eloise. "I never had a chance to ask her about it. Honestly, I didn't think to later on."

"Everybody loved him," mused Melanie. "Nobody said a bad word."

"Pretty convenient that they forgot about Joyce," said Chuck.

"They didn't forget," I said. "They didn't care. It was her fault. He got to walk away from it."

"This makes me sick," said Patton. She'd been so quiet behind us with Dallas that I'd forgotten they were there. "So unfair."

"Well," said Melanie. "You better come in."

"Me?" I said surprised.

"No, not you. I'm not that forgiving. Not yet anyway. I was talking about sitting down and telling current law enforcement everything I remember about the crash, Joyce, and my investigations. If this is going to blow up, we ought to get ahead of it." She gestured to the cops and then looked at me. "You've got the bad news to deliver, haven't you?"

I looked down at the photo of Christopher Lutz in my hand. "I don't know how."

"My advice," said Melanie, "send a registered letter. You don't want to go out to that farm. Ann was a crack shot back in 1984. I doubt she's lost the skill."

Fan-freaking-tastic.

CHAPTER TWENTY

Ann Thooft didn't shoot me, but only because she didn't get the chance. Melanie's advice, while sensible, wasn't how we Watts did things. I couldn't send a registered letter to a client. This was a face-to-face kind of thing. Dad always delivered the bad news himself. "If I'm man enough to take the job, I'm man enough to deliver the results in person."

Easier said than done, but I had a plan. We got in the car and I called Holt. No, I didn't wuss out and tell him before scampering back home. I told him I knew why Anton kidnapped me, but I wouldn't tell anyone but the people who hired me, Kimberly, Kevin, Gregory or whoever in that group still wanted to know.

"You have proof?" Holt asked.

"I do."

"Real proof? Like proof, proof?"

I glanced over at Chuck. He was scratching Pickpocket, who'd crammed himself between the steering wheel and Chuck's chest. No help there. I wanted to say the right thing. I had to say the right thing and it wasn't going to be easy. Nothing was easy just then. I was sitting for the first time since getting dragged across the Sentinel parking lot.

The Motrin had helped with the swelling of my rear, but the pain was worse and I didn't have a ton of patience.

Please don't grill me right now.

"Yes," I said. "Proof, proof."

"Is it what we thought?"

I couldn't remember what we thought or when we thought it. All that extra detail goes out the window when your butt's burning. "How about I just give Kimberly the answer and you tell me?"

"I don't know if she can handle it. Ann's been going off and Kim's crying constantly."

That's not changing anytime soon.

"I can only imagine, but Holt, they hired me to find out what happened. I did and I'm going to charge you for it. Do you want the answer or not? If not, I'm going to the hospital," I said.

"Are you alright?" he said with real concern and it warmed my heart considerably.

"I'm fine, but my bodyguard and her brother are there after the whole shoe factory incident. I should probably check in."

"Of course, I keep forgetting about that. I hope they're alright."

"They are," I said. "So what about it? Do you want the answer tonight? I'll do it as gently as I can."

Holt thought it over and came to the conclusion I had hoped he would. "I have no right to keep the truth from her for another day. Where should we meet you? I don't want you to come here. Ann will see the car."

I told him to meet us at Crabapples and when we walked in the entire restaurant stopped talking. It was pretty full for a Sunday evening and I hadn't anticipated that. I wish I could say it was our giant poodle and my hideous sweatpants that garnered the attention, but it was the case. Everybody knew. The change in the air told me that.

Carrie rushed over, wearing a sort of winter caftan with her hair slicked back into a chignon. It was a rainbow of colors but still very contained.

"Did you figure it out?" she asked breathlessly as she led us to a table tucked back by the bar.

"I did."

"How bad is it?"

"That depends on what you consider to be the worst option," I said.

Carrie was confident as always. "Was Anton Thooft a serial rapist, child molester, or murderer?"

"No."

"Then it's not so bad."

"When you put it that way, I guess not," I said.

Chuck was unmoved. "He was a kidnapper and Mercy would probably have gotten murdered by the person who blackmailed him into doing it."

"So it was blackmail," she said. "Kimberly will be relieved."

I sat down gingerly and ordered a glass of red. I deserved it. Chuck got some horrid protein smoothie for his so-called gains. He looked the same to me, but he was certain he'd have to turn sideways to get through a door any day now, like that was a good thing, and the horrendous gas would be worth it. For the record, nothing was worth that smell. Nothing.

When Carrie came back, she gave Chuck his smoothie, chock full of soy protein powder, edamame, peanut butter, and broccoli. If you think that sounds terrible, I can only say it looked worse. Then she put something in front of me that most definitely was not the lovely Italian red that I desperately needed.

"What the?" I looked at the tall glass filled with orange liquid and had round black blobs at the bottom.

"You don't need alcohol," she said. "You need anti-inflammatories."

Chuck nodded. "Turmeric. It's good for you."

Where's Aaron when I need him?

"Do you hate me?" I asked. "I need wine or hot chocolate."

Chuck banged my painkillers on the table and said, "You need these."

I hissed at him, but I took one as it was my only option other than storming the bar and grabbing a bottle. I was so slow-moving I doubt I would've gotten more than a swig down.

Carrie pushed the gross orange concoction closer to me. "Try it. You'll like it, I swear."

I tried it. I did not like it, but I didn't vomit and she took that as affirmation. "So did Anton know that you'd be killed when he gave you to whoever?"

Excellent question.

"No clue," I said. "But he would've done it even if he had."

She drew back. "You don't really think so."

We just looked at her and she plucked at her caftan. "What did the Thoofts say?"

I glanced over her shoulder. "We're about to find out."

Carrie looked horrified and said, "Here? You're telling them here? Why not the station?"

"I wanted wine," I said.

"Things really don't work out for you."

"They mostly do. I am alive."

A wonderful smile came over her face and she hugged me. "That's the best way to think. I'm sorry I said otherwise." Then she hastily got out of the way as Holt, Gregory, and Stephanie came through the door and walked over, all three dragging their feet.

"What can I get you?" Carrie asked.

The men ordered beers and Stephanie asked for a Long Island Iced Tea before sitting down to stare at us silently.

"I'm surprised to see you," I said to Stephanie.

"I was at the house telling Kimberly what happened with Kevin and I thought I'd tag along," she said.

"Still changing the locks?"

"Already done." Stephanie wasn't red-eyed. She was resolute and Gregory looked like he was just a little bit scared of his sister-in-law.

"Where's Kimberly and Kevin?" I asked.

Holt took a sip of beer before he said that Kevin tried to punch him when he asked him to come and Kimberly had elected to stay home with her boys. She sensed something very bad and would rather have it from her husband. I couldn't blame her. If someone had bad news like that for me, I'd rather have it from Chuck than some stranger.

"You haven't told her anything?" Chuck asked.

"No," said Holt, nodding at the other two. "They all know that I know, but I was waiting for proof."

"Proof of what?" Gregory gripped his beer, his life preserver, and what color he had drained away.

I put a fat folder on the table. I wasn't nearly so organized as Melanie. One folder would do.

"An unknown suspect blackmailed your brother into kidnapping me," I said.

Gregory blew out a breath and loosened his grip. "He wasn't going to...do things to you?"

"No, I don't believe he was. Not personally."

Gregory ran a hand through his long mullet and took a deep drink. "That idiot. Like we cared that he was gay."

"You knew?" gasped Stephanie.

"I knew," said Holt. "You both knew?"

What a family!

"Pretty much everyone knew," I said.

"That's not true," said Gregory. "Anton said I was the only one he could talk to."

"That's what he told me," said Stephanie.

"And me," said Holt, whose face turned into a deep frown. "So if everyone knew..."

"My parents don't know," said Gregory. "There's no way."

I bet they did.

"It doesn't matter," I said. "That's not the blackmail."

"I've always known there was something truly weird going on," Stephanie said. "What is it?"

I laid out the evidence, taking them through it, step by step. Holt knew the basics and was resolute, but Stephanie was shocked. She began blathering on about Ann and her honesty. Gregory, on the other hand, was silent. He drained his first beer and then a second.

"You knew," I said.

"Not exactly," he said.

"Was it how Kimberly was just there when you got home from Kansas?" Chuck asked. "That would've tipped me off."

Gregory shook his head and a thin lock of blond hair fell in his eyes. He brushed it away angrily. "No, I was only eleven. I didn't care about anything but the farm. It's all I ever wanted to do. I wasn't good at school like everyone else, but I was good at that."

"Then what?" Stephanie asked. "Did somebody say something?"

They had. Kids at school. Other parents. Friends. Gregory might not have been a rock star student, but he tucked away every little comment about how Kimberly was so different than the rest of the family from her coloring to her singing. She didn't fit and, although no one ever said she was adopted, he felt it down deep next to his heart.

"I love her," he said quickly. "I just never felt like she was part of me like Kevin and Anton. It was like something was missing."

Something was.

I tucked away the evidence but left the last bit hidden in the folder. I had to work myself up to it. I really could've used that wine. Gregory had accepted what his mother had done rather stoically so far. Holt and Stephanie, too, seemed surprisingly at ease once they got over the initial shock.

"You're taking this very well," I said.

"People do that, don't they?" Stephanie asked. "Those other adoptees, their parents never told them they were adopted either, right? They should've told Kimberly, but it's not the worst thing in the world."

Chuck looked at me, his blue eyes glinting with understanding he communicated to me. They didn't get it, even though I said that Ann was pregnant, somehow that had gone over their heads. I'd expected questions. *Did my dad know? Where's that baby?* Something like that, but they took the path that was most easy to travel.

"I'll tell Kimberly tonight," said Holt. "And maybe she'll want to talk to Ann and Anthony about it tomorrow. Gregory, can you tell Kevin?"

"I will." Gregory looked at me, a little dazed. "Do we write you a check or what?"

"I'm not done," I said.

He took a deep breath and said, "Obviously, I can't speak for

Kimberly and Kevin, but I think I'm done. It's out now and I don't really care about the rest."

Chuck leaned forward. "Trust me, you do."

Gregory stood up. "I get that you'd care about who got my brother to do this thing to you, but I can't deal with that right now."

"There's more to it," I said.

"The deal was that you find out why," said Holt.

Stephanie started to rise, but I put a hand on her arm. "I've finished what you've hired me for, if you don't care about who caused it, that's your prerogative. But—"

"But what?" Gregory asked. For the first time, he sounded angry. It might have been my imagination, but I thought I saw fear in his face.

"I have to tell you the rest," I said. "It's information you paid for. You deserve to hear the whole story."

"We heard it." His voice went up and the restaurant stopped buzzing and turned our way.

"Please sit down," hissed Stephanie. "This is bad enough without making a scene."

Gregory dropped down into his seat and drained the last few drops of his beer onto his tongue. "Alright. Fine. What's left? We already know why she did it."

"Do we?" Stephanie asked.

"My mother wanted a girl," said Gregory, rolling his eyes. "When she had Kevin she cried for days, but she got over it and then she adopted Kimberly. It's fine. We'll get through it."

Stephanie crossed her arms. "She cried?"

"Well, she had two boys already and she wanted a daughter really bad," said Gregory. "I remember Dad saying when she got...pregnant with Kimberly"—Gregory's voice slowed to a crawl—"that she was the last one. Four was perfect."

Stephanie grabbed my wrist painfully. Another bruise. Why not?

"You said...you said..."

"She was pregnant," said Holt. "But you meant that she pretended to be pregnant."

I patted Stephanie's hand. "No. That's not what I meant."

Gregory turned around and yelled at the bar. "I need whiskey. Somebody! Whiskey!"

Carrie snatched a bottle off the top shelf and ran over to pour a generous glass. "On the house." Then she ran off.

Stephanie clamped her hands over her mouth and said through her fingers, "Oh, my God. Her baby died."

Gregory threw back the whiskey in a big gulp and asked, "Where's the grave? Did they even get to grieve? Dad didn't seem upset, but we hardly saw Mom. She stayed in Kimberly's room for weeks. She must have been distraught and I didn't even notice."

"You were a kid," said Stephanie. "She didn't tell you. How could you know?"

I looked over at Holt, who'd said nothing. His half-empty beer sat on the table with his hands in fists on either side. I had a flash of him throwing it at me, but, when he met my eyes, I knew he wouldn't. Holt had put it together and it was all he could do to contain himself.

"She didn't lose the baby," I said.

Gregory heaved a huge sigh of relief. "Thank goodness. So she faked it. That's bad, but better."

Chuck pulled my chair up close to his and Pickpocket got between me and Stephanie. My guys taking care of me.

"She had a baby, Gregory. It was a boy, so she exchanged it for Kimberly," I said.

"That's not true," he said in a vicious whisper. He sounded like Anton and it sent a chill through me. "My mother wouldn't do that."

I took out Eloise's evidence and showed them the buys and how Kimberly's birth date was wrong.

"So there was another baby," Gregory said. "So what? It doesn't mean that it was my mother's."

I put the photo of Christopher Lutz in front of him. "This is the boy that was born on that day."

"He's the spitting image of you," said Stephanie and she began to cry. "I knew something was weird, but I didn't think it would be this bad."

"It can't be," said Gregory. "It can't."

To Holt's great credit, he took Christopher's picture and asked me, "Is he okay?"

That warmed me more than the wine would've. "I think so. He got loving parents and a couple of sisters, who are probably adopted, too. He lost a leg in a motorcycle accident a while back, but from Facebook it looks like he's recovered enough to ski and water board."

"Does he know about us?" Gregory asked in a low whisper.

"No, but this is all going to come out publicly and he will. His wife got in contact with the Children of Whiskey Ridge group, so I'm sure she'll notice when the news hits."

"He didn't contact them?" Stephanie asked.

"No and he didn't want to hear about her theory," I said.

Gregory tucked the photo back in the folder and said, "I hope he doesn't find out."

"Why?" Holt burst out. "He's your brother."

"That's why. I don't want him to know that she gave him away like that. I want him to be happy."

That hung in the air for a few minutes and then I eased myself out of my chair. I'd thought that at the end of my very first case, there would be shaking of hands, thank yous, or, at least, acknowledgement of a job done, if not well done, but it wasn't like that at all. There were three stunned people sitting at that table probably wishing they'd never laid eyes on me. Thinking Anton was a psycho might have been preferable to the answers they asked for.

We didn't say goodbye. They didn't either. Chuck paid for our questionable drinks and we got out of the warm Crabapples and into the chilly evening.

"To the hospital then?" Chuck asked.

"Please just take me home," I said.

He opened my car door and Pick jumped in. "Don't we have to go to the hospital?"

"Are Aunt Miriam and Aunt Willasteen still there?"

"Probably."

"I don't deserve whatever those two have to say."

Chuck helped me in and said, "You know what, you don't. But I'm putting you straight to bed." He waggled his brows at me.

"Have you gone insane?" I asked. "I had little bits of glass and metal pulled out of my butt today. It's enormous."

He grinned at me as sleazy as could be. "I know."

"Unbelievable."

"I like big butts and I cannot lie," he sang.

"Oh, my God," I said. "Close the door."

"You other brother—"

I slammed the door, but that didn't stop the singing. Chuck danced around the car, doing what might've been the typewriter and I dissolved into laughter. Just what I needed.

CHAPTER TWENTY-ONE

Two days later I was walking alongside the highway, thinking that had to be one of my worst ideas yet. It was freezing and quite possibly pointless. We'd been stumbling around for an hour and I was so over it. We didn't need Anton Thooft's burner phone. I didn't care *that* much who blackmailed him. I wanted a hot chocolate and a Worf burger. Cheesy fries wouldn't go amiss either. Maybe some of Aaron's new cheesecake. It was boozy, just the thing to defrost me from my bright red nose to my feet that had lost all feeling.

"We're almost to the exit!" yelled my dad from the median.

"I wonder if we could've hired someone to do this," said my mother.

I gave her a look. "Dad hired us because we're free."

"We're not," said Avery Sampson. "But we're doing this gratis for you, Mercy."

Leo Frame, who had dressed correctly for the tundra, winked at me and said, "I'm sure you appreciate a good walk."

"This is dangerous," I said. "We could get flattened."

"You're just cold."

"Damn straight."

"Mercy!" Mom exclaimed.

"Mom, you shouldn't be here at all," I said. "You're still recovering."

She gave me her lopsided smile. "I wouldn't miss this. It's like a treasure hunt."

"If you say so."

"I do and we're going to find that phone and then we'll go to lunch."

I smiled. "Now you've got my attention."

"You can get in the van," she said.

"I'm not getting in the van," I said. "You get in the van."

Mom stuck out her chin. "I'm fine."

She wasn't particularly fine. She was stumbling over small rocks and having trouble with the incline, but I knew that look. She wasn't getting in the van that Claire was driving behind us so slowly that she'd glued her false eyelashes on while doing it and then proceeded to answer Dad's million and half emails. Some of them were even for me. Lots of people wanted to hire us to find out whether they were Whiskey Ridge kids, and Tiny was already on five cases, doing the preliminaries while wrangling Aunt Willasteen and Fats. My plan, although Fats was plenty pissed at me, had done the trick. The elderly aunts had bullied Fats into taking the meds and she hadn't thrown up since. Sister Clarence was having long talks with my bodyguard about forgiveness and I had faith that someday Fats would stop threatening to snap me in half and stuff my body down a sewer drain. The baby was considerably more active and that alone was probably saving my life at the moment.

Dad had done six TV interviews and, as promised, I did my Tank interview and nothing else. St. Seb was a mad house once again and Stratton had to bring in the State Troopers to handle the crowds of reporters and curiosity seekers. To my surprise, she was good with it. Every hotel in town and the surrounding area was full as were the restaurants. The town scrambled to put on an impromptu Christmas market with a spooky theme and it was drawing even more visitors, who couldn't wait to spend their money.

More than anything, I wished I was there, drinking mulled wine and eating venison goulash, but no. I was walking the never-ending walk, staring at the ground and thinking we weren't going to find that phone. My idea sucked. Anton Thooft didn't toss a phone. He never had a second phone and I was making myself miserable for nothing.

We curved with the exit ramp and Dad and Chuck dashed across two lanes into the gulley on the other side. There were three miles left before we reached the spot were Anton died, and I found myself dreading it. I didn't want to see that spot. Not that I had some kind of affection for the man, but because I had affection for the people who did. I hadn't heard from Kimberly or anyone else from that group and I didn't expect to. They'd paid the bill for my services and I figured that was as good as it got. That's what Dad said anyway. What I found was painful, I was painful, and I'd never see them again. I got it, but I kinda wanted to know how they were doing. Mom said that you can't have everything. She was right. You can't. Unless everything included a wickedly itchy butt from healing cuts. That you can have.

Mom, the guys, and I cleared the ramp and I looked back to see my Dad climbing out of the gulley by grabbing tufts of crabgrass. Behind him, a long arm shot up.

"I found it!" Chuck yelled, waving a small black phone around.

Thank you! Thank you! Thank you!

A car whizzed by and I yelled, "Be careful!"

On cue, Dad raised his fists in triumph, a gust of wind kicked up, and he tumbled backward into the gulley.

"Tommy!" Mom yelled and I had to grab my crazy mother to keep her from dashing in front of a truck.

"He's fine!" yelled Chuck and Dad popped back up, sans hat with dead grass in his hair.

"Totally fine, Carolina!" Dad yelled, grinning from ear to ear.

He and Chuck waited for a break in the traffic and then ran across to us. Dad tried to get the phone, but Chuck gave it to me.

"You were right," he said.

My teeth had started to chatter, but I managed to get out, "Hoorah."

Avery and Leo herded us into the van as a State Trooper rolled up with lights flashing. Dad went to handle that situation as only he could and it gave me plenty of time to pour Mom a cup of hot tea out of our supersized Thermos, admire Claire's eyelashes, and message Spidermonkey.

Predictably the phone was dead, but we'd planned for that. Leo got out a backpack stuffed with cords of every description so we could charge it. Dad got in and said, "We're clear," but he insisted on informing Rich, so we'll have to hand it over at some point."

"That was a given," said Chuck. "Anything, Mercy?"

"Hold on," I said.

The phone blinked green and powered up. It wasn't password protected and I was in. Unfortunately, there wasn't much to get to. Anton had sent a grand total of one text. One! And it said, "I've got her." There was no reply and only a number. I called it and it was disconnected. I expected that, but I was still disappointed.

"We need maps," said Dad and Mom slapped down his hands because he kept trying to reach back and grab the phone.

"I'm getting there," I said.

Maps was more informative. Anton had used his burner to get around the CWE. He'd gone to all the places I was known to inhabit, including Kronos, Uncle Morty's apartment, Ode de Caffeine, Colombia Clinic, SLU hospital, Egon's Cherry Pit, and, of course, Hawthorne Avenue. His last destination was the most important. Anton Thooft was taking me to a tiny regional airport five miles away. My stomach twisted and I gave the phone to Chuck. Anton almost made it. If I hadn't had my arm in a cast. If I hadn't woken up so quickly. If I hadn't known what to do.

Chuck put an arm around me and lowered his head to mine. "Try not to think about it because it didn't happen."

I nodded. Easier said than done.

Claire turned us around and we headed to the airport, zipping along with such speed that it made me acutely aware of how close I'd come. I'd been incapacitated. It wouldn't have been hard at all to get me out of that trunk and into a plane.

We arrived at the tiny terminal ten minutes later and I elected not to go in. It was too much, so, instead, I sat in the van with Mom and Claire, watching Claire put her spare set of eyelashes on Mom. About fifteen minutes later, Chuck came out of the terminal and ambled over.

I recognized that walk. It was the everything's-fine-nothing-to-see-here walk, but I wasn't buying it, especially when he climbed in and avoided my eyes for a second.

"So we called Rich and he's headed over," he said.

Mom took a breath and then asked, "Good news?"

"Um..."

"By good news," she said, "I mean do you have a lead?"

They had a lead. Sort of. A Vision SF50 had landed a week before my kidnapping. Being a pricey model in red and black it had attracted some notice. The two men on the small jet had been polite but not social and were apparently unconcerned by the number of people who came out and took pictures of their aircraft. We had a picture with its tail number clearly visible. The two men wearing nondescript suits and sunglasses matched the vague description of the two that had murdered Lester. We had no names, no real names anyway. They called themselves John Smith and John Jones. Imaginative, I know. The men stayed at a nearby motel and showed up at the field at six in the morning on the dot and left at midnight. They had all their food delivered and sat in the jet, waiting. They had filed a flight plan with an unspecified date for Chicago.

The day of my kidnapping at the exact time that Anton Thooft was chased off that exit ramp to be shot a few minutes later, the suits activated their flight plan, climbed aboard, and took off. They landed in Chicago and disappeared into the city. The jet was a rental and that was probably a dead end. A shell corporation out of Panama had rented the plane and a quick search by Spidermonkey showed it to be a dummy corp, but he'd keep working it.

"What do you think?" I asked.

"I think they were going to put you on another plane," he said, "and get you out of the country."

"What makes you think that?" Mom asked.

"Because there was no point in flying Mercy to Chicago unless she was supposed to go somewhere else. I think we'll find another rental that was waiting and then canceled."

Mom looked at Claire and asked her to go check on Dad to see how long they would be. Claire shut off Instagram and glanced at me. "You're not going in at all?"

"Nope," I said.

"*You* don't want to ask any questions? That's so *not* you."

"I don't think I care right now," I said.

She frowned and told Mom, "I think this is enough. We should go."

"I agree," said Mom. "Please tell Tommy."

Claire hopped out, fluffed her hair, and dashed for the tiny terminal through the gusting wind.

Mom turned in her seat and said, "So it was The Klinefeld Group and you were going overseas."

"Maybe," I said. The Klinefeld Group just didn't feel right to me, but I had no other answer.

"Somehow, they know that you found out something useful in St. Seb," said Chuck.

"We were so careful," said Mom.

"Not careful enough," he said. "I wouldn't be surprised if they had someone there watching in St. Seb and just Mercy's demeanor tipped them off."

"We did cut down our communications," I said. "If I was watching us, I'd think something was up."

Mom opened her purse and handed me a little black rectangle. "It goes on your bra strap and it's now a requirement."

"A panic button?" I asked. "Seriously?"

"Look at where we are and ask that again."

I didn't look. I didn't need to. "Fine, but you should have one, too."

Mom tapped her chest and said, "I do. Morty set these up for us."

"Nikki let him work?" Chuck asked.

She smiled. "Only on this. They're set up to alert Tommy, Chuck, and local law enforcement wherever we happen to be twenty-four-seven. If you are out of the house, you have it on. Period."

"Must be expensive," I said to my perennially penny-pinching mother.

She took my hand. "We can afford it and I want you to be safe."

"Us to be safe."

"Right. Us."

I clipped the button on my bra strap. "It's already active?"

"It is," said Mom.

Chuck took a look and asked, "You're sure it will call me, if she presses the button?"

"Yes. Automatically."

"It works internationally?"

"Of course."

He relaxed back onto the seat and heaved a sigh. "Thanks, Carolina. I needed that."

"I know and you need something else, too."

Chuck raised an eyebrow. "Oh, yeah?"

Mom didn't get a chance to answer because Campbell and Rich came screaming into the parking lot, kicking up a hell of a lot of dust amid squealing tires. Rich got out of his car and looked at me through the window of the van. I don't know what it was about my expression, but he took a step and then nodded before turning around to go in the terminal.

"Don't worry," said Chuck. "Spidermonkey already got everything off the phone."

"I wasn't worried, but I'm not in the mood for an interview or anything," I said.

"Good," said Mom, "because you're leaving right now."

"Huh?"

She gave Chuck the van keys and opened her door. "Go home. You have things to do." She tried to wink, but she still couldn't do it right so it was more like a tick.

"No way," said Chuck. "I was promised Luanne's Pit BBQ and I'm not giving that up. I found that phone and I want my reward."

Mom got out and said, "Your reward is at home." She closed the door and rushed to the terminal through wind that practically blew her off her feet.

Chuck made a confused face at me. "Is your mother saying what I think she's saying?"

I smacked his arm. "No, you big dufus."

He nuzzled my neck. "I'm all for it."

"You're an idiot."

"But I'm your favorite idiot."

"Think about it," I said.

"I am, believe me."

I pushed his head away and tapped his forehead. "Hello, super cop. Nobody is home."

"I'm sure The Girls are."

I rolled my eyes. "At my parents' home." I pointed at the terminal. "Everybody's there."

Chuck jumped out of the backseat. "Why didn't you say so?"

"Come on. It was pretty obvious."

"It was not."

We bickered and Chuck called my dad, telling him I was upset and desperate to get home. Dad protested, but Chuck just said to hitch a ride with the cops to the commuter lot where we'd left the other cars. He'd leave the van there and drive me home in his car. Dad squawked, but Chuck hung up on him.

"That was satisfying," he said with a devilish grin.

I kissed the back of his neck. "Don't I know it."

CHAPTER TWENTY-TWO

When I awoke with a start over an hour later Chuck had parked in the Bled garage next to the Jaguar and was already on the phone.

"What are we doing here?" I asked with a yawn.

"I was going to let you sleep for a while," he said.

I got out gingerly and stretched my stiff legs. "You're out of your mind if you think I'm not looking in that liquor cabinet myself."

"You fell asleep in the middle of a sentence."

"And now I'm rested."

He sighed and turned his attention back to the call. "What about the plane? I didn't catch that."

"Who is it?" I asked.

"Rich. There was a Learjet rented and waiting. Canceled on the day you were kidnapped."

"Any footage of our guys?"

He nodded and held up a finger. "Uh-huh. We should be able to track that."

I stretched and pointed at the door to the garden. Chuck followed me to the house and he keyed us in. Joy heard us coming in and came out of the kitchen to ask if I wanted some hot chocolate. Aaron had given her a recipe and she was keen to try it out. Even though I was defrosted the lure of hot chocolate was pretty strong and I followed her into the kitchen.

"Try this," said Joy, handing me a chunk of dark chocolate.

It melted on my tongue like warm butter. "That is exactly what I needed. Peruvian?"

"Close," she said. "Ecuador."

Chuck came in and started pacing beside the long island. "I'll get on that."

"What?" I asked.

"Rich wants his uncle disinterred for a new autopsy." He started dialing. "I'm calling a DA I know so we can get it moving."

"Can't that wait? We've got a thing."

"It'll only take a minute. Your parents have just left for Luanne's." He turned away and I was about to climb out of my skin. I'd had chocolate and I was good to go. Waiting wasn't my strong suit anyway and I knew my parents, or more especially my father. I wouldn't put it past him to come right back and get to work. Food was always optional for Tommy Watts.

"I'm going," I said.

"No." Chuck snagged my arm. "I'm coming."

"Where are you going?" Joy asked.

"To my parents'. I want to get something."

The housekeeper wheeled her chef's knife above an enormous block of chocolate. "It'll be ready when you get back. I hope I do it right."

I grinned at her. "It's an Aaron recipe. You'll do fine."

Joy gave me a thumbs-up and began chopping as I eyed the door.

"I'm almost done," Chuck said to me and then held up a finger. "I'm looking for Darnell Hill. This is Chuck Watts. Can you transfer me?"

Almost done, my foot.

My phone buzzed and it was our neighbor Sandy. She rarely called unless it was to check up on Mom so I answered despite my urge to get out of the house. "Hey, Sandy."

"Hi, Mercy," said a man. "It's Terry."

"Oh, everything okay?"

"Yeah. I was wondering if I could clean up that mess. Sandy says it's Carolina's purview and we shouldn't overstep. But your mom's still recovering. Would it really bug her if I did it?"

"No idea what you're talking about," I said.

Chuck raised a brow and I whispered, "Terry from next door."

He nodded and went back to trying to locate the missing DA.

"Of course," said Terry. "You've been busy. That adoption thing is wild. I'd love to hear all about it. You should come over for ribs. I do great ribs."

"I know you do and I'd love to," I said. "What do we need to clean?"

Terry explained that on the night of the insane Christmas party some moron had been in our alley with fireworks and had blown up potatoes. There were a bunch on the ground. They'd frozen and then thawed and frozen again. There was going to be a mushy mess, but Mom and Sandy had a deal. Mom took care of the alley, sweeping and whatnot, plus the back alley. Sandy took care of the sidewalks in front and up to the houses. Our sweet neighbor had tried to take care of the whole shebang after Mom's attack, but Mom had kicked up a fuss, saying she could handle it. She couldn't handle it. She couldn't go into the alley at all, being that it was the scene of the crime. I couldn't either and Mom's friend Dixie had taken over the duty, but exploded potatoes was beyond the call of friendship. That was down to family.

"I'm sorry," said Terry, "but I think they'll stink."

"I'll take care of it," I said.

"Mercy, I'll do it."

"No, no. I'm going over right now. Why potatoes?"

Terry laughed. "Why any of it? The whole avenue was a wreck. Now everyone's haggling over who has to pay for the cleanup crew."

"That'll be fun," I said.

"I didn't know rich people could be so cheap."

"Don't get me started."

"I want you started. Those idiot butlers are still in jail. Their bosses won't bail them out, even though they armed them to protect their properties."

"Typical. I'll be right over."

I hung up and said, "I'm going to clean up frozen potatoes."

Joy shook her head. "Terry can do that."

"You knew?"

"Mrs. Haas had pumpkins. I think they were throwing them at each other. What a mess. There were seeds everywhere."

"Wait," said Chuck. "I don't want you alone."

"I'll take Pick."

He grumbled, but I exposed the new panic button and he gave in while asking which courthouse the DA was at. I didn't know there were that many to choose from, but I'd only been in the straight up criminal court.

"Ten minutes. Tops," he said and I rolled my eyes before heading to the library to get the poodle off his cushion. The fuzzball was not pleased, but I promised sausage and that got him moving. Since it was freezing, I put on his tartan jacket and booties. It made me feel ridiculous, but Pick danced around excited in his fancy duds.

We headed out into the blustery wind and jogged the whole way, despite my burning butt. It was not happy to move, but my freezing fingers insisted. As cold as I was, my mind was working. Potatoes in our alley. Why? We weren't close to the action at the Klemp mansion at the other end of the street. We were mostly unscathed with only a few spent firecrackers in the yard and some minor damage to the trees from the Roman candles.

Pick and I arrived in front of my parents' house and I was about to go to the front door when I saw the evil Siamese in the window, staring at me. So familiar. They didn't usually sit there, but they weren't acting like maniacs like they did on the day of Mom's attack. So that was good.

I headed up the walk, but Pick yanked on his leash, wildly trying to get away from them. I couldn't blame the poor poodle. Biting him was their favorite thing. Only Chuck could get the Siamese to back off, if Mom wasn't around, and he would be there in ten minutes or so he said.

The side door would work. If we got in quick, I could lock the cats out of the kitchen, but I'd have to go in the alley. No matter. I had to anyway because of those stupid potatoes, but I had to use all my will to do it. It hadn't sounded so bad when I was talking to Terry. Just the alley that I'd known all my life. But I hadn't been down there since Mom's case was closed and I could still see her there, lying helpless on the ground.

I let Pick turn me to the right toward the alley and the wind kicked up, freezing my ankles and driving that awful image from my mind. At the entrance, Pick backed up and yanked at his leash, making a grumbling sound.

"There's nobody there," I said and Pick answered with a deep growl.

The poodle was right. It felt wrong. Bad and off in some way, but I could see clear down through the wrought iron gate into Mom's side garden all covered with frost. The potato mess was equally clear. There was spatter a few feet in and three gross Idaho bakers lay on the ground and they looked like stink was coming in a huge way.

The trash cans were next to the side door. I could just toss the potatoes in there and worry about the spatter later. I went for the potatoes and Pick growled in earnest, baring his big teeth. The feeling got worse. A pain in the gut.

"Okay," I whispered and I stepped back, but not quick enough. A figure stepped out of the side door's alcove. It wasn't very big and neither was she. About five foot, wearing a black puffer coat with the hood up over a fat padded neck brace.

Fat head.

"Of course," I said, stepping back again and pressing the panic button. I didn't know if I got it pushed correctly. It was under a shirt, sweater, and coat, but what else could I do? She pointed a .22 at me with a shaking hand as she stepped around the cans with an awkward gait. It was a wonder she could get around at all. In addition to the neck brace, she had an eye patch, a walking cast, a purple can-shaped bruise on her forehead along with burn pattern, and bandaged hands.

Without thinking, I asked, "What happened to you?"

"You happened to me," she said in a hoarse whisper. From the look of her, I imagined she'd damaged her voice by screaming. "Don't move."

"Don't shoot me," I said.

"I'm not going to shoot you."

"Are you sure because I'm not feeling good about it."

"I'm sure."

The muzzle of her weapon bobbed around like crazy and her one eye was blinking rapidly.

I took a step back and the shaking got worse.

She's going to shoot me on accident.

"Be careful with that," I said.

"You...you go back and unlock that gate," she said.

"No."

"What?"

"No. I'm not doing it," I said.

"What do you mean?" she asked. "I'll...I'll shoot you."

I put a hand on my hip and sighed like I wasn't totally freaked. "You just said you weren't going to shoot me."

"Well, I will if I have to."

"Why would you have to? Who are you?"

"Never mind," she said, her voice getting worse and harder to understand. "You'll unlock that gate. I'm not doing this again."

"Again?" I frowned and attempted to stall. "How many times have you done this?"

"It doesn't matter. I've got you now."

"Did you blow up that potato?"

She pursed her cracked lips. "It was supposed to be a silencer."

"Did you drill a hole?" I asked.

"Nobody did that in the movies."

"So you *were* going to shoot me?"

She gestured with the gun for me to walk past her. Not going to happen. Even if I wanted to, Pick wouldn't have let me. His growls were so loud, I was surprised that Sandy and Terry couldn't hear them.

"No thanks," I said. "So the potato didn't work out. What's up with the leg?"

"Move."

"No. Tell me about the leg or get to shooting."

"It got caught in the cord when I pushed out the air conditioner," she said.

"You really want to kill me." I have to admit I was astonished. This woman was about sixty years old and beat to hell. What did I do to her?

"No, I just have to deliver you."

"So whoever can kill me," I said.

"No, no." Her eye widened. "They promised that they just want to ask you some questions."

There was nothing to say to that. It was too ridiculous.

"You thought an a/c unit wouldn't kill me?"

"I thought you'd get knocked out and I could put you in my trunk."

Oh, she's an idiot and I'm alive because she's incompetent.

"Well, I'm not getting in a trunk. You can forget about that," I said.

Her whole body was shaking now. "You are."

"Not."

"Unlock that gate. My car's in the alley."

"Never gonna happen," I said.

"I'll...I'll shoot your dog," she said. It was supposed to be an ominous threat but came out like Minnie Mouse with strep throat.

I, on the other hand, sounded the way I felt. Pissed off. "If you shoot my dog, I will take you apart joint by joint. I'm a nurse. I can do it."

"You have to get in my trunk."

I waved a hand up and down in her direction. "Look at yourself and get the picture. This is not going to work out for you."

"I'm going—"

My phone started buzzing in my purse.

"I have to get that," I said.

Her laugh sounded like ripping paper. "No way."

"My boyfriend's a cop. He's meeting me here any minute."

"Yeah, right."

My phone buzzed again and again.

"He's going to notice if I don't answer," I said and I could see her waver. No wonder she got beat up by an air conditioner. "He's better with a weapon than you. I guarantee it."

"Just unlock the gate," she said.

"I'm not doing it and he's going to come here fast."

The woman gritted her teeth.

She's never going to buy this, but...

"I'll just say I'm fine. You're watching me. There's nothing else I can do."

She took a ragged breath and said, "Okay. Just say you're fine or I'll shoot the dog."

I'll be damned.

I opened my purse, pressed the 911 emergency button on my phone, and grabbed my Mauser. "Pickpocket, sit," I commanded and the poodle actually sat. Shocking.

I dropped my purse, put both hands on the Mauser, and started advancing on her. "I've been trained to use this. Have you?"

"I...I..." She pressed herself against Sandy's wall.

"I suggest you drop that weapon. I don't need *you* alive."

She scooted along the wall toward the gate. "Stop."

"I don't stop. Haven't you heard? I'm a Watts."

She tripped on a crack in the sidewalk, stumbled and dropped the gun.

"That's better," I said.

She fumbled with her jacket as she backed up, reaching the edge of our house almost to the gate. She pulled out a black canister and said, "I'll spray you."

She can't do anything right.

"That's a fogger," I said.

"It's pepper spray," she said.

I held the Mauser on her and said, "A fogger type of pepper spray has a range of six to eight feet. I'm over ten feet away."

"I'll still spray you."

"Go for it." I crept closer and backed her up. She raised the pepper spray and held it out straight as she stepped backward past the edge of the house. I kept coming. She backed into the gate and sprayed.

It did not work out for her. The wind was so gusty that it rolled the thick fog of pepper spray around her, wrapping her in its noxious embrace. She screamed and dropped to the ground, not that far from where I found my mother. A better image for me to remember, I have to say.

She screamed and writhed on the ground, and I picked up her weapon as a siren echoed down the alley, followed immediately by Chuck with his weapon drawn.

"What the hell?" he yelled.

"Chuck Watts, may I introduce you to my latest kidnapper. I didn't catch her name, but she's about sixty and super stupid."

He sniffed. "Did you spray her?"

"She sprayed herself." I waved my hand over her. "I think you'll find she did all those injuries to herself."

"Is she wearing a patch?"

"Oh, yeah. She also has a nifty can-shaped ring on her forehead."

"From what?"

"Remember that smoke grenade that Dallas threw out of the Sentinel?"

"You can't be serious."

I shrugged. "She tried to drop an a/c unit on me."

"Bitch."

"I'm not crazy about her," I said.

We watched her writhe around until the cops got there. Contrary to popular belief there's not a lot to be done about pepper spray. You just have to wait it out. It's not like you can wash your eyes out with soap and she got it in the mouth, too. It would be bad for days. Diarrhea, nausea, the whole painful deal. I was good with it. If you try to put me in a trunk, you deserve what you get.

An ambulance showed up about ten minutes later, just after she booted all over the place. Fan-freaking-tastic. Another thing for me to clean up, made worse by her rolling around in it. The EMTs were not at all happy and it took a while for them to haul her caterwauling butt away. She wasn't exactly cooperative. Nazir and his new partner Waz got the case and we only gave them preliminary interviews because the guys were having a hard time keeping it together. Nazir tried not to laugh and failed. Wiping his eyes, he told me to come down and make a formal statement the next day. I said I would and they left with peals of laughter echoing down the alley.

"So that was The Klinefeld Group's second string," said Chuck as I unlocked the gate and Pick raced through and spun in a circle.

"It wasn't them," I said.

"Has to be. Who else would hire those dudes at the airport?"

"I'm telling you it's not them. They're not stupid and blackmailing that woman to snag me is stupid."

"It doesn't make much sense I admit," he said.

I climbed the back stairs and unlocked Dad's security system. "Because it's not them."

"She won't be able to tell us anything, but it has to be them."

"Wanna bet?" I opened the door and stepped into the butler's pantry.

"Sure," Chuck said. "What are the stakes?"

"I'll eat a bucket of Aaron's crab puffs if it's them."

He took off his jacket and tapped his chin. "I'll clean the bathroom for a month if it isn't."

"Two months."

"Get real."

"We're talking crab here," I said.

Chuck stuck out a hand. "Deal."

I leapt into his arms and kissed him. "Deal."

"You ready to see what Stella put in that cabinet?"

"Yes, I am," I said. "Nothing's going to stop us now."

The doorbell rang.

Dammit.

The Girls stood on the front porch of my parents' house wearing their mother's vintage mink coats, matching hats, and twisting their hands in worry.

"Are you alright, dear?" Millicent asked.

"That woman, who sent her?" Myrtle asked.

I brought them inside and cranked up the heat. They really shouldn't have been out in that weather. It was getting worse by the moment.

"Didn't Joy tell you that everything was fine?" I asked.

"She did, but you might have been sugarcoating the situation and Carolina isn't here to take care of you," said Millicent.

Chuck came down the hall. "I'm here and Mercy handled it like a professional."

I put a hand on my hip. "I am a professional."

"You know what I mean."

"No, I don't."

He helped The Girls with their coats and said, "I meant to say you were amazing and I couldn't have done better myself." Then he muttered something about years of training, but I chose to ignore that. I had years of Tommy Watts training and you couldn't beat that with a stick.

"In any event, I'm fine and Linda Snodgrass is in the hospital under arrest," I said.

The Girls took my hands and looked me over carefully.

"You seem unscathed," said Myrtle. "How did you—how do you say it—take her down?"

"Well, she sort of took herself down."

They frowned and I explained.

"That doesn't sound like The Klinefeld Group," said Millicent.

I elbowed Chuck. "Told you."

"We'll see," he said, checking his phone. "Your parents are heading back. Are we doing this or not?"

"Doing what?" Myrtle asked in a whisper.

"Nobody's home," I whispered back.

The Girls clapped their hands in delight and hustled back to the butler's pantry, leaving us in the wake of their bespoke perfume.

"I guess we're doing it," I said with a laugh.

"Come on." Chuck dragged me down the hall and we found The Girls already taking the bottles out of the liquor cabinet. Once it was clear, Chuck and I used flashlights to examine every inch. Nothing.

"I can't believe it," I said, dropping into a kitchen chair.

"Access must be from the back," said Chuck. "Makes sense with having it built in like it is."

Myrtle and Millicent stood up, straightened their twin sets, and picked up the flashlights.

"May we try?" Millicent asked.

"Be my guest," I said.

The Girls went over the cabinet and found nothing as I knew they would.

"I don't believe that Uncle Josiah would've made it so the cabinet would have to be broken out to access whatever Stella hid," said Myrtle.

"I agree," said Millicent. "He prized good workmanship and wouldn't have wanted it destroyed."

"What do you suggest?" Chuck asked.

"Well, my dears, you know all the secret compartments he built in this house are not to be seen, hence the secret part."

"Okay," I said.

"Uncle Josiah made them so they couldn't be seen, only felt. That's why Tommy probably hasn't found them all. One could spend a lifetime feeling around this house trying to hit upon the hidden."

"We felt it," said Chuck.

"Thoroughly?" Millicent asked.

He shrugged. "I thought so."

"Let us try. We are his nieces. He was giving us puzzle boxes before we were born," said Myrtle.

"I get it," I said. "But Uncle Josiah didn't make this cabinet."

"But he loved it and that says something."

"Go for it."

The Girls smiled and went in the pantry to run their soft fingers over every nook and cranny. I poured myself some of Dad's special German peach schnapps and was about to throw it back completely despondent, when Millicent turned around. "We found it."

Chuck and I jolted to our feet.

"What?" I asked.

"A tiny little indentation," said Myrtle. "Nothing really unless you know it's something."

We gathered around the cabinet, holding our breath.

Millicent reached in, pushed something, and the base of the

cabinet popped up. The illusion was perfect. The ornate marquetry hid the compartment completely.

Myrtle carefully opened the compartment and we all leaned forward.

"It's empty," I said, tears threatening to overwhelm me.

Millicent took my hand. "It's not empty, my dear. Look there. A page of something."

Chuck reached in and lifted out a single piece of yellowed paper. "It's a poem." He held it up and The Girls beamed. I was bewildered. Josiah Bled had ripped a page out of *Where the Sidewalk Ends* by Shel Silverstein.

The Girls hugged me and Myrtle said, "Uncle Josiah gave that book to Carolina for you."

A zing went through me and I raced out to the living room. I searched the bookshelves until I found *Where the Sidewalk Ends* amongst all the other books Mom had read to me as a child. I knew that book. It had a missing page. The blank spot had annoyed me when I was little. It was like someone had stolen something special from us. Mom always said she'd get another copy to see what we were missing, but she never did. I turned to the empty spot with the jagged remnants where the page had been ripped out.

The Girls and Chuck walked in, and Myrtle placed the page inside the book. Complete as it hadn't been my whole life.

"He must've taken out what was in the secret compartment right before he left with Tommy," said Millicent.

"And put the poem in," said Myrtle. "It's a clue for you, Mercy."

"Me?" I asked. "I wasn't even born yet."

"He knew you would be wonderful," said Millicent. "He said so."

"I could've been a dipstick."

They hugged me and Myrtle said, "No chance of that."

"Which side was up?" I asked. "Which poem?"

"'Listen to the Mustn'ts.'" said Chuck. "'Joey' is on the other side. Are they important to you?"

"Me?" I asked. "I've never heard of either of them before."

"He's talking to you now," said Millicent. "Uncle Josiah is telling you that you can do anything. You can find whatever he took out of there."

Myrtle took the book from me and opened it to the title page. "Look here. He signed it."

There next to the title was Josiah Bled's neat signature. I'd seen it a million times, and it always struck me as odd. For a man so wild and impetuous, drunk and daring, his signature was contained and quiet. You'd think it would be an illegible scrawl, but Josiah signed the way he never lived.

"Check out the date," said Chuck.

"The day he left," said Millicent.

I'd seen and recognized that date, but I pointed to something else, a small arrow pointing to the light bulb drawn on the page. "Showing us the direction?"

"Let's look at the poem," said Millicent and Myrtle turned the page to the poem "A Light in the Attic". We read it together. A lovely poem, but in itself the reading meant nothing. The seeing it did. Josiah had underlined five words "dark and shuttered" and "a flickering flutter."

"What do you suppose that means?" Chuck asked.

"I have no idea," I said. "But I think we'll find out."

"Really?"

I smiled. "Uncle Josiah knew we'd get this far, so what's a little farther?"

"I hope you're right."

I am.

CHAPTER TWENTY-THREE

The next night I sat in my favorite booth at Kronos with a mug of hot chocolate and a double chocolate metaphysical malt. I didn't order either, but I wasn't complaining. Aaron made my beverage choices and he apparently thought I needed bucking up. He wasn't wrong.

Kimberly had texted me that morning to request a meeting and it was a terse exchange without a hint of her usual warmth. To say I wasn't looking forward to it was the understatement of the year, but I had to take the meeting. As Dad said, it was my job to meet with clients, angry or otherwise, and his advice on how to handle it wasn't particularly helpful. "Suck it up, Buttercup," he said and then he took a call from NBC. Awesome. Thanks.

I was early for the dreaded meeting, but Kimberly was late. When she walked in at seven fifteen, I didn't recognize her until she made a beeline for the table. The blonde hair was gone, replaced by a rich chestnut brown and the dull mom clothing of khakis, tennis shoes, and Mickey Mouse had taken a hike, too. Kimberly wore a well-fitted violet cashmere dress with patterned tights and knee-high heeled boots. She was stunning and every dude in Kronos noticed.

"Wow," I said without thinking.

Her eyes rimmed in kohl and dramatic lashes widened and she surprised me with a shy smile. "Do you like it?"

"You look...like yourself," I said. "I hope that's okay to say."

Kimberly slid in the booth and before she could say anything, Aaron rushed over with hot chocolate, a strawberry metaphysical malt, and a basket of arancini. He didn't say a word, looked over our heads, and then hustled back to the kitchen.

"He thinks you're upset," I said by way of explanation.

"How did he know strawberry's my favorite?" she asked.

"It's a mystery."

She took a sip of the malt, groaned, and said, "That's amazing."

"Everything he makes is and it's usually exactly what I need."

Kimberly looked at the drinks in front of me. "So you're upset."

"Mostly I'm worried about how upset you are since I never had the chance to give you my report personally."

"I've been better, but you're right I look like myself. The way I always wanted to look but couldn't."

"Your mom?" I asked.

A flash of pain coursed over her face and she nodded. "She persuaded me to dress the way she did, dull and not to be noticed. I wanted to be noticed. I didn't know how much until I found out."

"I'm sorry it worked out the way it did."

"Did you know from the moment you met me?" she asked.

"That you were adopted? No, I didn't, but seeing your brother's and mother's behavior over the years it became obvious that they were hiding something to do with you."

"They were hiding a lot of things. I just came from Black Heart Books. Jamie's a lovely person. I don't understand why Anton hid him from me."

"From what I can tell he felt compelled to hide most things about himself."

"So no one would really know him." She hesitated and gripped the malt. "Because of me."

"Because he feared exposure and what it would do to the family, I would guess," I said. "It's not your fault."

"I think I will forgive him someday."

"What about your mother?"

That was a harder question and it took a while to answer. "People keep telling me she's an old lady and that I should forgive her, but that doesn't make any difference. Time, I mean. Just because she got away with it for forty years doesn't mean it's somehow okay."

I only nodded and kept my mouth shut, for once, because I agreed. Letting people off for their crimes because they were good at it didn't track for me. "How is everyone else doing?"

"Fine. Holt's been great about the whole mess. Gregory and Kevin are stunned. My dad kicked my so-called mother out. She's moved in with her sister."

"He's decisive," I said.

"And he won't change his mind. She manipulated him and stole his son. He loves me"—she smiled—"and he can't stop saying it, but his son is gone."

"Have you contacted Christopher Lutz yet?"

"Stephanie and Holt talked to his wife and she told him who he is." The smile fell off her face. "He doesn't want to know us, not that I blame him. She gave him away like a skirt that wasn't the right color. She didn't care about him at all. When Holt told her who her son is, she didn't care. She wasn't interested at all."

"What about you?" I asked. "Are you ready to look for your birth parents?"

She shook her head. "Holt and I have discussed it, but no, not yet. I have to wrap my head around what my mother and Anton did before I can begin to think about them."

I was afraid to ask, but I did. "What did Ann say?"

Kimberly quietly revealed Ann Thooft's point of view. She wanted a girl and that was the end all be all of her ambitions. Anthony said four kids were his limit, so when Dr. McBride did the ultrasound and she saw her last chance was a boy Ann cooked up a plan to switch her baby with one from the camp next door.

"And McBride just went along with it?" I asked.

"I don't think he had a choice. She knew what he was doing at the camp."

"She blackmailed him?"

"I think so."

"She was determined," I said.

"And there was no going back," said Kimberly, "once she started."

Ann told her husband she was having a girl and gave him an ultrasound photo of someone else's baby. It took a couple of months, but they found a baby girl. The young mother was due right around Ann's due date, but she changed her mind and never came to the camp. That left Ann in the lurch, but, luckily, as she put it, there was another young mother pregnant with a girl. The problem was she was only thirty-two to thirty-four weeks pregnant.

"Doesn't sound like it was a problem for Ann," I said.

Kimberly's cheeks pinked up. "She'd already told Dad I was a girl and she didn't care what happened as long as she got one. Four pounds is really small. My friend Christine's son was four pounds. He was in the NICU for a month with immature lungs. I could've died and they knew that, but that bastard McBride induced me anyway and they did it days earlier than they absolutely had to to see if I would live."

"In case..."

"I had to be replaced." Kimberly's face got redder and her breathing rapid. I put her hands on the hot chocolate.

"Drink. I swear it helps."

She took a sip and closed her eyes.

"You survived," I said. "Try not to concentrate on what didn't happen. It's a long dark road. Take it from me."

Kimberly took another sip and then looked at me. "You've had a few long dark roads."

"I have." I took my own advice and drank Aaron's magical elixir. "But they've come out alright so far."

"That woman they arrested, was she like Anton?"

"She was."

I told her a short version of what happened and what we'd learned afterward. It hadn't taken Spidermonkey five minutes to put together who Linda was and why she was after me. Her husband was Harvey Snodgrass, the seventy-year-old ex-CFO of Titian Electronics. He retired—and I use that term loosely—not long before The Klinefeld Group made its move on the Bled collection using the art museum's board. Spidermonkey had heard through the grapevine that Harvey had been caught with his hand in the till and Titian gave him a golden parachute to go away and not reveal that he'd looted their pension fund. Part of the deal was the empty board seat at the art museum, vacated because of Detective Rich's Uncle Orson's death.

When Linda Snodgrass stopped caterwauling from her own pepper spray, she readily confessed to everything. She'd been blackmailed, but she had no idea who was behind it. A man, who called himself an emissary, gave her evidence of her husband's crimes and with an added bonus of evidence that Harvey Snodgrass murdered Orson Imich to get his board seat, including photos of the old man's arm, showing a puncture. The man said his employer would tell the police that Harvey had injected Imich with amphetamines to induce a heart attack. It was all neatly laid out, means, motive, and opportunity. He claimed to have Harvey's fingerprints on the syringe and Linda knew it was possible. They could have a syringe. Harvey was a diabetic and there were plenty of syringes in their trash. Linda was terrified. Harvey was in ill health, suffering from arrhythmia himself and prison would kill him. She knew he hadn't killed Imich, but he would go to prison if revealed so she agreed to deliver me to an airfield in Illinois. She swore that they promised not to hurt me. They only wanted to ask me questions about something.

Linda saw Anton Thooft's attempt on the news and knew she couldn't overpower me like he did and decided the only way to deliver as required was to incapacitate me, but she wasn't the brightest bulb. Her first try was when Rocco and I walked to my parents' house and we heard a scream. Linda tried to shoot us, aiming for the thigh, as if that made it better. But my would-be attacker had seen one too many crime shows and knew about ballistics just enough to hurt her. She decided it made sense to catch the spent casings as they ejected so no one would find them. She didn't know that they'd be hot. The first shot went wild and the casing burnt her hand. The scream was Linda. The second was the car in St. Seb that missed me because Pickpocket saw a squirrel. Linda got whiplash instead. The third was the air conditioner that she thought would knock me out so she could stick me in her trunk and it broke her ankle. That it was in broad daylight didn't seem to give her pause. When Nazir pointed out that nobody was going to let her put an injured woman in her trunk, she disagreed heartily. She would say that she was taking me to the hospital and nothing could dissuade her of the notion.

Because Linda couldn't take a hint, she decided to try shooting me again on the night of the Christmas parties. It was easy to get access to the avenue because of the Klemps' party and she parked her son's crappy Hyundai right in front of our house. Unfortunately for Linda, her silencer had broken on her first attempt when she burned her hand and dropped her weapon. She was afraid to go buy another one in her condition. Nobody was more memorable than Linda Snodgrass at that point, so she decided to use a whole potato. That, without a hole, blew up in her face, injuring her eye. Then, I aimed the Roman candle at our alley and grazed her, giving her burns to her face and hair. Second to last but not least, she figured a smoke grenade was the way to disorient me enough to get me in her trunk. I had to admit it was her best idea, but then Dallas threw out the grenade can and beaned her in the head giving her a moderate concussion and probably a scar for life.

"She just didn't give up," said Kimberly in astonishment.

"I have to give her that. Linda Snodgrass isn't a quitter."

Kimberly switched back to her malt, her face a normal color. "Who are these people?"

I followed suit and took a big drink of Aaron's best cold concoction. "I don't know."

"I saw on the news that they think that not-for-profit was behind getting Harvey Snodgrass on the board. What about them?"

"Is that why you wanted to meet with me? To find out who was behind it all?"

She nodded. "You did a great job, don't get me wrong."

"But?" I asked.

"But I still want to know who did this. I mean, why you, why us?"

I leaned back and looked at her pretty face. "Are you sure it matters?"

Kimberly met my gaze steadily. "It does. I want to know what Anton said, how hard it was to convince him to do it." Her voice lowered. "I want them to go to prison. They killed Anton and they almost got you killed. Don't you want to know who they are?"

"I don't know that we can find the answers. Everyone and their brother are trying to track the planes and the men on them, but it's not looking good. Linda's information is a dead end and so is Anton's burner phone."

"Are you sure?" she asked.

"If my guys can't get anything out of it, there's nothing to be gotten," I said. "Those men were hired guns any way. I doubt they knew any more than Linda. I was just a job to them."

"Who wants you bad enough to go to all that trouble?"

"Could be The Klinefeld Group like you said, but I don't think so. This was too ham handed."

Kimberly crossed her arms. "I think it is them. Somehow, they're involved. I read your report."

"Oh, yeah?"

"Yes. You said this all started in Germany. My brother was paying someone off over there. Cash from an ATM. That's personal. Face to face. The Klinefeld Group is German, isn't it?"

"Yes."

My mind started going. Kimberly was right. It all came back to Germany. The suspicious death of original Jens Waldemar Hoff in Berlin 1963. The cop who investigated it, hit and run 1965. Stella Bled Lawrence. Josiah Bled. The war. Whatever was in that liquor cabinet. It all came from Germany and kept The Klinefeld Group coming after us. Anton Thooft was a link and it was a trail I could follow.

"I decided last night," said Kimberly. "Nothing you said changed my mind."

"About what?" I asked.

"I want you to keep going. I *need* you to keep going."

That makes two of us.

Aaron trotted over and poured us fresh mugs of hot chocolate and laid down a printout in front of me. Flights out of Lambert over the next two days. The little weirdo always knows.

"I guess I'm going to Germany," I said, raising up my hot chocolate.
Kimberly lifted her mug level with mine. "To the truth."
I smiled. "And wherever it may lead."
Clink.

The End

USA Today bestselling author A.W. Hartoin grew up in rural Missouri, but her grandmother lived in the Central West End area of St. Louis. The CWE fascinated her with it's enormous houses, every one unique. She was sure there was a story behind each ornate door. Going to Grandma's house was a treat and an adventure. As the only grandchild around for many years, A.W. spent her visits exploring the many rooms with their many secrets. That's how Mercy Watts and the fairies of Whipplethorn came to be.

As an adult, A.W. Hartoin decided she needed a whole lot more life experience if she was going to write good characters so she joined the Air Force. It was the best education she could've hoped for. She met her husband and traveled the world, living in Alaska, Italy, and Germany before settling in Colorado for nearly eleven years. Now A.W. has returned to Germany and lives in picturesque Waldenbuch with her family and two spoiled cats, who absolutely believe they should be allowed to escape and roam the village freely.

www.ingramcontent.com/pod-product-compliance
Lightning Source LLC
Chambersburg PA
CBHW020903060726
47591CB00004B/1055